INTO DARKNESS

TERRY GOODKIND is a number one *New York Times* bestselling author. His Sword of Truth series has sold over 20 million copies. Before writing full-time, Terry worked as a wildlife artist, a cabinetmaker and a violin maker. He writes thrillers as well as epic fantasy and lives in the desert in Nevada.

BY TERRY GOODKIND

TERRY GOODKIND

INTO DARKNESS

A Children of D'Hara Novel

Episode 5

HEAD of ZEUS

First published by Head of Zeus in 2020

9 7 5 3 1 2 4 6 8

A catalogue record for this book is available
from the British Library.

ISBN (HB): 9781789544718
ISBN (E): 9781789544787

Printed and bound by
CPI Group (UK) Ltd, Croydon, CR0 4YY

Head of Zeus Ltd
First Floor East
5–8 Hardwick Street
London EC1R 4RG
WWW.HEADOFZEUS.COM

INTO DARKNESS

1

When hands gently lifted Kahlan from the ground, she came awake. Not fully awake, but awake enough to be aware of the red leather of a number of Mord-Sith surrounding her. She was aware, too, of the pain. That terrible, deep pain that told her that her pregnancy was in serious trouble.

Overriding the pain was a sense of helpless panic that there was nothing she could do about it.

In her dim, dazed vision, she saw Shale leaning close. Kahlan grabbed her sleeve.

"The babies . . . are they all right?"

Those carrying her by holding the edges of the blanket she was lying on paused as Kahlan desperately held on to Shale's sleeve. Even in her semiconscious state, she caught the side-long glance the sorceress gave some of the Mord-Sith.

"Hurry and get her inside," Shale said to the others.

Kahlan looked around as they started out again. Her vision grew dim at times, but she could see that they were carrying her into some kind of crude shelter. When she rolled her head to the side, she saw a lean-to wall at the back. It looked to have been hastily constructed of sapling poles covered in pine and spruce boughs. The Mord-Sith gently laid her down on a bed of grasses and fern fronds. The whole shelter was roughly made from materials at hand, but at least it helped protect her from the cold wind.

Cassia knelt down beside her and laid another blanket over the top of the one already there to keep her warm. It was cold out, but Kahlan felt hot. She was already so hot she was sweating. She had to blink sweat from her eyes.

Shale turned a little and cast a hand outward, sending flame into wood that had already been carefully stacked for a fire behind her. As soon as it blazed up, Kahlan felt the added warmth of the crackling flames.

The next moment, she was overcome with a flash of cold shivers. The sheen of sweat suddenly felt like ice on her face. At least the lean-to helped reflect the heat back now that she was suddenly cold.

Moments later, though, the heat again felt oppressive. Sweat once more poured off her face and stung her eyes. As soon as she didn't think she could endure how hot she was, she turned back to shivering with sudden chills. The breeze that made it into the shelter felt icy.

When the sorceress passed close enough, Kahlan once again grabbed her sleeve. "Shale, talk to me. I'm burning up one moment, and the next I'm freezing. What's going on?"

"You have a bit of fever."

"But are my babies all right?"

Shale patted her shoulder and flashed a brief smile. "You need to rest. That is the best thing you can do for them right now. Please, Mother Confessor, you need to lie still."

Instead of following instructions, Kahlan tried to sit up. The sorceress rushed to push her back down onto a pillow made of a folded blanket.

"You must not to do that, Mother Confessor. Just lie still. Try to go back to sleep."

3

"I'm not going to go to sleep until you tell me what's going on. Are my babies all right?"

Shale pulled her lower lip through her teeth as she considered whether or not to answer the question. She shared looks with some of the others standing over Kahlan.

"Shale?"

"You are having some difficulty. Nothing that can't be set right."

Set right. From Shale's tone of voice, Kahlan didn't know if the sorceress believed that it could be "set right." Kahlan looked around. Given the Mord-Sith's grim expressions, she didn't think they did.

"Where is Richard? Why isn't he here? He should be here with me. What happened? What's going on?"

Shale sighed as she realized from the confused panic in Kahlan's voice that she wasn't going to settle for anything less than the truth.

"You are having some difficulty with the pregnancy."

Kahlan was already aware of that much of it. "Difficulty? What does that mean? What difficulty?"

"The babies are in danger of miscarrying."

Kahlan blinked. "But I can't lose them."

Shale pulled the blanket up a little, tucking it under Kahlan's chin. "Lord Rahl and Vika went to find a plant I need to heal you—to save your babies. Once he returns with that herb, I will make you a medicine that should set you right."

Kahlan clearly caught the word "should." It wasn't a word that inspired confidence.

"What plant?"

"It's called mother's breath."

Kahlan had grown up in the Confessors' Palace and the Wizard's Keep. She didn't know much about the woods and plants, except what Richard had taught her. When she had been young, wizards, too, taught her a little about herbs. She couldn't remember ever hearing of mother's breath.

"Will he be back soon, then?"

Shale smiled. It was clearly forced.

"Just as soon as he finds me some mother's breath so I can make you all better. You need to lie still until then. You will make it worse for the babies if you try to move too much. Lying still is the best thing you can do right now to help them."

Suddenly fearing that she might be hurting

them by trying to sit up, Kahlan relaxed back onto the makeshift bed. She did feel better at hearing that Richard was going for a medicinal plant. Richard knew a lot about healing herbs. She appreciated the Mord-Sith and the sorceress being there, but what she really wanted was Richard at her side, telling her that everything would be all right.

Kahlan stared up at the roof of pine and spruce boughs, searching for courage to ask a terrible question.

"Am I going to lose my babies?"

Shale leaned in, her face tight with concern. "No, no, Mother Confessor. I don't want you to have such a thought. I'm with you, and Lord Rahl will be back with what you need. Now that we have you inside a shelter and out of the cold wind, the best thing you can do for the twins is to rest until he returns. It's important for the babies that you don't try to move right now."

Kahlan felt a tear running down the side of her face. "Please, I can't lose them. I've already lost my first child." She fought to keep control of her voice. "I can't lose the twins. Tell me what's going on. Don't lie to me to try to make me feel better. Being kept in the dark is not helping me. I want to know the truth of what's happening."

Shale regarded her with a long, solemn look. "All right, I suppose you have a right to know." She took a deep breath before she began. "For some reason the babies are trying to be born before their time. It's too early. I don't know the reason this is happening. I have seen this occur before in women I've helped back in the Northern Waste.

"The truth is, if they are born now, they will die within minutes, if they are even born alive. With the way this kind of thing goes, that would be unlikely."

Kahlan stared up at the woman. She heard the words, but she was having trouble understanding them. This couldn't be happening. Everything had been going well with her pregnancy. These were the children of D'Hara. They had to be born and grow up to protect their world.

Kahlan realized she was panting in fear as well as pain. "But you've handled this kind of thing before, haven't you?" she asked Shale. "You said that you attended many births, even difficult pregnancies. You've seen this before?"

The sorceress nodded. "That's right. From the time I was young, I went with my mother and she taught me to use my gift to help where it was necessary. I would guess that I've attended hundreds of births."

"But what about trouble like I'm having? Have you helped with that as well?"

Shale pursed her lips, considering for a moment.

"I told you I wouldn't lie to you, and I won't. I've seen situations like this maybe six or eight times."

Kahlan looked up expectantly. "And were you able to help? Were you able to save the babies?"

Holding Kahlan's gaze, she slowly shook her head.

"I'm afraid that in every case like this that I've seen, despite what I did, not one of the babies survived."

Kahlan swallowed back her fear. "What about the mothers?"

Shale, with a grave look, shook her head again. "None of those mothers survived, either."

Kahlan's muscles went slack. Her weight sank back. The world seemed to be spinning.

That was the end, then. The end of everything.

Shale put a hand gently on Kahlan's shoulder. "But we have things on our side that I didn't have any of those other times."

Kahlan looked up. "What things?"

"In every one of those cases someone had to come to get me, so I wasn't there from when it started. With you, I was right there at the beginning, so I was able to use a bit of my gift to try to stabilize the situation right from the first—before it was already too late, the way it was with those other women."

"Can you heal me, then? Heal the twins? Can you do something for us?"

"Before I came here from the Northern Waste, I would have said no, it is beyond what is possible. But since I have arrived, I have seen things that I would not have thought possible. I have seen Lord Rahl heal wounds that could not be healed. I have seen you bring him back from the dead. I have seen Lord Rahl do things that I used to know with certainty could not be done.

"If you and Lord Rahl have taught me anything, it is that we are all more than we may think we are, that we should never give in to despair and defeat, that we should never give up.

"I intend to save you and the twins, even if I

have never been able to do such a thing before. That is the long and short of it. I will keep all three of you alive until Lord Rahl returns with the herb that can reverse what is happening so that you can carry the twins until it is time for them to be born."

Kahlan felt more tears run down the side of her face. "Thank you," she whispered.

Shale leaned in and placed one hand on Kahlan's forehead, and the other on her swollen belly.

"Now, I am going to put you into a deep sleep in order to slow down what is happening. I will do everything I can to help the twins stay in the safety of your womb until your husband returns with the mother's breath. When he does, it will heal you.

"Until then, you need to sleep. The next time you wake, if I am half the sorceress I think I am, half the woman you have taught me to be, you will be well on the road to being set right."

Kahlan wanted to say something, but before she could, magic swiftly brought darkness that took her.

2

Richard lifted his shoulder, trying to shelter his ear from a frigid gust of wind. His fingers and ears ached from the cold. As the sun sank behind the mountains, not only was the light fading fast, but the temperature high up in the mountains seemed to be dropping even faster.

The cold, though, was the least of Richard's concerns. He urgently needed to get even higher up in the mountains to the tree line to find the mother's breath plant if he was to save both Kahlan and their unborn babies.

Vika had told him that mother's breath had odd, lopsided leaves. She held up her fist with the back of her hand facing him. "The shape of the leaves looks like this. If you ever saw it once, you would never forget it, but it's rare. I've only seen it a couple of times in my life, and then only up in the mountains near the tree line."

Richard dared not let himself worry about how rare it was. He just needed to get up to where it grew so he could search for it. He told himself that he was going to find it, and that was that.

The tree line, though, was still quite some distance away and much higher up the mountains. It was slow going trying to find an uncharted way up among the rocks and often dense trees of the steep and rugged terrain. It was difficult enough in the day, but he knew that in such mountainous country where there were no trails, it would be virtually impossible for the horses to climb once it was dark.

He also knew from Shale's urgency that time was critical to Kahlan's survival, so darkness or no darkness, one way or another, he intended to press on. Since the horses couldn't continue on in darkness, as soon as he found a place to leave them, he intended to keep going without them.

An all-too-familiar memory came to mind. Zedd had always said that nothing was ever easy.

Richard forced the thought from his mind

as he turned his attention toward an opening between a stand of young spruce trees. Beyond was a jumble of rock with just enough space for the horses to pass through. It was the only way he could find that looked to have any chance to lead them higher.

Richard was using all his knowledge and experience as a woods guide to find a way to steadily make it to higher ground. Occasionally, game trails helped. Even so, without a real trail, they had a number of times come to the base of impassable cliffs that forced them to find another way around so they could keep going up. Other times, what had looked like a good route ahead ended at a drop-off that forced them to backtrack and find another way in order to keep going.

Richard tried to scan the mountainside higher up while his horse carefully picked its way over the loose rock between tall rock formations rising up to either side. Water seeped down the faces of some of the speckled rock, leaving green and brown streaks. Plants growing in the cracks hung down in places, making it look like green walls. Tangles of roots here and there made the footing tricky. He wanted the horse to hurry, but he knew that it was climbing as fast as it could. It was almost as if it could sense his urgency.

As they made steady progress ever higher, they entered low clouds. The soft gray blankets rolled over the jutting towers of rock as if trying to find a way down. As they climbed upward into the clouds it made the granite the horses had to walk over slick and the footing dangerous. In places the horses had difficulty on the steep ground only made worse in the wet. Their hooves slipped repeatedly before they could find adequate grip.

He knew that in such steep country going back down would be considerably more difficult for the horses than going up. It would likely be too dangerous in many places to ride down. For much of the way down he knew they would have to do the descent on foot, letting the horses pick their way without having to also deal with a rider who would make it more difficult for them to balance.

But first they had to find the plant Shale had sent them for. That was all that mattered.

Vika followed behind without comment. She was his sworn protector, after all, and in addition to wanting to find the mother's breath, as Mord-Sith, Richard's safety was her first responsibility. She knew how desperate he was to keep going despite how dark and dangerous it was getting, so she didn't object. With the way the trees found places to grow in among the rocks they were picking their way over, even without the fog the canopies were too dense for them to see higher up and how much farther they would need to go.

Not long before, through an opening in the trees and despite the thickening fog, in a rare moment of clear sky he had been able to catch a brief glimpse of the mountains towering above them. Through that opening in the trees he had seen that the tree line was still a great distance away.

As it grew darker, he was having trouble picking out a passable route. On top of the darkness, the fog was making it difficult to see very far. Besides cutting visibility, the fog was creating an icy mist that was both miserable and slippery.

As they came up into a broad area that was somewhat level, their progress blocked by a fragmented granite wall, Richard frantically looked for a way up. Worried they were again going to have to backtrack, he suddenly spotted something in among the trees atop that vertical granite barrier.

"I think I see a trail."

Vika rode up beside him and frowned. She looked to each side, seeing that there was clearly no way around.

"A trail? Are you sure?"

Richard pointed up at the top of the granite. "Look over there to that split in the granite wall. I think it might be a way up."

"We can't take the horses up that. It's way too steep."

"Yes, but it looks like there are boulders and rock jammed into that crevice that would allow us to climb up it on foot. Look at the top of the wall over to the left by that mass of tree roots coming down over the edge. What do you see?"

Vika rested her wrists on the horn of her saddle as she stood in the stirrups and leaned forward, squinting up at the top of the wall.

"That's strange. It's foggy and hard to see, but it looks like it might be several stones stacked atop one another."

"Exactly." Richard dismounted. "It's a cairn."

She frowned over at him. "What's a cairn?"

"It's a way to mark a trail in difficult areas where it would be easy or even dangerous to get lost and go the wrong way. If I'm right, and it's not something natural, it would mean we have come across a long-forgotten trail."

Vika held her long, single blond braid in her fist over the front of her shoulder as she frowned up at the top of the wall. "Why would there be a trail up here?"

"It could very well be an old trail leading over a pass. It has to be from before the boundary that ran up the spine of these mountains. If I'm right, it may be a way not only to get up higher to the tree line, but to get over these mountains. It could be a trail that leads over a pass and into the Midlands."

"The horses can't get up there, that's for sure."

"You're right about that," Richard said as he dismounted.

Once on the ground, he started to unbuckle the saddle girth strap. "We are going to have to leave them and go the rest of the way on foot. If it really is a trail, this would be an incredible stroke of luck. Once we find the mother's breath and heal Kahlan, then we might even be able to get over the mountains on this trail. That would save us a lot of time getting to Aydindril."

Vika scanned the area before she climbed down out of her saddle. "It's pretty flat here, but what if the horses wander off?"

"It's a risk we will have to take. Let's get the saddles and tack off them," he said.

"Should we take anything with us?" she asked.

Richard nodded. "We'd better at least take our packs."

"We should also take some dried meat and whatever supplies we can carry," she suggested.

"I have some oats tied to the back of my saddle. I will leave some of it out for the horses. That should keep them around." Richard gestured to the left. "There is a little water running down off the rocks over there. It's collecting enough for them to get a drink. After we get the saddles off we need to break out the travel candles. The light is fading fast, but if that really is a trail up there, the candles will help enough that we should be able to keep going."

Vika glanced up toward the mountain they

could no longer see. "Candles in the tin traveling cases won't provide much light."

"With the fog, even if it was still light out, we wouldn't be able to see very far anyway. With the candles you can wait at that cairn up there while I scout ahead to see if I can find the next one. When I do, you can come catch up and then wait at that one until I find the next. In that way, if it really is a trail marked with cairns, we can keep going even in the dark."

Richard dragged the saddle off his horse and set it on a rock. As Vika did the same, he spread some oats on a flat area of rock. The horses were eager to eat. After giving them a pat on the neck, he swung his pack and his bow up on a shoulder. Vika untied supplies from her saddle. She hoisted her pack up onto her shoulder.

Once Richard lit a strip of birch bark with a steel and flint and it flared up into flame, he then used that to light the candles. They immediately started out into the foggy darkness, climbing up the narrow split in the granite wall.

3

Not long after daybreak they had made it up near the tree line and left the trail to search for mother's breath among where the snow had started to stick in patches. As eager as he was to find the plant, he had to be careful when he moved across the rocky ground they were searching. If he fell off the mountain, he wouldn't be able to help Kahlan, and in the place where they were searching, there was certainly a danger of falling. With the fog now down below them, there was no telling how far it was down some of the drop-offs.

The trail they had found was marked well enough with cairns and took a route that made for much easier climbing, at last saving them a lot of time. Richard was sure the trail had to have been laid out long before the boundary between the Midlands and D'Hara had gone up because, like the mountain range, the boundary divided the lands, so there would have been no purpose for a trail over a pass that would have been cut off once the boundary was there. It was fortunate that the cairns were still standing after all that time, and even more fortunate that he and Vika had happened across it.

It had worked surprisingly well for Vika to wait at each cairn they found while Richard went ahead to find the next one. Then she would climb to him by the light of his candle and wait at that cairn while he went on ahead to find the next. It was slow going to do it that way, but still a lot faster than wandering aimlessly up the mountains and having to backtrack from dead ends or being forced to climb in difficult and dangerous areas, especially when there was no way to tell if after a lot of hard climbing it would end up providing a way to continue. Sometimes it didn't.

They had climbed on the trail, following the cairns, throughout the entire night. Richard was too driven to find the plant that could save

Kahlan to stop and sleep. Vika was Mord-Sith. Mord-Sith were trained to do without sleep.

Once it had gotten light enough to see, they had been able to make much faster progress following the trail. But their method of continuing to cover ground throughout the night had helped make critically important progress. Now that they were finally up to where the trees were thinning out and they had daylight, they left the trail to search at the base of where the snow had begun to stick, hoping to find mother's breath not yet killed by the ever-descending snow line.

"Lord Rahl!" Vika called out.

Richard had been using his hands to help keep his balance on the steep ground as he searched under brush and the lower sides of rock ledges that were still free of snow. Shale had told him that she needed living plants with their roots; she couldn't use them if they had been killed by the snow.

He stood and looked off to his right. "What is it?"

"I found it!"

It felt as if his heart came up in his throat. He scrambled over a rounded projection of rock and through several patches of snow, then held on to low-growing, thick juniper brush to help keep from sliding down loose scree.

Richard found Vika sprawled on her belly in front of an opening in the rock. The rising sun was at their backs, so it lit the entrance to the small cave.

Vika pointed. "Look! It's mother's breath. It's protected in here from the snow, so it's still alive."

There were three plants to her left, where she was pointing, and a couple more to the right side, just inside the cave's maw. They had fist-shaped leaves just as she had told him. She had been right; after seeing those odd, lopsided leaves, he knew they were a plant that he would never forget. Just inside the opening of the cave, where Vika was on her belly, wouldn't quite be high enough to stand in, but it was enough to protect the plants.

Richard looked deeper and suddenly saw what Vika hadn't noticed in her desperate search for the rare plant, and her excitement at having found it.

In the snow to either side of the cave, and in the soft ground of the entrance, were the prints of a large cat. Farther back in the cave, where rays of the rising sun reached, he spotted a variety of bones.

Farther still, back in the darkness, Richard saw a pair of eyes reflecting the light.

When he thought he heard the low rumble of a throaty growl, he drew his sword.

Vika looked back over her shoulder when she heard the distinctive sound of his blade being drawn. "What's the matter?"

Richard gestured with his sword. "There's a mountain lion back in there."

Vika froze. "What do we do?"

Richard carefully put one knee down beside her and leaned in, holding the blade protectively out over the top of her. He put his left hand on the back of her shoulder to keep her down as he spoke quietly, so as not to alarm the animal hiding back in the darkness.

"Dig up the three plants right there by your left hand. Shale said she needed the whole plant, so dig out the roots. We need to get all of the roots you can dig out. Three plants should be more than enough. Leave the other two on the other side to help them regrow. While you dig these three out, I'll watch and make sure that mountain lion stays back."

"All right," she said as she quickly pulled her knife from the sheath at her side, drove it into the ground, and used it to help her start digging.

With her fingers and the blade she dug down through the relatively soft, rocky dirt, frantically flicking it back like a badger digging a den. As she worked, the animal back in the cave crept forward into the light enough for Richard to see its face and yellow eyes. It was indeed a formidably large mountain lion, and by its low, rattling growl, an unhappy one at that.

The creature drew back its upper lip, revealing big teeth, as it opened its mouth a little to let out a louder guttural growl. As it took another step forward with a big, broad paw, Richard poked the blade toward its face just enough to make his defensive intentions clear.

It took two steps closer, head hunched down, ears laid back, eyes locked on him. Powerful muscles in its shoulders flexed as it growled while taking another step closer.

"Don't make me kill you," Richard said to the beast. "I don't want to kill you, but I will if I have to. Just wait a moment until we're done here and then we will be on our way."

For the time being, the blade was keeping it back. The mountain lion stopped, almost as if it understood his words. More likely, it understood the blade in its way.

Vika dug with her fingers as fast as she could, throwing the dirt back, trying to dig down and expose the roots without damaging them. All the while Richard and the mountain lion stared each other down.

Vika clawed at the ground and was finally able to bring the first plant out of the deep hole she had dug. It had a long, thick taproot. She got almost all of it out, shook the dirt off the roots, set it aside, then went back to excavating the other two. Richard could see that it wasn't easy digging while on her belly, but she worked as fast as she could, letting out little grunts of effort. Her fingers were bloody, but that didn't slow her down.

Richard carefully reached down with his left hand, as he kept the mountain lion at bay with the sword in his right, and set the mother's breath already out of the ground safely up on a small ledge that formed the roof of the cave. When Vika, panting with the effort, brought out the second, he took it from her and set it up with the first. Having loosened the ground as much as she needed to with her knife, she returned it to the sheath and went back to clawing out the dirt around the roots of the third mother's breath plant and flicking it behind.

"Got it!"

With the third plant in her left hand, Vika squirmed back. When she was back far enough, she got to her hands and knees under the protection of Richard's sword and collected the other two as he continued to guard her.

After she had the three mother's breath plants clutched in her hand, the two of them slowly retreated from the mouth of the cave. The mountain lion matched their movement, slowly slinking out with them while maintaining a safe distance, until it emerged from the darkness and into the light.

Richard gripped Vika's arm with one hand and pulled her behind him while he held the sword out with the other. Together they moved off to the side away from the angry animal.

Once they had left it enough room to escape, the mountain lion emerged from the cave, gave them a long, uncomfortable look, and then gracefully bounded off to their right, over the snow and among the sparse trees.

"It's heading toward the trail," Vika said as she pulled out a blanket to wrap up the plants. "That's an odd coincidence."

Richard watched where the mountain lion was slipping away. "We're long and well past the realm of coincidence."

4

Quiet darkness was settling into the woods when Richard spotted Nyda on watch long before she spotted him and Vika. When she finally did see him, she ran out and whistled a birdcall he had taught the Mord-Sith to alert the others that they had returned.

Rikka then emerged from the thick underbrush behind him. He hadn't spotted her. He was glad to see that they were using the tactic of positioning one person on watch so as to be spotted and distract anyone approaching. If it turned out to be a threat, the one still hidden could then take out that threat from behind. Even though he was glad to see them using their heads, he had more important things on his mind.

Richard and Vika were both exhausted from the long ride up the steep terrain, climbing the trail in the dark the entire night before, the hunt along the steep and difficult ground for the mother's breath, the tense encounter with the mountain lion, and then the difficult journey back down the mountains to where they had left Kahlan, Shale, and the rest of the Mord-Sith.

As they galloped into camp, Richard leaped off his horse. Berdine ran in and took the reins of both horses as Vika jumped down and handed Richard the blanket with their precious cargo. Shale was adding a stick of wood in the fire when she saw them ride in.

She stood and then rushed to meet them, brushing crumbs of bark from her hands. "Do you have it?"

Richard flipped open the blanket to show her. "How is Kahlan?"

Shale gently lifted out all three plants, using it as an excuse to divert her gaze. She looked amazed that they had actually found some mother's breath.

"Three! This is wonderful, and you managed to recover them with their taproots intact. I had dared not hope you would find even one. This is exactly what we need."

"I asked how Kahlan was."

Shale looked up from under her brow. "The Mother Confessor is asleep."

Richard gently grabbed Shale's upper arm. "I asked how she is."

The sorceress considered the intensity in his eyes briefly before answering. "She was losing the babies and her life along with theirs. The only thing I could think to do until you returned with the mother's breath was to use my gift to immerse her in a form of very deep sleep. I had to put her in that place between life and death. You called it the cusp. My hope is that inducing such a profound sleep will slow down all the functions in her body enough to keep her from miscarrying. It was the only way I could think of to save her and the twins. So far, she still has the babies and she is still breathing."

"But she will be all right." It came out more like a command than a question. He didn't like to hear that the sorceress had pushed Kahlan to the cusp between life and death. He didn't like it one bit. But he didn't want to second-guess her decisions. He knew the extent of the emergency, and that Shale would do everything she could to save Kahlan. "Now that we have the mother's breath, will she be all right?"

The sorceress hesitated. "I hope so. At least for now she and the twins are alive and together. With the mother's breath we have a chance. Now, I must hurry and prepare the medicine she needs."

"What can I do to help?" Richard asked as he followed close behind her as she hurried back to the fire.

Shale paused and considered a moment, looking toward the lean-to beyond a crackling fire before gazing at the three plants resting in her hand.

"I need to prepare the remedy, but that is going to take several hours. Since you were able to bring three plants, and considering the seriousness of the situation"—she handed Richard the one with the longest taproot—"maybe there is something you can do to help. Take this one, go to her, break off the bottom tip of the root, and then let the milky fluid drip into her mouth. She needs to swallow it. Do it only when you have it over her mouth so you don't waste any. It is a very rare and precious substance."

"If I'm going to let some of the milk drip into her mouth, why do you need to prepare a remedy?"

Shale didn't shy away from his gaze. "Lord Rahl, please do as I ask, and hurry."

Richard was concerned that she was deviating from the plan of preparing the plants first. He knew a great deal about plants and herbs, but he didn't know anything about mother's breath or how it needed to be prepared. He did know that there were plants that when prepared properly could heal. But he also knew that when raw and not properly prepared they could kill.

"Will it harm her to give her the raw milk of the plant? Are you sure you shouldn't prepare it first?"

Shale touched her fingers to the hollow of her neck as she considered it a moment. It was apparently a question that worried her, too.

"To tell you the truth, I can't be sure. I've never heard that mother's breath is poisonous, but also, I've never heard of giving a miscarrying woman the milk of the plant raw, rather than in a prepared remedy. I do know that the healing power of the plant lies in the milk." She held up a hand and rubbed her first two fingers together with her thumb. "It's a sticky substance, much stickier than the milky sap in any other plant. I believe that sticky quality is what may be the key to how the plant helps stop a miscarriage.

"I was told by an herb woman I knew that she believed the sticky milk of the mother's breath plant strengthens the bond the mother's body has with the unborn babies, keeping them in her womb. But to be honest, I've never heard of the milk being given raw. My thought is that women are always given the prepared potion but that may be because living plants are never at hand, whereas the preparation can be made up ahead of time and kept in stock, sealed in jars, ready for when needed in an emergency."

"Then to be safe, why not just wait until you can prepare the plants the way you were taught?"

Shale gave him a meaningful look. "Because it took you a long time to find the plant. Too long. I realize that's not your fault, and it is remarkable that you were even able to find it at all, but as far as the life of the Mother Confessor is concerned, it took too long. That's the reality.

"The only reason she hasn't miscarried and she is still alive is because I was there right when it started and so I was able to put her into that deep state of sleep before it had advanced too far. Traditionally the remedy is prepared by an herb woman for those times when it is urgently needed. That is often later when a healer has been summoned, so much time would have already passed by the time any help reached the mother. My intention was to prepare the plant in that way. But it took you a long time to return. Too long."

"But if you were to prepare it—"

"To be honest, Lord Rahl, even though she is in a deep sleep, I don't think your wife can last long enough for me to prepare the plants. My hope is that the raw milk will stop the miscarriage and keep the three of them alive and together until the preparation is ready. For all I know, the raw milk might even work better and then the prepared potion wouldn't even be needed.

"But what I can't say is that it won't do harm. In my judgment we have to chance it."

"It's a big chance," he said.

"It is," Shale agreed with a nod. "I leave the choice to you, then. You are her husband and would know best what her wishes would be.

You decide for her. What would she want you to do?"

Richard didn't have to think about it. "She would say that it's the only chance for her and the babies, so we have no choice but to try it."

Shale offered him a brief smile. "Hurry, then, and give it to her."

Richard gripped the plant in his hand as he nodded. "How long will it take you to prepare the other two?"

She looked over at the fire. "To boil it down and prepare the remedy will take a few hours. I think you have made the right decision in the meantime. You must give her some of the raw milk now."

Richard looked down at the plant she had handed him. "Could it hurt her? Could it hurt her if it's raw, or hurt the babies?"

"I already told you that I just don't know." The sorceress glanced over the fire to the still Mother Confessor. "But I think that the problem may actually be if it works too well."

Richard frowned. "What do you mean?"

Shale looked back at him. "I mean that it may bind the babies into her so well that it may prove difficult for her to give birth."

"Well then, maybe—"

"Lord Rahl, there is no time. It is already long past when she should have been given the potion that I have yet to cook. By all rights, she shouldn't even still be alive. I doubt she will be for much longer. If you have made your decision, then you must do it now or she will be lost."

Richard let out a troubled sigh as he gently gripped the plant in his fist. He knew that there was really no choice. He just wished it were not a choice he had to make.

Shale put a hand on his forearm as if to steel him. "Hurry now. Go to her."

5

Richard's fear for Kahlan had him feeling like he was watching himself from somewhere high above the campsite as he rushed around the fire to the lean-to. If he had made the wrong decision, he could very well be about to poison the only woman he had ever loved, the only woman he ever could love.

He found Kahlan laid out just under the shelter of the lean-to on a bed of grass. She was covered with blankets. He marveled at how exquisite she looked in her deep sleep. It was the perfect innocence and beauty of a child. He hoped the sleep was a peaceful one. He knew, though, that if Shale really had succeeded in putting Kahlan in that nowhere place between the world of the living and the world of the dead, it was anything but peaceful there.

The Keeper of the underworld would be whispering promises to her, urging her to take that last step and enter his eternal realm of rest. Richard knew all too well that it was a seductive call and difficult to resist. But he knew, too, that she would be trying with all her will to resist so that her babies would have the chance to live. If she was able to resist that longing to be free of pain and suffering, it would be for them.

Cassia was there as well, on the opposite side of Kahlan from the fire, sitting on the ground beside her, holding her hand in both of hers. As Richard knelt down beside her, Cassia offered a hopeful smile as she moved back out of the way.

"How is she?" he asked back over his shoulder.

Cassia's voice was heavy with anguish. "She hasn't moved since Shale put her in a deep sleep. I was relieved, though, when she did because the Mother Confessor was struggling terribly in pain. I ached myself at seeing her in such agony. At least she is breathing more easily, now."

Richard nodded and turned back to Kahlan. He pushed her chin down until her mouth fell open. With his thumbnail, he clipped off the bottom of the taproot. One drop of the milky white sap dripped on her cheek before he could get the tip of the root over her mouth. As he held the plant over her with one hand, letting the milky fluid slowly drip into her mouth, he swept the drop up with a finger and wiped it onto the inside of her lower lip.

Even though she was still not conscious, Kahlan's tongue worked at the contact with the milky fluid. When the dripping slowed to a stop, Richard pushed up on her jaw to close her mouth. He knew she needed to get it into her stomach, so he was relieved to see her swallow.

After she had swallowed a few times, he opened her mouth again, then snapped off the taproot halfway up. When he did, more fluid again began running out, dripping into her mouth. Once the flow finally stopped, he closed her mouth again until she swallowed, then opened it and snapped the root off where it turned to the green stem. An even more plentiful, thicker flow started to drain from the rest of the plant. He understood, then, why Shale had told him that it had to be a living plant. A dead and dried-up plant would have no milky sap.

When the flow stopped, he worked his fingers to gradually wad up the plant in his fist. He squeezed to force out as much fluid as possible. When he was sure the dripping was finished, he handed the crumpled plant to Cassia.

"Take this to Shale. There may still be some milk in the plant that she can add to the medicine she's making."

Cassia nodded and then raced off to take the crumpled plant to the sorceress. Sitting on the cold ground beside Kahlan, Richard watched as Shale tore the plant into small pieces and added it to the steaming pot she already had cooking on the fire. She reached into a pocket of her trousers and pulled out a pouch. From the pouch she added a few pinches of some kind of powdered preparation to the pot.

As she stirred the boiling potion, Richard lay down close beside Kahlan to help keep her warm. He gently ran a hand over her round belly, hoping she would know that he was there with her. As much as he wanted to stay awake, he was exhausted and soon nodded off into a troubled sleep.

He hadn't been asleep long when he heard Shale speaking to some of the Mord-Sith. He sat up and rubbed his eyes. The brief nap had done nothing to banish his exhaustion. To his side, Vika sat on the ground, watching over him and Kahlan. He knew that she had to be just as tired as he was.

"Why don't you lie down and get some sleep?"

"I will," she answered. "But not until after the Mother Confessor gets the medicine Shale is preparing."

He looked over at Shale, squatted down beside the fire, leaning over the pot she had set on the ground, continually stirring the preparation. She lifted the stick out, letting the concoction drip off to test its consistency. She dipped her little finger into it to test if it had cooled enough. Apparently, it had. She gave an order to one of the Mord-Sith. Vale quickly stood and rushed to one of the saddlebags. She dug around until she came up with a piece of cloth.

Shale urged both Nyda and Vale to hold all four corners of the cloth. When they had, she slowly poured the pot of liquid in the cloth to filter the preparation and let it drip into a tin cup she had placed on the ground. Once the liquid had mostly dripped through, she took the cloth and twisted it around and around. She grimaced with the effort of squeezing out all the remaining liquid.

When she was finished, she threw the cloth and its contents onto the fire. Blue and green flames and glowing sparks shot up from the cloth as it burned, lighting the trees all around in flickering, colored light.

After dispensing with the filter cloth, she picked up the cup and hurried to Kahlan. She knelt down on the other side and set down the cup before putting a hand to Kahlan's forehead, checking on her fever.

"That's good. Her fever is down," Shale told Richard. She gestured. "Sit her up for me."

He carefully and gently scooped an arm under Kahlan's shoulders and lifted her. Kahlan's head slumped to the side. Shale straightened her head and then put her fingers on Kahlan's temples with her thumbs over her eyes. She softly spoke some kind of chant. Richard couldn't hear the words well enough to understand them. He doubted that even if he could hear them well enough he would have known what the words were. He assumed it was some sorceress's—or

even witch's—spell. Sorceresses, and likely witch
women, often relied on spells.

Whatever it was, it caused Kahlan to gasp in
a deep breath along with Shale. Richard noticed
that Shale synchronized her breathing with
Kahlan's for a moment. Finally, the sorceress took
her hands away and Kahlan opened her eyes.

Richard jumped a little in surprise. "Kahlan!"
He was excited to see her awake. "How are you
feeling?"

The sorceress swished a hand. "She can't
hear you. She is still in that deep place. I don't
want her to choke or drown when I give her the
preparation."

Indeed, Kahlan seemed completely unresponsive. Though her eyes were open, it didn't
seem like she saw anything. Still, Richard felt
hope at seeing her beautiful green eyes. There
was life in them, and that was cause for hope.

As he held Kahlan up, Shale brought the tin
cup with the milky potion to her lips. As she
tipped it in, Kahlan began to drink it. It took
a while for her to slowly drink it all. When she
had, Shale took the cup away and motioned
for Richard to lay her back down. As he did,
Kahlan's eyes closed once more.

Shale stood and let out a weary sigh. "Now we must let the mother's breath do its work—both what you gave her and what I prepared. When it has done all it can, and if it is enough, she will wake on her own from the deep sleep and be fully back in the world of life. Until then, let her rest. Tonight determines if she will survive this ordeal or not. Until then, we all need to sleep to be able to face what tomorrow holds."

Richard couldn't take issue with that. He nodded as Shale went to her nearby bedroll. She looked exhausted. Richard was as well, but he was worried that the medicine might not work. He was terrified that he might lose Kahlan this night. But at least she seemed to be resting peacefully. What terrified him more was that she might instead rest peacefully for eternity with the good spirits.

He leaned close. "Life is a struggle," he whispered to her. "Fight for me, for us, for our children."

When he was finished and sat back up, Cassia touched his shoulder. "Berdine and I will watch over her tonight. You and Vika need to get some sleep."

Richard didn't want to sleep. More than his better judgment, it was his exhaustion that made him lie down beside Kahlan. He kissed her cheek and then gripped her hand in his.

6

Richard was having a wonderful dream that Kahlan was kissing him. As it always did, the feel of her soft lips on his seemed to open up the feminine half of the universe to him. It was a profound completion of his reason for being. It made him whole.

As he was kissing her, something made him open his eyes. He abruptly realized that it wasn't a dream.

It was not yet dawn, but through the trees he could see the eastern sky just beginning to brighten a bit. Her hair had fallen down to flow around his face. Flickering firelight gave her face a warm glow as she pulled back and looked down at him with that radiant smile he knew so well.

TERRY GOODKIND

"You were sleeping so peacefully, I didn't want to wake you." The smile widened with mischievousness. "But I couldn't resist kissing you."

Richard let out a deep breath of relief as he embraced her, holding her tight to him. His fears melted away in that moment.

He finally gripped her shoulders and lifted her back away from him. "How do you feel?"

Her mouth twisted playfully. "Pretty good now that I've had a kiss."

"No, I mean everything else." He looked at her skeptically. "Are you all right?"

She shrugged. "I feel surprisingly well, actually. I think I was having a terrible nightmare and it felt like I was asleep forever in some faraway place. I didn't like being in that place. While I was sleeping, I thought I heard you say that life is a struggle, and I should fight for you, for us, and for our children. So I did and woke up."

Seeing that Kahlan was awake and up, Shale threw off her blanket and rushed around the fire. "Mother Confessor! You're awake. How are you feeling. Don't try to stand. Any pain? Are you hurting anywhere?"

Kahlan struggled to sit up as Shale tried to push her back down. "I feel like I've had a very long and restful sleep, actually. I feel fine." As the Mord-Sith rushed up around them, Kahlan frowned. "Why is everyone acting so strange?"

"You don't remember?" Richard asked.

Kahlan made a face as she half smiled. "No. Remember what?"

"You . . . were having difficulty with your pregnancy," Shale said.

Kahlan's face suddenly went ashen. "What?"

The sorceress waved her hands to dispel the fear from Kahlan's suddenly pale expression. "No, no, everything is fine, now. Lord Rahl found a plant I needed to make you some medicine and it fixed you right up. It was not a big thing, really. You were exhausted and just needed a bit of medicine and rest, so I helped you go to sleep. Don't worry, everything is fine, now."

Kahlan looked skeptically at all the faces watching her as she ran a hand over her round belly. "Are you sure?" She looked under the blanket. "Where are my trousers?"

When everyone was silent for a moment, Rikka finally spoke up. "I washed them for you,

Mother Confessor. I dried them by the fire. They are ready whenever you want them."

"I made some breakfast," Berdine said with a big grin. "I thought you would be hungry when you woke up. We have fresh fish and rabbit. Which do you prefer? I have to say, I like the rabbit best."

"Well, actually, I am pretty hungry. The fish sounds good." She tipped her head to look out of the lean-to. "It looks like the weather is no better."

Richard glanced out. "At least it's not snowing down here. Fortunately it's not raining any longer, either. At least for now. The weather in these mountains can change in an instant, but I don't think it's going to be getting much better for a while."

"Well," Kahlan said, "we need to get moving south to try to find a way to get around these mountains if I'm to have these babies at the Wizard's Keep."

"There can be no going south," Shale said with a frown. "Not with that boundary wall of death thing."

"The boundary . . ." Kahlan's brow twitched a little as she put a hand to her forehead. "That's right. I seem to have forgotten that we had run into the boundary . . . ."

"Lord Rahl found a trail leading to a pass over the mountains," Vika said, hoping to dispel Kahlan's sudden concern.

Kahlan's mouth fell open. "A trail over a pass? That would mean the boundary wouldn't matter and we can cross the mountains here. That would get us directly to Aydindril." She looked up hopefully. "If there is a pass, we could get over the mountains right away. That would significantly shorten our journey."

"The sooner the better," Shale said. "You aren't getting any less pregnant. I would feel a lot better if we weren't out in the wilderness when the time comes to give birth."

Kahlan still seemed somewhat confused. "So then I'm all right? The twins are all right? Was I having some kind of trouble?"

Some of the Mord-Sith exchanged glances. Everyone noticed that Kahlan seemed not to remember what had happened. Richard could see no reason to tell her how close she had come to losing the babies, to say nothing of her life. It would needlessly frighten her to know how grave the situation had been. From the looks

on all the other faces, it seemed that none of the
rest of them thought it would be a good idea to
tell her, either.

Berdine suddenly smiled brightly. "Lord Rahl
found a plant that made you all well again."

Kahlan looked over at him and put a hand on
his chest. "Was it any trouble?"

"None at all," Vika said from behind Richard.

Richard wasn't as happy about the pass as
the rest of them. It seemed everything had
been conspiring to force them to cross the
mountains in this place. Someone was behind
the strange woods they lost so much time in.
Someone had usurped his ability and used it to
put up those boundaries. Kahlan had begun to
miscarry and he had to find a very rare plant
to save her and the babies. There just happened
to be some of those very rare mother's breath
plants up the mountain trail they just happened
to come across.

Whatever hidden hand was behind all of the
recent events seemed determined to get them
up into these mountains. And there just so
happened to be an old trail for them to use.

"As soon as we have something to eat then
we should probably get going," he said. "There

is no telling how long this break in the weather will last. It would be good to make some distance while we have the chance."

She flashed him a smile. "I would like that. The sooner we are to Aydindril the better. I feel well rested. I'm up for some traveling."

"I'm afraid it's going to be a difficult journey," Richard cautioned her. "It's a demanding climb from here to get to the trail, and the trail itself is not an easy one. I'm afraid that once we get to it, there is no way to take the horses up that trail and over that pass."

"Well," she said, thoughtfully, "I expect the horses will enjoy their freedom. I'm sure they will be glad not to have to carry us and all our gear any longer."

Richard smiled. Kahlan always tried to find the bright side of things. He was sure she was worried about what lay ahead for them, but she didn't want to show her concern. As the Mother Confessor, she always tried to keep everyone positive. Richard wasn't feeling nearly so positive. As pregnant as she was, it was going to be a difficult journey on foot.

Worse, he knew that they were being guided by a hidden hand.

7

F at snowflakes drifted through the still, cold air, dissolving away the instant they touched Richard's face and the backs of his hands. Dark, brooding clouds overhead seemed to hang still in the pass, casting the day in gloomy light. Richard could just make out the smell of woodsmoke. They all lay in a line on their stomachs in the fresh snow, heads just high enough to peek over the edge of the ridge in order to squint into the distance.

Richard was not liking what he was seeing.

"Why would such a strange place be way up here?" Rikka asked.

Nyda pulled the small willow stick she had been idly chewing from her mouth. "Maybe it's a stroke of luck."

"It's not a stroke of luck," Kahlan said, clearly as unhappy as Richard was at what they all saw in the distance.

"Why not?" Nyda asked. "Shelter, warmth, food, rest. That sounds like a stroke of luck to me. What could be wrong with that?"

"It's a trap," Richard said in a distracted voice as he peered into the distance. "That's what's wrong with it."

Nyda put her chew-stick back in her mouth as she let herself slide back down the snow-covered slope a little ways, retreating from the edge of the ridge so she could sit up without taking the chance of revealing herself to anyone beyond. She planted a boot against the base of a birch tree to halt her slide. "You really think so?"

"Everything that has happened has contrived to put us up here, on this trail, with nowhere else to go," Vika said with obvious displeasure as she looked over the edge of the ridge, watching into the distance with the rest of them. "Do you really think that coming upon this place is just chance?"

Nyda sighed. "I suppose not."

"This is the trap that has been pulling us in

ever since we left the People's Palace," Richard said.

With a cunning look, Nyda spun her Agiel up into her fist. "Maybe I should go take a look."

"Not a good idea," Vika said.

Nyda dropped her Agiel, letting it hang from the gold chain around her wrist. She pulled the stick out of her mouth again. "Why not? A Mord-Sith might be the right thing to set the mood up there and change our luck."

Vika looked back over her shoulder. "The Law of Nines, remember? We need the nine of us to stay together."

"Vika is right," Richard murmured as he watched for any sign of people. He was sure that the Golden Goddess was still searching for them, so he didn't want anyone who might be out beyond to see them. There was no telling how many eyes the goddess could be looking through as she frantically hunted for him and Kahlan.

The town in the distance, off through the heavy timber, had been built hard up against the pass, spanning the broad distance from one towering bluff to the other, some of the buildings piled up on top of one another in what looked like an unplanned, haphazard fashion, making them appear hunched together against the elements. It was hard to tell at such a distance, but it looked like there was a stone wall built all the way across the pass, entirely blocking the way through. He supposed it was possible it was simply built that way to take advantage of the lay of the land. But in his gut, he knew there was more to it.

The massive fortress town grew right up behind the stone wall, the wall itself so high it rose up above some of the treetops. The tree line and barren ground above overlooked the town from each side of the wide pass.

As far as Richard could tell, the only way over the pass was through that walled fortress. He had trouble imagining the reason for a fortress in such an isolated place. Of course, it was possible that it wasn't really a fortress at all, and it only appeared that way from a distance. Again, his gut told him that wasn't the case.

Up inside the wall built across the pass and beyond the jumble of structures, he could just make out a much taller, more impressive-looking structure of some sort. It looked like maybe it was made from a pale-colored or white stone.

It had to be a difficult life in such a remote place. As such, it seemed an odd place for a grand structure of any sort to be towering in its midst.

Richard didn't think there could be more than a few thousand people at most living in the town. The smell of woodsmoke told him that the place was not abandoned. If it was not abandoned, then the goddess might be able to use the people living there to finally spot and attack them.

Unfortunately, the only way across the pass was to go through that fortress town.

Kahlan put her hand on his forearm. "I don't like it. Like you say, it's a trap. Everything that has happened to us since leaving the People's Palace has been leading us right to here."

Richard nodded. "I'm afraid you're right."

She rolled a bit to the side, looking like it was uncomfortable to be lying on her swelled belly. "So what are we going to do about it?"

In the middle distance, on the path leading through the snow-crusted trees and among the rocks rising up from the thick white blanket of snow covering the ground, and across another snow-covered rise, he could just make out the tracks of a big mountain lion. He didn't have to wonder if it was the same one he and Vika had encountered when searching for the mother's breath.

"Well," he finally said, "Zedd told me once that one should not willingly walk into a trap."

Shale scowled over at him. "Is that another one of your Wizard's Rules?"

Richard looked over and showed her a crooked smile. "If it isn't, it should be."

"Is that all of what Zedd had to say about it?" Kahlan asked.

"Actually," Richard said, "the rest of it is 'unless you have no other choice.'"

"Well, it looks to me like this would qualify as 'no other choice,'" she said.

They all turned to look up at the gray clouds when rumbles of thunder echoed through the mountains. The low, ragged clouds that were silently gliding in obscured the higher peaks, and by the looks of them, they promised some bad weather.

"I grew up in mountains like this," Vika said. "Thunder and snow high up in the mountains are a worrisome pair."

"So what are we going to do?" Kahlan asked,

ignoring Vika's comment and obviously growing impatient. "I'm not in favor of walking into a trap. Someone wants my babies. I don't intend to simply walk in there and hand them over or have them taken from me. But I'm cold and I want to get beyond these mountains and down into Aydindril, where it will be warmer. We can't lie here forever watching that place."

Richard let out a long breath. The rising breeze carried away the cloud of that breath as he appraised her green eyes. "I agree." He showed her a smile. "I have a plan."

Kahlan arched an eyebrow. "A good plan?"

He wasn't in the mood to debate the merits of it. He was more concerned about avoiding whatever kind of trap waited for them in the walled stronghold blocking the pass. He was also concerned about the way the wind was coming up and the weather was closing in. The night before had been miserable huddled in the protection of a quickly built pine-bough shelter, with no fire, as they ate some of their dwindling supply of dried meat and hard travel biscuits.

"First," he said, "I need to know if you're up for a difficult attempt to get over these mountains in order to avoid walking into the trap that's waiting for us."

Kahlan frowned at him. "What are you proposing?"

Richard put an arm over her shoulders and pulled her close so she could sight down the length of his other arm to where he was pointing.

"Look at that notch to the left side of the pass, just before the slope of the second mountain over starts to rise up again. See what I'm talking about?"

Kahlan squinted into the distance. "I can't tell for sure. You always could see better than me. And you know more about such country than I would."

"Well, there's an indentation in the side of where that mountain rises up." He gestured to indicate the slope on the left side of the pass. "That notch is higher than the pass with that walled town built across the trail, but it might be a way over the mountains without having to go through the town. See? Up there not far above the tree line."

"I see it," Shale said as she pushed in close on the other side of him, finally seeing where he was talking about.

"I see it too," Vika offered.

"What of it?" Kahlan asked. "What are you thinking?"

"Like I said, it might be a way over the mountains. A way to skirt that walled fortress built across the pass."

"You mean a way to skirt that trap?" the sorceress asked.

Richard nodded. "Yes. I think it could give us a way to avoid walking into a trap and instead go right around it. If it is a way across, we could avoid anyone seeing us, and we just might be able to make our own luck and get over the mountains and into Aydindril and then to the Wizard's Keep."

"Then what are we waiting for?" Kahlan asked, blowing some warm breath into her cupped hands again.

"I'm waiting for you to tell me that you're up for it. It's going to be a difficult climb. It's not a trail, so we will have to make our own way. It will be hard climbing."

"I'm pregnant," Kahlan said, "I'm not helpless, and I'm not eager to spend any longer up here than necessary. Let's get going while we still have light."

8

The light was fading fast by the time they got closer to the notch Richard had spotted from back in the forest. Some of the way was steep and dangerous. They had struggled to make it through the snow up above the tree line.

In several places Richard had to climb up, lie on his stomach, and then reach down to help Kahlan, because her pregnancy made it more difficult for her to pull herself up, and also Berdine, because her arms weren't long enough to reach the edge. Once, when there was no practical way around, Richard had to quickly fell a pair of trees so they could cross a deep chasm. As they got higher, frigid winds funneled through the canyons to sting their faces with ice crystals.

In spots the thick blanket of snow hid deep ravines and rifts in the uneven, rocky ground. After Kahlan sank up to her armpits in one of those rifts, and he and Vika had to pull her up and out, Richard cut a long staff and took the lead, testing for ground under the way ahead to make sure it was solid. He cut a similar staff for Vika. She walked beside him, and together they tested the ground ahead. He had the rest of them follow in his and Vika's footsteps so that they wouldn't drop into a hole where they could easily be hurt, or worse.

As they got closer to the towering mountain, it was easier to see the notch in its lower slopes. The sun was setting beyond, to the west, to where they needed to go, and even though it was cloudy, the brighter light of the western sky silhouetted the shape of the mountain to reveal the cut in the rock.

"Numbers mean things, right?" Berdine asked as they trudged through the snow. "I mean, like the Law of Nines. You said before that numbers have meaning."

Richard looked back over his shoulder. "Yes, sometimes. Why?"

Berdine squinted, shielding her eyes with a

hand as she peered up at the gray sky. "Well, there are thirteen ravens circling us. Does that mean something? Thirteen?"

"They've been following us since we left the trail," Richard said.

"Really? I didn't notice them before," Berdine said, her voice trailing off as she turned, looking up. "But now that they are overhead, I noticed them going around in a circle as they follow us. So, does it mean something that there are thirteen?"

Richard poked his staff into the ground ahead, testing. "Hard to tell. A lot of numbers have meaning. Some are more important than others. It often has to do with circumstances surrounding the numbers or even the context that makes the number significant. I can tell you, though, that ravens are crazy smart, and they are as curious as cats."

"Oh," Berdine said, not really knowing if that answered her question or not. "I just thought that maybe thirteen meant something."

Richard glanced back over his shoulder at the witch woman. Her face was unreadable. He decided not to get into it and instead started out again.

Like the rest of them, he was bone-tired. Walking in deep snow was a lot of work. Kahlan was following behind Vika, trying to walk in her footsteps, but even though the person ahead was breaking a trail, it still took a grueling effort to pull each leg out of one hole and put it in the next. He could see that Kahlan was near to dropping from exhaustion. He wanted to stop and rest, but with the day drawing to an end he knew she would want to keep going while they still could, and she would want even less for them to stop because of her.

There was still enough light for them to see their way by the time they made it to the notch. As they worked deeper into the cut through the mountain he had seen earlier, sheer rock rose up to each side. It looked like slabs of the granite making up the mountain had broken off and fallen away, leaving the opening for them to make it through. The fractured rock created small shelves that allowed snow to build up, making white ledges that stood out against the gray rock.

In the sky between the soaring granite walls, he could see the thirteen ravens circling high overhead. Sometimes ravens followed hikers, hoping to snatch small animals such as voles that were flushed out by the noise and vibration of people walking.

He didn't think these ravens were looking for voles.

Richard was relieved to see ahead that there was easily going to be enough room for them to make it through the opening, although the snow had built up in the sheltered gap between sheer walls, making it deeper and progress even more difficult. But at least it was a way to finally get across the mountains and around the trap. With the light fading fast they were all eager to get through the opening before they had to stop for the night, so, despite their exhaustion, they pressed on through the deep snow.

No one wanted to waste their breath to talk. No one wanted to give up until they were at last through. Each of them struggled to simply put one foot in front of the other.

To make matters worse, the wind had picked up and snow was beginning to fall harder all the time. It collected on their eyelashes and it had to be blinked away to see.

Every few difficult strides through the deep, packed snow, they had to pause to get their breath in the thin air of the higher altitude. They were all keen to get far enough to finally see beyond and confirm that they had indeed managed to find a way across the mountain range by skirting the trap of that strange fortress town across the pass.

Richard expected that once beyond the walls to each side of the notch and finally on the way down, they would all need to at least stop and rest, if not stop for the night, but he would prefer to press on long enough to make it down to the tree line and get back into the shelter of the forest before they stopped. He could see the tops of trees beyond, so he knew that the ground descended just ahead and the next day they would finally be able to start down out of the cold and snow of the towering mountains, down to where winter hadn't yet fully taken hold.

As Richard poked his staff in the snow ahead and took another step, the air all around unexpectedly began to glow green. There was no mistaking that color for anything else.

Vika, her head down as she wearily plodded forward, was out a little ahead of him. She took another step and a hard, green wall lit in the air all around her.

Richard reached out, grabbed her arm, and yanked her back before she even realized what she had almost walked into. She looked up, stunned to see that she had nearly entered the world of the dead without even realizing it. She had been so focused on making headway that she was only watching the pole she was using to check the ground where she wanted to put her foot next.

They all stood stunned, staring at the greenish glow to the air before them. There was no need to talk; they all knew what it meant. They all felt the same sense of bitter disappointment.

Kahlan dropped to her knees in tears. Richard pulled the blanket she had around her shoulders up tighter around her ears to keep her warm. He hugged her, then, holding her head to his shoulder. He hated to see her in a state of such despair and on the edge of giving up. Shale touched her shoulder, as did several of the Mord-Sith. They all felt that same sense of wordless despair, but Kahlan seemed to be the one who most exemplified what they were all feeling.

"It's clear that we can't go any farther," Richard said as he looked up at the rest of them all huddled around. "We need to go back."

"I'm so tired . . ." Kahlan wept.

"The sun is down and it's getting dark fast," Richard said. He looked up at the others. "We need shelter for the night. We need to get her warmer. I'm sure we can't make it back down to the tree line. These rock walls offer some protection, but not enough."

"We need to go back just far enough to be clear of this boundary of death and then make a snow cave," Shale said. "We do that often in the Northern Waste. It's a quick way to have shelter and it can save your life on a cold night."

Still holding Kahlan's head to his shoulder, Richard nodded. "That would make the most sense."

Shale pointed. "That spot just back there, where the snow is drifted up against the jog in the face of the rock wall, would be good. The snow will be deeper there and compacted from the wind that drove it in there."

"Let's hurry and get it done before it gets too dark," Richard said. "We'll all feel better when we can get out of the wind and have something to eat."

Directed by Shale, the Mord-Sith began digging into the tightly packed snow. Once they had a good start on a cavern, Shale had them stand back. With them safely out of the way, the sorceress cast her hands out, sending a roaring stream of orange and yellow flame into the cavity. It curled around, melting the snow in deeper. She held her hands out, to keep the fire going, until it had melted a big enough space down inside for them. The snow walls to the side that had been melting quickly froze into a glaze of ice.

Richard glanced up at the black clouds through the snow that was beginning to fall in earnest, swirling around in gusts through the split in the mountain. "The storm is upon us. We need to get out of the weather."

Shale nodded. "Take the Mother Confessor into the back, against the rock wall. It will be warmest against the rock from the heat of the fire. It should be hot enough to let us all get warm. The ice walls will keep the heat in for a while, and I can use my gift to warm the rock when we need it."

"That sounds wonderful," Kahlan said through chattering teeth.

9

At first light they dug their way out of their cozy snow cave. After they all emerged, they began making their way back down the mountain to the shelter of the forest. Their breath drifted slowly in the bright, clear air. The fresh snow from the night before had completely covered their tracks with a new layer, making it even more difficult to walk than it had been the day before. The momentum of going downhill, though, was a bit of a help. Still, it took a lot of effort to make it back down to the forest and below the ridgeline where they had first spotted the town built across the mountain pass.

"What are we going to do?" Kahlan finally asked when they stopped to rest on a rock outcropping that was blown clear of snow but was ice cold.

It was a question they all had on their mind, but no one else had wanted to ask.

Richard scanned the thick woods. "We need to make a good shelter, clear some snow away, and build a fire. We all need food and rest to get our strength back."

"No," Kahlan said. "What I meant is what are we going to do about the boundary stopping us? I don't see any other way but to go to that town to get through the pass."

Richard shook his head. "I'm not ready to do that. We know there are people there. If the goddess can use them, we could suddenly find ourselves fighting an army of Glee. We need to avoid that at all costs. We need to recover and think this through before we do anything."

"So, what are we going to do, then?" Kahlan pressed. "We obviously can't go back."

Richard gave her a look. "We are going to make camp."

He didn't want to tell them what he had in mind. So instead, he went about cutting some young trees and stripping them of limbs to make poles. He used one of the bigger poles to span between the crotches of a couple of trees and used a vine to secure them. As he cut down more saplings the Mord-Sith placed them against both sides of the one bigger pole spanning between trees to make a roof of sorts, leaving a space on one end for an opening to get inside. Richard made sure the space inside was big enough for all of them.

He finally gestured. "Shale, could you clear the snow away in front of the door for a fire?"

The sorceress used fists of air driven by her gift to blast the snow from the ground for their shelter. It cleared the snow down to the forest floor. Scraping away wet leaves and branches uncovered solid rock that was broad enough to be a good place for a fire.

Some of the Mord-Sith went about collecting pine, spruce, and balsam boughs to place against the poles to form a roof to protect them from the wind if it came up again and hold in the heat. It took several hours to complete the roof.

While they were doing that, a couple of the others collected dried deadwood for a fire. They stacked up the wood and as it began growing dark Shale sent fire into the stack. In short order they had a good blaze going. The fire crackled as it burned the pine, sending sparks swirling up into the air.

While Richard set fishing lines in a nearby stream, and Kahlan squatted before the fire warming her hands, Berdine, Vale, and Rikka spread out all the bedrolls inside the shelter. There wasn't a lot of room inside, but the tight quarters would help keep them all warm. Nyda and Cassia brought more dried wood from the surrounding woods and stacked it to the sides so there would be a supply throughout the night. The crackling fire lit the trees all around, sending sharp shadows into the darkness.

After they had collected enough wood, they all gathered around the fire for a meager meal from the supplies they still had left. They were all hungry and there was only sporadic conversation as each of them tore off pieces of dried meat and salted fish. It wasn't very enjoyable, but at least it helped quench their gnawing hunger. They scooped up snow in tin cups and set them close to the fire to melt the snow for drinking water.

After they had all eaten, the Mord-Sith decided on watches. Richard let them talk him into sleeping the whole night. He knew he was going to need the rest. Once their meager dinner was finished, they all crawled into the shelter, except Vika and Nyda, who had first watch.

Richard hugged Kahlan close to him. He ached all over from the strenuous hike up to the notch and back, and he knew she felt just as sore. It was a lot of effort that had in the end been for nothing. They were all disheartened that their way had been unexpectedly blocked by the boundary. At least it felt good to have Kahlan tight up beside him. He enjoyed the quiet pleasure of holding her as long as he could, but in mere moments, sleep took him.

At the first hint of light, Richard woke when he heard Rikka putting more wood on the fire. He sat up and stretched as quietly as he could. Kahlan was still asleep. But when he started to climb out from under the blanket that had been around both of them, she woke up.

He told her to go back to sleep. He was relieved that she lay back down while he made his way out of the low shelter. He searched around until he found some tender saplings, then set to work. He used his knife to split them and then bend them around to make a hoop.

With a supply of leather thongs from his pack, he wove a net across the loop of wood.

About the time he finished, everyone woke up and came out. They dug travel biscuits from their packs and had a quick bite to eat as they all rubbed sleep from their eyes.

"All right," Kahlan finally said, "we're rested. So what are we going to do now?"

Richard, his forearms resting on his knees, chewed the hard biscuit for a moment before answering.

"Well, you all are going to camp here and get some rest."

Shale, Vika, and Kahlan all looked up suspiciously.

"And what do you intend to do while we all 'rest'?" Kahlan asked.

"I'm going to go into the mountains on the other side of the town. I'm going to see if I can find another way around."

"You mean you are going to go see if the boundary is over on that side, too," Kahlan said, obviously realizing what he was up to.

"We need to know for sure if there is a way through or not."

"Then we should all go," Kahlan said.

Everyone else shifted their gazes between the two of them, not wanting to get in the middle of what was Kahlan's obvious displeasure at the plan and Richard's clear determination.

"No," he said, "we should not all go. I can travel faster by myself. There is no reason to expose you to the dangers and the difficult hike if it turns out to be for nothing, like it did on the other side. If I find a way through, I'll come back and by then you all will be rested and ready to travel."

"You're not going alone," Vika finally said. "I'm going with you."

"Not this time."

"Why?" Kahlan said. "Why can't you at least take Vika?"

"Because with me gone, I want everyone else to be here to protect you, that's why."

Vika clearly looked upset. "Lord Rahl, I—"

"I want you to stay here and protect the Mother Confessor. We don't know what dangers might be about. She carries our children, our hope for the future of our world. I want her protected." He stood, lifting his pack, slinging it up on one shoulder. He picked up his bow from where it was leaning against the shelter.

"The subject is not open to debate. Check the fishing lines. Hopefully you can all have some fresh fish. I'll be back as soon as I can."

"You said that we have to all stay together," Berdine said, "for that Law of Nines thing."

"I'm doing what I think best," he said. "It doesn't take nine of us to trudge through deep snow to scout the terrain. Scouting ahead is what I'm good at."

Berdine pointed off through the trees to where the ravens had roosted. "Can you at least shoot a few with your bow so that their number will be less, like ours will?"

"It can't be done," Richard said.

"Why not?"

"Because the ravens would not allow it."

Berdine wrinkled up her nose. "Not allow it? What are you talking about?"

Richard gestured to the birds perched on branches in the pines. "Watch."

He turned his back on them as he quickly strung the bow. He gripped it in one hand as he pulled an arrow from the quiver over his shoulder. He quickly nocked the arrow in the string, and then turned around toward the ravens. Before he could even raise the bow to aim, all the ravens started squawking as they took to wing and, in an instant, had vanished back into the trees.

Richard cocked an eyebrow at Berdine as he replaced the arrow in the quiver and hooked the bow over his shoulder.

"Like I said before, ravens are crazy smart. But those are not merely ravens. I want Kahlan protected while I'm gone." His gaze swept over everyone watching him. "Is that clear?"

Once Shale and all the Mord-Sith nodded, he sat on the edge of the rocks and bent to tie the snowshoes he had made to his boots.

"That's pretty creepy," Berdine said as she looked again to see that the ravens had vanished. "It's like they're watching us."

"They are, so they will be back," he said. "Now, all of you watch over Kahlan for me until I get back. Please," he added.

Without waiting for them to raise objections, Richard started out, pleased to discover how well the snowshoes worked. It would make it a lot easier to cover ground quickly.

10

As he expected, one of the thirteen ravens left the others to follow him as he quickly made his way through the woods. It flew through the forest, weaving in and out among the branches as if they weren't even there to get out ahead of him, and then with a quick flutter of its black wings settled on a branch to wait for him to pass underneath. As he did, it would turn its head to look down at him with one black, glossy eye.

The bird's black eyes reminded him of the eyes of the Glee. It was wearisome the way there was always someone or something watching them so that they were never completely alone, to know instead that they were always being observed for any sign of weakness and for the right time to attack.

He knew that if he wanted to, he could kill the raven—what he had done before with the bow was just to show the others that these were not merely wild ravens so that they would be on alert—but he also knew that killing it would accomplish nothing, so he didn't want to reveal his ability before it became necessary.

Besides, the animal itself was innocent. It was merely being used, much the same way the goddess looked through the eyes of unsuspecting people. He actually rather liked ravens, although they were often quite noisy.

Richard was happy to find that the snowshoes made for much easier progress over the snow. They weren't perfect, but they worked. Rather than his legs sinking in with each step, he could simply walk on the surface almost as well as he could on the bare ground.

He didn't know why he hadn't thought of it the day before as they had struggled to make their way up the mountain to the notch he'd spotted. He guessed that he was letting himself become too focused with worry of what was going on and with what he had been hoping would be their way out. He supposed that he simply wasn't thinking straight.

He reprimanded himself that such lapses could be fatal. They were in a lot of trouble, more trouble than any of the others realized, and he needed to think clearly. That was the only thing that was going to save them.

He wasn't concerned about leaving the rest of them back at camp. He knew they weren't in danger there. The danger was in that fortress town built across the pass. That was where the spider waited at the center of this web.

They had discovered that to the left of the fortress town in the pass the boundary blocked their way. He needed to see if there was a way around the pass on the other side so that they could make it to the Wizard's Keep without having to go into that fortress. He had to know if they had a choice or if the boundary continued on to the right of the town.

As the day wore on, he continued to push, making more progress than he ever could have if he had let Kahlan and the others come with him. Kahlan never complained about the physical challenges, but with her being pregnant it was difficult for her to push as hard as she would like to or as hard as he could alone. Before she had become pregnant with the twins, he would never have had any doubt that she could keep up with him. At times, if anything, he had trouble keeping up with her. But he knew that now she couldn't.

When he finally made it above the tree line, he stopped and turned back to see the raven sitting on a bare limb, watching him. He turned and started ahead, panting with the effort and the thin air at this altitude.

After a time, he paused and with a hand shielded his eyes from the bright sunlight as he scanned the mountainside. While the place he spotted was far from ideal, and he knew it likely wouldn't be a way they could cross the mountains, he headed for the spot anyway, because it would serve his purpose to confirm what he suspected. In such a life-and-death situation, he dared not leave any stone—or escape route—unturned.

It was sometime in the mid-afternoon when he had to remove his snowshoes to start climbing bare rock that had been blown mostly clean of snow by the howling winds. At least those winds were now calm. It was hard climbing, but he was able to keep going without stopping to rest. Some of the places were so high that he had to jump and grab an edge with his fingers and then pull himself up. After such places, he had to lie on his back and catch his breath in the thin air.

His legs ached, and the altitude was not only causing him to become easily winded, it was starting to make him feel sick. The answer, he knew, was to reach the place that would tell him one way or the other what he needed to know, and then he could start back down.

As he pulled himself up and over the top of another ledge, he saw that the way ahead was relatively flat and would be a lot easier walking. As he started across, he could see trackless forests of trees crusted with snow blanketing the slopes beyond, on the way down. It would be impossible to climb down the cliffs on the other side of the place he had reached, but that wasn't important for now, so he kept going.

Partway across the broad ledge, he abruptly had to stop when the air all around him lit with green light. Another careful step and the wall of green appeared all around him.

It was the boundary he expected to find but

had hoped he wouldn't. He found no joy in confirmation that he had been right.

Richard backed away from the boundary until it became invisible again and he could see beyond, then sat down on a knee-high section of ledge. He put his face in his hands, disheartened at the discovery. He had known the boundary would in all likelihood be there. Finding it removed all hope that they could avoid what he knew waited for them in that fortress built across the pass.

When he looked up, he spotted the mountain lion sitting on its haunches some distance away, its color making it blend in well with the rock. When their gazes met, the animal rose up, stretched, arching its back with its paws stretched out in front. Long, sharp claws came out from its paws as it stretched, scraping across the rock. The big cat stared at him the whole time.

Richard lifted his sword a few inches to make sure it was clear as he stared back at the sleek creature. He let the weapon drop back in its scabbard, sending a clear message of his own.

"Tell your mistress that I'm coming for her," he called out to the mountain lion.

The creature stared at him for a moment longer, then turned and trotted off.

Richard knew who it was going back to.

He now knew for certain that they had no choice.

11

When Kahlan, sitting in front of the fire to stay warm, heard one of the Mord-Sith let out a birdcall, she stood. Shale rose to her feet beside her.

"Do you think it's Richard?" the sorceress asked.

"Yes, it's him. Nyda would have made a different call if it wasn't, if it was a stranger or some kind of trouble. He's finally back."

Cassia glanced back over her shoulder to the woods in the direction of the birdcall, then put another stick of wood on the fire before standing. A spit over the fire had rabbits roasting. The cooking meat smelled good, but Kahlan, wringing her hands expectantly, was too worried about what word Richard would bring to them to be hungry.

When she spotted him coming out of the trees with Nyda, she ran to him and threw her arms around his neck. Her loneliness and worry of the day melted away at the sight of him. Something about being pregnant made her want to be close to him all the more.

She kissed his neck. "I'm so glad you're back. I was so worried."

Even though she was relieved that he was safe, the grim look on his face had her stomach once again feeling like it was tightening in knots. She gestured back to the fire.

"Cassia and Vale set snares and caught some rabbits. There were also some fish on the lines you set out before. You're just in time so that we can have a good meal together. We all need it. Come and have something to eat. You must be starving."

She could tell that he was deeply troubled, so she didn't want to press as to why just then. She knew that he would soon enough tell them all what he had learned. By that troubled look, though, she knew it would not be good news.

He put his arm around her waist as they walked together to the fire and then sat cross-legged on the bare ground. The fire had been going since the day before, so it had warmed the rock they were all sitting on, making it a cozy refuge from the cold.

Cassia tore off a big piece of meat from one of the already-cooked rabbits sitting beside the fire to keep it warm. She grinned as he took the meat from her.

"We used snares—like you showed us," she told him.

Richard returned a smile. "I'm proud of you. You did good."

"So are you going to tell us where you went and why?" Shale asked, obviously not willing to wait for him to decide to tell them in his own way and time.

"I had to confirm that the boundary was also on the other side of the town blocking that pass. It was. It runs off in both directions."

That bit of news was disheartening, but not exactly unexpected.

"It wasn't worth all of us going just to find that out. Going alone I made good time and was able to confirm it quickly," he explained. "That means that we now know that the boundary makes a big loop all the way around us, and likely around the People's Palace as well. It's a noose drawing tighter around us."

Berdine leaned forward. "Drawing us into what?"

Richard took a bite of rabbit as he looked into her eyes and then gestured back over his shoulder with the piece of meat he was holding.

"Drawing us into that fortress built across the pass. I suspect that if we stayed out here, the boundary would close in around us until we had no choice but to go in there or die.

"Someone in there didn't want us getting away—getting to the Wizard's Keep, getting to where they couldn't get their hands on us."

Kahlan didn't say anything. None of it surprised her. It angered her, but it didn't surprise her.

"But why?" Berdine pressed as she tore off another piece of meat and handed it to him.

"Isn't it obvious?" Kahlan said in a quiet voice as her gaze sank to the crackling flames. "To get the children of D'Hara that I'm carrying."

When she glanced up, Richard was looking

into her eyes. From the look in his gray eyes it was obvious he agreed with her.

"If that boundary is covering all that territory," Shale said, "then what happens when people come upon it. There are people traveling between places. There are merchants and traders that travel between cities. Some people have business that requires them to travel. People are going to encounter it. What happens when they come to the boundary?"

"If they are unlucky or foolish enough to walk into it, they die," Richard said with finality. "As you get close the boundary starts giving off that green glow as a warning, but not everyone knows what it means. If they are too curious and keep going in to try to find out what it could mean, then once they take one step too many it will be too late for them to turn back."

"Doesn't whoever is doing this care about the lives taken by the boundary they created?" Cassia asked.

"No," Richard said. "They want what they want and that's all there is to it. They obviously don't care if it costs the lives of innocent people."

Shale threw up her hands. "Who? Who is

doing all of this? It has to be more than one person. No one person would be powerful enough to use your gift to put up that boundary of death. You said before that gifted people could join their gifts to do things that none of them alone could do. It has to be a number of people doing it. But who?"

"Someone seriously committed" was all Richard would say.

Kahlan knew that he knew who waited for them in the fortress town.

Shale lifted her hands and let them drop into her lap in frustration. "It's not just the boundary. It's also that strange wood we were lost in for so long. I suspect they not only created that but also started the Mother Confessor miscarrying to keep us from getting far. I just don't know who could be doing all of this."

Richard gave her a look. "You will find out soon enough." He turned to the Mord-Sith gathered around. "Pack up everything. We're leaving."

"Now?" Kahlan asked. "It will be dark pretty soon."

"I'm done wasting time and I'm done letting other people control us. The skies are clear. The moon will be up soon. The moonlight reflecting off the snow will easily provide enough light to see our way. We're going in there now when they won't be expecting us and putting a stop to this."

12

The snow crunched underfoot in the cold, still air as they made their way up the path marked by cairns. Kahlan could smell woodsmoke mingled with the aroma of balsam and spruce. Richard and Vika led the way, poking their staffs into the snow ahead to make sure it didn't hide any deep holes. Kahlan and Shale followed behind them, with the rest of the Mord-Sith guarding the rear. If the fortress up in the pass had sentries, they hadn't seen any, yet.

The moonlight on such a clear night was proving to be more than enough to help them see their way. It was a little harder to make out the lay of the land in the dark pools of moon shadows as they passed under dense canopies of trees, but with the light reflecting off snow they were still usually able to make out the trail well enough.

In a particularly dense, dark section of the woods, Richard had Shale light a torch he made so they could see. Since they were going to the town in the pass, they would be seen soon enough, so it no longer really mattered if they were spotted by the light of that torch. When they once again emerged into bright moonlight, Shale turned the torch down and doused it in the snow.

It turned out that the fortress town they had spotted from that ridge the day before was a lot farther away than they had initially thought. As a result, as they finally drew closer after a long and strenuous hike and were better able to see the details of it, it became obvious that it was not only much larger than they had initially thought, but more complex.

At parts of the wall to either side, the wall itself continued up to become the walls of multistory buildings, their square windows looking out over the approach to the pass. Those windows looked to be more domestic than watchtowers. A great many more structures were crowded in behind them, rising up higher on the ascending slopes to each side, like building blocks stacked tightly together.

The pass itself was broader than it had appeared to Kahlan from a distance, meaning that the town partly built into the wall with more blocky buildings tightly stacked behind was larger than she had at first realized. The imposing wall stretched from the sharp rise of the mountain on the left to a similar soaring mountain on the right. Now that Kahlan was closer and could see that wall better, it was obvious to her that it was well built and looked quite formidable. Stained with water and age, it also looked ancient, as if it had been there for thousands of years.

As the trail led them closer to the base of the wall, they were finally able to spot a large, arched opening near the bottom. Two halves of a gate door stood open. The massive doors were made of wood held together with iron straps. Inside, beyond the doors, there was a portcullis made of crossed iron bars, but it was drawn up enough to easily allow admittance. The portcullis had spikes along the bottom to crush anyone if the heavy gateway were to be suddenly dropped on them. Through the tunnel that was the arched opening in the wall and beyond the portcullis, Kahlan could see broad steps bathed in moonlight.

Vika pointed with her staff. "What kind of tracks are these?"

Kahlan looked down and saw that in the trail they were following there were a lot of tracks from a big animal.

"Mountain lion," Richard said without even needing to look down.

"That's what I thought." Vika frowned over at him. "They go right into that opening in the wall up there. Why would a mountain lion be coming and going from this fortress?"

"I guess we're about to find out," he said, clearly not yet wanting to say what he seemed to already know.

Kahlan didn't especially like his answer that wasn't really an answer. He knew more about what was going on than he was saying. She had to admit, though, that she did as well. She guessed that she was no more eager to put words to her suspicions and fears than was he.

She glanced up from time to time but didn't see any guards patrolling along the top of the wall. As they went into the arched tunnel under the massive wall, it revealed at last how massively thick it was. The buildings up on top were obviously as broad as the wall itself. Everyone continually scanned the area, looking for trouble.

Kahlan thought it was just a little bit too easy for the gates into the wall to be wide open and the portcullis drawn up out of the way, like the maw of a beast inviting them in. As they started climbing the broad hill of stairs, Richard gave the Mord-Sith a hand signal. They spread out, some racing up the stairs, with others dashing off diagonally to the sides as they ascended.

When they finally reached the top of the long rise of stairs, Kahlan was stunned by what she saw. Spread out before them were row upon row of plants to each side of the wide path. Off in the distance beyond the fields of low plants were more of the blocky buildings, presumably homes. They were stacked along the base of the mountains to either side, all on top of one another, stepping their way up the steep slopes.

Richard paused and bent to lift a big leaf of one of the plants as he looked up at Shale. There was a long row of the plants with the same fist-shaped leaves.

The sorceress stared in disbelief. "Mother's breath."

Beyond the row of mother's breath, there were expansive rows of many other herbs, some tall and spindly, some short and lush, some with blue flowers and others with yellow. Bright blue butterflies flitted along over the plants in the moonlight, pausing at flowers, presumably to drink nectar. There were vast rows of different kinds of plants stretching off to each side of the cobblestone path. Kahlan recognized some of the herbs, but not most of them. Some of the plants were exotic, crooked shapes unlike any she had seen before.

Far out ahead, beyond the fields of herbs, up against buildings, there were pens with animals. Kahlan could see pigs and sheep. Given the size of some of the other pens, she was sure that there must be milking cows in some of the buildings that had to be barns.

The place beyond the fields of herbs and the animals was not a village; it was more like a small town. There were square buildings built of stone stacked up along the rising ground to each side of the pass. Out ahead in the flatter ground beyond all the fields and animal pens there were yet more of the blocky buildings crowded together.

While most of the buildings were small, some were larger, with two, three, and in some cases four stories, but it looked to Kahlan like it was possible that each of those square buildings was an individual home. Like the stone walls themselves, all of the windows were square and devoid of any exterior decoration. Nor were any of the buildings at all fancy or adorned in other ways. The roofs were uniformly tile, making all the buildings appear simple and much the same. A few of the windows had lamplight coming from inside, but most were dark.

"It's not cold here, inside the wall," Richard said as he looked around at the growing fields of herbs.

Kahlan looked around, then, too, realizing when he said it that he was right. Not only wasn't it cold, but there was no snow. It felt like a gentle spring night, with no sting of approaching winter. All the plants looked green and healthy. It was as if the wall also kept out the snow and cold.

Shale looked around in wonder. "The air is mild, mild enough to grow all these rare herbs."

"I think we all know that there has to be some kind of magic involved," Richard said.

The Mord-Sith all returned from scouting to form a protective ring around Richard and Kahlan. The ring tightened when they saw a man in the distance making his way toward them down the cobbled mountain-path road. He lifted an arm in a friendly greeting. He walked with an odd side-to-side sway to his gait, as if his knees didn't bend very well.

"Welcome," he called out when he was still some distance away, his arm repeatedly waving in greeting.

Despite his obvious difficulty walking very fast on his stiff legs, he did his best to hurry to meet the visitors. He finally came to a stop, wheezing a bit as he caught his breath.

"Welcome," he repeated. "We were expecting you tomorrow, not this late at night, but welcome anyway. I'm Iron Jack."

Kahlan could see where he got his name. He was quite stout-looking, with a thick neck, a full red beard, and a full head of wiry red hair. His thick features revealed that he was well beyond middle age, but he looked like a man made of iron, with his red hair giving him a rusty look, the kind of man who had been in many a battle in his years and had the scars to prove it.

Kahlan stepped forward, holding her hand back at her side in signal before Richard could say anything.

"I am the Mother Confessor."

Richard arched an eyebrow at her when the man showed no reaction, least of all reverence.

Cassia stepped forward as she spun her Agiel up into her fist. "Perhaps you are hard of hearing. This is the Mother Confessor. You should be on at least one knee, and two if you had any common sense."

He smiled as he gestured dismissively. "My knees don't work so well anymore. Sorry, but I'll not be able to kneel."

He didn't look at all concerned; Cassia did.

"Then maybe I can help you to—"

"It's all right," Kahlan said as she gently took Cassia by her upper arm and pulled her back. "It's clear that the man has bad knees."

Cassia looked in a mood to bite spikes in two. "His neck isn't bad. He can at least bow his head."

Iron Jack's cheerful face suddenly didn't look at all cheerful. "If it would speed matters along . . ." He performed a perfunctory bow of his head. "Mother Confessor. Welcome."

Out of the corner of her eye, Kahlan saw Richard use two fingers of his left hand to lift his sword from its scabbard enough to make sure it was clear. She had seen him do that same thing as a prelude to the possibility of violence countless times since he had become Seeker.

But this time, the sword didn't lift away from the scabbard.

Instead, the scabbard lifted with the sword as if the two were welded together. Richard tried not to betray his surprise, but Kahlan could read his reaction in the change of his posture. Kahlan didn't usually become overly concerned when someone didn't show the proper respect for the office of Mother Confessor, but with Richard's sword suddenly not available to him, her level of concern rose several notches.

She returned her gaze from Richard to Iron Jack so as not to draw attention to what was clearly a problem.

"What is this place?" she asked the man before her.

"Why, you didn't know?" Iron Jack lifted an arm and swept it around in grand fashion. "You have arrived in Bindamoon."

"Bindamoon? This is Bindamoon?" Shale asked with a frown of surprise as she took a step forward. "I know of Bindamoon."

Iron Jack's tense expression eased and he beamed again. "Then you know what a wonderful place it is."

Richard shot a suspicious look at the sorceress. "You're from the Northern Waste. How do you know of it?"

"Some of the people in the Northern Waste trade in Bindamoon for rare herbs. Healers consider this place sacred. They make pilgrimages here to collect the rare herbs they need."

Richard turned back to the blocky man. "You said that you were expecting us."

"That's right," the man said, as if no explanation were needed.

Richard clearly wanted to hear that explanation. "How is it that you were expecting us?"

"The queen told us that you were coming."

"The queen," Richard repeated in a flat tone.

Iron Jack twisted around to lift an arm toward an elegant, soaring structure built on a prominent rise of rock in the distance.

"Yes, the queen. That would be her winter palace, up there."

"We need to see this queen," Richard said. "Now."

Iron Jack, the mirth again vanishing from his gnarly features, lifted his eyebrows. "Oh, I'm afraid that isn't possible."

13

"And why isn't it possible?" Richard asked.

The man shrugged in reaction to the question. "It's the middle of the night, in case you hadn't noticed. No one would be wanting to wake the queen at this time of night, and I'm sure you wouldn't, either. You will wait until morning."

Richard clearly looked displeased. "The morning? You expect us to wait until morning to see this queen of yours?"

Iron Jack smiled without humor. "That's right. You may see her in the morning—if, that is, she wishes to see you, and when she wishes to see you. She is, after all, not at the beck and call of travelers. Until then, I will take you to our guest quarters, where you may await word on a possible audience."

"That sounds more than reasonable," Shale said as she tugged Richard's sleeve to get him to let her speak for them.

When he frowned back at her she gave him an odd smile as her eyes widened and she leaned toward him a little with meaning. Kahlan could see that the sorceress had her reasons for not wanting to push the issue and she wasn't going to say those reasons out loud in front of the stout man. She was simply hoping to get Richard to go along with her.

Richard finally turned back to Iron Jack. "Considering the late hour, I agree that it would be a rude imposition. Why don't you take us to these guest quarters?"

Shale looked relieved. Iron Jack appraised Richard with a sly smile. Kahlan thought for a moment that the two men might suddenly break into a battle right then and there among the fields of herbs and blue butterflies.

Iron Jack finally broke eye contact and turned to lead them off past the fields of herbs toward the mass of buildings. When they reached a series of paths that branched off, he took one leading to the right. It soon started ascending the steep slope into the town, wending its way among the tightly packed buildings that, while square and uniform, were placed askew, apparently wherever would work best on the rising mountainside.

Heavy wooden beams every few feet were set across the cobblestone path to make steps of sorts as well as help keep people from slipping in the wet as they climbed through the canyon of buildings.

Walls made of flat, tannish-colored stone set in dark mortar rose straight up to each side. The path wouldn't have been wide enough for a wagon. When they came to a small handcart sitting tight against the wall by a door painted dark green, they all had to turn sideways in order to squeeze past.

They finally reached a long, low, blocky building in a row of low, blocky buildings set in front of another. Since each of the buildings had a number of doors, the long buildings were apparently divided into a series of separate rooms. Iron Jack opened the first weathered, wooden door they came to.

"These are guest accommodations for

visitors, merchants, traders, and those passing through Bindamoon and needing a place to stay for the night." He pointed to the row of doors in the low stone buildings. "There is a different room for each of you. I don't know what sort of food would be at hand at this hour, but I will have someone bring along something to eat to each of your rooms."

"Thank you, Iron Jack," Shale said, stepping in front of the others before anyone else could say a word. "We could all use a bite to eat and some rest."

He bowed his head with another sly smile as his gaze passed among all those watching him. "Have a good night's rest, then. I will come by in the morning to take you to the queen, if she is of a mind to greet visitors."

Once the man was gone, Richard ushered all of the Mord-Sith through the open door, rather than letting anyone go to one of the other rooms. He then urged Kahlan and Shale inside and, once inside, shut the door. The sorceress lit a lamp on a small table and another on a shelf in the stone wall. There was a bed, and other than a table with a bench on each side, not much else, not even a window.

"I don't want us splitting up and going to different rooms," Richard said.

"I have to agree with your sentiment," Shale said. "All is not right here, and not what it seems."

Berdine arched an eyebrow sarcastically. "You don't say?"

The sorceress turned from Berdine to Richard. "Iron Jack is gifted—maybe a sorcerer or possibly even a wizard. I don't know exactly what he is, but I do know he is gifted."

Richard shared a look with Kahlan.

"He's a wizard?" Kahlan asked. "You mean like Richard?"

"No one is a wizard like Lord Rahl," she said.

"But is he powerful?" Kahlan asked.

Shale shrugged unhappily. "I don't know a great deal about wizards and such. All I can say with any certainty is that he is powerful enough to cause us a world of trouble."

Richard slipped the baldric off over his head. He held the point of the scabbard out to Vika and Cassia.

"Take hold of the scabbard while I try to draw the sword."

Despite their looks of confusion, the two

Mord-Sith gripped the scabbard and together spread their feet. Richard held on to the hilt and pulled the sword with all his might. The two women bent their knees and backs into it. As Richard pulled and they held on tight, their feet slid as he dragged them both across the wooden floor.

Kahlan was alarmed that the sword would not come free. She could see that the scabbard wasn't bent or dented. Richard finally conceded that it wasn't going to work.

Shale frowned with concern. "Here, let me see it."

When he handed her the sword with the baldric still attached, she held it in one hand and ran her other hand down the length of the elaborately engraved silver and gold scabbard.

She finally handed it back. "I can't tell the exact nature of it, but I can tell you that the blade has been locked in by a spell of some sort."

Richard tried jiggling the handle in an unsuccessful attempt to draw out the sword before looking up at her. "Can you break the spell?"

Shale arched an eyebrow. "You're a war wizard. Can't you break the spell?"

Richard's only answer was to smile. Kahlan

couldn't understand the meaning behind the look. Before she had time to consider his expression, Shale shook her head in sympathy.

"It would take more power than mine to overcome the magic holding the sword in the scabbard. It was likely a relatively easy trick for someone gifted to merely weld it in, as it were, so that it can't be drawn. It would be a much simpler way to disable the magic of the sword itself than to actually defeat such immense power."

Richard simply nodded as he slipped the baldric back over his head anyway, apparently not willing to abandon the weapon even if he couldn't draw it for now. Kahlan had a hard time believing that he couldn't pull it from its scabbard.

"The Seeker is the weapon," she reminded him. "The sword is just a tool."

Richard smiled at her. "You're right."

"Iron Jack may be gifted in some way," Vika said, "but Lord Rahl is a war wizard. Lord Rahl is more powerful and can handle that red-haired fool. He has killed legions of Glee with his power. He can certainly pull the head off that obnoxious Iron Jack if he has to."

Shale sighed. "I hope you're right, and I don't mean to discount Lord Rahl's ability—I've certainly seen things that I can't begin to understand—but I think there is more to Iron Jack than meets the eye."

Kahlan stepped closer. "Like what?"

Shale shook her head, clearly distressed. "I don't know but think about why we are here."

"You mean the boundary?" Kahlan asked.

"Yes, and don't forget about the strange wood, among other things. The boundary was put up by someone or some group of people using Lord Rahl's gift. If they are that powerful, then . . ."

Vika planted her fists on her hips. "Then you think Lord Rahl isn't powerful enough to handle them?"

Shale looked anguished to be taken the wrong way. "I'm not saying that, I'm only bringing up the fact that people powerful enough to steal his ability and use it to create the boundary are at the center of this, so it seems obvious they manipulated us in order to get us to this place. I only mean to say that we are dealing with something profoundly dangerous, and we should not assume anything—not about Iron

Jack or anyone else we might meet here. Bold people often end up dead."

Vika's glare eased. "Well, I would have to agree that Lord Rahl is often too bold for his own good. He would usually be better off if he let us handle things."

"Whatever is going on," Richard said, seemingly irritated by the way they were talking about him, "it is profoundly dangerous, and we need not to have tests of magic with anyone until we know what we're up against."

Shale nodded with relief. "That's all I meant."

Before they had time to discuss what they were going to do next, there was a knock at the door. When Richard opened it, a shy woman holding a tray looked inside and blinked in surprise. She then leaned back to look to the other doors. Richard leaned out for a look himself. Kahlan could just see through the open doorway that there were other women also carrying trays at the other doors, confused that their knocks weren't being answered. They all wore the same formal brown dresses with white aprons of servants.

"You aren't all in your rooms," the woman said with obvious surprise and uncertainty as to what she should do about it.

"They will all be going to their rooms in a bit," Richard told her in a friendly tone to ease the worry on her face. "We're all in here talking about our arrival at this amazing place of Bindamoon."

His words did the trick to put her at ease. The young woman finally smiled. "Bindamoon certainly is an amazing place."

"And how do you like the queen?" he asked, offhandedly.

The smile evaporated. She bowed her head, fearing to look up into his eyes. "I am but a nobody, sir. I have never met the queen, so I would have no reason to have any thoughts on her, much less an opinion."

"I see," Richard said as he took the tray with a bowl of soup.

Relieved of her tray, she took a step back to motion the others to bring theirs. As they filed in, several of the Mord-Sith took the bowls of steaming soup, pots of hot tea, and cups and placed them all on the table. Once they had emptied the trays, they glared at the women. The women, fearful of meeting the gazes of the Mord-Sith, bowed their heads as they tucked their trays under an arm and filed out.

The one who had come first bowed deeply several times. "Please enjoy your meal."

After she hurried away Richard shut the door. "I don't want us splitting up and going to separate rooms. I want all nine of us to stay together."

"I couldn't agree more," Vika said.

The rest of the Mord-Sith all nodded that they were of the same opinion.

Shale, over at the table, turned back to the rest of them after staring down into the soup. She stirred a finger over one of the bowls.

"I don't advise eating any of this."

"Is there a problem with it?" Kahlan asked.

"I believe that I can detect some kind of nasty magic floating around in it."

"You mean the food has been spelled?" Richard asked.

"Yes, I believe so, but I don't know what kind of spell it could be. It's possible that it could merely be an innocent spell to help us sleep, but I think it best if we don't eat it and find out too late that it is something more."

With the heel of his hand resting on the hilt of his sword locked into the scabbard by some sort of magic, Richard drummed his fingers on the wire-wound handle.

He frowned in thought as he looked around at the others. "Why are we here?"

"To see the queen?" Berdine asked.

Richard shook his head. "No. We came here because the boundary left us no other way around the mountains. But the path, while leading us into this trap, also revealed a pass that can get us over the mountains. That's what we need to do: get through this pass and cross over the mountains and into the Midlands.

"Why would we need to see the queen? What we need to do is leave this place before the Golden Goddess sees us through the eyes of people here and sends more of the Glee to kill us. We've been lucky up until now in fighting them. I'd rather not press our luck and have to fight them again."

Shale passed a worried look between Richard and Kahlan. "What about Iron Jack? He is gifted. And you can't use your sword because of some magic he has used on it."

"Hopefully he went to bed." Richard showed her a grim expression. "But if he tries to harm us and if I have to, I will put my sword, scabbard and all, through his heart."

"At last," Vika said, throwing up her hands, "you are finally making sense."

Her sisters of the Agiel all nodded their agreement.

14

Other than a skinny gray cat looking for a meal among the refuse in scattered piles and trash that had drifted into corners of buildings, the dark, narrow streets of the mountain-fortress town were deserted. Something about darkness gave the place a forbidding feel. Kahlan got the distinct feeling that Bindamoon was not a place where one would want to be outside at night.

Moonlight reflected off cobblestones worn smooth and shiny by countless feet. The variety of laundry hung on ropes strung between opposing windows overhead cast ghostly moon shadows across the passageways. Without any wind, woodsmoke from chimneys curled down the tile roofs to settle into the canyons and alleyways between the towering walls, looking like fog as it slowly crept along the ground.

Kahlan was relieved that there hadn't been guards posted at the guest quarters to keep watch over them. At least, there were none she saw. She supposed that they assumed the spells in the soup had rendered them helpless, or unconscious. Or even dead.

Shale had said that she didn't sense anyone near. Richard, worried about how the gifted might be able to use magic to conceal their presence, and not exactly sure of the extent of Shale's ability to determine such things, had gone out alone to scout the area anyway and make sure they weren't being watched. Once he was satisfied that there was no one about, he and Vika took the lead as they left the buildings Iron Jack had taken them to. They left the soup and pots of tea untouched and cold on the table.

Berdine shadowed Vika, with Kahlan and then the rest following behind. They stayed close together as they made their way through the cobblestone streets as quietly as possible. None of them spoke for fear of waking the sleeping residents or giving away their position if there were any watchmen in the city. She also knew of magic that could detect and even overhear distant voices, so they used hand signals when necessary.

The windows overlooking the tight, winding passageways were all dark. While there was a main road leading through the town, Richard didn't want to take it for fear of being spotted out in the open, so they took a route through the tight cluster of buildings stepping up the steep rises to the side of the pass. As far as Kahlan could tell, other than the main road through the pass, there were no large thoroughfares among the densely packed buildings, just a maze of narrow streets and alleys.

Those narrow streets and alleyways weren't laid out in any particular pattern she could discern. It seemed that the buildings were simply built where they could fit in atop the rocky terrain. That meant that to go in the desired direction, they needed to take a zigzag route among the stone buildings.

Every once in a while, they caught a view of the moon as they continued making their way generally west by way of twists and turns. As difficult as it was to navigate among the tightly packed buildings, Kahlan found it preferable to being out in the open on the main road through the pass. If they could be spotted by any of the people of Bindamoon, they could also be spotted by the goddess.

Richard pointed up at a window as he tiptoed under it. With his back close to the wall, he crossed his lips with a finger in warning. Kahlan glanced up and in the moonlight saw a heavyset man in a dark window scratching the back of his fat arm as he yawned. He stepped close to the window to look out at the mountains. He probably couldn't sleep. Kahlan wished she could; she was exhausted and, on top of that, being pregnant with the twins meant that everything required extra effort. Her fear of being caught by the menacing and gifted Iron Jack kept her moving without complaining as she, too, put her back up against the wall while passing under the window.

At the first opportunity, Richard hurriedly turned them all to the left around a corner and down a different street. He put a hand to their backs as they went by, urging each of them to hurry along so that the man wouldn't see them if he happened to look down. Kahlan breathed a sigh of relief to have made it past unseen.

The maze Richard took them through led them ever higher up the slippery cobblestones. The heart of the town was a warren of passageways, some of them with steps to climb the steeper alleyways. In some places there were courtyards to the side screened by solid wooden gates. Kahlan looked through the spaces between the wooden slats and was able to see small tables and chairs. There was nothing threatening in any of the enclosed spaces she looked into.

No matter how far they went, the buildings were all constructed the same way. The moonlight among the vertical stone walls was enough for them to see by, but barely, and not enough to banish the spooky shadows in angular, twisting corners. Kahlan worried about what might be lurking in those shadows.

In many places they had to step carefully lest they walk in the muck that people dumped out of the windows. Large populations of rats scurried along close to the walls. The alleyways stank of the waste thrown out from chamber pots. The streets didn't smell much better. The stench mixed with the woodsmoke creeping along the ground to make a pungent tang. In places the overwhelming smell made Kahlan feel sick to her stomach. She was eager to get away from Bindamoon and out into the fresh air of the surrounding forests.

As the sky began to brighten with the approaching dawn and they came to the top of a cobblestone passageway, they got their first glimpse between buildings at what lay out beyond the town. It wasn't a good enough view to satisfy Kahlan, but through the vertical slit between walls she was at least able to see open countryside. The expectation of getting away had them all hurrying to get beyond the buildings of the town and out into the concealment of the forests.

When they finally reached the outer edges of the town, where some of the buildings sat right atop the wall where it met the mountain, they all finally got their first good look over that wall and down the trail on the western side of Bindamoon. In the brightening daylight, Kahlan could see that the path went off into snow-crusted trees. She knew that anyone would be able to follow their tracks in the snow, but she also knew that the path would eventually descend below the snow line, where it would be much easier for them to disappear into the thick trees and brush among the rocky outcroppings.

She could see that lower down the pass there were dense green forests blanketing the slopes to either side that would help conceal them. In the center of the descending ground among the hills, far below, she could see a broad valley with a large stream snaking back and forth through flat grassland. She could also see the path in places as it wound its way down toward that expansive valley.

Beyond the grassland with that meandering stream, the countryside was open. There were no mountains to block their way.

What Kahlan was looking out at was the eastern ranges of the Midlands where it met D'Hara.

She felt a swell of excitement at seeing that open ground. Her heart beat faster. Each breath came quicker. She was almost home. She felt tears unexpectedly well up at the thought of finally being in the Midlands.

"It's our way out," she whispered to Richard with tear-choked words.

Richard circled an arm around her shoulders

to give her a quick hug. "We will be to Aydindril before you know it."

Below them they could see that the road went through the opening in the western wall of Bindamoon. She knew, though, that once on that road they would be out in the open, where they could be easily spotted from either side of the town. To make matters worse, it was getting brighter, as the sun was close to rising behind them. It couldn't be avoided, so they hurried down out of the buildings to the road that would get them as far away from the town as swiftly as possible.

Once they were on the main road that led through the wall and out of town, everyone kept a watch all around. Fortunately, they didn't see anyone. Lights from lamps began coming on in a few windows behind them, but Kahlan didn't see anyone looking out.

The road led to an arched opening in the wall that was much like the one in the wall they had come through when they had entered Bindamoon from the east side, meaning that the town was a walled fortress with a wall guarding it from both sides of the pass.

Kahlan was relieved to see that the portcullis

was drawn up. As they passed into the dark, arched tunnel through the wall, they all kept looking back to make sure no one was watching or following. Kahlan's gaze flicked from window to window, but she still didn't see anyone watching them. The huge wooden doors, like the ones on the eastern side of the town, also stood open.

She was alarmed to see, up on the wall, a small group of ravens looking down, watching them pass beneath.

Beyond the wall, the road dwindled back down to a well-worn trail. They hurried away as quickly as possible without running, putting distance between them and the town. As soon as they were out of the protection of the town, the cold air returned. With the mild conditions inside Bindamoon she had forgotten just how cold it had been outside.

Kahlan felt a sense of relief when they finally made their way in among sparse trees. Most were pine, and the ground was open. In places there were groupings of white birch. She could see that off ahead the woods became increasingly dense. She looked forward to getting into dense woods, where they couldn't so easily be spotted, although, she realized, the ravens would probably follow and keep track of them. Once they reached the Midlands and were away from Bindamoon, she thought, the ravens might finally abandon following them. She didn't care if they flew around outside the Keep once she got there.

Suddenly, without warning, the air around them turned green. Kahlan had been lost in her thoughts as they marched along; Richard thrust an arm in front of her to prevent her from inadvertently taking another step and walking into the world of the dead. As everyone lurched to a stop, the strange green glow was all around them. Going any farther would bring up the darkness of the underworld.

"Bags," he growled. "I was afraid of that."

It was unusual for Richard to curse. In this case, she couldn't say she blamed him. She shared the same frustrated rage.

"What do we do now?" Vika asked.

Richard backed them all away from the green wall of death. He glared back toward the fortress town.

"We no longer have a choice," he said. "The boundary completely blocks any way to get out.

We're going to have to go back to Bindamoon."

Kahlan gestured off to the sides. "Maybe if we checked to the sides there might be an opening in the boundary wall—a way around it if not through it."

Richard shook his head in anger. "You know as well as I do that's a false hope. Someone wanted to get us here to Bindamoon and to keep us here. They were willing to kill any traveler or trader who might come along and walk into the boundary in order to make that happen. This place is a trap and they aren't going to let us escape it so easily."

When they turned back, off in the distance they could see Iron Jack, hands planted on his hips, standing on top of the wall, watching them.

15

With the boundary now blocking any hope for escape, they had no choice but to turn around and trudge back toward the tunneled opening in the wall. Satisfied to see that they were returning, Iron Jack turned and vanished from the top of the wall. Kahlan wondered where he was going.

Richard fumed in a quiet rage. His silence was telling. She knew that when he got like this it was best not to ask him anything unless it was important. The focus of his anger rightly belonged on whoever was doing this to them.

As was his way, he had first tried to avoid a conflict. Now that those who had created this trap had made avoiding conflict impossible, he was prepared to meet it head-on.

Kahlan struggled to put one foot in front of the other. She was exhausted, both physically and mentally. It seemed like everything was grinding her down. Her worry, though, was for the twins, not for herself.

It seemed like forever ago that they had started out from the People's Palace, and yet the distant Wizard's Keep seemed no closer. In her mind, the Keep had come to seem more an impossible dream than a place they would ever reach.

They had been traveling for so long her belly had grown quite large. She was relieved to feel the babies kick from time to time, because it meant they were still alive. Everyone sacrificed their own food to give to her, knowing she needed it for the growing babies.

Because they had lost an unknown stretch of time in the strange wood, she was no longer sure of when the babies would come, other than knowing that it was still a ways off. But with as big as she was getting, that time was clearly getting closer, while the Keep wasn't.

She reminded herself that she was still the Mother Confessor, and no matter her concerns and doubts, this was no time to show weakness.

She gestured to the sides. "There is still some forest here, outside the wall. I don't like that place inside the walls. We know they already tried to spell us—or poison us—with the food, and we know that the man up there bound your sword into its scabbard. Obviously, it's dangerous in there. Why don't we just go into the woods and set up a camp while we come up with a plan?"

Richard kept his gaze resolutely ahead as he continued to march toward the opening in the wall. "How is camping out here going to get us to the Keep?"

"I don't know," Kahlan said in a weary voice, "but how is going back in there without a plan going to get us to the Keep?"

"I have a plan."

Kahlan gave him a sidelong glance. "And what would that be?"

Richard didn't look over at her. "The people who are preventing us from getting to Aydindril by doing all these things to stop us, like the way they used my gift to bring up the boundary, are after those babies you are carrying. They are willing to let people who wander into that wall die. They are after the hope of our world and willing to kill innocent people to get what they want. I can't let this threat stand. I'm going in there and putting a stop to it."

Kahlan again stole a sidelong glance at him. "That's your plan?"

"That's all the plan I need."

Kahlan didn't think that was the case, but she didn't want to argue with him. He was not the one wanting to get her babies.

The witch woman looked distraught with concern. "But if they are powerful enough to do all the things they have done to draw us into this trap, and as you say they are willing to let innocent people die, do you think it wise to walk right back into their trap?"

Richard shot her a quick glare before looking ahead as he continued on. "They think they are smart and powerful because they have contrived to use my gift to put up the boundary to lure us to this place. What they have actually done is to attract lightning, and that lightning is about to strike them down."

Out of the corner of her eye, Kahlan saw Vika and some of the others smile. They were eager to face the threat and put an end to it. Kahlan was as well, but it wasn't likely going to be as easy as it sounded.

Although it was a rather foggy memory, she knew that she had already started to miscarry once. She feared losing the twins. She had lost a baby before and didn't want it to happen again. In the past she never would have hesitated to back Richard, but now that she was about to be a mother, it added a complication to everything. She had always been willing to put her own life on the line, but now she had to consider putting the lives of the twins at risk, to say nothing of all the people of their world.

On the other hand, if they were to protect their children from the Glee, they needed to get to the Keep, where it would be safe to give birth. Of course, while they might be safe there, the rest of the world would not be. That meant that to protect her children, and everyone else, the situation actually demanded that she fight more ferociously than ever before.

How they would eliminate the overriding threat posed by the Glee she couldn't begin to imagine, but she knew that the worst thing they could do would be to hide forever in the Keep while everyone else faced the onslaught of the Glee. They had to stop the immediate danger, and once it was eliminated, they needed to find a way to stop the Golden Goddess.

That thought added resolve to her determination. It was time to show whoever was stopping them exactly why she was the Mother Confessor. Richard was right: whoever had trapped them in this place had to be stopped, one way or another. As for the threat of the Glee, she couldn't imagine how they could overcome predators who could simply come into their world at will, but in the back of her mind she knew that such a threat could be faced only by a war wizard.

The more she thought about it, the more she realized that Richard was right. They had to go back into the town and end the threat, or they would never make it to safety and then be able to find a way to stop the goddess. Their world would never be safe until they did. Unfortunately, she was pretty sure who was at the center of all their current problems, and that was the one thing she truly feared to face, but this time there could be no backing down.

They all marched resolutely through the dark tunnel and emerged again inside the town. None of the narrow streets and alleys were straight, so it was hard to know the best route. There was often a warren of sharp corners and wedge-shaped intersections confronting them. In some places they had to pass under arches with parts of the buildings crossing overhead and in other places go under lines with laundry. Richard didn't seem deterred by the maze. He took them on a route that headed ever closer to his destination: the tall, white palace.

As they came around a corner of a wider passageway, they were confronted by Iron Jack, fists on his hips, standing to block their way. To the sides behind him it looked like there was a converging intersection of several narrow alleyways. Kahlan had been wondering how long it would take him to make an appearance. He obviously had guessed where they were headed.

"I will escort you back to your guest quarters," Iron Jack said in a threatening tone.

"We're not going to any guest quarters," Richard said. "We are going to see the queen. Either you can take us there, or we will go on our own."

The burly man gripped his kinky red beard as he cocked his head to the side and peered at them with one eye. "That would require an audience."

"That's not a problem," Richard said. "I am the Lord Rahl, leader of the D'Haran Empire, and I intend to grant your queen an immediate audience."

"That's not what I mean," the man growled.

"No, but it's what I mean."

"I'm the gifted man who rendered your sword useless," he reminded Richard. "You would make a very big mistake if you think to defy me."

Richard didn't look to be moved by the threat. "You can take us to this queen, or you can stand aside and we will go see her ourselves."

Iron Jack's sly smile grew wider as his eyes narrowed. "I'm afraid that I can't allow that. If you try, I will put you down."

Richard marched ahead. As he did, he rammed the heel of a hand against the man's big chest, slamming him back up against the wall of a building with enough force to make his teeth bang together.

"Good luck with that," Richard said on his way past.

Kahlan hurried to catch up and then followed

close on Richard's heels. Vika and the rest of the Mord-Sith, each with an Agiel in a fist, also rushed to keep up, adding their glares at Iron Jack on their way past.

Kahlan was glad to see that Iron Jack didn't follow them. She hoped he had gotten the point and wouldn't challenge them again.

Shale leaned closer to Kahlan and spoke in a low voice. "That man worries me."

"Why?"

"Because while I can't determine how gifted he is, I don't think I have the power to stop him if he comes for us."

Kahlan didn't look at the sorceress as she hurried along. "Richard does."

16

When Kahlan looked up between buildings, she finally got a good glimpse of the soaring palace. It wasn't dark and sinister-looking. Instead it looked light and elegant. While the base was obviously quite large, it didn't have a lot of grounds around it the way a typical palace would have had. It did, though, seem impossibly tall and graceful. Small, round spires, each with a conical tile roof and an arched window, stuck up here and there in various places along the towering height of the palace. Colorful pennants flew from each of those pointed roofs.

When they got closer, Kahlan spotted a flock of black-and-white wood storks, slowly flapping their broad wings and then soaring together in the clear morning air. She realized from how small the birds looked against the white walls of the palace that the place was both bigger and taller than she had thought at first. The scale of it didn't seem real.

She also realized, now that she was seeing the town for the first time in daylight, that most of the buildings were actually washed with faint color. There were a light mint green, pale pink, light blue, and soft yellows. All of the colors had faded over time so that the stone showed through.

Bindamoon was in many ways cramped and unappealing, even with the long-faded colorful paint, but the palace, glowing in the early morning sunlight as it overlooked the town, was actually rather magnificent. She realized that it was a mistake to ascribe a sinister aspect to a building inhabited by what could only be sinister people.

Considering all the twists and turns they had to make, there clearly wasn't a direct route through the town to the palace. That left them to try to find their way through the maze of structures as they worked their way ever closer to the palace rising up above them.

The buildings of the town seemed to have sprouted around the soaring palace like mushrooms around a tree trunk in damp weather.

As they got close, they didn't need the view between buildings; it loomed over them. Here and there Kahlan saw people in the windows of the surrounding buildings, looking out, greeting the early morning. In a few places, women leaned out to pull in laundry that had dried overnight. Occasionally, in the distance, she saw people hurrying among the buildings, but she didn't see anyone nearby.

As they were going up a cobblestone street that rose gently toward the palace, Iron Jack suddenly stepped out from a side alleyway to once again block their path.

"This is as close to the palace as you will be getting until the queen says otherwise," he announced.

Richard grew calm in a way that she knew all too well. Trouble was about to begin. She saw, then, several more men waiting in the shadows behind Iron Jack. Without being obvious about it, she pulled her knife from its sheath at her side. She saw Shale do the same.

She was surprised to see Richard reach over

and grip the hilt of his sword. He couldn't possibly have forgotten that it was bound into the scabbard by magic, so she couldn't imagine what he was doing.

He stood for a moment, head bowed, eyes closed, the muscles in his jaw flexing, his right hand on the hilt of the sword at his left hip, the muscles in his arm relaxed. She realized he was letting the power of the sword flow into him, letting its rage join with his. She suspected he was also summoning his own gift.

And then he began to draw the sword.

The blade came out silky smooth. Its distinctive ring echoed through the canyons of buildings as the blade, stained black by the world of the dead, emerged from the scabbard. The gleaming black steel greeted the dawn, ready to do battle.

Iron Jack looked stunned. "You can't do that! I myself sealed the sword and scabbard into one with powerful magic!"

Richard glared at the man. "I am the Lord Rahl."

"Not my lord. I answer to no one but the queen."

"You, and the queen, answer to me and to

the Mother Confessor," Richard said in a deadly voice.

Vika stepped up beside Richard. She made a show of spinning her Agiel up into her fist.

The rest of the Mord-Sith moved protectively around Kahlan. Each of them had her Agiel in her fist at the ready. They looked fed up with Iron Jack's nonsense and seemed more than pleased that Richard was as well. So was Kahlan.

Growing up, she had never had any interest in flaunting her authority. Her mother instilled a sense of responsibility as a Confessor, not self-importance. It was simply something she had been born with, not something she had that she would hold over others. As Mother Confessor, she knew how to wield that authority when it was necessary. And when it was necessary, she found that she didn't especially like that authority dismissed or disrespected, because respect for the Mother Confessor was not about her, it was about everything she represented.

Richard was much the same. He had never lusted after power. He never sought to be the Lord Rahl. But he had come to accept the responsibility and he, too, was fed up with his authority being ignored in something so important. He was, after all, the leader of the D'Haran Empire, and as such he ruled over these people. Including Iron Jack and the queen.

They were about to find out why.

As Iron Jack watched, Richard drew the sword across the inside of his forearm, giving the blade a taste of blood, something that made the sword's anger lust for more. Kahlan could see the sword's magic dancing in the Seeker's eyes.

Richard brought the blade up to touch his forehead. He closed his eyes.

"Blade, be true this day," he whispered.

"Is that supposed to scare me?" Iron Jack asked.

"This blade can't harm an innocent," Richard said. "It can only harm an enemy. I suggest you decide for yourself if you should be afraid."

Iron Jack ran a hand down his red beard as he took a step back. Rather than accepting Richard's command to stand down, he suddenly lifted his hands with an attack of his own.

When he did, every one of the Mord-Sith around Kahlan toppled to the ground as if a rug had been pulled out from under them. Iron Jack had attacked, not with a blade, but with his gift. As they struggled unsuccessfully to get back to their feet, they were visibly in pain from the magic Iron Jack had used. He smiled in satisfaction at seeing them on the ground.

They all knew that Iron Jack had magic, but any of the Mord-Sith, when he used that magic against them, should have been able to capture his magic and use it against him. That none of them could clearly spoke to the unique power of his gift.

Shale moved closer to Kahlan, her knife at the ready, obviously not willing to put her faith in her gift against such a man.

Iron Jack defiantly spread his feet to show that he intended to block their passage. "As I said, no one sees the queen until she wishes it. You may have somehow overpowered the magic fusing your sword tight in its scabbard, but you will not overpower me."

The man again lifted his hands in anger.

Suddenly, in the distance, Glee flooded out from around the corners of buildings. In a heartbeat they took out the men in the background, before they knew what had hit them. Tall, dark creatures, all teeth and claws, raced down the cobblestone passageway.

The Glee weren't materializing out of thin air the way they usually did. Steam didn't rise from them as always before. They didn't come streaming into Richard and Kahlan's world all together for an attack.

This time, they were using a new tactic: they had been hiding in ambush and Richard and Kahlan had walked right into their surprise attack.

The Glee had just learned an important strategy. Ambush gives the attacker a tactical advantage. That kind of attacker gets to pick the place and the moment of attack, while the defender is caught unaware and forced to respond, which puts them at a disadvantage because action usually beats reaction.

17

Richard was pleased to see that Iron Jack's ire was so fixated on him that he didn't even notice what was happening back over his shoulder until one of the tall creatures raced in and crashed into him. As it did, it grabbed him from behind. The Glee's new tactic of ambush meant never letting the opponent see you coming. Iron Jack hadn't seen them coming. Before the stunned bearded man could grasp what was happening and react, dark, slimy arms had already circled around him from each side.

Jack twisted frantically in an attempt to get out of the bear hug, but the powerful arms held him in tight against the Glee that had him. Shards of light flashed from the man's hands as he tried to use some kind of power to get the better of his attacker. The Glee bent its head first one way and then the other to avoid each of the flashes of light, but another creature nearby was torn apart by the release of the man's gift and fell dead.

Before Iron Jack could do anything to get away, the Glee that had him sank its teeth into the back of the man's neck to hold him. The creature then pulled its claws in opposite directions as Iron Jack was being held by the teeth in his neck. One claw ripped open Iron Jack's chest. At the same time, the other claw pulled in the opposite direction to tear out his throat. He didn't even have time to cry out before the Glee dropped him in a bloody heap to come charging for Richard.

Fortunately, because they surprised Iron Jack first, Richard was ready, and the magic coursing through him from his sword was ready to respond with swift violence.

As the Glee charged in, Richard had already begun his counterattack. The tip of the blade came around with such speed that it whistled as it sliced through the air. When the creature saw the sword, it reflexively lifted its arms to defend itself. Richard gritted his teeth with the effort of the swing.

The blade took off both the creature's claws and its head in that one lightning-quick strike. Richard held the blade up straight and took a step back, at the same time turning sideways and out of the way. The momentum of the clawless, headless body carried it past him to stumble across the cobblestones and collapse.

With Iron Jack dead, the Mord-Sith were suddenly able to scramble to their feet, and none too soon. More Glee charged down the street. The Mord-Sith raced to cut them off before they could get to Kahlan. Needle-sharp teeth clacked in anger. Most of them held an arm and claws cocked back, ready to strike. They were met with either an Agiel in one hand or a knife in the other.

Claws flashed through the air. Mord-Sith ducked under those claws as they swept by overhead and then sprang up to drive in for the kill. The Glee were clearly as vulnerable to an Agiel as any person would be. Wounded Glee fell in agonizing pain, holding arms across their injuries, or turned to scribbles and vanished, bleeding, back into their own world. Dead Glee simply dropped to the ground. Their blood ran down the slope in between the cobblestones.

As Richard noted what the Mord-Sith were doing, he was already moving into the attack. He swung his sword with deadly effectiveness. The magic from his sword, the same magic he had summoned to help free the blade from the scabbard, raged through him, demanding the blood of the enemy. He gave it all the blood it could want of any Glee within range. As he drove his attack directly into the enemy, Glee fell all around him, many without a head, others cut nearly in two, and some run through with his blade.

He turned and saw that Kahlan already had her knife to hand. It quickly became clear that she was the one the Glee wanted. They had come to rip the twins from her womb. She spun around when she heard one of them that had snuck around behind her and drove her knife into one of the big, glossy black eyes. The creature covered its eye as it shrieked. At the same time, it stumbled back awkwardly and, as it did, vanished to its own world. Even as she was pulling her blade back, Richard was there to protect her from others charging in to get her.

Shale, too, turned her abilities, rather than her knife, to the attack. With her eyes rolled up in her head, she lifted her hands, her fingers slowly waggling. As she did, masses of white snakes appeared, slithering across the cobblestones, going for the Glee.

The morning air was filled with the screams of the dark creatures as the snakes sank their fangs into them. From their awkward, jerky, contorted movements as they were struck by the snakes, it was clear to Richard that not only were the snakes venomous, but the venom acted so swiftly as to be almost immediate in its action. Glee, with snakes firmly attached to their legs, arms, and bodies, stumbled back, gurgling in choking pain as the venom quickly began to paralyze their lungs.

Shocked people appeared in windows, looking down on the frantic battle. Some screamed and ran back into dark rooms. Some, their mouths hanging open and hands gripping the windowsills, leaned out to watch.

Knowing the snakes were Shale's and meant for the Glee, Richard ignored them. It was

Kahlan most of the Glee were going for. She was the one they most wanted to kill. It was Kahlan he had to protect.

In that moment, as the fury of the sword's magic twisted together with his own and stormed through every fiber of his being, he lost himself to the madness of the battle. He became that madness. The Glee had come as hunters. Richard was now the hunter and they the prey.

As he responded to the attacks, he suddenly came to comprehend in a new and clear way how the Glee moved, the extent, the range, and the limitations of their movements. He began to see exactly how they used their claws to strike, with their teeth being their backup weapon. It was often a quick flick of a strike, but other times they used those claws to intimidate their prey for a fraction of a second to make the prey freeze just before they struck. That allowed them to be more accurate and deadly when they did strike.

The reason for the tactic, he saw, was that the Glee had most of their power when their arms were used in close combat. The farther they reached, the less power they had. The way they had killed Iron Jack had been their biggest strength—holding the prey in close as they tore it apart.

Once he grasped the technique in their strikes and how they set up for an attack, he was able to predict how they would move, which claw they would use first, and when they would strike with it, or instead, if their claws were not able to be used to their best advantage, use their teeth to try to kill.

He began to understand the fight with them in a whole new way. It all made sense in an entirely new light. He understood the battle from their perspective, rather than seeing it from his perspective, defensively.

Once he had the full scope of the realization, those attackers, rather than seeming like frightening creatures coming for him and Kahlan in a crazy, hysterical frenzy, became instead a part of the larger dance with death.

That meant he was no longer fighting them in the same ways he had previously. Now he was using their nature against them, turning it back on them, using their limitations and weaknesses as openings. For the first time, he was, in a sense, fighting them on their terms, and in that way, because he could anticipate what they would do next, he abruptly put them at a distinct disadvantage.

In that moment, he came back at them in a new way, in a way that completely overwhelmed their multiple tactical advantages of teeth and claws. Their limitations in range and movement became his advantages and openings.

In that moment, he stopped trying to kill them and switched instead to the quicker task of cutting off their powerful, deadly claws. It was a revelation. He didn't need to kill them. He simply needed to deny them their primary weapon. If the Glee didn't have those razor-sharp claws, they were nearly defenseless. They couldn't grasp or cut or rip or hold prey in order to use their teeth.

His sword spun through the air without pause, cutting at a dizzying pace. He moved around Kahlan, protecting her, disabling any enemy that came for her. She took out several with her knife as he momentarily moved around the other side of her. His sword lopped off claws as fast as they came within reach of his blade. He understood, now, where and how those claws would be coming, and which of the two were the actual threat. Severed claws tumbled through the air as he lopped them off at the wrist or forearm. The still-twitching claws littered the ground.

The creatures shrieked as they lost their precious claws. Some held out stubs in disbelief, and tried to reach out to grasp so they could attack with their teeth, but without their claws, it was easy for Richard to take off the heads of those determined enough to continue to come for him rather than escape back into the safety of their world. Seeing what happened when they came in at him, and seeing so many of their fellows with stubs of arms and no claws as they vanished back into their own world, they began to rightly fear to swing their own claws and lose them.

As they hesitated, the snakes struck and sank fangs into them. Once they had their fangs in the soft black skin, they would not let go. As that happened, Richard spun through their midst, taking the claws off the ends of their arms. Without their claws, they couldn't effectively try to tear at the snakes to get them off.

All around, panic spread among the shrieking and dying Glee. As their boldness and aggression turned to terror and timidity, those who still could started to turn to scribbles to flee back to the safety of their own world before Richard or the snakes could get to them.

Without a target, Richard finally paused, panting to get his breath as he let the tip of his sword lower to rest on the cobblestones. He looked all around, searching for any threat. The rage of his sword still thundered through him, demanding more blood. The ground was littered with hundreds of claws and dozens of heads, as well as the bodies of those that couldn't vanish before death.

18

With his sword, Richard gestured ahead for everyone to move on toward the palace and away from the scene of the brief but frenzied battle. While the Glee who went back to their own world would be testament to others of the trouble that awaited them here, tyrannical leaders, as the Golden Goddess apparently was, were often more than willing to throw the lives of countless followers into the fray.

With the battle over, Richard didn't want to be anywhere nearby in case the goddess, in a fit of anger, decided to send another wave of fighters. Attacking after a battle had seemingly ended was a good way to catch your opponent with their guard down. Richard didn't want to let his guard down, so he urged everyone away from the scene of the fight.

Though he might have won this skirmish, he knew that he had to solve the vastly bigger problem of stopping the goddess from sending any Glee at all. Winning a battle was of no use if he couldn't win the war. Every battle exposed them to the possibility that, this time, they might lose. If they lost, everyone in their world would ultimately lose.

Even if Richard and Kahlan could get to the safety of the Keep, that wouldn't provide any safety for everyone else. They would continue to be vulnerable. In the end, that was his weakness as a leader, and the goddess's strength. There was virtually no way for normal people to protect themselves, especially if the Glee came in massive hordes, and Richard couldn't protect everyone. People everywhere would be prey at the mercy of savage predators.

He took Kahlan's hand to help her balance as she stepped over the thick, tangled ring of severed claws and slimy bodies surrounding her. All those claws were now still, but it was a very visible reminder that they had been meant for her and her unborn babies. He knew that more would come. The Glee were relentless. He felt sick at not knowing if he was ever going to be able to stop them once and for all.

Richard let go of Kahlan's hand so she could help Shale, who looked weak and exhausted after unleashing masses of white snakes. The snakes she had conjured were gone now, either withdrawn by the witch woman after they were no longer needed or taken back to the home world of the Glee as they fled with the snakes still attached to them. Those snakes were in a way part of her, so when they were taken away with fleeing Glee, they were in a sense ripped away from her connection to them.

In the aftermath of the effort, the witch woman looked like she might collapse. Cassia rushed in on the other side and helped Shale stay upright as she stepped among the mounds of claws and the remains of the dead.

With the sword still in his hand, the magic of it still surged through him, filling him with rage. The sword hungered for an enemy; that was its way, its purpose. With the threat so fresh, the shrieks and howls still echoing through his head, Richard was not quite ready to relinquish the rage of the sword's magic spiraling through him. He wanted it at full force and at the ready just in case.

As the Mord-Sith started up the narrow cobblestone street, closely protecting Kahlan, he held back to reassure himself that there were no more threats lurking around any of the corners. Seeing none, he finally sheathed his sword and, in so doing, extinguished the rage. Once that fury of magic was finally cut off, it left him feeling weak and exhausted from the effort of the fight.

When the hair on the back of his neck tingled and stiffened, he looked up and saw a single Glee standing in the sun atop a two-story building, looking down, watching him. Somehow he had known that it would be there. The rest of those with him were helping each other and talking among themselves as they made their way up the narrow street. They didn't see the Glee. He didn't think that this lone creature wanted anyone but Richard to see it.

As he stood staring up at it, the Glee opened its arms a little and spread its claws to reveal webbing between its razor-sharp claws. Richard felt that it was a sign—that it was trying to convey the message that it meant no threat.

And then it bowed at the waist, as if out of respect.

He spotted, then, in those slow movements as it bowed, something he had never noticed before. There was a slight, iridescent, greenish sheen to this Glee's skin. It reminded him a little of the iridescent green sheen on the backs of some black beetles. He hadn't seen this quality to the flesh of any Glee he had fought.

Even though he hadn't noticed this slight greenish sheen on this particular Glee before, there was no doubt in his mind that this was the same individual he had seen several times before, when on previous occasions it had also signaled that it intended him no harm.

When the Glee stood back up, it shared a long look with Richard. From time to time as it stared, its third eyelid blinked across its big, glossy black eyes. It cocked its head a little, possibly as if appraising him. Richard felt a sense of peace with this creature.

He reminded himself of one of his most basic beliefs, that an individual was not guilty because of the crimes of others. It was something very personal for him, because he had once been hated as the Seeker because of how corrupt people before him had been when they had possessed the sword, its power, and the post. Because of their notorious behavior, it was assumed that all Seekers were evil. He had likewise been condemned as evil because of the sins of his father. He knew that although all the other Glee he had seen and fought had been trying to kill them, this one individual had not, so he had to remember not to judge it by their actions.

And then it turned to scribbles and in a fleeting moment was gone.

Richard wished there were a way to talk to that Glee, to find out its intentions and what it wanted.

Kahlan paused a ways up the narrow street and turned back. "Are you coming?"

"Sure," Richard said as he sprinted to catch up with the others.

"So," Shale finally said as they moved on up an even narrower alleyway to continue to make their way toward the palace, "tell me how you managed to get your sword out of the scabbard when it had been welded in there by Iron Jack's magic."

"Wizard's First Rule," he said.

Shale paused to turn back and give him a squinty-eyed look. "What?"

"I was always able to get the sword out," Richard said.

Shale flopped her arms against her side in frustration. "Well, if that were really true, then why couldn't you get it out before? You had Vika and Cassia hold the scabbard while you pulled on the handle. You couldn't get it out then."

"Actually, I could," Richard told her.

Shale clawed her fingers as she growled in exasperation. "No, you couldn't. I saw it. It was welded in by Iron Jack's magic and the three of you couldn't pull it apart. What's more, when I felt the scabbard, I could feel the magic bound into it holding it together."

Richard shrugged. "I could feel the magic, too."

Shale held her head with both hands as she growled again. "And you couldn't draw it! Why could you draw it now, but not back then?"

Richard finally showed her a smile. "Shale, I could have drawn it whenever I wanted. I asked for your help and you said you couldn't do it. As you said yourself, I'm a war wizard. But I wanted Iron Jack to think he had bested me."

The witch woman leaned toward him a little. "What?"

"I felt Iron Jack's magic tingling around the hilt. It was only Additive. There was no Subtractive element to it. So, I only pretended I couldn't get it out of the scabbard because I knew he would be able to sense if his spell was broken. For that reason, I was careful not to. I wanted him to think instead that I had tried and failed, so I was defenseless. I wanted him to believe that so he would feel emboldened. I wanted him to think he had everything under control so that he would lose his sense of caution and act true to his nature."

Shale straightened her back and stared at him for a moment. "You mean you were concerned that if he feared you, he might put on an innocent and friendly act?"

Richard smiled again. "Now you're getting the idea. I felt no need to show off and pull the sword when he thought his magic had locked it in the scabbard. I wanted to see what he would do when he thought he was in complete control."

Shale turned to Kahlan. "Your husband is a very devious man."

Kahlan nodded. "Annoying, isn't it?"

19

Richard didn't see anyone near the entrance to the palace. No guards, no supplicants, no staff. There was no insurmountable wall or any other method to keep people out as was typical around places of power.

Now that it was daytime there were lots of people hurrying about their business back in the narrow streets of the town. None of them came near the palace—not even close. It was obvious that no wall was needed.

If he was right, and he was almost positive that he was, they had good reason to give the place a wide berth, which would obviate the need for a wall, or guards.

While the palace was not massive in the sense that other castles or palaces he'd seen covered a lot of ground, it was nonetheless still sizable. Rather than being imposing by its girth, it was instead gracefully tall, taller than most palaces he'd seen. There was only one palace he could recall that soared to such heights with similar splendor. That palace didn't need high walls or guards, either.

He shared a look with Kahlan, and he could see in her green eyes that she was thinking the same thing he was.

As he looked up the soaring white stone wall, he could see in the places where it stepped back as the palace went ever higher that there were ravens perched on the edges of various levels, cocking their heads to look down at them.

Thirteen steps in gray marble with white swirls through it stretched out quite some distance to either side. At the head of those steps there was no grand entablature decorating the entrance; there were no intricate, ornamental moldings. Instead, atop the landing was an elaborate door set back into the white stone. The massive door looked to be made of bronze. The entire surface was covered in rows of orderly, embossed writing, designs, and symbols. Each row was unique.

When he led the others up the steps for a closer look, he saw that he recognized some of the lines of symbols on the massive door. They were in the language of Creation. He ran his fingers over the raised designs as he mentally deciphered their meaning. They were general warnings to stay away, but there were also some critically clear specifics.

With his fingers still on the symbols, he looked back over his shoulder at Kahlan. "This says that none may enter without first being commanded to appear."

Kahlan stepped up the final step to stand beside him to study the door. She gestured to one of the lines of the writing.

"It says the same thing there."

"Do you recognize any of the other writing?" he asked.

She scanned the door, then used her fingers to touch some of the lines of symbols to keep her place as she examined the strange designs. She finally gave Richard a grim look.

"At least a dozen of the languages here on this door are those used in the Midlands. That makes sense, given the location of Bindamoon right in the middle of the line of the mountains that divide the Midlands from D'Hara. And, as Shale said, even people from the Northern Waste came here. It would seem that many different people came here for the rare herbs they grow in those fields. It would make sense for there to be a lot of languages represented, so that anyone who came up here could read the warnings.

"I speak most of these languages. Each message is a warning that says the same thing as you read, that none may enter without first being commanded to appear."

Richard glanced back at the others. "I guess it's pretty clear by everything that's happened that we have been commanded to appear."

"With all those languages being clear warnings," Shale said, "do you think it wise to go in there?"

"Wise or not, this is the heart of the threat. We're going in and I'm putting a stop to it."

No one looked like they had any intention of arguing.

Richard turned a lever, then drew back a bolt. It made a dull clang when it reached the end of its travel. He put both hands against the tall brass door and pushed. He pushed, then pushed harder to get it to start to move. With a great deal of effort, and several Mord-Sith coming to help, the heavy door silently swung inward until the opening was wide enough for them to slip through and enter.

The hushed interior was not nearly as bright as it was outside, but there were a number of high windows that at least let some light stream down from above. Hundreds of candles in ornate metal stands all around the interior lent the place a mellow glow.

Their footsteps echoed softly back from the distance. If the outside of the palace was rather simple and plain, the inside was the complete opposite.

On each side there were a half-dozen steps up to raised vestibules. Above them were convex entablatures decorated with complex moldings. The massive stone structures were held up by rows of fluted stone columns that enclosed each of the areas. The capitals atop those columns were intricate, curling acanthus leaves carved from a pale greenish-gray stone Richard had never seen before.

Between the entablatures were enormous arches leading deeper into the side wings. Each end of those massive arches was held up with four fluted stone columns composing a single support structure. The bases of those arches were so sizable that they had small, internal arches on all four sides of their bases, each held by a stone column, all of them together holding up the more massive main arch. The whole thing was so complex it sent the eye dancing over the elaborate, involved, and interconnected shapes.

The windows beyond those arches were made up of what had to be hundreds of small pieces of beveled glass in a gridwork of stone mullions. That beveled glass sent prisms of colors scattering all across the walls and columns. Beneath and beyond those windows, Richard could see ornate side chambers, lit by countless candles.

In the center of the room, the arches before those antechambers formed a perimeter to support a central dome. Massive square support structures, with square, fluted pilasters, anchored each of the primary arched sections. Inside the top of the dome, small windows all around let in light from exterior rooms above and around the interior dome. All of the stone of the entire place was various shades of greenish-gray, giving the place a uniform, muted theme.

In the center of the massive room, beneath the dome, was a floor with cream and gray stone making up large squares that marched all the way around a central design of a wreath made out of gold-colored stone set against a background of white. In the center of the wreath were more concentric designs that stepped down in size. The floors to the sides, going off into the antechambers, were gridwork designs made of the same cream and gray stone.

In between the fluted columns and the fluted pilasters there were recesses with life-size statues in the same greenish-gray stone. Some were of people, but most were of strange, con-torted figures that didn't look quite human— or possibly were people in great pain. All the figures were clothed in flowing robes carved out of the same stone. The carved robes were so realistic that it made it look like there was a brisk breeze blowing through the place.

Richard had seen a number of magnificent places since leaving his home of Hartland. This was up near the top in the sheer splendor of the complex yet graceful architecture. He had never seen cold stone looking so warm in its intricate stateliness. The whole place made him feel small and inadequate. He supposed that was really the purpose and the point of it all. Those who entered should be humbled before the master of this domain.

Richard and those with him, all standing in a close cluster, stared around at the ornate stonework of the arches and the dome. It was achingly beautiful, but at the same time it was a clear statement that they were in the place of powers not to be trifled with.

In the center of the circular design in the floor, under the dome, the mountain lion sat on its haunches, watching them, its tail slowly sweeping back and forth across the floor.

When the mountain lion was sure that they had all looked around enough, it stood. As they all watched, it turned and started walking away, deeper into the palace, clearly expecting them to follow.

20

Richard watched as the mountain lion casually walked off into the distance. "We're supposed to follow it."

"Why do you think that?" Berdine asked.

He gave her a look. "Because it was sent to fetch us."

Berdine's nose wrinkled up. "How do you know that?"

"Because I've seen it before at another important moment, and I don't believe it was a coincidence."

Vika turned a troubled look toward Richard. "So then you think it's the same mountain lion we saw up on the mountain when we found the mother's breath?"

"Of course it's the same one. When we found

the mother's breath, it left to tell its master."

"And so you think its master lives here?" Berdine asked.

Richard gave her the same look again, as if to say it was a silly question. "Why else would a mountain lion be walking around inside this palace?"

"Oh," she said, "I guess I see your point."

"Odd choice for a house pet," Shale said.

"It wouldn't be the strangest one I've seen," Richard muttered under his breath as he started out after the mountain lion. "Come on. We don't want to lose sight of it."

Shale leaned in. "But—"

"Hurry," Kahlan said as she put a hand to the small of Shale's back to get her moving.

The mountain lion led them across the broad, circular design in the floor under the towering dome. The animal stopped before a vestibule of sorts in the distance. Curved staircases on either side surrounded it on the way to an upper level with rooms beyond and to either side.

The mountain lion looked back for a moment to be sure they were following, then ambled onward. That vestibule, with more of the greenish-gray columns to either side, stood before a broad passageway that wasn't as wide as the antechambers off to the sides of the domed area had been. This seemed to Richard more like it was an entrance into a central hall of some sort leading on into the interior. The significance of the central hall was evident from its elaborate architecture.

The same fluted columns of greenish-gray stone lined the long room. A great many ornate metal candlestands held what had to be hundreds of candles that not only lit the way ahead with soft light but lent a pleasant scent to the place.

To the sides, between pairs of fluted columns, inside stone frames, there were large square panels of incredibly beautiful red marble with swirls of green, gold, and black veins runn-ing through them. Each one of those massive red granite slabs seemed to glow in the soft candlelight.

It occurred to Richard that the swirly red marble panels reminded him of a floor covered with blood that had been cut out and then hung up for display. He paid closer attention to the red slabs as he passed by them, scrutinizing them to make sure they weren't actually patterns of blood. Even though he stared closely at each one, he still wasn't sure.

Farther down into the dark end of the magnificent but somber passageway, the pairs of columns were set closer together. Rather than the red marble that was displayed between the previous columns, between each of these there were faces, again carved in the greenish-gray stone. They were similar to the statues Richard had seen before, except these were only life-size busts. Each one leaned out, making it seem they were trying desperately to come right out of the wall.

All of the grim faces stretching out from either side were distorted in agony, or longing, or terror. Some of them reminded Richard of the carvings of tortured souls he had seen in the Old World. Like those statues he had seen there, he had seen the real thing in the underworld.

Other faces looked like they might be human, but if they were meant to be human, they were ghastly examples of torment and torture. The others, the ones that weren't human, Richard couldn't even guess at, but they, too, had horrified expressions, with mouths opened wide as if they had been frozen in mid-scream. The farther they went into the ever-darkening passageway, the more grotesque and distorted the faces became, with flesh carved to look like it was torn open so that the bones and teeth beneath the ripped cheeks were visible.

The wide hallway was enough to sap the courage of anyone who got this far, but it didn't dim his determination. If anything, it reinforced his resolve to stop the person responsible for depictions of such horrors, but more importantly those responsible for what they were doing to Kahlan.

Shale looked from one side to the other, staring for a moment at each one of the faces looking like they were trying to push themselves out of the walls to escape.

"Why would anyone carve such awful things?"

Richard glanced back at her. "Well, I like to look at beauty, but there are people who choose instead to look at ugliness. That alone tells you a lot about them, don't you think?"

Shale looked from Richard back to the busts. She shook her head in disgust. "I fear to think what this tells us about the people who live here."

At the end of the long passageway, farther away from the light of the high windows and lit only by candles, Richard realized that the hallway didn't simply get dark, it actually ended in a dark opening, but not the kind of opening that went with the rest of the place. It was a hole crudely chiseled into the stone of the mountain the palace had been built into.

It looked like nothing so much as the rough opening into a mine. Or the underworld.

Unlike everything else he had seen in the palace that was ornate and highly detailed, this was merely a roughly round opening cut into the rock with crude tools used for excavation. The mountain lion vanished into that dark maw. He saw the tail flick up briefly, and then it was gone down into the darkness.

When they got close enough, they could see that there was a bit of flickering light inside from somewhere far down below. As Richard paused at the opening to try to see where the mountain lion had gone, he saw then that there were steps leading down.

"I don't think this is a good idea," Shale said. "We're walking right into the heart of this trap."

Richard turned back to her. "And how do you instead propose we free ourselves of that trap unless we face it and put an end to it?"

Shale's features twisted unhappily. "I don't know, but I don't like it. There are remnants of a spell of some sort lingering here."

Richard frowned at her. "What kind of spell? Can you tell?"

Shale shook her head. "It's just a trace of something, but I can't tell what." She sniffed the air. She frowned. "I can sense them, but I can't tell what sort of spells they might be. Whatever it is, it's interfering with my sense of smell."

"Well, we know that this trap was set with powerful magic," Kahlan said, "so there are bound to be spells lingering about this place. Sometimes magic does that—leaves traces."

Vika stepped ahead of him into the opening. "Rikka, Vale, come with me. The rest of you wait here. We will go down first and see if it's safe."

Richard gripped her arm and forcefully pulled her back before she could start down. "Are you out of your mind? Of course it's not safe. Now, stay behind me."

She looked so shocked by what he said that she did as he told her.

Richard started down with Kahlan at his side, expecting the rest of them to follow. Vika followed as close behind him as she could without stepping on his heels. Shale was right behind Kahlan. The others flowed down the steps behind them.

Only the first of the steps were carved well. On the way down, they soon became rough-hewn slabs in some places, and steps simply carved directly out of the stone of the mountain itself in others. Their uneven shape made footing treacherous. The treads and risers were different depths and heights, requiring care with every step they took. Sometimes it was a long stride and sometimes so short that they almost fell. Richard held on tightly to Kahlan's hand as he held his other out behind to urge the others to be careful. He didn't want them falling on top of him and Kahlan and causing them all to go tumbling down to somewhere far below.

As they cautiously descended the curving, irregular run of steps, he realized that the stairs followed the uneven excavation down along the rock walls. When they got farther down, he was finally able to see that they were descending to the edge of what was a vast, roughly circular chamber. He was astonished by how immense it was, both in width and height.

Like the opening above, the walls had been

cut with excavation tools, leaving a rough, un-
finished surface. It looked to Richard that
in places on the walls great slabs of rock had
collapsed down, actually aiding in the excavation.
It resembled a mine more than a room, except
that it was huge beyond any normal room, or
any mine for that matter. He had seen chambers
in natural caves that were this immense, but this
was not a cave and not natural. He couldn't
imagine its purpose.

Rather than it getting darker, they began to
see flickering firelight from below that helped
them see the steps better. Keen to find out what
this place was and what was going on, he had
to force himself to be careful and not to hurry.
The fact that it was a trap, with the mountain
lion leading them into it, also tempered his urge
to hurry.

He started to realize that this strange underground chamber had to actually be the true
purpose of the palace. The place above was
merely a façade. Like a man irresistibly drawn to
a beautiful woman with an evil heart, Richard
felt that he had first been charmed by the beauty
of the palace architecture, but he was now being
drawn to the evil heart of this place.

The stairs turned as they approached the bottom. He saw, then, that they were coming down behind enormous statues of ravens that were at least three times his height. Their wings were extended in front to hold stone bowls of flaming oil that provided light. The smell was similar to that of burning pitch. It also left a haze to settle in the cool air of the pit.

When they reached the bottom of the rough stairs, and they came around one of the ravens, he saw that there were more of the stone ravens all around the room in a circle, thirteen in all. They all faced inward to the center of the chamber.

Between and beyond the stone ravens, he could see that there were caverns all around the base of the room, going back into the stone of the mountain itself. Torches lit the tunneled passageways, but he couldn't see what they led to.

Off in the middle of the room, he saw a line of intimidating people watching them approach. They were all women.

In the center of that line of silent women sat a tall, elegant throne. He could see the light from the burning pots dance and flare on the gold-leaf vines, snakes, cats, and other beasts carved into the arms and framing the tufted red velvet-covered back. A canopy draped with heavy red brocade and trimmed with gold tassels jutted out overhead, making an imposing statement.

The mountain lion sat beside the throne.

Richard had seen that throne before.

As he cautiously closed the distance, he recognized the woman sitting in the massive structure.

It was his mother.

21

O ut of the corner of her eye, Kahlan saw Berdine's jaw drop. "Mama?"

Rikka lifted an arm to point. "No, that's my mother."

Vale went to her knees as her eyes welled up with tears. "Mother? Is that really you?"

"This is impossible," Shale whispered even as Kahlan knew that she, too, would be seeing her own mother.

When Nyda reached out in longing and started to rush ahead, Richard swept an arm around her waist and yanked her from her feet. He set her down behind him. Kahlan caught Rikka's arm to stop her from going any farther.

"Everyone stay where you are," Richard said in a commanding voice before any of the others could rush to the woman they all wrongly believed was their mother.

Most of the Mord-Sith looked in stunned confusion between the women and Richard. The woman sitting on the magnificent throne smiled benevolently. Kahlan knew that Richard, too, was seeing his mother. The only difference was, like Kahlan, Richard knew who this really was.

"Shota, stop it," Richard called out in a voice that cut through the hiss of the burning lamp oil and echoed around the chamber.

Kahlan had been pretty sure for quite some time who it was that had been drawing them into this trap. Richard had known as well, but like her, he had not wanted to put words to that belief lest that somehow make it true. They had both hoped they were wrong, and that it would turn out to be something else.

Kahlan's mother smiled, then, in a loving way, but Kahlan had already steeled herself against Shota's cynical deception. This was a witch woman playing her games; it was not any of their mothers. She didn't allow herself to let her emotions be twisted by what she knew to be an illusion.

Shale looked at Kahlan in wordless confusion.

"That spell you felt at the opening to this place?" Kahlan whispered to her.

"Yes? What of it?" Shale asked.

"It was to keep you from smelling witches."

Realization swept away the confusion in her features.

"Shota," Richard said again, "stop this cruel hoax."

Once Shota saw that Richard and Kahlan weren't about to play along, and that they weren't going to let any of the others be sucked into the deception, she stood and descended the three platforms the throne sat atop.

Her variegated gray dress gently billowed as if lifted by a gentle breeze. When she caught one of the points of the skirt, it was as if the breeze died out and it settled down. As the dress went still, her fabricated looks also died out, melding back into the face of the witch woman Kahlan knew all too well. She was glad, at least, that Shota was no longer taunting her with the image of her mother.

Kahlan glanced at the women lined up to either side of the throne. Their piercing glares were chilling. Even though they all looked very different, they all radiated the same aura of mystery and danger.

A self-satisfied smile spread across Shota's full, red lips. Her almond eyes sparkled with her smile. Kahlan had always thought of the stunning woman as a rose encrusted with ice crystals.

Shota glided across the room toward them, her eyes fixed on Richard the whole time. Kahlan found it irritating the way Shota had always acted a little too charming toward Richard. Richard, of course, didn't respond to her charms, but it nonetheless irritated her.

"Cruel hoax?" Shota asked in her silky-smooth voice.

Kahlan had never thought it fair that a woman as beautiful as Shota should also have a voice that could charm a good spirit out of the underworld.

"My intent was merely to bring a cherished memory to life so that each of you could once more look upon your beloved mothers." Shota arched an eyebrow. "How is that cruel? It was a gift created through great effort on my part."

"Your intent was to bring each of us pain and to crush our hearts," Richard said. "Nothing more, nothing less."

She smiled reproachfully. "Richard, a Seeker

needs his anger. If you will recall, I've warned you before not to let it cloud your judgment. And yet, it is a mistake you have made too often in the past."

Richard didn't go for the bait and instead glanced around. "What is this gloomy pit? Why aren't you in Agaden Reach?"

Shota swept an arm around in a grand gesture as if to show him the massive room, all the while smiling at him. "This is my winter palace. Isn't it splendid? Do you like it?"

Richard never took his eyes off her, the same way he wouldn't take his eyes off any lethal threat. "Not really. I think I prefer the swamp you live in. It's more honest."

"Ah, well, the Reach is nice, I must admit," Shota cooed. "But I come here to Bindamoon, on rare occasions, when I have important business to conduct."

"We met the man you sent to welcome us," Richard told her.

Shota's brow twitched. "Man?"

"The bearded fellow with the gift. A gift he intended to use against us."

Realization came over her features. "Ah." Her expression soured. "Iron Jack."

"That's the one," Richard said.

She flipped a hand dismissively. "A sycophant, a stooge. He fancies himself useful to me, thinking it will earn him favors. He is always trying to impress me. He doesn't realize that he merely impresses me as a worthless freak. He is a bothersome little man."

"He won't be bothering you anymore," Richard told her. "He's dead."

Shota shrugged as she smiled. "Good."

Kahlan was a bit surprised by the reaction. She had thought that Shota had sent him. Richard didn't mention that Iron Jack had been killed by the Glee.

Kahlan gestured, indicating the palace above them. "And so you have that place above, now, so that you can call yourself a queen? What are you queen of, exactly?"

Shota turned a cold look on Kahlan. "That is what the people in this place prefer to call me. Queen."

Kahlan frowned. "Why?"

Shota regarded Kahlan with the kind of penetrating gaze that only added to her menace. Shota had never liked Kahlan, and she took every opportunity to make that clear.

Shota glanced down at Kahlan's swollen pregnancy. It was not a look of approval. The witch woman's perfect shape made Kahlan feel fat and ugly in comparison. Against her will, she could feel her face start to go red.

"They choose to call me the queen because they fear to say my name aloud." The smile again spread on her lips, but failed to reach her eyes. She arched one eyebrow. "With good reason."

Frowning, Shale leaned closer to Richard. "Mind telling me what's going on?"

He held out an arm in introduction. "Shale, this is Shota, a witch woman Kahlan and I know all too well. Deluded by prophecy, she swore that if we ever dared to have children, she would kill them. That is the witch's oath that all along has been at the center of everything. That is the true witch's oath that has shadowed us, nearly gotten us killed, and in the end brought us here. The witch's oath had never been created by Michec. It had been Shota's all along."

Shota smiled at Richard and bowed her head in recognition of him grasping Michec's role. "He was a useful idiot."

Shale looked baffled. "But why?"

"Because," Richard said, "she fears our children. Isn't that right, Shota?"

Shota's eyes turned hot and dangerous. "I guess I can't fool you, Seeker."

Kahlan had noticed from the beginning that all the women to the sides of the throne were glaring right at her. She did her best not to look at them, but it was next to impossible not to. Each one was different, and each one, in her own way, looked intimidating.

Shota, annoyed that Shale had spoken before being spoken to, slowly stepped closer to her, her boot strikes echoing around the massive stone chamber. She came to a halt before Shale. She lifted her chin a little to look down her nose as she studied the sorceress's face for a moment.

"Well, well, what have we here?" she asked as she leaned forward then to peer intently into Shale's eyes. "A half-breed. How utterly revolting." She straightened back up. "Had you any shame, my dear, you would have long ago killed yourself." Shota's disapproval turned again to a mocking smile. "Not to worry." She cocked her head. "I will help with that when I'm finished with you."

"I can only assume that you are responsible for the boundary that appeared to force us to come here," Richard said to draw Shota's attention away from the sorceress. "That means that you are responsible for the loss of any innocent lives of the people who have been killed when they walked into it without realizing what it was. I want that terrible boundary brought down right now." Richard leaned toward Shota, fixing her in his raptor glare. "Right now."

Shota shrugged. "As you wish." She twirled a hand around overhead. "Done," she said in a voice that might have been used to announce dinner was ready.

Richard looked a little surprised to have her so easily agree, and a little dubious that she had actually undone something of such massive power. More than that, though, he was not at all happy about the boundary being put up in the first place. "How many innocent people do you suppose you murdered with that thing?"

Shota regained her imperious attitude. "I regret the loss of any innocent lives, but it was unavoidable in order to prevent what would be a much greater loss of lives. So, in that sense, you two are actually the cause of such deaths."

Richard continued to glare at her. "How do you figure that?"

Shota walked slowly to her ornate throne to stand for a moment as she gathered her thoughts.

She lifted a finger without looking back. "You saved me from the Keeper once."

"And this is how you show your gratitude?" Richard asked in a rising, angry voice.

After a moment, the witch woman turned and strolled back to stand before Richard and Kahlan. "I told you both that because of what you had done, I would be forever grateful. I meant it."

She touched her fingertips to the side of Richard's face. "I actually rather like you. You are a noble individual. You and the Mother Confessor both. You both have fought for the survival of your people, and in so doing fought for my survival as well. You have done good and brought peace to the world. For all that and more, I respect you both and wish you no harm."

22

" S o you decided to trap us here because you *like* us?" Richard asked. "You put lives of innocent people in danger because you *like* us? You more than likely caused the deaths of unwitting travelers because you *like* us?"

Shota gently gripped Richard's throat as she glared with menace into his gray eyes. "I warned you that all the children a Confessor bears are Confessors. Over time it came to pass that most give birth only to girl children. I told you that if you give the Mother Confessor a child, it would be a boy, and that boy child would be a Confessor. Beyond that, even a girl child with Confessor power and the gift of a war wizard from two lines of wizards, one with Subtractive Magic, would be an abomination. I told you that for those reasons you must not have a child with this woman."

"So you're back to that, are you?" Richard folded his arms across his chest. "Back to the nonsense about prophecy?"

"It is hardly nonsense. Fathers wed to Confessors are supposed to have been taken by her power so that if by chance she happened to bear a boy, the husband would without question end its life. You changed all that by finding a way to be with her without being taken by her power. As a result, neither of you has the will or the strength to kill the tainted children the two of you conceive."

She paused a moment as her grip on Richard's throat tightened. "I have the will, I have the strength, and I am willing to use it. I gave you my word on that. I gave you a witch's oath on that. And you both defied me."

"It's our lives," Richard said in a surprisingly calm voice, as if trying to reason with her. "It's our children's lives. You have no dominion over any of our lives and no right to deny our children the right to live their lives. I will protect those children, as will Kahlan. We will teach them to be good people who care about others."

Kahlan could see that it was like trying to reason with a stone wall.

"You two have selfishly put your own wishes ahead of the greater good. Once they are old enough, the power those two children possess will be profound. Your teaching will not be able to control such corrupting power."

Richard's features hardened. "You need to stop this right now, Shota. I will not allow you to harm us or our children."

Shota slowly shook her head as she gazed into his eyes. "Better you battle the Keeper of the underworld himself, than me."

Richard gripped her wrist and pulled her hand away from his throat. "You think so much of yourself, do you? We already faced your witch and your oath in the form of Moravaska Michec. You should know that he died with my hands around his throat and Kahlan twisting her knife in his heart."

Shota flicked her hand dismissively. "A warlock. Such men are a poor excuse for a true witch."

"He was a witch man," Kahlan said. "You are a witch woman. A witch is a witch."

"Hardly," she huffed. "Witch women and

witch men are from two entirely different lines. A witch man is not a witch by being born of a witch woman. Similar to Confessors, witch women don't give birth to boys. At least, none that live long. A witch man is the son of a witch man and a woman with no power. He does not carry the same heredity and power as a witch woman.

"While they like to think of themselves as more than they are, and while they certainly have great power and can cause a great deal of trouble, they are but a mere shadow of a *true* witch. His power was but a flea on the back of a wolf compared to mine. I let him have a try at enforcing my witch's oath, but in the end, he was an inferior witch and proved himself as much.

"He originally attached himself to Darken Rahl because he intuitively grasped the reality of his limitations as a witch and so he sought to add to his power through his association with a powerful wizard. Darken Rahl allowed him to indulge his sick desires because he was useful in the same way a vicious dog can be useful. Michec was a cruel man whom people feared— with good reason. But he made the mistake of thinking that because people feared him, that made him a more important witch than he actually was.

"With Darken Rahl gone, he sought an alliance with the Glee for the same reasons he had served Darken Rahl. He believed it made him a more powerful witch. His deluded beliefs ultimately proved to be his undoing."

"He was witch enough," Richard said, drawing Shota's glare away from Kahlan. "He was more powerful than you give him credit for. And we stopped him from carrying out your witch's oath, just as we will stop you if we have to."

Shota showed him an icy smile. "You think so, child? You can't begin to grasp how wrong you are about that. Michec groveled before me, the grand witch, as all witches do. He swore to carry out my oath, as all witches must. In his failure, he proved he was not a witch worthy of the task or my protection."

"I don't care what, in your vanity, you think of witch men," Richard said. "But I do care about your need to continue to pursue your nonsense about our children and what you saw while looking into the flow of time. Prophecy is dead. I ended it because prophecy is a corrupting influence and it was a danger to the world of life. Your blind obsession with it is proof of its corrupting nature."

Shota lifted her chin indignantly. "It was a true vision into the flow of time, into how events will unfold."

"The nature of prophecy is that it looks into possibilities that branch out endlessly from root events as the world moves forward and continually changes. You plucked one leaf from the tree of prophecy while ignoring the entire forest."

"The world may have changed, but the flow of time did not."

"You can't see into the flow of time anymore, can you?"

Shota squinted at him. "No, thanks to you. You destroyed one of our most valuable tools, a tool that belongs to witch women."

"It did not belong to witch women. It was an expression of possible futures belonging in the underworld. Once it was brought to the world of life, witches long ago latched on to it in order to deceitfully gain power for themselves. It was an underworld force that had never belonged in this world."

Shota took a threatening step closer to him. "I used the flow of time to know how certain events flow and unfold. I used it in the past to help you."

"And had we followed your advice born of prophecy, then on more than one occasion, we would all be dead by now."

"You were smart enough to use the prophecy I gave you to succeed in ways neither I nor you could foresee. But without that prophecy, you might not have saved anyone. That is part of the way the flow of time works. As you say, it branches into many possible futures.

"I know far more about that flow of time and prophecy than you ever will, and that flow foretold that if you have a child with this Confessor it will be a monster. Such a child would risk bringing back the terror of the dark times, and worse, considering the power these twins will be born with. They will be bonded as twins and by the power they would be born with.

"But you refuse to heed that warning of a dark future and instead would ignorantly visit upon the world a male Confessor. A male Confessor! You are selfish children, the both of you, without any care for how what you are doing would destroy lives of so many others if these monsters were to live."

She looked pointedly over at Kahlan, then turned back to Richard. "I won't."

Richard lifted his hands out in frustration. "You don't understand prophecy the way you so smugly think you do, Shota."

She arched an eyebrow. "You have used prophecy to survive."

"Yes, because prophecy was something that only a wizard with Subtractive Magic can rightly understand. That's because prophecy is an underworld element. I alone understood its changeable nature and thus its limitations. I acted within those limitations, not in defiance of them."

She dismissed his words with a flick of a hand. "This is a different form of prophecy, meant for a witch woman only."

"Prophecy is prophecy, no matter how you wish to dress it up."

Shota considered his words only briefly before ignoring them. "I used the flow of time to see that if you two conceived a child, it would be a monster. And now, you have conceived twins, the worst possible sign of the terrors to come."

Richard sighed in exasperation. "We're going around in circles. You said that we would conceive a monster, right?"

"You already know that I did."

He gestured expansively. "All right, for the sake of argument, let's say you were right." Richard held up a finger as he leaned toward her. "But what you may not realize is that your look into prophecy has already come to pass. That flow of time has run its course and is over. It already happened."

Shota folded her arms. "What are you talking about?"

"When the chimes caused magic to fail—caused the magic of the necklace you gave Kahlan to fail—we didn't know that your necklace wasn't working as you designed it, and as a result, we conceived a child. Unfortunately, Kahlan lost that child before it could be born. If your prophecy is true, that means the first child conceived, the one Kahlan lost, was in fact the monster you so fear, the very one you saw in the flow of time.

"That means that the prophecy you saw in

the flow of time has already happened and has already been fulfilled. Since Kahlan became pregnant but lost that first child, that means the child you saw in the flow of time that would be a monster, is already long dead. The world has already been saved from the dark times you saw in the flow of time caused by that monster."

Richard gestured at Kahlan as he went on. "This pregnancy is now a different one. This time, these children Kahlan now carries are exactly what the world needs to survive. They are not the monsters that would destroy the world, but rather they are the other side of that prophecy, the balance to it that magic requires: the saviors of the world."

Shota scowled at him for a moment. "It is not possible for them to be saviors of our world."

"Yes, it is, because without them, our gift— mine and Kahlan's—will eventually pass out of existence when we die. The Grace each of us was born with will carry us and our gift beyond the veil. Right now, our gift, Kahlan's and mine, is what is holding magic together and preventing the Golden Goddess from completing her lust to take our world and kill everyone in it.

"Don't you see? Without our magic carrying on through these children of D'Hara, the Glee will be able to ravage our world. If you think the dark times were bad, you have not seen the terror visited upon people by the Glee. We have seen a small bit of it, and I can tell you that no one will survive. If these children don't live, then no one will.

"If you were to kill these children, you would, in essence, be killing everyone."

With her hands on her hips, Shota regarded Kahlan for a long moment before looking back at Richard and again folding her arms.

"That's a nice story, but I can't risk the world on a nice story. I won't risk it. I know of the Golden Goddess. What you don't see is that she is not my concern." She unfolded her arms to poke Richard's chest with a finger. "The Glee are your concern, your responsibility, as the Lord Rahl. It is up to you to protect our world, and as such it is your responsibility to deal with the threat posed by the Glee. It is as simple as that.

"My concern is the monsters you have conceived. It is my responsibility—since you abdicated it—to make sure the twins you two have conceived never come to be."

Richard's hands fisted at his sides. "I don't have any way to fight a threat from another world! Any hope for the future will slip away without these gifted children!"

Richard took a settling breath to compose himself before going on. "Shota, your fault, your flaw, is that you are so focused on your narrow belief, that you are not able to see the bigger picture. You are fighting the last battle from dark times long forgotten."

"It is you who are not seeing the big picture and the obvious solution," she said. "You simply need to stop the threat from the Golden Goddess and her kind, *wizard*. When you do that, then our world will be safe from the Glee. That is your duty as Seeker and as the Lord Rahl. Do your job. My concern is that these children are not allowed to live in this world. That is my job.

"Had you not ended prophecy, I would be able to look into the flow of time and see if anything has changed and if your theory could possibly be true. But because you took it upon yourself to end prophecy, that opportunity is lost to us. Because the consequences would be too grave to risk doing otherwise, the original prophecy must stand.

"My witch's oath stands. It will be carried out."

Richard's eyes took on the hawklike glare that Kahlan knew so well. "Shota," he said in a low, dangerous tone, "if you have forced us to come all this way so that you can kill us along with these innocent children yet unborn, you have made a very big mistake. You have no right to their lives or ours, and as the Lord Rahl of the D'Haran Empire, I am telling you to once and for all to end your obsession.

"Believe me, you do not want to fight me." He gestured to Kahlan. "Nor do you want to fight the Mother Confessor. Have you ever seen a mother bear protect her cubs? I have. She is ferocious. You cross her at great peril."

23

Kahlan felt solace at Richard's words. Shota, however, looked like she was having none of it. Kahlan wondered how long the witch woman's patience would last before she decided to simply kill them.

Shota opened her hands as an empty smile spread on her lips. "Richard, just as you have so often misinterpreted my actions in the past, you misunderstand my resolve to be of assistance in this difficult time. You must believe me when I say that I have no malice toward you or the Mother Confessor. Nor do I have any desire to do battle with either of you. Most of all, I certainly have no intention of harming either one of you. I already told you: I am grateful to you both. Everything you falsely interpret as threatening is merely my desire to help you both."

Richard glared with incredulity. "You expect me to believe you are only interested in *helping* us? You want us to think that by murdering our children you are *helping* us?"

Shota stepped close so she could rest an arm over Richard's shoulder. She smiled warmly and batted her eyelashes, as if trying to charm him. Kahlan had absolutely no doubt that Richard was not charmed or attracted to the witch woman. Even so, it made her blood boil to see her trying to seduce Richard with her "charm."

"Think of me as doing a difficult chore for you, one that must be done, so that you don't have to do it," she said with a shrug. She idly ran a finger of her other hand down his chest, making Kahlan fume all the more. "I admit that my insistence on being of service to you could be taken the wrong way, but be assured, I certainly intend you no harm."

"If you intend us no harm, then why did you force us to come here?" Kahlan asked, drawing the witch woman's attention away from her husband.

Shota withdrew her arm from where it was

resting on Richard's shoulder and turned to
Kahlan, clearly annoyed to be interrupted in
mid-seduction. "I brought you here so you
could give birth to the children you carry. I
will see to it that you will be safe and comfortable while you are here until then. Once you
give birth, both you and Richard, and"—she
gestured offhandedly beyond Richard without
taking her eyes off Kahlan—"your gaggle of
Mord-Sith, will be free to leave and go about
your lives."

"My children will not be born here, in this
vile place, so that you can slaughter them."

Shota's grin widened. "I'm afraid that you
are once again getting the wrong idea. You see,
you have no say in this. We will do our best to
make you comfortable for the duration of your
visit to my palace. After you give birth, as I said,
you will be free to leave. But you will not be
leaving with those children."

Kahlan's hands fisted with fury. "You can't
have my babies so that you can murder them!"

Shota pressed the tips of her fingers together
and bowed her head for a moment, as if patiently
thinking of how to explain something to a
stubborn child. Her head finally came back up.

"You claim to be protectors of your people. Well, so am I. Although we disagree about aspects of it, our goals are actually the same: the safety of our people. That is in fact what this is all about. You are blinded by maternal instinct, which is only natural, but it prevents you from having the vision and strength to do what is necessary for the greater good. I have both, so I am going to help with what must be done."

Kahlan fought back tears of rage. "The greater good?"

Shota's expression turned dark and dangerous as she leaned in. "I am finished with trying to reason with you two foolish children. It shall be as I say."

Kahlan knew how dangerous this witch woman was, but she was at the end of her patience. "Shota, if you do not withdraw your witch's oath and let us go, there will be no turning back—for either of us. Know that, as the Mother Confessor, I will grant you no mercy and allow none."

Shota looked amused. "You think your Law of Nines will help you? I'm afraid that it no longer applies."

Richard glanced around at the group with

him. The Mord-Sith, all in their red leather, looked not only resolute but positively dangerous as they watched the conversation, waiting to be let off their chain.

"What are you talking about?" he asked.

Shota lifted her arm out behind, indicating the odd-looking group of women lined up to either side of her throne. "You see, I have come here, to Bindamoon, to my winter palace, to convene a coven."

Kahlan scanned the line of grim women to either side of Shota's throne. There were six on one side of it, and five on the other side. Although all of the women looked very different from one another, they had one thing in common: they did indeed all look like witches. They all fit the stories she had heard as a young girl from the wizards who taught her. And they certainly all looked dangerous.

She suddenly realized the flaw in Shota's grand scheme.

"I don't want to tell you your business," Kahlan said, "but a coven is thirteen witches. With you and the rest of these ladies, here, there are only twelve. You're missing your last witch."

"Do tell," Shota said with an amused smile.

Kahlan shrugged. "We killed Moravaska Michec, your thirteenth witch. Without the thirteenth witch, your call to coven can't authenticate the essential dictate so that you can initiate its power."

"Michec? A witch man? In a coven?" Shota said with distaste. She huffed dismissively. "Don't be ridiculous. He could not possibly be part of a coven. He's of more use to me dead than alive." She once more smiled as she leaned toward Kahlan. "But thank you for the suggestion of using him."

Kahlan couldn't imagine how Shota could use a dead Michec. Ignoring the distraction, she gestured to the women standing in the background.

"Well, I hate to tell you, but in that case you're a witch short of a coven. Like I said, including you, there are only twelve witches. Without thirteen witches you are not able to invoke the power of coven."

Shota smiled without humor. "Yes, I know. That's why I had you bring me the thirteenth witch."

Kahlan blinked, suddenly worried by Shota's calm confidence. "What are you talking about?"

Her eyes flashing with menace, Shota walked over to Shale. With her face mere inches away from Shale's, she pointed back behind. "Go and take your place with your sister witches."

Kahlan suddenly realized that Shale had been oddly quiet almost the entire time. Kahlan saw, then, that she seemed to be in a trance of some sort. She stared ahead without blinking.

Shota, still pointing back at the line of women, snapped her fingers. "Now."

Without a word of protest, or question, or even acknowledgment, Shale walked woodenly toward the women standing to the sides of the throne. When she reached them, she took up a place at the end of the line of five on one side of the throne, making six to match the six on the other side.

With Shale bringing the number in the line to twelve, and Shota making the total thirteen, Shota now had the witches she needed to invoke the power of coven.

"Shale," Richard called out, "what are you doing?"

When he started to charge toward her to get her back, Shota lifted a hand toward him, as if she were dismissing him. Kahlan didn't know what kind of power she had available to her with a coven, but she knew from stories wizards had told her that it was formidable.

Suddenly, Moravaska Michec materialized as if his corpse had been pulled directly up from the underworld. He looked as intimidating in spirit form as he had in life. Kahlan regretted now even having mentioned his name and giving Shota the idea. The dead man was semi-transparent in his spirit form, but the part that was visible looked like half-rotted remains. Blood that had gushed from the wound in his chest where Kahlan had driven her knife into him covered his front, and his intestines hung out from a gaping belly wound, dragging across the floor as he advanced.

His mouth opened with a roar that shook the room and made Kahlan feel as if her eyeballs were rattling in her skull. Michec abruptly shot across the room, not on his feet, but through the air as if he had leaped, his intestines fluttering out behind him.

He struck Richard with enough force to catapult him back so powerfully that he stopped only when he slammed into one of the stone ravens. As he did, the spirit of Michec, his summons completed, dissolved back into the world of the dead.

Richard scrambled to his feet, refusing to be shaken by what Shota had conjured.

"Shale!" he called out. "Don't do this! Don't let Shota do this to you! Come away from them!"

Kahlan could hardly believe that the woman who had saved her life several times would suddenly join with Shota against them. She joined Richard in crying out Shale's name, pleading with her to come away from the others.

"If it pleases you both," Shota said in a surprisingly sympathetic tone, "know that this is not by the choice of your half-breed witch. It is by my choice alone, by my command alone, as the grand witch."

Her tone turned iron-hard. "But a witch woman with such a mix of powers is an abomination, as would be your children. I will use her as long as it pleases me. When I am finished with her, I will eliminate her, as I would any such crime of nature."

Kahlan could feel the blood draining from her face. "Shota, you can't do this. A coven invokes the underworld, and with it, Subtractive Magic.

You said yourself that a witch with a mix of powers is a crime of nature."

Shota leaned toward her with a deadly look. "I warned you before. You did not listen. This is the consequence."

Kahlan knew that even in the best of circumstances, her gift and Richard's didn't work against witch women the way they did against others. Witch women had the ability to turn whatever powers you used back at you, often with fatal results.

But now that Shota had invoked coven, her power would make using their gift against her next to impossible.

She hoped that Richard remembered the warning Nicci had once given when explaining the complications of the magic involved when trying to use their gift against a witch woman.

Even so, they were being put in the position where trying might be their only option, since not trying would mean their death anyway.

24

Richard raced forward, going for Shota, but in response she again cast out an arm. A wall of shimmering light stopped him cold. He dropped to the floor, clutching his middle in agony.

As Richard hit the floor from what Shota had done to him, every one of the Mord-Sith spun her Agiel up into her fist. They had seen enough. All six of them, their single braids flying out behind them, leaped over Richard on their way to Shota. They screamed in lethal fury as they were still in midair.

They had only just started their attack when specters of horribly deformed dead appeared to catch each of the Mord-Sith in spirit arms. Like Michec, they appeared semitransparent, but they were solid enough to snatch up the Mord-Sith, the bones of the dead showing through their tattered flesh. Even as they were being lifted from the ground, each of the Mord-Sith attacked the specters with her Agiel in one hand and a knife in the other, but it had no effect on the phantoms from another world.

All of the Mord-Sith were swiftly carried backward, powerless to stop the underworld beings holding them, until each of the six were smashed into a stone raven, between its opened wings. A stone wing of each of the six raven statues swept around the Mord-Sith to trap them there. The spirits, their task completed, vanished back into the world of the dead.

The other wing of each of the six ravens held out its stone bowl of burning oil. The large stone wings were plenty big enough to hold the Mord-Sith fast. Dust and bits of stone drizzled down from where the stone wings had broken as they turned in order to grab and hold the Mord-Sith.

Out of the corner of her eye, as Richard struggled to get to his feet or possibly to conjure some kind of power to fight back, Kahlan saw two of the witches leave the line of their sister witches and start toward her.

Shota continued to hold the hand out toward Richard, as if pressing him to the ground, her power preventing him from getting up or doing anything else to stop her. She brought her other hand up when she saw Kahlan try to run to Richard. Whatever kind of magic Shota was using, she was effortlessly able to bring up a solid wall of air to prevent Kahlan from moving any closer despite how desperately she tried to push against it.

As Kahlan struggled to move through the thick air, her feet sliding against the floor as she shoved her shoulder against it, two women rushed up from behind and seized her arms. One was a short, squat, bulky woman in an outfit made of patches of different kinds of burlap sewn haphazardly together. It hung from her broad shoulders all the way to the floor, making her body look square. The wrinkles and lines of her face were pinched in toward her close-set eyes and wart-covered nose. Her downturned mouth made her look like she had a mouthful of bile she couldn't spit out. Her thin, frizzy hair stuck out all around her head like a dirty white thundercloud.

Kahlan tried to pull her arm back out of the

witch's grasp, but the woman, while not tall, was at least three times as wide as Kahlan, and held her arm in the powerful grip of her fat fingers. Her mass made Kahlan feel like she was trying to pull against an oak tree that had her in its clutches.

The witch who grabbed her other arm was as thin as the other was burly. The tattered, hanging, dark dress she wore looked like she gutted fish in it daily and the filth had never once been washed off. The skin of her bare arms was wrinkled and withered, almost looking like tree bark. Her bony fingers had long, sickly yellowish fingernails that were ragged on the ends and scratched Kahlan's arms. The witch also had filthy rags wrapped around her head, one part around the top to hold in her shock of unruly, inky-black hair, and another part down and around her head going under her chin and tied back on top as if it was trying to keep her jaw from falling off.

A number of long strings of bones, teeth, and feathers hung around her neck, swinging back and forth and clattering as the witch yanked on Kahlan's arm. She had similar strings of collected animal parts around her wrists, some of them still in the process of rotting. The gagging stench of dead things was overpowering.

Her large, round black eyes did not look human. She had the dead stare of a corpse. Although she was much smaller than the woman who had Kahlan's other arm, she was, with that dead stare, more frightening than the blocky, angry-looking woman on the other side, and by the hand clutching Kahlan's arm, just as strong.

Together, the women began dragging Kahlan backward with an urgency she wouldn't have thought either could muster. She fought against them, but she was no match for their strength, and they were not even using their powers.

Looking back over her shoulder, Kahlan could see that they were dragging her toward one of the dark openings at the bottom of the towering wall. As they went past the throne, another witch left the line to join the other two and walk, leaning in, facing Kahlan as she was being pulled backward, her heels dragged across the stone floor.

This witch, unlike the two who had iron grips on her arms, was not monstrous. She was, in fact, shapely and, in a dark sort of way, pretty. She wore a black, formfitting bodice that was cut low and edged with black lace. Her skirt, which hung nearly to the floor, was made up of what had to be hundreds of knotted and beaded strips of leather. Some of the beads sparkled and reflected the light of the burning bowls of oil held by the stone ravens. They allowed her bare knees to part the strings and show through when she walked. Around her neck she wore a broad, black lace choker.

Her hair was red, long, and stringy. It mimicked the look of her strange, stringy skirt: the veil of small, ropy strands of hair hung down in front of her face the way the skirt veiled her legs. Beyond the screen made of the strands of hair, her pale blue eyes lined with black, despite their beauty, were far more menacing than any of the others' eyes.

As she walked close in front of Kahlan, leaning in, while she was being dragged backward by the two older witch women, the strands of her skirt swished around her legs, allowing the beads to clatter together, making a distracting, enchanting, almost musical sound. That beguiling sound for some reason made it difficult for Kahlan to think clearly. As they walked face-to-face, the young witch leaned in more, to within inches of Kahlan's face, with a look that made goose bumps race up Kahlan's arms to the nape of her neck.

"Stay green for me," she said in a low, smoky voice that matched both the beauty and the menace of her blue eyes, "until I can cut those squirming little brats out of your womb and twist off their heads and eat them while you watch."

Kahlan didn't know what "stay green" meant, but the intent was clear enough.

Kahlan was helpless as she was dragged backward toward one of cavelike openings at the bottom of the towering wall and into the labyrinth of tunnels beyond. With the third witch leaning in, her face inches away, the musical jangle of the beads wove a tune that made Kahlan feel limp.

Even so, with fear choking her breathing, Kahlan gathered all her strength as she drew a big breath and then screamed Richard's name.

Even as he was held fast by Shota's power, he managed to turn to the sound of her shriek, and the terror in it.

Richard's fury was evident at hearing the fright in her voice as she cried out his name.

He threw his arms up as he screamed in rage. Whatever he did broke Shota's hold on him and staggered her back a step.

The witch woman's anger looked the match of Richard's. She again forced her hands out. At first, the air shimmered, but then spiderwebs of lightning ignited from her fingertips. As she did that, Richard did the same, but the crackling lightning coming from his hands was the black void of Subtractive Magic. The way it twisted and whipped around, it looked like it was tied to his hands and frantically trying to get away. Where it hissed and snapped against the walls, it cut through the stone. In places the stone above that had lost its support began to fall, making the walls look like they were beginning to come down.

And then they both halted what they were doing as they each seemed to gather their strength to redouble their efforts. They both cast their power out at the same time. Kahlan leaned her head a little to the side to look around the redheaded witch glaring at her. As they both projected their gift, Kahlan saw a wavering wall where that power collided suddenly come to life. The room shook with the thunder from the continual, flickering lightning they both were generating.

Neither of their magic could get past the other's wall of power, and the collision of their opposing powers created a blinding explosion of light in the center of the massive chamber. That sizzling light expanded outward in all directions, blasting into the stone to all sides—but far more critically, that sheer plane of power also shot vertically with a thunderous boom. Kahlan recognized that it was a hot brew of Additive and Subtractive Magic coming together. Both of their powers were clashing together in ways that weren't ever supposed to happen.

As the discharge of that explosive energy shot upward, it cut through the ceiling, the same as it sliced through the walls to the sides, going straight up through the entire palace, severing walls and floors above in the massive, ripping blast. Kahlan could hear the thunder of walls and ceilings on all the floors above collapsing inward.

And then, with so much above them destroyed, the ceiling of the massive chamber started caving in.

The other witches all ran for the safety of the

caverns at the rear of the great chamber. Shota began retreating with them as she continued to use her power to hold Richard at bay and keep him where he was.

The redheaded witch in front of Kahlan slammed the heel of her hand into the center of Kahlan's chest to force her back. At the same time, the two holding her arms yanked her back with them into the darkness of the tunnels.

The ground shook and the air filled with rolling, choking dust as unimaginable tons of rock from the palace above as well as the mountain itself began cascading down into the vast chamber just as the witch women dragged her back into the safety of the labyrinth.

Kahlan tried to reach out as she screamed Richard's name, but even as she did, she knew he would never be able to hear her in the deafening thunder of everything from above collapsing in on him.

She lost sight of him in the cascade of stone and the swirling clouds of dust.

25

In the oppressive silence, Richard realized that he heard distant, muffled voices. He couldn't make out who was talking, or what they were saying. It didn't seem to be important to him just then, so he didn't dwell on it. His head hurt.

When he realized that he was beginning to wake up, he rather wished that he wasn't, because, besides his head throbbing, he was just beginning to realize that he hurt all over. In order to try to alleviate the discomfort, he attempted to reposition himself. But when he tried to move, he found that for some reason he couldn't.

In his mind, he did his best to determine if it

was that he was being physically prevented from moving, or he was somehow paralyzed.

That sensation of not being able to move brought on a wave of alarm that woke him the rest of the way. He looked around but couldn't see anything at all. He felt with his hands, trying to figure out where he was.

In the pitch blackness, he felt something smooth, cold, and dusty mere inches above him. As he felt around, it seemed to be entirely over the top of him, but angled downward as it got closer toward his feet. There was more space under the thing above him up where his head was, so he was able to move his arms a little, but not his legs.

As he groped around, he felt ragged chunks of stone packed tight all around him. Everything was covered with what felt like a thick layer of dust. He regretted moving, because it lifted the dust into the air and he couldn't avoid breathing it in. He coughed, trying to get it out of his lungs. By the taste, he knew that it was stone dust.

As he was regaining consciousness, or waking up—he wasn't sure which—he began to remember seeing Shota unleash Subtractive

Magic. He had known that if he didn't act quickly, he would be killed. But he remembered that it seemed at the time as if his legs wouldn't move the way he needed. Maybe it had simply been sheer terror that kept him in place and prevented him from running.

He wasn't entirely sure what he had done at that point, other than simply reacting out of instinct. His gift as a war wizard, from somewhere deep inside him, came forth and did what was necessary to save him.

But he did remember being alarmed at how the explosive collision of Subtractive Magic had cut through the walls and ceiling. He didn't know how far those voids went off into the side of the mountain, but he realized that they instantly cut all the way up through the entire palace. It had to have cut support structures and beams in addition to floors, ceilings, and arches all the way up through the towering structure.

He remembered the terrible shrieking blast of Subtractive and Additive Magic mixing and then the roar of the entire place coming apart as it started falling in, and not being able to make his legs work. Even as he started remembering it, though, the whole thing felt like something that happened long ago, or maybe in a dream, or even to someone else.

He was so thirsty he couldn't think clearly. He worked his tongue against the top of his mouth, trying to moisten it, but the dust in his mouth was turning to a chalky paste and only making matters worse.

Putting all the pieces together in his mind, he realized that the entire place and probably some of the mountain had come down on top of him and he was obviously trapped, probably under one of the slabs of a floor from above. A lot of the rubble was packed around his legs so tightly he couldn't move them.

He realized that while he was jammed into a small space, at least the thick slab above him had saved him from being crushed under what had to be the weight of the entire palace. As lucky as that was to have survived in the small pocket under the slab, he felt a rising sense of panic at realizing that he was buried alive. There was no hope of digging his way out from under a mountain of rubble.

He reached up and felt his throbbing head. It was wet. He put a finger to his mouth to taste the wetness. He could tell by the coppery taste that it was blood. That explained his head hurting. It felt like it hurt both on the outside and inside.

Again he heard the distant voices. He had thought in the beginning that it must have been something he heard in a dream, but now that he was fully awake, he knew it was a person calling out to him.

"I'm down here!" he yelled as loud as he could.

He didn't get a response, so he called out again, forcing himself to yell louder. He was feeling desperate as he fought back his growing panic. He called out again, louder yet.

"Lord Rahl?" came a distant voice.

"Berdine? Is that you?"

"Yes!" The voice came closer. "Yes! It's me! I'm here!"

He heard people frantically talking. The sound came closer until he could make out individuals. Apparently, whoever was up above with Berdine was excited that they had gotten a response. Now that he knew there were people out there somewhere, he started squirming, thinking he might be able to work his way out.

He soon realized, though, that it was simply

impossible. The stone was packed in so tight that none of it would budge. He couldn't make any of it move so much as an inch. He was stuck solid in the rubble.

He began to remember his alarm as the entire palace above them had started to come down. Shota had somehow managed to touch off Subtractive Magic. The only way to prevent her from killing him had been to use a mix of Additive and Subtractive Magic to counter it. It had been his only chance. When those powers had come together, it had created a knifelike blast of Subtractive Magic that had cut all the way up through the palace and at the same time to the sides through the mountain under the palace.

He hadn't known that a witch woman could do such things. Apparently, from what Kahlan had been saying, a coven amplified her power and gave her additional abilities. For all of her assurances that she had no intention to harm them, she was quick to attack him with lethal power.

He remembered, too, that gifted people could join their abilities to amplify their power. The joining of the power of all those witch women had obviously managed to bring forth the boundary. That alone was a demonstration of the power that Shota now had at her disposal.

He could hardly believe that Shale had joined them. No, it wasn't her doing, he reminded himself. She was being used. He remembered that Shota had said as much. He could tell by the empty stare that Shale was not acting on her own.

"Lord Rahl!" Berdine's voice was closer, and more desperate. Even so, it still seemed like it was some distance away. "Lord Rahl, are you still there?"

"Mostly, I think. There is a big slab of floor, or ceiling, over the top of me. It created a pocket and kept me from being crushed. But my legs are encased in the rubble and I can't move them. How long have I been stuck down here?"

"This is the end of the second day," came the response.

Two days. Richard was stunned.

"Is Kahlan with you?"

This time the answer was slow in coming. "I'm afraid not. We haven't been able to find anyone other than you."

That answer sent a shiver of panic and pain

through his heart. She had to have escaped. He told himself that she had gotten out in time.

"Who's with you?" he called out.

"All of us. When everything started collaps-ing, the falling ceiling toppled those big stone birds. They sheltered us from all the stone falling in long enough for all of us to run into the tunnels and escape. We only just made it in time. We had hoped you were right behind us. The entire palace fell into that underground room and with all the dust and falling debris we couldn't see if all the witch women escaped."

Escaped with Kahlan, she meant. Richard didn't know which would have been a worse fate—to have her die quickly, or have the witch women take her away to do what they intended. He knew that despite what Shota said, she was no longer willing to tolerate Richard and Kahlan being alive to disobey her wishes.

"Part of the mountain collapsed off to the side," Berdine called out. "We have a lot of town people up here with us. They are all helping."

He thought that was odd. "What do you mean, helping?"

"Helping dig you out. We've all been working for two days to dig through the rubble, hoping to find you alive. We were not going to stop, but we were beginning to give up hope."

"I'm stuck down here."

"I know. But a lot of the town people came right away to help us. We've been digging inward from the section of the mountain that fell away. Your power cutting through the walls caused a big section of the mountain to slide away, so we're digging in from the side. We've been searching, calling out, and digging for two days, day and night, hoping to find you. But a lot of the stone from the palace is in big, heavy chunks and some of it needs to be broken apart in order to move it out of the way. Now that we know you are alive, and where you are, we can concentrate on getting to you."

Richard let out a weary breath. He didn't want to tell her that his head was bleeding, and he was dizzy. It felt like the dark world he was trapped in was spinning and tilting.

"Don't worry, Lord Rahl. We're coming for you. Hold on. But I fear it will take some time."

Richard nodded, then realized they couldn't see him nod. "I'll wait right here."

"Lord Rahl, just try to relax. It will take us

some time to get to you, but we won't give up. I can promise you that."

Richard felt tears welling up for Kahlan and their children. He feared to think what had happened to her.

For a moment, he felt overwhelmed by all of the insurmountable problems. In that instant, he thought that it would be better to just give up.

And then, he could feel his mind slipping into darkness deeper than the darkness of where he lay.

26

Richard heard people grunting with effort. And then, as a large chunk of stone was rolled aside, his dark hole was suddenly lit by a small shaft of light. It made him squint in the sudden brightness.

"Lord Rahl!" He recognized Vika's voice, and he could hear the desperation in it. "Lord Rahl!"

"I'm still here."

"Thank the good spirits," she murmured.

Richard briefly thought to ask her if the good spirits were up there helping them dig.

"Water," he called in a weak voice, instead. "Can you get me some water?"

"Water? Yes, we will get some," Vika said. "We've made a tunnel of sorts to get to you. It shouldn't be long before we have you out. Just hold on, Lord Rahl. We'll have you out soon."

"I need water," he mumbled.

"Rikka is running to get some. Hold on."

He could hear people grunting as they either lifted stone out of the way if it was small enough to handle, or rolled it back if it was too big and heavy to pick up. Hammers rang out against steel chisels as men tried to break up the larger pieces in their path. Others shouted instructions as they worked. Richard realized that he could hear a surprisingly large number of voices.

The light coming into his cavity in the rubble lit what he thought would be his grave with even more light as the people frantically worked to open the way in to reach him. The shaft of light revealed all the dust swirling around him. Richard wondered if they would be too late. He could feel himself losing the strength to remain conscious. They had told him that he had been there for two days. Stuck in the dusty space under the slab without water, it seemed like forever.

From time to time he heard things above him collapse and large blocks tumble down the hill of debris. It sounded like more walls might occasionally be falling in, or maybe ceilings that had little support might finally have given way— or were starting to give way. He was well aware that if things shifted wrong, or something big enough were to fall, he would be crushed. The thought of that made his chest tighten with the embrace of panic. Every time he heard stone above groan, or fall, he held his breath, waiting for the end.

He constantly had to fight back dread at being trapped under a mountain of rubble, never to get out. To keep his mind from wandering into frightening thoughts, he remembered Kahlan's face, trying to recall every detail.

Suddenly, a hand touched his shoulder. He jumped right out of his memory.

"Lord Rahl, it's me," Vika said.

She was close. Grunting and panting, she had somehow squirmed her way through the little tunnel they had made to his grave.

Richard reached up and put a hand over hers. It was bloody from digging through the rough, jagged stone chunks and rubble.

"I'm here," she said, groaning with the effort of getting in close enough. He could hear her pulling something up along her body. "I brought you a waterskin."

He squeezed her hand. "Today, Vika, you are my favorite. Be sure to tell Berdine."

Vika laughed a little as she pulled her hand back. She pulled the waterskin the rest of the way up along her body and then pushed it through the final part of the opening, which was barely big enough for her arm. Once it was in, she pushed her arm back through and grabbed his hand. He didn't know if she was reassuring him, or herself, but he held on to the hand as he guzzled water while holding the waterskin with his other.

"Take it easy. Don't drink it all at once or it will make you sick."

Richard nodded and pulled it away to get his breath.

"I have to go," she said. "We need to make this hole big enough to pull you out."

Richard felt too weak to answer, so he didn't. Vika huffed as she worked her way back out of the tight hole. As soon as she was back out, the work resumed. He could hear people shouting and groaning with effort as they worked.

Richard took another drink, then had to

rest again with the half-empty waterskin on his chest. It moved slowly up and down with his shallow breathing. The pull of the darkness was too great, and it gently took him again.

He was awakened by hands gripping his shirt and pulling on him. He cried out as they tugged, because his legs were trapped and it hurt when they tried to pull him. A wiry man wormed his way in under the slab beside Richard. His head was facing Richard's feet.

"Hold on, Lord Rahl. Let me see if I can free up your legs so we can pull you out."

He worked as quickly as he could, pulling the tightly packed rock and rubble out from around Richard's legs. He found a shallow place to the side where he could push some of it. For some he had to wiggle his way back out, pulling larger chunks along with him. He was soon back to continue the excavation.

After working at it for a time, Richard was finally able to move his legs.

"All right," the man said, "I think we have you clear. We'll go easy. Let us know if you are still stuck, but we need to get you out. There's no telling if the rest of what's above you might shift and come down all of a sudden."

"What's your name?" Richard asked.

The man seemed surprised by the question. "I'm just a nobody, Lord Rahl."

Richard smiled. "You are not a nobody. Right now, you are a very important somebody to me."

"I am Toby, Lord Rahl," he said in a gentle voice.

"Thank you for coming for me, Toby."

Toby patted Richard's shoulder as he backed out. "I'd do anything for the man what rid us of that cursed witch. Now you lie still, Lord Rahl, and let us do the work."

The man squirmed the rest of the way back out of the shaft they had made. Once again thick fingers gripped Richard's shirt. He felt himself beginning to move, and then they stopped pulling.

"Is everything free now, Lord Rahl?" Toby asked. "Nothing hurting when we pull?"

"I seem to be free. You can go ahead and give it another try. I'll let you know if I'm having a problem."

Once he was out a little farther, to the more open part of the little cave, other hands were able to reach in under his arms to help pull. Because they were on their stomachs, it was an awkward angle to pull from. They would pause and then someone would count down and say, "Pull."

They kept repeating the coordinated tugging. Inch by inch Richard was gradually worked out of his tomb and back through a jagged tunnel of what he judged to be a jumble of unstable debris. At one point, his boot dislodged a rock and the narrow tunnel back where he had been under the slab collapsed with a roar that pushed out a cloud of dust.

That made them pull all the harder and faster. The farther they drew him out, the more hands they could get on him to help. Richard finally emerged to see dirty, grimy faces in torchlight all around him.

Berdine rushed in to give him a quick hug. Legs in red leather were all around him. He saw that it was now night. Some people had torches, while others had lanterns. The sea of faces in the flickering torchlight was an eerie, but welcome sight.

An older woman pushed the Mord-Sith back out of the way and worked herself in through the tight crowd while holding out a lantern in one hand. With bony but strong fingers, she turned his head one way to have a look, then the other.

"He needs help," she announced back over her shoulder. "Lift him onto that litter and get him across the way and into the healing house so we can tend to him."

People rushed to do as the old woman said, lifting him by his arms and legs just enough to slide a litter under him. Four big men lifted the litter.

Trying to be as gentle as they could, they carried him down off the sloping rubble pile and into the narrow streets. Richard bounced up and down in the litter as they trotted along, all the while the old woman urging them to hurry. Looking up, Richard could see by the torchlight that they went around corners and down narrow alleyways until they crossed the pass road that divided the town, over to the side where Richard and his group of nine hadn't been.

They finally went through a doorway into one of the stone buildings and set him down on a raised platform.

The red leather reappeared around him; someone laid a hand on him as if to reassure themselves that he was alive. As they did, Richard's mind went back into darkness.

27

When Richard woke, there was daylight streaming in through a small window. He was about to sit up when he realized that he didn't have any clothes on. When he looked down, he saw that there was at least a towel covering his groin.

He sniffed the air, seeming to recognize an aroma, trying to place it. Finally, he remembered. It was the smell of an aum plant, something from back in his home of Hartland. It seemed like forever since he had smelled it. It was a difficult plant to find, but Zedd had taught him where to look for it. It usually grew in the deep shade of the forest under a nannyberry tree, which was easier to find first because of its thick crop of dark blue berries.

He reached up and pulled something wet off his head and held it out to look at it. It was a big leaf from an aum plant that had been crushed to make it pliable and conform to the contours of his head. That was what he had smelled. Aum both eased pain and, importantly, helped wounds to heal quickly.

Vika shot to her feet when she saw that he was awake.

"He's awake," she called out to the old woman.

The old woman turned away from what she was doing at a table against the wall and smiled down at him. "There you are. You are looking much better."

The room with stone walls wasn't large, but it was filled with tables, a long stone bench against one wall, and standing cabinets all across another wall.

The old woman picked up a stone bowl from one of the tables. She used the pestle in the bowl to crush and stir the contents, then tapped it on the side, removed it, and set it aside. She came close and lifted his head as she put the bowl to his mouth.

"Drink this. It will help you to clear your head."

Richard glanced at Vika. She gave him a reassuring nod, so he drank it. It had some pungent herbs in it, but it mostly tasted of honey diluted in tea.

When he was finished, she patted his shoulder. "I'll go get the others."

Shortly after the woman left, the rest of the Mord-Sith rushed into the room.

"Lord Rahl!" Berdine squealed. "You look so much better!"

Richard squinted up at the faces leaning in, looking at him. "Where are my clothes?"

"Your clothes?" Cassia asked.

"Yes, my clothes."

Nyda gestured. "They're over there. They were positively filthy with all that stone dust and dirt, so we had to wash them."

Richard frowned up at the faces leaning in over him. "Well, who took them off me?"

The faces all smiled.

Richard rolled his eyes.

"You were really dirty, too, from all that dirt and grime," Berdine said. She grinned. "So we had to wash you, too."

Richard could feel his face turning red.

The old woman rushed back in with half a

dozen more old women, all of them in similar long, dark dresses with ample skirts. Richard was glad to have them interrupt the Mord-Sith.

The original woman who had given him the drink held her hand out to the others. "Lord Rahl, we are Bindamoon healers. We have all been seeing to your care. I'm Rita."

"So you have been healing me?"

"We all worked on you," Rita confirmed. "You were seriously hurt."

She lifted the stack of aum leaves off his forehead, to the side, to have a look. She turned briefly to allow the others to have a look at the wound on his head. They all seemed pleased. Rita laid the moist aum back down, patting it gently into place so it would be in contact with the wound.

He realized, then, that there were poultices in several places on his legs and a big patch of aum on the left side of his ribs. It was a pale yellow, similar to the poultice Zedd used to make, but it had a different smell.

"You're lucky to have been injured here, in Bindamoon," Rita said. "We grow some of the rarest herbs here, herbs very helpful for healing. Because of the herbs we have, people come to

Bindamoon to be healed. Some we can help, some we cannot."

"Aum is hard to find back where I come from," he said. "You mean you actually grow it?"

Her brow lifted in surprise. "You know of aum?"

Richard nodded. "My grandfather taught me about it, and how to find it."

"Well, no trouble finding it here," she said with a smile. "It's a valuable medicinal plant, so we grow rows of it." She turned a little and pointed. "We use fresh when we can, and we tie the plants up by their stems and hang them up in drying sheds, over there, until they are cured for when it is out of season. We trade most of it to help support our town and use some of it for people who come here to be healed. You are in one of our healing houses where we tend to people."

Richard looked around and saw a variety of jars and canisters, along with a number of washbasins as well as a half-dozen lanterns on a well-worn, heavy wooden table supplementing the light from the small window. There were shelves under the cabinets with smaller bottles neatly lined up.

"How long have I been asleep?" he asked.

She let out a concerned sigh. "You were brought here two nights ago. Because of your injuries, we had to give you some things to keep you asleep. With so many wounds we feared infection. Some of the herbs we use work better when the person is sleeping. The medicated sleep helped you get over the worst of your injuries. They are now all nicely on the mend. Especially your nasty head wound. We couldn't be sure everything inside was all right until you woke, but we can now see that your eyes are clear and you don't appear dizzy."

"I truly appreciate your help," Richard told her. "But I really need to search for the Mother Confessor. She was—"

"I'm afraid she's gone," Vika told him. "The people told me that all the witches left with her."

Richard blinked. "Left with her?"

"On horses," Vika confirmed.

Richard looked up at Rita. "You have horses here?"

She gestured with gnarled fingers. "Over on this side of the road, opposite from where the palace once stood, there are stables—the queen's stables. The witch women all left and took the Mother Confessor with them."

Richard sat up in a rush, holding the towel over himself. "She's alive then?"

"Yes," Cassia said. "But we learned that they left with her that first night."

Richard put a hand to his head, trying to calculate how long it had been since he and Shota had their battle. "How long ago? How long have I been asleep, or unconscious . . . how long have they been gone?"

The Mord-Sith shared sidelong glances.

Vika's expression revealed her worry. "Quite a while, now, I'm afraid."

Richard stood, still holding the small towel in front of himself. "How long is 'quite a while'?"

"Altogether it's been over five days since they left," Vika said.

28

He turned to Rita. "Are there more horses in the 'queen's' stables?"

She nodded. "Quite a few, but they belong to the queen. She never allows anyone in Bindamoon to use them. The people here must care for them for her. The man called Iron Jack saw to it that the queen's orders were carried out and no one from town was ever caught riding them. He was very cruel in that task, as well as others."

"Well, no one need fear Iron Jack any longer."

She leaned in. "Oh? I have heard rumors that say he was killed by demons. Are the stories true?"

"The man is dead, that much is true," Richard

said as he held the towel over himself. "He can never hurt any of you again."

"This is wonderful news," one of the other women said. Several of the others nodded their agreement.

Richard gestured with an arm. "Out. Everyone out. I need to get dressed. I must get to the Mother Confessor."

The healers glanced at one another with renewed concern.

"I don't know if that is such a good idea just yet," Rita said as she held up a cautionary finger. "It would be best if you rested for a few more days in order—"

"There are vastly more critical things than me getting more rest. I've been sleeping for days. Believe me, I am plenty rested. Now, please, all of you, out, so I can get dressed."

The healers grudgingly gave in and filed out, looking back over their shoulders with concerned looks as they left. They closed the wooden door behind themselves. The Mord-Sith stood at ease and showed no indication that they thought the orders included them as well.

"You too," Richard told them with a swish of his hand. "All of you, please wait outside."

Berdine grinned. "Lord Rahl, that is rather pointless now. I mean, after all of us helped—"

"Out!" Richard could feel his face going red again. He briefly wondered if there was a way his gift could prevent that from happening. If there was, he wanted to learn the trick.

The Mord-Sith all let out deep sighs, as if he was just being silly, but to his relief they finally left him to get dressed alone, closing the door on their way out.

Richard found all of his clothes washed and neatly folded on a chair. His sword hung off one side of the back. His pack, bow, and quiver hung off the other side. His mind raced as he hastily got dressed. He needed to get to Kahlan, but Shota and her coven had quite a head start. He knew, though, that Kahlan would be doing what she could to slow them down, hoping that he would catch up—hoping, too, no doubt, that he was still alive.

Finally dressed in his freshly cleaned clothes, his sword at his hip, and his pack and bow each hanging over a shoulder, he pulled open the door.

He was not prepared for what greeted him outside.

The healing house stood at the edge of the town on the opposite side of the pass road from the palace. The hillside before him gently descended down toward the western wall below where he stood outside the stone building. The entire hillside was packed with people, all silently staring up at him. It looked to him like the whole town was assembled there.

The healers were off to his right, keeping watch, presumably in case he succumbed to his wounds and collapsed. The six Mord-Sith were there waiting for him just outside the door. Once he stepped out, they took up places beside him, with three to either side. Vika took her place immediately to his right, signifying that she was his lead protection.

The people looking up at him stared in silence. He had no idea what was going on, but he was pretty sure that they had never seen a Lord Rahl before, so he thought that maybe that was it.

Richard recognized Toby, but not the two big men in leather vests beside him. When Toby saw that Richard was looking at him, he glanced around, then took a few steps forward. He swiped the flat hat off his head and held the hat in both hands, nervously turning it around and around.

"Toby," Richard said, "I want to thank you and all the others who helped get me out from where I was trapped. You people saved my life. I am indebted to you all. I will never forget all you and the healers have done for me."

Toby shook his head. "No, Lord Rahl. It is we who are indebted to you."

"What do you mean?"

Toby gestured off across the pass road to where the towering palace had stood. Richard could see that the entire structure had collapsed. An enormous pile of rubble was all that remained of a once-elegant structure. It was a reminder of the tremendous destructive power of Subtractive Magic.

On the lower side of the mountain's prominence, where the palace had stood, the ground had sheared away and slid down to cover a number of the stone buildings. He could tell by the way the ground had dropped away on the downhill side that it had exposed the area closer to where the massive chamber beneath the palace had been. That was where Richard had been trapped. The Mord-Sith had been down in that chamber, so they would have known where Richard was. They had undoubtedly been the ones to direct rescue efforts.

It was fortunate that the rock of the mountain itself, having been sliced through and weakened by Subtractive Magic, had slumped down and off to one side the way it had, because it made it possible for his rescuers to dig in from the side, which would have been considerably closer to him, than to try to dig down from atop the enormous pile of rubble. Had they needed to do that, he knew, by the time they reached him it would have merely ended up being an effort to recover his body.

"I'm sorry that when the palace came down it buried so many of your homes," Richard said.

"You destroyed that terrible palace of the queen," Toby said.

"You mean Shota, the witch woman," Richard corrected.

People all through the crowd nodded at that. They had been afraid to say her name aloud, but now that he had, they readily acknowledged it.

"That's right," Toby said as he kept turning his hat in his hands. "The people in those buildings heard the powerful uproar of your magic, and the sounds of the palace coming apart, so they were able to escape before the whole place came down. Those homes can and will be rebuilt. I'm thankful that none of the people who lived there were hurt and they are all safe."

Richard nodded with relief. "That's good to hear."

Toby lifted his thumb to the side. "These are my two boys. They helped dig you out, as did many of the people of Bindamoon. We have lived our lives under the cloud of that witch and her sister witches, to say nothing of Iron Jack. Whenever she was here, in Bindamoon, we feared to even come out of our houses. Everyone feared that if she saw them, she might strike them down for any reason or no reason."

"Well, she's gone now, and Iron Jack is dead," Richard said. "She no longer has a palace to come back to. I intend to see to it that she never comes back here."

At that, everyone went to their knees. They all did it together, as if they were of one mind. The six Mord-Sith came around and in front of the people on the hillside, turned toward Richard, and went to their knees as well. Everyone bent forward, putting their foreheads to the ground.

Together, in one voice, they began.

"Master Rahl guide us. Master Rahl teach us. Master Rahl protect us."

Richard hadn't expected them all to give the devotion. He stood silent and tall as they continued.

"In your light we thrive. In your mercy we are sheltered. In your wisdom we are humbled. We live only to serve. Our lives are yours."

As all the voices died out, silence slowly fell over the expanse of the hillside. And then they repeated the devotion. When they were finished, they spoke it for a third time.

Richard felt a catch in his throat. This devotion was his link to people, a link forged through his gift. They were the steel against steel for him; he was the magic against magic for them.

He had used that magic to bring down the hated palace of the woman they feared to name.

More than that, the devotion was his protection for their world, linking all the magic of the world in a web of security that kept the Golden Goddess from coming unimpeded to slaughter everyone and feed on them as he had seen happen back in the lower reaches of the People's Palace.

His magic, and Kahlan's, was the protection for their world, and it linked them all together. The devotion was an acknowledgment of that shared bond.

The two children Kahlan carried were the continuation of that magic, that power, that bond that was the protection for their world.

Richard swallowed. "Thank you all. I can't begin to tell you what it means to me."

A cheer went up to let him know that it meant something to them as well.

"We've never been before the Lord Rahl to give the devotion," Toby said. "The queen—I mean Shota, the witch woman—wouldn't allow the devotion to be given."

"I appreciate everything you've done for me, both to dig me out of that rubble, and to heal me. I was in good hands. But now, I need to chase down those witches and put an end to what they are doing to destroy all our futures."

One of Toby's sons pointed. "The stables are over there." He grinned. "Since you are going after Shota, maybe you would like to take some of her horses to her?"

Richard returned a brief smile. "That's the idea."

29

With Vika and the rest of the Mord-Sith following right behind, the crowd followed them to the stables, eager to see to it that he had whatever he needed. Lord Rahl or not, Mord-Sith were fearsome, so they all preferred to follow at a respectful, and safe, distance. He hoped that these people had seen that Mord-Sith had been weapons used by evil men in the past, but that they were not the monsters they were once feared to be.

That deferential distance, though, pleased the Mord-Sith. Friends or not, this was the Lord Rahl, their charge. Their responsibility was to keep him safe. Nothing frustrated them more than when he, in their opinion, disregarded their protection and went out of his way to put himself in danger. In other words, live his life. He sometimes thought that they believed he should stay at the People's Palace where they could watch over him and he could simply rule from there.

The stable grounds were larger than Richard had expected. There were fenced corrals with lush green grass. The mild temperature of the mountain fortress provided the same perfect growing conditions for the grass as it did for the herbs they grew in large fields.

Richard and the Mord-Sith made their way among the complex of supply buildings and barns. He was eager to get going. His worry for Kahlan was a constant distraction.

As they were crossing the stable grounds, behind them Glee suddenly poured out from hiding places among the buildings. The dark creatures had let Richard and the Mord-Sith pass so that they could attack the massive crowd following them.

Richard instantly recognized that it had the makings of a massacre, which was exactly what the Glee had planned. He also recognized the method to their battle plan.

As the gangly creatures continued to pour

out from behind the buildings, people shrank back in terror. The Glee quickly filled the gap between Richard and the crowd. Their tactics had evolved. This time the creatures wanted to attack directly into the tightly packed throng of people, both to kill as many as possible and to make it harder for him to fight back and stop them.

Richard knew he had only one chance.

He gestured to the Mord-Sith. "Wait until I tell you!"

He drew his sword as he raced through the band of Glee intent on attacking the towns-people. Running at full speed, he crashed right through the horde of dark, slimy creatures, knocking some of them out of his way when he had to, before they had time to react. They expected him to take up a defensive position back where he had been. They hadn't been expecting him to charge right through their midst. Though their legs were long, and they could run fast, Richard could run faster. Besides that, the sword whirling through the air, cutting them down from behind as he hurtled through their midst, surprised and distracted them, caus-ing many to turn and slowing others down.

As soon as Richard broke through and gained the ground between all the people and the Glee, he spun around to attack them head-on.

"Now!" he called out to the Mord-Sith to be heard over the hisses and screeches of the Glee.

His sword whistled through the air as he sliced through the advancing invaders, swiftly lopping off claws as they used them to attack. Dark, glossy heads thudded down on the ground, bounced, and rolled among the advancing Glee. All of the severed claws and heads were a distraction that turned them away from their intended target of the stunned crowd. Infuriated, they instead all charged in at him. The people unwittingly helped him by continually falling back or running away, opening up fighting space and keeping the Glee from reaching them.

At the same time as Richard was hacking his way through the enemy coming at him, the Mord-Sith, now ordered into the battle, attacked from behind with Agiel in one hand and knives in the other. The Glee found themselves trapped between deadly attacks from the front and the rear at the same time. Many became confused, not knowing who to defend themselves from. Others began turning to scribbles to escape back into their own world to avoid certain death. Many more hesitated too long and it cost them their lives.

What Richard had learned about fighting them from the previous attack served him well. He had learned how the Glee moved their arms and claws, where those claws were dangerous, and where they were useless on their back-swings or when their arms were extended. They also fought as individuals, not as a cohesive force, which made it easier for him to take out individuals.

Their main weakness was that each of them wanted to be the one to sink their claws and needle-sharp teeth into the helpless towns-people, not fight a battle. They each had their own agenda to be the first to get at the people and feed on them. As such, they had no regard for protecting one another, working together, or forming a united front. He scythed his way through their ranks, and claws, arms, and heads began to litter the ground as he perfected his technique of taking advantage of their weaknesses.

It became almost a game to him, a dance with

death in which they had no chance to touch him as he spun and dodged through their midst.

At their rear, the Mord-Sith attacked them from behind and took down unsuspecting Glee, bringing surprised cries of pain as they were stabbed, or hit with the horrific power of an Agiel. Hearing the shrieks of pain, many turned to the new threat, which left them vulnerable to Richard's blade. Many realized that mistake too late to save themselves.

The creatures in the center of that hammer and anvil paused in confusion. They hadn't expected to be suddenly trapped between two dangerous threats interrupting their single-minded lust for the slaughter of the townspeople. They began to realize that what they had at first thought would be overwhelming numbers was not nearly enough and was dwindling by the second. As Glee fell dead, their assault began to fall apart. They had expected the panic of the townspeople to aid them in their attack, but now, instead, panic swept through their own ranks. They were quickly being overpowered by Richard's whirling blade on one side and the Mord-Sith dodging and weaving in to press their lethal attack from the other.

Even as the dark creatures were falling dead or seriously wounded all around them, the remaining Glee, gripped by terror, almost all at the same time turned to scribbles and vanished.

As soon as they were gone, the Mord-Sith moved quickly among the wounded on the ground and cut their throats. Panting from the effort, Richard scanned the area for any further threat, prepared for another surprise attack.

Exhausted not only from the physical effort but from the storm of rage pounding through him from the sword, he sheathed the weapon so that he could recover.

A group of healers in the dark dresses and full skirts rushed in and surrounded him.

"Hurry," Rita called out.

Richard could see a couple of others racing toward one of the buildings. The Glee were all dead or vanished, so he didn't understand what was going on or what they were so concerned about.

Rita and a gaggle of others rushed in around him and started pulling up his shirt. Not knowing what they were doing, he tried to push their hands away, but they were as persistent as a swarm of wasps. He kept trying to pull his shirt back down as a different woman on the other side pulled it back up.

He tried to lightly slap Rita's hands away. "What is wrong with you?"

She seized the tail of his shirt and shook it to show him. "It's not what is wrong with me, it's what is wrong with you."

Richard looked down and saw that the side of his shirt was soaked with blood.

30

T he healers who had gone off to one of the buildings emerged and raced back with a variety of supplies.

Rita lifted his elbows. "Hold your arms up. Your wound has torn open from your effort at fighting and it's bigger now than before. We will need to stitch this up."

Richard was wishing he had Shale around to heal the wound with her gift. But then he remembered that Shale had become part of the coven, even if it was against her will.

Rita grumbled, reprimanding herself for not sewing the wound better before. She pushed the sides apart to open the wound so she could inspect it. It made Richard groan with pain. Another woman handed her a bit of poultice as another handed her a needle and thread. She immediately swiped some of the yellowish concoction into the wound and then set to work stitching it together.

Richard winced and held his breath each time she pushed the needle through his skin and drew the sides of the wound together. With each stitch she pulled the thread tight with a little tug. Each time she paused before the next stitch he caught his breath. When she was satisfied, she bent and bit the thread to break it and then tied off the ends.

"I hope that holds it," she muttered.

Another of the healers leaned in for a look. "It looks like it should. You did strong stitches. They should be more than enough to hold it tight."

"As long as he doesn't get into another battle right away," Rita said.

One of the others scooped another big glob of a different ointment of some kind out of a bowl. Richard could smell aum. Another woman dabbed the bloody wound over his ribs with a rag to clean it up. Richard winced and recoiled. It wasn't the stitching that hurt so much as the wound itself.

"Stay still," Rita groused. "Hold your arms up out of the way."

She obviously didn't appreciate that he had ruined her previous work. The woman with the ointment slapped a handful of it against the wound. As soon as she did, another pressed a folded cloth over it. As she held the cloth in place, Rita took a roll of binding material from one of the others and started wrapping it tightly around him. He grunted from the pain of how tight it was, but at least the aum was already beginning to numb the ache of the wound.

"I know that you aren't going to take our advice to rest for a few more days," Rita said, "so I had to put in extra stitches and it was necessary to make the binding tight. I don't want the wound opening up when you are riding horseback. I hope you don't need to get in another battle with those monsters for a little while at least."

Seeing that it was important, Vika grabbed the roll from Rita. "Here, let me help. I can make it tighter."

Vika was not nearly as gentle as Rita had been. She made the wrapping so tight that Richard feared to exhale lest she cinch it down when he did and then he wouldn't be able to breathe in again.

"Stop complaining," Vika murmured as she continued to wind the binding around his chest, concentrating on what she was doing.

"That's good," Rita said, taking the end from Vika once she had used the whole roll. She split the end, then pushed it through several of the layers of bindings and tied the tail so that it couldn't come undone.

"You are a natural at this," Rita told Vika. She shook a finger at the Mord-Sith. "I want you to keep an eye on the wound. If he starts to bleed again, unwrap it and put some more of this salve on it, then put a clean cloth over it. After that, wrap him back up. I'm afraid that is all we can do without him taking some time to rest and heal. But we all understand the urgency of going after the Mother Confessor."

Vika took the tin after Rita checked that there was enough in it before screwing on a lid. "I will. Thank you for helping Lord Rahl. I will watch over him in your place."

Rita smiled and patted Vika's cheek. "Good girl."

"We need those horses," Richard told Toby.

One of the men pointed a thumb back over his shoulder at the sinking sun. It was hovering over the western wall out to the pass. "It will be dark in a couple of hours, Lord Rahl. Don't you want to wait until dawn to leave?"

Richard glanced to the pass trail under the setting sun. "If I missed saving the Mother Confessor from that coven of witches by a couple of hours, or a couple of minutes, or even a couple of seconds, I could never forgive myself, and our world would never forgive me."

The man and those around him acknowledged what Richard said with solemn nods.

Richard intended to ride hard and cover ground as swiftly as possible. There were plenty of horses, more than he had expected, so he told the men that he wanted horses for him and the six Mord-Sith, and an extra for each of them so they could rotate their mounts when the horses got tired.

The crowd outside the stables watched as men led horses out of stalls in a couple of the stable buildings. A pair of men for each horse, to save precious time, helped get the horses saddled and bridles on. While they were doing that, other women and men rushed up with supplies for their journey and tied them to the spare horses. Richard could see men tying bags of oats to the spare horses as well.

"Let's get going," Richard told the Mord-Sith once he saw that the horses were ready.

As they all mounted up, Rita stepped forward and put a hand on Vika's leg. "Watch over him, will you?"

Vika smiled. "Like a mother hen."

Richard believed her. But he had to admit the support of the binding did seem to make the wound feel better. The aum helped as well.

"Lord Rahl, thank you," Toby said as he, too, stepped out of the crowd, hat in hand. "We are in your debt."

"And I in yours."

"If we can ever be of help, with herbs or anything else, everyone in Bindamoon stands ready to render any assistance we can."

Richard gave the man a nod of appreciation. "We need to get going. The children of D'Hara need me."

Without delay, Richard flicked the reins and gave his horse a gentle press with his heels. The horse responded immediately, charging ahead at a swift trot. The Mord-Sith stayed right with him.

The extra horses ran behind on long tethers. He ran his horse down the trail road the rest of the way through the town and toward the western wall and its arched opening.

"Lord Rahl," Vika said as she rode up beside him as they went through the arched tunnel under the wall, "how in the world are we going to find that witch woman, Shota, and her coven?"

"That's the least of our worries. We simply need to head west."

"Why west?" Berdine asked.

"Because," he told them as he looked back over his shoulder, "Shota will be taking Kahlan to Agaden Reach."

Berdine wrinkled up her nose. "What's Agaden Reach?"

Richard passed a look among all the faces watching him as they rode. "A very bad place. It's surrounded by jagged peaks of the Rang'Shada Mountains, like a wreath of thorns, and then a dangerous swamp."

"Ah," Berdine said. "Of course it is."

31

A wintery gust of wind quickly reminded Richard how cold it was outside the town walls. It sent a shiver through his shoulders. He knew that he would soon enough become accustomed to the cold again, but in the meantime it was unpleasant.

He had to read the way ahead by how the snow followed the contour of a slight depression in the ground created by the trail as it wound its way into the snow-crusted trees. Once they were into the thick of the forest, the narrow but open area through the woods more easily revealed the trail. He knew, though, that once they got down out of the mountains, the snow would be gone, it would be warmer, and the path down from the pass behind them would be much more obvious.

The wound in his side hurt with each step the horse took under him. He did his best to ignore the pain. He checked a few times, relieved to find it wasn't bleeding. Vika watched him checking.

After the sun was down and it grew both darker and colder, Richard glanced over at Vika. "I'm not tired. The moon on the snow provides enough light. I'm going to keep going. I don't intend to stop unless we're forced to." He swept his gaze over the rest of them. "Is that a problem for any of you?"

Vika glanced over at him suspiciously. "You aren't planning on leaving us behind, are you?"

Richard frowned. "No, of course not."

Vika shrugged. "Then there is no problem. We are Mord-Sith. We will ride as long as you want to ride. If you get too tired to ride, you can ride on my horse behind me."

Even though Richard wasn't in a smiling mood, he smiled briefly at that. "Thanks. I'll let you know if I need you to carry me."

"Riding is a bit rough, though," she said. "You just be sure to let me know if that wound in your side starts bleeding again. If it does, I will need to fix it."

Richard turned his eyes ahead to the moonlit,

snowy trail. "I need to be strong to stop Shota and get Kahlan back, so you just make sure I stay healthy."

Vika showed him an earnest smile. "By your command, Lord Rahl."

A few hours later, when Richard departed the trail and took a route leading down through a broad valley, Rikka rode up close to him. "Aydindril is to the north, Lord Rahl. Are you sure they aren't going to head there to take the Keep in order to be safe from the Glee? Surely even the witches don't want to tangle with the Glee."

"No, they're taking Kahlan west, to Agaden Reach." He gestured ahead to some of the depressions in the snow. "Those are their tracks joining us now, but they are days old."

Richard had assumed that they would follow the trail, so he hadn't taken the time to stop and look for tracks in the dark. He was a bit alarmed to see that their tracks were now intersecting their route. That meant that he hadn't realized the coven had somehow taken a shortcut up until that point. That would put them even farther ahead than he thought.

"I can't see any tracks," Berdine said. "It's too dark."

"I can see them well enough," he told her. "The wind and sun have worn them down over the days they had a head start, but fortunately there hasn't been more snow to cover them." He was angry at himself for not looking earlier for their tracks to cut away from the trail to take a shortcut. Even though it was dark, if he had spotted that deviation he would have seen where they had gone. "Even if it does snow, now, this confirms where they are headed. That is what matters."

For most of the rest of the night, they rode on through the dead quiet, snowy woods. They descended steadily through the mountainous forest and eventually down into the sparsely wooded hill country. As they got lower, tufts of long grass started to appear in open patches of the snow. Richard could see that in the distance, revealed by the pale moonlight, the valley out ahead was clear of snow.

Even so, they had to maintain a slower pace than he would have liked, because it would be dangerous to go too fast in the dark—snow or no snow. A horse could break a leg or easily come up lame if it stepped in a dangerous place it couldn't see. If they lost horses, they would lose a lot of time to the witch women they chased. If they had to take to traveling on foot, it would mean a disastrous loss of time to get to Shota.

The whole while they rode in silence, Richard's mind churned with questions about what he was going to do when they got to Agaden Reach. He ran through endless possibilities, trying to think through every likelihood, and even things less probable. None of the outcomes looked good to him.

When dawn broke behind them and gradually brought color and light to the landscape, and more open ground, Richard was finally able to pick up the pace. By midday, the horses were winded. He brought them all to a halt on a broad, flat plain so they could move the saddles over to the fresh horses.

The horses chomped on grass while they had the chance. A small stream meandering through the flat ground provided water for them to drink deeply. Berdine and Nyda broke out some of the fresh food from the supplies the townspeople had packed.

Nyda waited until he finished cinching up the saddle, then handed him some freshly cooked pork. Berdine gave him a chunk of cheese from a different pack. Seeing the cheese reminded him of the way Kahlan had hated cheese but craved it now that she was pregnant. That craving came from at least one of the unborn children.

He ate the cheese in three bites, washing it down with water, then held the chunk of pork in his teeth as he saddled up again. In mere moments they were on their way on fresh horses and with some much-needed food. None of the Mord-Sith had voiced a single word of complaint. Of course, they wouldn't even if they had any. Charging onward without resting was something they were used to.

By the second night a thick cloud cover had rolled in, completely blocking the moon and stars. It quickly grew so dark he couldn't see his hand in front of his face, much less the lay of the land. With a flint and steel he lit strips of birch bark from a stock of them he had in his pack and used that to light travel candles so that they could at least see each other.

Richard knew that he couldn't risk the horses in the dark over unknown terrain, so they were forced to stop for the night. Since they had not stopped to sleep the night before, they were all exhausted. There was no way to see if there was a good place for shelter, and Richard didn't think it was worth searching the surrounding countryside with a candle to look for wood to build a fire, so they all rolled themselves up in their bedrolls. Despite the chill, they all quickly fell asleep, all of them too tired even to eat.

The next day dawned overcast and gloomy, but it was warmer, and better yet they had made it down out of the mountains. Before them lay the rolling hills and broad valleys of the Midlands, which would be much easier and faster traveling. There were trees, but they were in scattered clusters along hillsides overlooking meandering streams through stretches of gravel beds.

They rode hard and switched horses at regular intervals to keep them fresh, using those opportunities to grab some food, which they ate while riding. Fortunately, the people in Bindamoon had packed oats for the horses. For the next few days there would also be grass for them to eat.

Richard knew that they would need to cross the Callisidrin River in order to get to Agaden

Reach up in the vast spine of rock that ran north-east up through the Midlands. He wanted to cross the river north of Tamarang in order to avoid anyone seeing them, so that the Golden Goddess likewise wouldn't see them. They were fortunate that, so far, since leaving Bindamoon, they hadn't encountered any people. He was thankful they hadn't been forced into another battle with the Glee.

Richard pressed ahead as fast as they could throughout the day. As darkness began to gather, Vika rode up beside him. She reached over and put a hand on his forearm to bring him out of his brooding thoughts.

"Lord Rahl, we need to stop," she told him.

Richard gestured ahead. "We can still see well enough to keep going."

"You're bleeding," she said. "We need to stop so I can tend to your wound."

Richard put his hand on his ribs. His shirt was wet with blood. He sighed in annoyance. "We don't have time for this."

"We can stop, and I can take care of it while we get a quick bite to eat and let the horses graze for a bit, and then we can keep going if you want."

Richard knew she was right. "All right. We have a long way to go. I don't want this wound to get worse and slow us down."

"That's why I need to fix it now," Vika said.

"How much farther is it?" Nyda asked.

"It's still quite a ways," he told her. "But worse, not long after we cross the Callisidrin River, we will have to leave the horses and make it the rest of the way up into the rugged Rang'Shada Mountains on foot. Ordinarily it would take close to a week of climbing once we get to the mountains and have to leave the horses. If we're to catch up to them, we need to do it in less time than that. The last part of it up and into the Reach will not be easy."

Richard hoped that Shota and her coven would not be traveling as swiftly as he and the Mord-Sith had been and that he was closing the distance. They, too, had to make the same strenuous climb up into the mountains on foot, so he intended to press on as quickly as possible to catch them before they could do whatever it was Shota had planned.

She had said that they would wait until Kahlan delivered the twins, rather than simply kill her and thus the unborn babies. But since the battle at her winter palace, he knew that everything had changed.

The witches most likely intended to get Kahlan to Agaden Reach, where Shota would feel safe on her home ground, and then end Kahlan's pregnancy. He feared to contemplate how she intended to accomplish her ends.

32

The few rays of the late-day sun that made it through the thick balsam limbs reflected off a layer of long-fallen leaves, making a golden-colored path ahead of them leading the way between dark woods to each side. The beauty of the place was overlaid in Kahlan's mind by the sinister nature of where they were taking her. The smell of wet, decaying leaves piled up in corners of rocky outcroppings and under the dense brush only added to her sense of foreboding.

She was being taken to a place where she was told she would be held until she gave birth and then her babies would be killed. Shota said that she would then be released. While Shota was brutally honest about what she intended to do with Kahlan's babies, she didn't think Shota was being so honest about the second part of it. As if that mattered to her now.

When Kahlan looked up through the upper branches of trees, she finally saw the snowcapped peaks that were the formidable spires that surrounded Agaden Reach like a ring of thorns. The view was quickly lost again as they followed a trail that disappeared ahead of them into thick forest of fir and pine trees. She took out some of her frustration kicking pine cones out of her way as she hiked along the trail.

The canopy high above cut off most of the light, so the plants that grew in abundance on the forest floor, such as the ferns, were those that thrived in shade. Most of the brush, unlike the ferns that were turning brown, would keep their leaves all winter. They helped add to the shadowed gloom.

Kahlan could see that past all the women, out ahead, they would come to a branch in the trail, with the right fork leading lower and the left fork leading higher. Without delay or hesitation Shota took the left fork. The rest of them followed in a single-file line.

The witches following close behind Kahlan,

and bringing up the rear, kept a close eye on her, making sure she didn't try to go another way or suddenly bolt and run. When they hadn't been looking, Kahlan had tried to vanish into the thick underbrush several times. The swift punishment taught her a painful lesson that escape was hopeless. At least for now. She was determined, though, that if she saw a chance to get away, she would take it.

Ravens followed them, as they had since they'd left the fortress town of Bindamoon, sailing effortlessly through open limbs of winter-bare branches of oaks, maples, and linden trees. In the thicker foliage of the weeping spruce, tamaracks, and red pines, where they couldn't easily sail, they swerved and darted through any opening they could find. Sometimes they flew above the forest canopy, only to swoop down unexpectedly, giving Kahlan a start as they suddenly appeared to surprise her.

The leaves, long since fallen, leaving the branches bare, blanketed rocks and in other places lay rotting in damp piles. The boots of the women ahead scuffed over rocks hidden under leaves. As weary as Kahlan was, when she wasn't paying enough attention, those hidden rocks sometimes tried to twist an ankle when she inadvertently stepped on them wrong. Thick lines of leaves suggested deep gaps in the rock that could break a leg, so she was careful to avoid stepping there.

The bull of a witch with the sour expression lumbered along just ahead of Kahlan, swaying from side to side to keep her low, squat bulk moving. Despite the obvious effort of walking, she didn't seem to tire and never complained. In fact, she had so far not spoken a word. The scary, bony one with the big, black eyes was directly in front of her. They were the two who had pulled her out of the way of the falling rock when the palace had begun to collapse. They had dragged her into the tunnels, saving her life and at the same time capturing her. As they were hauling her away, Kahlan hadn't been able to see in all the swirling dust if Richard had escaped the mass of falling stone. Since he'd been in the center of the enormous room, she didn't see how he could have made it out in time.

The scariest witch guarding her, while not at all ugly as most of the others certainly were, was the ill-tempered witch with the stringy red hair veiling her face. Kahlan had learned that her name was Nea. She followed behind Kahlan as they hiked through the woods, glaring at her the entire time, waiting for Kahlan to try to run, or to give her some other excuse to hurt her. For seemingly no reason, other than her bad temper, she occasionally murmured blood-curdling threats and promises. The worst were what she intended to do to her babies.

From the interactions Kahlan had observed during their journey, Nea was apparently Shota's lieutenant, her favorite, the one she trusted most, and the one she had put in charge of watching over Kahlan. Every once in a while, as they walked, Nea would lean forward and whisper in Kahlan's ear what she intended to do if Kahlan would just give her an excuse. Kahlan believed her.

Kahlan, though, wasn't so much worried about herself as she was for the two unborn children she was carrying, and she knew quite well what these witch women had planned for them. Kahlan couldn't stand the thought of the twins never having the chance at life.

When she saw soft ground with the leaves mostly clear from the center, all the witch women ahead of her walked off to the side to avoid the mud. Kahlan deliberately walked straight on through it in order to leave her tracks. She knew that if he had somehow been able to survive, Richard would come for her. He would recognize her tracks and know for sure where she was being taken. Sometimes, when a branch was close to her when she passed, she would break the tip and leave it hanging down as a sign for him.

She also did whatever she could along the way, from minor things like feigning having difficulty getting up a rise of rocks or having to often empty her bladder from the pressure of the twins, to bigger things like sitting and saying she needed to rest, all in order to delay them. She used all those little diversions to slow the coven down, hoping Richard would catch up with them. She didn't know what he could do to stop all of these witches, but, well, he was Richard, so she was sure he would come up with something if only he could get to them in time.

Kahlan did her best not to consider the possibility that Richard wasn't still alive, but her mind frequently didn't cooperate and fed her a steady stream of fears to haunt the dark corners of her thoughts. It would make her feel a sense of growing panic if she let herself think about him being crushed under a mountain of rubble, so she did her best not to.

After the trail went up a steep switchback and then doubled back on itself, she could look down and see through the branches of white cedar and spruce trees where they had just been a short time before. After they had doubled back, the path came to another fork. This time they took the one to the right. Knowing where it went, she dreaded the choice that was made for her.

The trail the witch women took immediately began an increasingly difficult climb up a series of switchbacks and up over ledges. In places it was so steep it required them to use their hands to hold on to the gnarled roots of the trees growing close in on each side of the trail. Those handholds helped them to continue to climb ever upward. The sour-faced witch woman ahead of Kahlan often had to wait for the assistance of the younger, stronger women ahead to help hoist her up.

The climb required that Kahlan frequently use her hands, so much so that the rough roots gave her cuts and increasingly painful blisters.

The web of roots coming down the rocky ground surrounded chunks of granite, holding them in place like powerful, living claws so that it couldn't fall. Since they provided places for water to collect and moss to grow, the twisting roots frequently made for slippery footing, or slimy handholds.

More than once, Kahlan's boot slipped off a root and she had to catch herself with a tenuous grip on a rock or a root above as her feet momentarily swung free out in space. Each time it made her gasp. She worried about doing anything that could hurt the babies, so she did her best to quickly regain a foothold rather than let herself drop back down to a previous ledge. Once, Nea reached up, caught her ankle in a powerful grip, and placed her foot atop a shelf of rock so that she wouldn't fall.

Kahlan panted with the effort of the climb. She was drained and exhausted by the time she could again see the snowcapped spires around Agaden Reach off through the trees. But down in the dark woods where they were climbing the trail, it was growing increasingly difficult to see where she could put each foot to help support her when they had to climb. The farther they went, though, the more often she had increasingly open glimpses of that crown of thorns. She knew they would soon be up to the tree line and then they would have to make their way across open, windswept ledges.

When she reached a level place, Kahlan plopped down in exhaustion on a smooth piece of rock to get her breath.

Nea immediately was in her face. "What do you think you're doing?"

"Why don't you try climbing this steep trail when you're this far along in a pregnancy? See if you can do it."

Sorrel, one of the nastier of the witch women up ahead, gave the bull of a witch a hand up. Once she had helped the big woman up, she then knelt to lean back down over the top of where Kahlan sat. She had long, pointed nails, and both of her hands looked like she regularly dipped them in red wax. Her hair was done in neat rows of short spikes, all of them tipped with the same red wax, or paint, or whatever it was. At least, Kahlan didn't think that it was blood.

"No one told you that you could sit down," Sorrel growled down at Kahlan.

Kahlan looked up at Sorrel's black gums, revealed whenever she snarled, wishing she could drive her knife through the woman's heart. But they had taken her knife and her pack, lest she get the idea to use her blade on one of them. Shota didn't want to take a chance on losing one of the thirteen witches, because that would break the coven. That coven gave her powers over and above those she possessed on her own. The kind of magic she had used back in the chamber below the palace had made those frightening powers all too evident. As if Shota hadn't been frightening enough without them.

"I'm exhausted," Kahlan told Sorrel as she gestured to the side. "Look, there's a pretty level place, here, on this ledge. It's sheltered by that rock face you're kneeling on. I think we should stop for the night. Besides being spent, we can't climb this mountain in the dark. I could easily fall and split my skull."

Grinning, Nea put a hand on Kahlan's shoulder and pulled her around to face her. "That would solve everything, then, now wouldn't it? We are only keeping you alive because that's Shota's wish, not because it's ours."

Worry for her unborn babies immediately

came to the forefront of Kahlan's thoughts. "Shota is the grand witch. You had better do as she tells you and keep me alive."

Kahlan didn't think that Shota really cared if she died, but it was a bluff that seemed to give Nea pause.

Nea reached up and parted the strands of hair hanging down over her face so that she could better peer out at Kahlan. "True, but if you took a nasty fall and broke some bones . . . who is to say it's the fault of anyone but your own clumsy feet?"

33

Shota pushed her way through the tight knot of witch women crowded around on the ledge just above Kahlan. She leaped down the last few feet, landing with surprising grace. She had fire in her eyes.

Kahlan stood. She didn't know exactly why. Somehow, she felt compelled to stand and face a coldly angry Shota, whether by her own volition or Shota's she wasn't entirely sure.

Kahlan remembered how terrified she had been the first time she had gone to Agaden Reach with Richard to face the witch woman. There had been times since then when her fear of the woman had ebbed and flowed, but at the moment, she was back to remembering how much she had feared that first encounter, when

Shota had put snakes all over her. The witch woman knew how much Kahlan feared snakes. Had Richard not been able to stop her and make her remove her snakes, they very well might have bitten her, and she surely would have died. But Richard was not with her this time.

"Do you think I don't know what you are doing?" Shota asked in a smooth voice, suddenly looking and sounding like Kahlan's mother.

Such an image hurt Kahlan's heart, but she dared not show how much it got to her.

"I don't know what you are talking about, *Shota*."

Kahlan put emphasis on the witch woman's name to let her know that she wasn't going to break down in helpless emotion at seeing an image that appeared to be her mother. It was thievery of cherished memories from her own mind in order to use them in cruel trickery. As much as Kahlan had loved her mother, she didn't appreciate Shota using her mother's image in such a cold-blooded manner.

"Do you think I haven't noticed you deliberately leaving your tracks, or breaking a branch here and there so that Richard can follow you?"

"I don't know what you're talking about."

Kahlan hooked some of her hair behind an ear. "I'm simply walking. I don't know how you expect me to walk and not leave tracks."

Shota, reverting to looking again like Shota—a very angry Shota—seized Kahlan's chin between her thumb and the knuckle of her first finger. She narrowed her eyes as she leaned in.

"Don't feed me that. I know what you're doing. I am also well aware that you have been trying to slow us down so that Richard can catch up with us and 'rescue' you."

Kahlan retreated to her Confessor face, showing no emotion.

"Why would you fear he would be alive?" Kahlan asked. "The entire palace fell in on him."

"Fear it? There is hardly anything to fear." Shota released Kahlan's chin, instead regarding her with an intense look that held her in no less of a powerful grip. "On the contrary, I made sure the palace fell in on him. But you foolishly hold out hope that he somehow got out in time. Am I right?"

Kahlan shrugged. "Well, you know Richard. He often manages to come out of impossible situations wondering why anyone would have been worried about him. So, were I you, I wouldn't be so smug that he isn't this minute coming up this mountain after you and your coven."

"You think so?" Shota nodded with a sly smile. "Well, I think you should know that down in that chamber beneath my palace, when I saw that everything was beginning to fall in, just before I escaped out the tunnel with you and my ladies, I turned back and cast a simple little spell to hinder his legs for just long enough to keep him from running to safety in time. He wouldn't have realized that my spell was there, and, because of it, he would have been unable to get away. As he stood there, momentarily helpless, the entire weight of the palace and a good part of the mountain all fell in on him."

Not wanting to give Shota the satisfaction of reacting with the horror and rage she was feeling inside, Kahlan maintained the Confessor face and didn't say anything.

"So you see, Mother Confessor, your husband, the man who fathered those two monsters you carry, is dead and buried in a grave so deep his body will never even be recovered for a state funeral. He is entombed under my palace, because of my spell. Quite fitting, don't you think, since he came to bury me."

"What's your point?"

"The point is, you no longer have a husband; we no longer have a Lord Rahl; those two children no longer have a father; and he isn't going to come to rescue you. So you might as well quit bothering with your little tricks."

Unable to maintain her Confessor face, Kahlan swallowed.

"You shouldn't be so smug about your safety, because if he doesn't come to kill you, I will do it myself—you have the promise of the Mother Confessor on that."

Shota straightened and folded her arms, looking down at her, amused by the threat. "Is that so? Well, I must admit, you are more vicious than I am. My intent is to let you live, not kill you. I simply want to eliminate the threat to the world posed by those two monsters you carry. Fortunately, with Richard dead, no more can ever be created."

Against her will, Kahlan felt a tear roll down her cheek.

"Now," Shota went on, "you can either get moving and get yourself and those unborn babies to Agaden Reach, where you will give birth to them, or I will see to it that you miscarry here and now."

Kahlan lifted her chin. "You mean like you tried and failed to do before?"

"With everything I have done, my aim was always to simply slow you down so that you wouldn't get too far away. Were you to get to the Keep I wouldn't have been able to get to you and do what is necessary for the greater good. I could have killed you any number of times, but I didn't. None of the things I did, such as that wood where you lost so much time, were an attempt to kill you, now were they?"

"You did something to make me start to miscarry after we were out of that wood, and after we were stopped from getting to the Keep by the boundary you put up, but Richard was able to help stop it. You were trying to kill me along with my babies."

"On the contrary." Shota couldn't seem to hold back a knowing smile, as if she were talking to an ignorant child. "I knew that if I cast a spell to have you start to miscarry, Richard would have to find you a plant called mother's breath, the only herb that could stop it. I made you start to miscarry and collapse in that particular place on purpose. I knew that when Richard went to look for mother's breath—mother's breath transplanted from the fields of Bindamoon and planted there for him to find—he would come across the pass trail, which would eventually lead you all to the pass and to me. My mountain lion returned to let me know that all went as I had planned.

"So, you see, it wasn't an attempt to kill you, but instead I went to a great deal of trouble to get you right to the spot where I wanted you. As I have told you, I don't want to harm you, but to simply eliminate the little monsters you carry.

"Unfortunately, Richard destroyed my winter palace. Now, I want you to finish the journey into my home of Agaden Reach, where you will be taken care of until you give birth. After that, you will be free to go. But like I say, if you are too difficult about it . . ."

Shota touched a finger to Kahlan's belly. She gasped with a sudden, powerful contraction. The pain was so intense that it doubled her over as Shota followed her down to continue holding the finger on her swollen belly.

". . . then I will simply have you miscarry right here and now and be done with it. So what is it going to be, Mother Confessor? Do you want to finish the journey and give birth in comfort and with help? Or do you want to simply miscarry right here and bleed to death on this mountainside?"

Shota removed her finger. When she did, Kahlan sucked in a breath and a cry of agony. At last, the painful contraction eased.

"All right, you win," Kahlan said, swallowing between pants as she caught her breath. "I won't cause any more trouble. I will go willingly."

Shota stared long and hard into Kahlan's eyes as if to satisfy herself that Kahlan meant it before slowly nodding.

"Smart girl. Now, no more nonsense. We will not be stopping." The witch woman lifted an arm to point. "It grows dark, but the tree line is right there. Out of the woods and in the open, with the moonlight reflecting off the snowcaps, there will be plenty of light to allow us to continue.

"We will walk the rest of the night to cross that snowcap, and then in the morning we will reach the swamp that guards my home. Once through that foul place, we will head down into my beautiful home of Agaden Reach. It will be warm, and you will be able to rest until you deliver. But for now, we push on."

Kahlan was still experiencing stitches of pain, although they were easing. She felt helpless. She feared that what Shota did might harm the babies. She didn't want her to do anything like it again.

She nodded her agreement.

Shota looked around at all the witches seeming to hang on her every word, Shale among them. Shota gestured with a flick of her hand. "Let's get moving. Now."

Kahlan had been well aware that Shota had shown no fear of being within range of her Confessor's power. More worrisome, she could feel a subtle difference in the restraint that she always had to exert on that power within herself, lest it be unleashed accidentally. The coiled fury of the power felt . . . muted. It was as if that restraint had clamped down tight when Shota had finally established the coven with all thirteen witches.

When Shota glared at her, waiting, Kahlan grabbed a root for a handhold and started climbing, following after the rest of them, with Nea right behind.

Something fundamental in the back of Kahlan's mind was bothering her. She couldn't put her finger on it, but she knew that the pieces didn't fit. Something didn't ring true, didn't add up, didn't make sense, but she couldn't quite reach it. Despite her best efforts to pull that question out of the dark reaches of her mind to examine possible answers, it remained just out of her grasp.

She knew, though, that if she thought on it long enough, it would come to her.

34

Not long after dawn, after a long and difficult night of crossing the frigid, wind-swept lower slopes of the spires that formed the formidable wreath of thorns protecting Agaden Reach, Kahlan and the witches guarding her finally started a difficult descent. Initially, they trudged through deep snow to make their way down the slopes. They had to avoid what looked like easier travel over open rock because it was mostly covered with black ice. The snow at least kept them from slipping and falling out on the sloping granite ledges where they could easily crack their skulls if they fell wrong.

To avoid the danger of the slippery ice-covered rock, they instead had to plow down through the snow that collected between massive fingers of rock jutting up all around. It was not only a more difficult route, but a more dangerous one because of how steep it was in those white rivers of snow. There were times when Kahlan thought she might not survive the steep drops they sometimes had to slide down. A few of the witch women fell during those descents and tumbled a long way before recovering their footing.

Like the rest of them, Kahlan had to aim for the upright columns of rock and then slam her feet against the rock to break the slide and keep from accelerating and being carried over a cliff. Some of the others, like the sour-faced bull of a witch, were quite awkward at it, but they all made it. After using the tall stacks of open rock at the end of each of those runs down, they then had to traverse the slope to make it over to the next one that didn't end in a sheer drop where they would fall to their death.

Anyone attempting to get into Agaden Reach who didn't know the proper route through the maze of towering rock outcroppings would have a difficult if not impossible task to find the one true way down the dangerous slopes. Taking a wrong turn on the way down, one that might look good at first, if it didn't turn out to be a dead end could instead turn out to be a place where it would be impossible to stop, with nothing below for thousands of feet. It was just another of the many hazards protecting Agaden Reach.

Kahlan's teeth chattered the whole time they were out on the moon-lit, open ledges below the snowpack. But the worst of the cold had been crossing the snow. She had been so cold it made her hurt all over and gave her a crushing headache.

The muscles of her legs burned from the effort of the controlled falls down through the fingers of snow and then, once below them, hiking down off the steeply sloping shelves of open granite, then over and through debris fields of boulders and the jumble of fallen rock. Her ankles felt like they were about to give out, but she knew she had to keep going if she was to have any hope for the twins to survive.

She didn't know how she would save their lives once they got down into Agaden Reach, she only knew she would have to find a way. She knew she couldn't count on Richard showing up. It was going to have to be up to her.

When the sun was finally up, they at last entered the dark woods, where they were at least sheltered from the cold wind. As they moved down through the steep, forested mountain-side, it gradually began to grow warmer. The farther they went, the warmer it got, until Kahlan's teeth finally stopped chattering and she didn't have to hunch her shoulders.

After a few more hours of making their way lower through tangled growths of tightly packed thickets of saplings and snarled vines, they at last reached the flat, swampy area that guarded the entrance to Agaden Reach.

Even though the sun had come up, it was dark and gloomy among the massive trees and vegetation, which grew thicker the farther in they went. Kahlan had always thought of this place as a moat, like those around some fortress castles, except this one protected Shota's home and was far more dangerous than any simple moat.

Kahlan remembered quite clearly going through these strange, hot, humid woods. After the frigid hike the night before, the oppressive heat was at first welcome. Before long, it became suffocating.

She remembered, too, how dangerous these

woods were. The swamp had unseen things that would grab anyone unwary enough to wander into the water, and in some cases, if they simply got too close to it, they could be snatched right off the trail. It was not at all rare to see human bones in the bogs or sticking up from the slimy, green, swampy places that had trapped them.

Kahlan knew that a wizard had once come to take Shota's home. He was not killed by anything in the swamp. He had faced something far more dangerous: the witch who lived there and wanted her home back. She had used his hide to cover her throne. The same throne now buried under a mountain of rubble.

Kahlan prayed to the good spirits that Richard wasn't also buried under all of that same rubble.

As she plodded ahead, Kahlan was well beyond her second wind. She was spent and could only shuffle along, putting one weary foot in front of the other, her mind numb. But in these woods, she knew that she had to pay attention to every step, or it might be her last, so she focused again and tried to watch where she put her feet.

The hot, humid swamp smelled foul. They passed through a number of areas, though, where the stench was especially bad. She held her hand over her mouth and nose, trying not to breathe in the gagging smell of death and rotting flesh. She hurried until they were past the worst of it.

Birds screamed raucous calls that echoed through the wet woods. The ravens that had followed them for so long sat in a row on a long, dead branch, watching Kahlan approach. They cocked their heads and looked down at her with one black eye as she passed beneath them. Sometimes they flapped their wings and cawed so loudly it made her ears hurt. Then, they flew on to another branch where they could continue to watch her progress.

Here and there boggy patches of water spanned back in under the thick, overhanging growth. Vapor hung just above the murky black water. In places, it drifted out and across the path. It swirled around her legs as she walked through the thick, heavy mist. It came up only about as high as her knees and left the bottoms of her trousers damp. It also carried with it the smells of dead things.

In other spots, the tangle of thick vines coiled like snakes on the trees, killing them. In the boggy woods to the sides the roots of large trees were so thick, gnarled, and broad that in places they spread out over the path. She knew that if her ankle got caught in one of those gnarled roots, she might break it before she could catch herself, so it took time and extreme caution to cross those extensive webs of roots.

Off across the water, in the deep shadows, she could see glowing eyes watching them. Others followed from off in the trees and brush. A few dark shapes now and then leaped from tree to tree, following them from the shadows for a time.

In some of the wetter areas, large trees stood on skirts of tall roots, as if trying to stay above the dark water. Smaller creatures hid back in those standing roots. The gray trunks of those trees were smooth and bare of bark and their branches were bare of leaves. Instead, they were draped with long trailers of dead, brown moss hanging still in the stagnant, humid air. It made the trees look like silver specters haunting the trail, watching who dared pass.

The spongy path in many places was mere inches above the expanses of turbid water to either side. With each step, water oozed up out of the soft, mossy ground and over her boots.

Sometimes the water to the sides rippled as something unseen under the surface followed them along for a time, then left a spiraling swirl as it submerged.

Off in the thick, dark, dense vegetation in the distance, unseen things whooped and howled. Every once in a while, Kahlan spotted a shadowed shape skitter through the lower branches or bound along the ground back in the brush. In the heavy air, other things off out of sight clicked and whistled warnings to others of their kind. Creatures she couldn't see and couldn't imagine noted the group's passing with apparent displeasure by growling low, guttural warnings.

In some places, the mist rising from the stinking, bubbling, thick black water carried with it the smell of sulfur. It was a smell strongly associated with the underworld, so Kahlan kept a wary watch whenever she smelled it, worried that something might appear from the world of the dead.

Sometimes the mist carried the gagging stench of rotting flesh. There was never any area where it smelled even remotely good. Kahlan was reluctant to draw a breath as her gaze continually swept the area to each side, watching for danger or the source of the stench. In places she saw the bloated, putrefied, half-submerged bodies of animals too rotted to identify. She didn't know if they had drowned in the foul water, or possibly succumbed to the toxic smells.

In a few places she saw rotting corpses that looked like they might be human floating only partly above the surface of scummy water.

Those ahead of her carefully picked their way over the tangled masses of roots of the gnarled trees. She remembered all too well that there were particularly dangerous roots in the swamp that no one would dare to walk across. The roots of those trees, the ones with squat, fat trunks, were tangled and looked very much like nests of balled snakes. Those roots had to be given a wide berth. She saw those every once in a while, but the path skirted them, and the witch women always walked on the farthest side of the path so as to stay as far away as possible.

And then, near just one of those squat trees with the tangled roots that had to be avoided, Kahlan suddenly missed a step.

She stopped; her eyes went wide.

The thing she had been trying pull from the

dark corner of her mind suddenly came rushing forward into her consciousness.

She realized what it was that didn't make sense.

35

One single question stood out in Kahlan's mind above all others.

Why would Shota want Kahlan to give birth just so she could kill the babies?

And why go to all the trouble to take her all the way to Agaden Reach to give birth? Not only that, but if she simply wanted to kill the babies, why not have her miscarry—which she had now twice proven she was entirely capable of doing—and then use a healer, like Shale, to help her recover if she really wanted Kahlan to live? If her intention was in fact to get rid of the babies and not kill Kahlan, that would be the easiest way. It would be over and done with.

So why would Shota insist that the babies

must be born first, if she simply wanted them dead so that what she saw as the threat of their existence would be ended?

On the surface it made no sense.

But beneath the surface, it was starting to make sinister sense.

In the beginning, Shota had told Richard and Kahlan that she harbored no ill will toward them. She had even said that she appreciated the things they had done for their people, as well as what they had done that had saved her from the Keeper of the underworld. She had even said that she rather liked them, and that she didn't mean them any harm.

She had tried to paint herself as reasonable—kind, even.

She had said that after the birth they would be free to go.

And yet, she proudly admitted that she had spelled Richard's legs so that he couldn't get away in time and the palace would collapse on top of him. That certainly didn't sound like she didn't intend them harm. In fact, she had used her power in a surprise attack to try to kill him just before that. Richard hadn't struck first; she had. Despite her benevolent claims, it was clear that her intent had been to kill him, not let him go.

After all of that, why would she then go back to her original story that she meant Kahlan no harm and that she would let her go once she gave birth? She had said that she intended Richard no harm, either, yet she had clearly acted to kill him.

Why did Shota seem so intent on keeping Kahlan alive and having her give birth *before* she killed the children? What purpose would it serve to have the children born before she killed them?

It now seemed pretty clear from everything that had happened that Shota didn't really intend to let Kahlan go once she gave birth. She intended to kill her.

So, if she actually intended to kill her in the end, but wasn't admitting as much, which Kahlan now believed was the case, then the previous evening, on the mountain before they crossed the snowcaps, why hadn't she simply let Kahlan miscarry and bleed to death? It would have been a simple solution to the greater good she kept talking about.

For that matter, why hadn't she let Kahlan

die way back when she started to miscarry after they finally got out of the strange wood? Killing the two unborn babies was her goal, after all, for that greater good as she saw it, so what difference would it have made had the babies died in a miscarriage and Kahlan died as well?

Shota's true intentions flashed like ice through Kahlan's veins.

Kahlan stood frozen with the sudden realization of what Shota actually wanted.

36

Kahlan was well aware that time was not on her side. If she was going to try something, it had to be now, when they least expected it. Later, down in Agaden Reach, with her time running out and the birth imminent, they would be expecting her to try to resist or flee.

The problem was, she knew that her Confessor power wouldn't work on Shota because the witch woman was now in command of the power of coven. That power protected her—protected all of them—as long as that power of coven was in effect.

The coven. Of course. With sudden realization, she grasped the only way that gave her any kind of chance against all of these women.

"Keep moving," Nea growled from behind, bringing Kahlan out of her headlong rush of thoughts.

She knew she needed some kind of excuse in order to create surprise. What had Richard always told her? If you had to act, if acting was your only hope, then act swiftly with maximum violence.

Thinking quickly, Kahlan saw her only opportunity. She went to a knee and bent forward so that Nea couldn't see what she was doing.

"I said to keep moving!" the witch woman screamed at her from behind.

Kahlan looked back over her shoulder. "My bootlace came untied. I have to retie it."

Nea folded her arms. "Well, hurry it up, then."

Sorrel, one of the more disagreeable of the whole disagreeable lot of witches, stormed back, shoving her way past the bull of a witch woman who had been just ahead of Kahlan. She angrily waved her arms. Her gums were dark, as were the rings around her eyes, adding to her already wicked looks.

"What's going on?" Sorrel demanded.

As the angry Sorrel had been charging back

through the group of witch women, Kahlan knew she was quickly running out of time. She struggled with all her might, using her fingertips to try to pry the heavy rock out of the mud where it was half buried right beside her boot. She hunched over in such a way that the others couldn't see what she was doing and would think she was tying the lace on her boot.

She held her breath with the effort of pulling on the rock. The mud sucked it down tight and made it resist coming up. She wiggled the rock then pried it with all her strength, her breath held and muscles tight against the effort, knowing it was her only chance, but the portion of the rock under the muddy ground was larger than Kahlan had thought at first, making it far more difficult than she had expected. She knew that she dared not abandon the effort. It could very well be the last chance she would ever get.

Sorrel rushed up in a rage, screaming curses and waving her arms.

"Answer me!" Sorrel yelled, her face going red with fury, matching the red tips of her spiky hair.

The rock popped free of the mud.

Instead of answering the woman, Kahlan

sprang up and whirled around in one fluid motion, bringing the rock with her. As she spun, she whipped the heavy rock around at the end of her extended arm.

Sorrel was just opening her mouth to yell something else when Kahlan slammed the heavy rock into the side of the woman's head. It made a loud crack as the thick skull bones shattered.

The witch's eyes went dead as her skull caved in under the speed of the heavy rock. Her right eye went glassy as it turned up and to the right. Her left eye, equally glassy, turned to point down and to her left. Kahlan imagined it looking to the underworld, where her soul was already sinking into eternity.

Sorrel dropped straight down into a limp, still heap.

As a pool of blood began to spread under Sorrel's body, the sour-faced bull of a witch—at first surprised, now looking livid at what she had just seen happen—suddenly rushed headlong for Kahlan. Her fat neck was sunken down into her broad shoulders, like a charging bull's, so much so that she couldn't easily look down at where she was going. Her angry scowl was fixed on Kahlan.

In a reckless rush, the big woman stumbled over Sorrel's body. In that instant, Kahlan seized one of her outstretched arms by a fat wrist and used the woman's falling motion and weight to swing her on around. With a grunt of effort, Kahlan propelled the witch woman's bulk out into the murky water.

She didn't fly far, but she flew far enough. Her angry cry was cut short when she hit the water with a massive splash that lifted not just the dark water but strings of water weeds and algae up into the air, some of it flopping out across the trail. The big woman popped back up to the surface, her hair matted to her head, coughing up water between gasps for air.

As she surfaced, splashing and paddling awkwardly to get to the bank, something apparently grabbed her leg, making her cry out. She screamed in pain, reaching for the bank at the same time. Whatever it was that had her abruptly pulled, and in a single big yank dragged her back and down under the water. She was gone in an instant. Bubbles came up from the deep as a blood slick grew at a rapid rate and spread across the rippling surface.

Almost at the same time, the bony witch

with the big black eyes, who had seen what
had just happened to her sister, charged toward
Kahlan, careful to leap over Sorrel's body,
intent on taking revenge. The witch's sticklike
arms flailed as she let out an animalistic cry that
was a shriek of anger and lethal intent mixed
together in one. It was the first sound Kahlan
had heard the woman make, and it was properly
bloodcurdling.

Kahlan was just coming up from having
dropped to a knee having lost her balance from
the effort of tossing the bony witch's very large
sister witch into the water. Without pause, as
she stood, Kahlan seized a sticklike arm and
spun the witch woman around, this time easily
because she didn't weigh much at all. Kahlan
wheeled completely around with her. As she
did, the woman's feet, clear of the ground,
sailed out as she flew around through the air
like a bony rag doll.

As she came around from a full turn, Kahlan
released her with a grunt of effort, letting her
sail through the air and into the nest of roots
of one of the squat, fat-trunked trees just off
the trail.

When the bony woman crashed down in the

midst of the roots, they instantly whipped out, knotting and coiling around her body the way a constricting snake would wrap its coils around a victim. Other roots captured her flailing arms and legs. Showers of sparks filled the air above the roots as the witch tried to cast some kind of spell, but it was too little too late.

Almost as soon as she had fallen in, the sparks died out as the witch woman was pulled under the mass of coils and writhing roots. Kahlan couldn't see it, but she could hear bones snapping and joints popping as the strange tree dragged her under its nest of roots and pulled her limb from limb. Almost as quickly as the roots had grabbed her, she was gone, and it was over.

At the same time, Kahlan heard Nea scream in rage and charge toward her from behind.

Nea was out for blood and revenge.

37

Kahlan turned halfway to the threat.

It was clear from the wild look in her eyes that Nea's rage had taken control of her senses. Surprisingly, she charged in with a knife—Kahlan's knife—rather than using magic. She apparently wanted to physically rip into Kahlan and take her down. She raced ahead knife-first, intending to slam the blade into Kahlan.

That was the last mistake the witch woman would ever make.

With the death of three witches mere moments before, the spell of coven was broken.

Kahlan's power was no longer suppressed.

Nea leaped toward Kahlan, throwing herself at her, intending to crash down on her knife-first.

Kahlan lifted her hand, palm out toward the blade, as if warding it off.

It all happened in an instant, but that instant was all the time it took.

The world went still.

Kahlan felt the tip of the knife, as it had just begun to touch her palm. Although it was a razor-sharp blade, to Kahlan it felt like no more than a breath of air on her hand. It was not necessary for her to summon her Confessor power; she merely had to withdraw her restraint of it, and she had already done that.

Time stopped.

The inner violence of Kahlan's cold, coiled power slipping its bounds was breathtaking. The astonishing magnitude of the force as it was unleashed was like touching the sun. It flared up from the very core of who she was and through every fiber of her being, lighting her soul with white-hot intensity.

Nea hung in the air, stopped dead before Kahlan, her hand with the knife outstretched, her feet clear of the ground, one of her knees parting the hundreds of knotted and beaded strips of her leather skirt. Kahlan could have counted the hundreds of stringy strands of red hair, lifted out in all directions, now frozen motionless in midair. It was like seeing a statue made of flesh and bone.

The rage in Nea's eyes had only just taken that first tick of transition to alarm. She had just begun to realize by Kahlan's posture, her resolute stance, her fearless bearing, that something was terribly wrong. Before she had been able to fully realize what was happening, it was already too late.

She was frozen in that instant of time just before the danger had fully registered.

Kahlan knew that behind her, the rest of the witch women were also still as stone, frozen in mid-movement. In the sky, a number of the ravens that had taken to wing at the initiation of the violence were impossibly stopped in mid-flight, their wings having just flapped, spread, or started to take another bite of the air, the fanned feathers at the back of their wings standing out individually, black, glossy, beautiful.

Something under the water to the side of the path had just disturbed the surface, and the ripples from it were now motionless. The mist drifting over the water had likewise stopped in place. The whole world waited, unmoving.

In the silent stillness of Kahlan's mind, she had all the time in the world, all the time she would need to do what she had done so many times before.

Nea's face was set in mid-snarl. Her teeth were bared. Beads of sweat dotted her glowering brow. Her pale blue eyes were wild, frozen in a picture of fury.

Of all the witch women, this one had been the one she had feared most because she always seemed dangerously deranged. Shota had put her in charge of Kahlan for a reason. She was not only Shota's next-in-command, but she was also ruthless and would not hesitate to take control of any situation, and she had the power to deal with anything.

Except this.

The control of what was about to happen now belonged entirely to Kahlan.

She knew that back behind her somewhere, Shota would be in mid-scream, trying to stop what Kahlan had already done to break the coven. That power was now lost to Shota.

The Confessor's power was now Kahlan's again.

She had yet to feel a single heartbeat. Even so,

she had taken in the whole scene in excruciating detail. She knew where everything and everyone was, all stopped in space.

Kahlan wondered if this redheaded witch woman yet knew that her mind was about to be gone. It was possible that she didn't realize that a Confessor's power also took a person's mind, but everything she was, and everything she had been, was about to be wiped away in a lightning instant by the unstoppable force of Kahlan's power.

The woman's mind, once emptied, would be replaced with a frantic, burning desire to do what Kahlan, and only Kahlan, as the Confessor who was taking her mind, wanted.

Even with taking control of this one witch before her, Kahlan was well aware that her position was still one of great peril. There were a lot of other witches.

And then there was Shota. She would not take kindly to what Kahlan had done.

Even so, it couldn't be helped. The way things were going, if Kahlan didn't act, and soon, it would all end badly. This way, at least, she had broken the coven and changed the balance of power. It didn't ensure that she would survive, but had she not done it she would have had no chance. This at least gave her an entirely different field of battle, one in which she was not powerless.

As Kahlan gazed again into the eyes of this woman before her, she felt no hatred, no remorse, no anger, no sorrow, no pity. In fact, she felt no emotion at all.

This act was the embodiment of Confessor power, and the Confessor face reflected its cold nature, and in a way part of its purpose. This was reasoned action absent of emotion. It was a calculated act of aggression to change what would have otherwise happened. Emotion had no place in that, and was no longer necessary, so it was no longer a component of what had to be done. It was already decided the instant that knife point touched Kahlan's palm.

Nea had no chance. None.

In that singular moment, if Kahlan was the absence of emotion, then Nea was the manifestation of it.

In that infinitesimal tick of time, Nea's mind, who she was, who she had been, was already gone.

Kahlan did not hesitate.

She released the rest of her restraints on her gift to unleash the full, blinding force of her power.

Time slammed back.

Thunder without sound jolted the air—exquisite, violent, and for that pristine instant, sovereign.

The trees all around shook with the force of the concussion. The violent shock of it lifted the leaves, bits of plants, and sticks littering the ground and blew them outward in an ever-expanding ring around Kahlan. The dust and dirt and debris driven before the wall of power knocked the rest of the women from their feet as it stripped vegetation off the nearby shrubs and trees. As the force of that silent thunder ripped across the water to each side of the path, it drove a ring of water and water vapor before it. Trees shook. Small branches were torn off and blown back.

Nea gasped as the full force of Confessor power slammed into her.

Behind Kahlan, all of the women, who had been thrown from their feet and tumbled back away, were now grabbing their elbows, knees, or wrists in pain. She could hear them groaning in agony from having been too close to Kahlan when her Confessor power was unleashed.

Nea dropped to her knees before Kahlan. She looked up through strands of red hair, no longer in hate and rage, but in pleading.

"Mistress . . . please . . . command me."

Kahlan looked down, feeling no sorrow for the woman. Her life as she had known it was now ended. Her memories, her wishes, her hopes were gone. She had forfeited all of that and more when she tried to kill Kahlan.

"Please, Mistress," Nea begged. "Please, command me."

"Kill Shota."

Almost instantly, knife still in her fist, Nea scrambled to her feet and charged past Kahlan, going for Shota.

38

As Nea shot past, Kahlan turned to see all the rest of the witch women, including Shota, getting to their feet, most of them groaning in pain from being so close when Kahlan had unleashed her power.

Nea, screaming in single-minded, lethal fury, raced through some and leaped over others as she bolted toward Shota.

Unlike the others, who were slowly struggling up, Shota, who had also been knocked from her feet, swiftly swirled around as she rose with the grace of silk billowing in a breeze. The flaps and folds of her variegated gray dress whirled with her like trails of smoke behind the flames of a torch as she advanced in a blur with otherworldly speed.

Kahlan blinked and there was Shota abruptly standing before the advancing Nea. Nea was still screaming, intent only on carrying out Kahlan's command.

She lifted her fist with the knife to drive it into her former leader.

Before the knife made it to Shota, Shota calmly tapped Nea's forehead once with a finger.

Nea instantly stopped dead in her tracks. At the same time, all of her blackened and cracked the way a log in a fire turns black and checkers into pieces before it falls apart. All of those black chunks one moment made a very odd-looking Nea, and the next moment crumbled like coals collapsing in a blaze. In mere seconds, all that was left of a totally committed Nea was a heap of glowing embers.

Kahlan could hardly believe that just that quick, Nea was no more. She supposed she was actually no more the instant Kahlan's power had taken her mind, but still, this was a disturbing development. One second there was about to be a battle, and then the next second it was over. Of course, Kahlan hadn't thought that killing Shota would be as easy as simply ordering Nea to kill her, but she had hoped that it would result in a longer battle that would allow her to escape.

That was not to be.

Beyond Shota and the blackened, crumbled remains of Nea spilled all over the ground, Kahlan saw all the rest of the wide-eyed witch women, including Shale, standing close together, shrinking back in horror at having seen both Shota's power and Kahlan's used in such horrifying fashion, to say nothing of having also just seen four of their sister witches die violently in a matter of seconds.

The four dead witches had been vicious and seemed to enjoy their roles in Shota's scheme and as Kahlan's captors, glad to inflict whatever pain that control required or was commanded by Shota. It was apparent from the way the rest of them in the background stared that they were not nearly so eager for battle. Faced with such savage power unleashed so swiftly, and with such devastating results, they all had to fear that any of them might be next.

Kahlan knew that Shale, at least, was not there by her own wishes, but by Shota's command. She wondered if it was the same for any of the others.

Shota gracefully stepped around the smoldering remains of her former second-in-command and came to a halt in front of Kahlan.

"Well, well, Mother Confessor, it seems you have managed to break the coven." She tipped her head close and spoke in a low, deadly voice. "But in so doing, you have lost the ability to use your power again until you recover your strength, and we both know that will take a while. In the meantime, you have left yourself defenseless against my abilities." She gestured back at the smoldering ashes. "Abilities which, I believe you now realize, need no coven."

"Wars are rarely won in a single battle, or a single victory," Kahlan said. "It may take a while before my power recovers, but that power will soon enough return. On the other hand, you have lost the power of coven for good." Kahlan arched an eyebrow. "Unless you have four more witches hiding in your pocket?"

A slow smile came to Shota's full lips. "Nea was a very, very good witch, but she made the mistake of underestimating you. I don't make those kinds of foolish mistakes."

Kahlan didn't try to outsmile the witch woman. "Then you had best let me go, before I regain the ability to call on my Confessor power again."

Shota glared. "That isn't going to happen."

Kahlan shrugged. "Then you will have to kill me before my power recovers and I have you on your knees at my feet, begging for me to command you. So go ahead and turn me to a pile of smoldering coals as you did your trusted right-hand witch. I wouldn't delay long, were I you. I was named Mother Confessor in part because my ability recovers quickly."

Shota's smile returned and widened. Kahlan thought it looked almost like a smile of admiration.

"Kill you? I told you before, my dear, I don't intend to kill you. You are far too valuable to the world. No, you will come with me down into Agaden Reach, where you will rest in comfort and security until you deliver your two children. After that, you will be allowed to go off on your way."

"And how do you think you could possibly accomplish such a feat before I am able to use my power again and I kill you?"

Shota dismissed the notion with a gesture. "It took a great deal of time and trouble to assemble the witches needed to form a coven, and you may have broken that gathering, but you make a serious mistake thinking that weakens me to the point of being helpless against you and your power. I have not only my own power, but the power of the witch women behind me that I can link should I need to."

"Then you best do it soon," Kahlan warned.

The witch woman's smile changed from admonishment to amusement. "You are correct, Mother Confessor. Wars aren't usually won in a single victory, and although you don't seem yet to grasp it, you are destined to lose this war."

"I don't believe in destiny."

Shota sighed, weary of the game. She ran the tip of her finger along Kahlan's jaw.

"Maybe you are right, Mother Confessor, but I have made plans enough to predetermine that the outcome will be as I wish it."

Kahlan felt something abruptly tighten around her ankles. Without looking down, she tried, but couldn't move her feet. She was too angry to let herself panic.

"Clever trick, Shota. But I will soon end this war with you once and for all."

Shota arched an eyebrow. "I'm afraid you

will never get that chance. You see, before you can recover your ability to use your power, you will be spelled into a deep and peaceful sleep and then taken the rest of the way down to my home, where you will not awaken before you give birth. Once you do, then I will kill those two children, as I have told you I would.

"I have given you enough chances to be reasonable for the greater good. For my own safety, since you have now vowed to kill me with your power once it recovers, after you give birth and your children have been killed, you will have to be put down for good. You will never recover from that peaceful sleep."

"You're a liar," Kahlan said.

"Do tell," Shota said, indulgently.

"You may indeed plan to kill me after I give birth—as you have actually planned all along—but you have no intention of killing my two children. None."

39

The smug smile vanished. "I don't know what you're talking about."

"Really?" Kahlan cocked her head. "If you really wanted these children dead, they would already be dead. You've just said you intend to kill me. So if your intent really is to kill these children, and you admit that you also intend to kill me, you would do to me right now what you just did to Nea. Then my unborn children and I would all be dead. Isn't that what you claim to want?"

Shota didn't answer.

"But you can't do that," Kahlan went on, "because you actually have no intention of killing my children, and if you killed me now you would be killing those two children—the children you so desperately want to be born alive."

Shota acted perplexed, as if such a notion was utterly outlandish. "Where in the world would you come up with such a fanciful idea? After I have for so long promised you that I would not allow the children you and Richard create to live, why in the world would you now come up with this crazy notion I would not carry out my promises and kill those two little monsters?"

"Because you intend to raise them."

Shota stood stock-still as she stared into Kahlan's eyes for a long, dragging moment.

"I can see that Lord Rahl does not wed stupid women."

"And certainly not one stupid enough to let you get away with it."

The menace returned to Shota's face. "Oh, but you are wrong, there. I have already gotten away with it, we simply need to play out the final acts and it will be done. At least as far as your part in this is concerned."

"You seriously think I intend to let you raise these two children?"

"You no longer have any say in it." Shota

gestured dismissively. "I will raise them in a way that you never could."

"You mean raise them as your two little underlings to follow in your footsteps, worship you as their mother, and do your bidding?"

Shota glared. "I have seen into the flow of time. I told you that I saw that you and Richard would conceive a monster. It is possible, although it is a remote possibility, that it is as you have said, that the child I saw in the flow of time was the one you previously lost. But having seen into that complex flow, I don't for a second believe that.

"One of the children you now carry is the monster I saw in that prophecy."

"Richard ended prophecy."

"That doesn't mean that prophecy wasn't real, or true, or that when it was here in our world I wasn't able to use it. You didn't see what I saw in that flow of time, and you can't begin to imagine it. Before Richard ended my ability to continue to use that flow, I saw this, saw what you two would create."

"Our children will be who we raise them to be. I told you, I don't believe in destiny. No matter what you saw, that doesn't mean one of these children will turn out the way you think."

Shota shook her head as she let out a weary breath. "You just can't grasp the entirety of this, can you? You see only your little slice of it, your naive wishes, hopes, and dreams. Monster or not, they are both gifted with power from each of you.

"You and Richard are not the ones to raise such a powerful pair—a girl with Confessor power combined with the power of her war-wizard father, and a boy war wizard with your Confessor power. Neither of you can begin to comprehend the enormity of what you have created.

"You say that these children are needed to protect our world from the Glee by maintaining the web of magic they provide, and you are right. The power these two hold will be a web of magic so intense that it will drive the Glee from our world for all time. It will protect our world and protect the magic of it.

"But you don't see the bigger picture beyond that which our world needs to free us from the immediate threat of the Glee. You and Richard are too weak, too softhearted, too indulgent of what people under your rule wish to do with their lives. Those ebbing and flowing wishes of the ignorant masses would eventually lead our world over the brink and into ruin that even the Glee could not accomplish.

"You two fought a long and terrible war against the Imperial Order. Do you think their destructive doctrine came from another world? No, it came from the people in our world, people who left to their own ignorant wishes will one day again fall under the seductive spell of such beliefs. It has always been that way, and it will always be that way, unless there is rule strong enough to exert control for the good of our world.

"These two children you carry, together, with the gifts they will be born with, will have the ability to rule the world with the kind of power and authority that will prevent that kind of thing from ever happening again.

"So you see, in a way, I, too, do not believe in destiny. I am the one who will prevent that terrible future from ever having the chance to fester and grow. What I do now saves countless lives in the future.

"With these two under my protection, care,

guidance, instruction, and preparation, they will be the two powerful instruments to both expel the Glee and control our world so that it can never be allowed to fall into the foolishness of ignorant masses too stupid to know what is in their own best interest. I will control those masses. With those two children, I will protect the best interest of the world. It will all be done for the greater good.

"You and Richard do not have the strength to raise rulers like that. I do.

"I will be the mother children such as these really need. The boy will see me as a vision of Richard's mother, and the girl will see me as a vision of yours. They will both see me as their mother, think of me as their mother, and have total trust in me as their teacher.

"They will both depend on me for everything. They will learn from me everything. They will come to believe from me everything. I will forge them both into the powerful force the world needs, into the powerful rulers the world needs in order for it to continue without the mindless, destructive beliefs of fools being allowed to flourish. In the past when people were allowed to force unworkable ideas on nations, it cast the world into wars in which countless masses died. I will not allow that to happen again.

"These two will rule with iron fists and their power.

"I will rule them both with mine."

Kahlan blinked in stunned surprise. She had known that Shota wanted both children in order to raise them and use their gifts for her own ends, but she hadn't realized the full extent of her ideas.

Shota intended to turn the twins into weapons she would shape and wield. It was she who would be pulling the strings of her two puppets in order to rule the world. It was now crystal clear that Shota had put a great deal of thought, to say nothing of effort, into her mad scheme. She was convinced of the need of doing this. She believed in what she was saying and that she was doing it for the greater good. She thought that she was ultimately doing the right thing.

Richard had always said that the most dangerous person was the one who truly believed that their cause was right. Shota believed that what she was doing was inherently right. It was the greater good as she saw it.

Kahlan knew that she had to stop the woman now, before she used her witch woman's power to put her into a numb sleep until the babies were born. By then it would be too late.

Because it would still be a while before her power returned, she could see no other way to do it.

Since Kahlan couldn't move her feet, while Shota was still close enough and before she moved away Kahlan leaned out with lightning speed and just that quick had her hands around Shota's throat.

She gritted her teeth and growled with the effort of squeezing the life out of the witch woman.

But before she could crush her windpipe, Shota did something Kahlan hadn't considered.

40

Kahlan gasped in pain as she felt the shock of a flash of power hit her. The abrupt jolt of it sizzled through every nerve in her body, making her involuntarily release her grip, and then, as she pulled her hands back, she suddenly felt the terror of snakes slithering up in under her shirt.

Another snake, with multicolored scales, climbed up over her back and coiled its fat body around her neck, constricting enough that it made it difficult to breathe. She tightened her neck muscles as much as she could, hoping to protect the blood supply to her brain so that she wouldn't lose consciousness. She didn't know if that would actually work, but it was the only thing she could do.

Another, with a diamond pattern along its back, came around her waist, then moved up and over her shoulder. The whole time its tail rattled a threat. Several long, thin, black vipers with red and yellow bands slithered right up the side of her face and into her hair. Colorful snakes writhed everywhere on her, tightening around her legs as they pressed their heads against her back in under her shirt.

Shota didn't back away—she didn't need to. Kahlan was immobilized with fear. There were so many snakes everywhere on her that she feared to breathe.

The smile that Kahlan had come to hate spread once more on Shota's full lips. "I strongly suggest you don't move, Mother Confessor. Agitated vipers"—Shota leaned in a little—"bite."

Kahlan didn't have to be told not to move. She was too terrified to move. Her mind raced, trying to think what to do. When Shota had done this the first time they met the witch woman, Richard was there and made her stop it. Richard wasn't there, now, to make Shota withdraw her vipers.

Without looking away from Kahlan's eyes,

Shota lifted a hand and snapped her fingers back behind at the other witch women.

"Niska, come here."

One of the women in the group rushed forward, shuffling her feet the whole way. Her shoulders were hunched in fear of the very angry grand witch.

"Yes, Mistress?"

Niska wasn't at all malicious-looking, but she certainly was strange, and Kahlan had no trouble whatsoever believing she could be nothing other than a witch woman. She was youngish and slender, wearing floaty, flimsy white robes pinned together above each shoulder.

What there was of the robes left her arms and lot of her flesh exposed, and every bit of that flesh was covered in writing.

It ran up her arms, line after line, on all sides. On her right arm, from her biceps to her shoulder, the writing went in bands around her arm. On her upper shoulders and chest the writing followed the contours of her body. When she moved, and the material of her robes parted, Kahlan could see that her thighs, too, were covered in line after line of writing.

There were several lines of symbols down

the bridge of her nose, and horizontal lines of symbols following the contours of her face onto the sides of her nose, where they met the lines coming down the bridge of it. Line after line of the symbols ran all the way around her neck and continued back under her fall of satiny black hair.

Kahlan could see in the light as she moved, by the way most of the strokes had a welted look to them, that it all had been tattooed in dark ink, not simply written or painted on her skin. Or else, she thought, perhaps the lines of writing had been branded into her flesh with magic.

Kahlan couldn't read the writing, but she did recognize the look of some of the symbols. They looked very much like the ancient symbols Richard had shown her several times. Those were the language of Creation. These looked like they were as well. The significance of that alone was unnerving.

Niska stood meekly to the side and slightly behind Shota. Her shoulders were stooped, and her head was sunken down into those shoulders. She worried her fingers against one another as she stared at the ground.

"Yes, Mistress? Do you wish something from me?"

Kahlan could tell by the quality of her voice that although Niska was submissive in front of Shota, encountered by herself, this slight woman would be formidable.

"Yes, as a matter of fact, I do," Shota said.

Off behind Shota, the other witch women watched, not knowing what was coming but, after the things they had already seen, clearly fearing it.

"Niska," Shota said in her silky voice as she twirled a finger, "I'd like you to spin a sleep spell around the Mother Confessor. I want it to be irreversible."

"Irreversible?"

"Yes, irreversible." Shota shrugged. "We will not have cause to break it, since after she gives birth she will have to die, so yes, it may as well be irreversible. That kind is easier, and stronger, so we won't have to worry that she might come awake in childbirth."

Niska bowed. "As you wish, Mistress."

Niska took a few steps away from Shota to give herself room, then began chanting words under her breath. As she went on in the singsong rhythm of the unfamiliar words, she pointed down at the ground and slowly began spinning a finger around and around.

As she mumbled the strange words, and her finger revolved, her hand took up the turning, and then her whole arm began making circles as it hung like a pendulum from her shoulder.

As her hanging arm revolved round and round in circles, the beautiful but incomprehensible words gradually became louder. They seemed to echo back through the trees and thick vegetation, their power resonating with the wild things back in the shadows, with nature itself, calling power forth.

Kahlan began to see, off in that dense vegetation and out among the trees across the swampy bodies of water, a thickening mist all around begin to form and gradually start to revolve. As the strength of the words Niska chanted became stronger and deeper, the mist became thicker, and it gradually picked up speed as it circled around them all gathered there on the path through the swamp.

As the circle of that mist gradually began to shrink inward, Kahlan could tell that she was at the center of that low, thick ring of haze.

As she watched it closing in around her, she tried to move at least her feet, but she couldn't. Her feet were bound together with a spell, but worse, there were snakes, hundreds of them it seemed, slithering all over her feet and up her legs. They were so many that some of them had to slither over the tops of others. She had no doubt that if she moved, they would bite her, so she reconsidered her attempt to move her feet. The only slight doubt in the worry that she would be bitten was that if the vipers did bite her, her babies would die with her, and since Shota was determined to have those two gifted children, she wouldn't want to lose the opportunity. Still, as angry as Shota was, Kahlan didn't feel at all confident that she wouldn't let the snakes bite to kill her and the twins along with her.

As Niska chanted and the revolving ring of thick mist came ever closer, Kahlan felt increasingly desperate, but she was also beginning to feel so tired that she caught herself starting to nod off. Each time, she jerked herself back awake, knowing that once that circling mist completely closed in on her, it would overwhelm her ability to stay awake and that would herald the end of her, and the end of her children's chances to have a good life.

She knew that once she did fall asleep, Shota would simply have to bide her time a little while longer, until Kahlan delivered, and then she would have the twins all to herself.

As desperately as she tried, she could think of no solution to the spot she was in.

Kahlan blinked with sleepiness, desperately trying to stay alert even as the weight of drowsiness pressed in on her. When she forced herself awake again, she saw a big white snake rise up along the length of her, slithering its way onward among the writhing net of other snakes. All the rest were different colors and covered with patterns. Only this one was white.

Kahlan jerked her head again, trying to stay awake. She looked beyond Shota and Niska to the others standing together in a group.

Kahlan saw, then, that Shale's eyes were rolled up her in head and her fingers were moving.

Kahlan blinked in disbelief when she suddenly realized what that meant.

41

Kahlan instantly recognized that this was her last chance, and despite her paralyzing fear of the snakes slithering all over her and the sleepiness incrementally tightening its grip on her, she had to take it. She didn't know if Shota would let her snakes bite Kahlan, but she had no other choice but to act.

The white snake turned its big head to look at her, its red tongue flicking out. It was frightening seeing such a deadly creature up close.

Before it was too late, quick as a crack of lightning, Kahlan ignored her revulsion and snatched the white snake right behind its head. As she turned it and thrust it out, its mouth opened wide, exposing long fangs as sharp as needles.

Kahlan slammed the snake against Shota's neck before she had time to react. The fangs instantly sank in deep, hitting the main vein. Even though it already had its fangs in, Kahlan held it there, pressing the head against the witch's neck. She felt the snake's powerful muscles flex as it worked its mouth to pump venom into the jugular vein.

The witch woman stumbled back with a shriek of shock and fear. The white snake had its fangs fastened in her neck and was pulled away from Kahlan's grip as Shota staggered back. She grabbed at her throat, weakly trying to claw the snake away. As she did, it whipped coils of its white body around her arm and neck, preventing her from pulling it away from her.

There was no faster way for the venom to get to Shota's heart than the vein in her neck. Because that was where the venom entered her bloodstream, it acted all that much faster than it otherwise would have. Her heart would circulate it quickly to her brain and through the rest of her.

Niska gasped in shock at seeing what had just happened. She stopped chanting and quickly stepped out of the way as Shota stumbled back, both hands fighting the thrashing white snake that had her by the throat. Without the chanted words, the circle of mist began to evaporate, losing its grip of sleepiness on Kahlan.

Shota collapsed with the snake's fangs still sunk deep into her throat. She mumbled something in the delirium of the lethal venom pumping through her body. Her hands fell away from the snake even as it continued to flex and pump venom into her.

Shota gasped once, deep and desperate, and then the breath left her lungs with a sickening rattle. After that breath had gurgled out, she lay still and breathed no more.

Kahlan realized that the snakes that had been crawling all over her were gone. They had died out with the witch woman who had conjured them.

She stood stunned at how fast it had all happened. Grasping the relevance of the white snake, the near-instant crystallization of a plan, and the execution of that plan had all happened in a flash.

She blinked in surprise as Shale raced up and threw her arms around her.

"Mother Confessor! You understood! I was

so hoping that you would realize that the white snake was mine."

In gratitude and relief, Kahlan embraced her tightly for a moment.

"I remembered the white snakes from when you used them before, on the Glee."

Shale pushed back and grinned at Kahlan. "That's right. I was hoping you would remember. Shota's power prevented me from using my gift against her—any magic used against her would only have reflected back to me. This was the only chance I could see to help you, so I had to take that chance while Shota was so focused on the snakes she had conjured. I knew she would have to watch what Niska was doing as well as make sure her snakes didn't recklessly bite you, or the babies would die as well. I knew she wouldn't want that to happen."

Niska came close and put a hand on Kahlan's shoulder. "I'm so sorry, Mother Confessor. I never wanted to be part of this. I would never have wanted to hurt you. Shota forced me to be part of her coven and do her bidding."

Kahlan nodded, tears in her eyes with happiness for her twins. "I know."

Kahlan circled an arm around Niska's thin

shoulders and pulled her tight in a quick hug to let her know that she understood and didn't blame her.

42

The rest of the witch women all gathered around Kahlan, each of them briefly touching her in genuine sympathy as they explained how Shota had dragged them into her plans. They apologized for participating in the whole terrible ordeal. They all talked over each other, trying to explain that they had been living their own peaceful lives when Shota, as the grand witch, had summoned them with the magic of her oath and forced them to be part of her coven and thus her larger scheme.

One of the rather frightening-looking witch women, with one scarred, empty eye socket, a mangled nose, and no lips, approached. It took all of Kahlan's strength not to recoil at the horror of her face. She touched Kahlan reverently.

"I have been persecuted my whole life for being a witch." Her speech was halting and slurred because of her lack of lips, making it difficult to understand her.

The scar tissue where her lips had been cut off had thickened and tightened, pulling back from her gums and teeth, giving her a frightening look. The empty eye socket and the way her bared teeth grinned like those of a skull made it hard to look at her. She wet her teeth with her tongue before going on.

"I am named Yara. As you can plainly see," the woman said, gesturing self-consciously at her face, "I have had vile things done to me by people who think my gift alone makes me evil. I hate that every day I must wear the scars of that hatred for all to see on my face."

She choked up with emotion for a moment as a few tears ran down her cheek from her one eye. "But the one who was the most wicked of all was Shota, because she of all people should have known better. She knew what I had suffered, what I must live with for the rest of my life, and yet she used me anyway, used my face, to create fear in you. You have freed me, Mother Confessor. Thank you."

With a tear still in her own eyes, Kahlan put an arm around her shoulder and gave her the same kind of hug she had given Niska. Kahlan understood all too well people who in the past had thought her evil because of her Confessor power.

She tapped the witch woman's chest. "You keep your beauty in here, but I can see it."

Another woman stepped forward to touch Kahlan's arm. She was a lovely looking young woman, with unsettling birthmarks below each eye that made it look like blood was continually gushing from her eyes. While she was off-putting to look at, her gentle voice was the counter to the disturbing birthmarks.

"I am Thebe, Mother Confessor. All of us hope you can understand that none of this was our doing. We hold no ill will toward you and hope you can find it in your heart to hold none against us. We hope you can forgive us for taking part, even if it was against our will."

"We were being used," an older witch woman with long, wavy white hair said. She had a large wart on one side of her long nose. The tip of that nose drooped as if it were made of wax and she had let it get too close to a flame and it melted the end. "Shota used us much like the way she intended to use your two children, once they were born."

"She lied at first," another, very short witch woman said. She had wooden pegs for legs sticking out from beneath her tattered dress. "She had planned to kill you all along after you gave birth and keep your babies for herself. That is the most evil thing one woman could do to another, and to her children. She was using us as well, but what she was doing to you and the children you carry was much, much worse. I am so sorry for what almost happened."

"None of us would ever think to harm anyone," Yara said, as best she could without lips. "We have all been tormented by people for being born as witch women before anyone comes to know us for who we are. We simply want to be left alone to live our lives in peace."

"But there were a few among us who had evil in their hearts," Thebe said. "They were eager to participate in Shota's grand scheme, eager to cause you pain. Those are the four who are now dead, as is Shota herself. I don't think any of us ever dreamed that you would survive this plot, but we are truly thankful that you did."

"We realize you have no reason to believe our sincerity," another said, "but I swear to the good spirits, it is the truth."

"I can vouch for the honesty of what they are saying," Shale said. "I have spent time with these women. I know the heart of each. The hearts of the ones you killed were black, but these witch women are my sisters and their hearts are good."

"I understand." Kahlan spread her hands. "I am also sorry that all of you have suffered as well. Like my husband, I don't assign guilt because of the sins of others. We each should be judged for who we are and what we do. My hope is that all of you can now go back to your homes and live in peace. Know that I hold no grudge against you. My hope for you all is that others won't, either."

They whispered among themselves for a moment, until there were nods among them all.

"We have all discussed it," the one with the wavy white hair said, "and we all agreed that any of us will come to your aid should you ever ask us. We would be eager to try to make amends in any way possible."

"No amends are necessary, but I will remember your offer should I ever need your help."

Kahlan let out a deep sigh. "Although she doesn't necessarily deserve it, Shota has in the past helped Lord Rahl and me, so in view of that alone, I think you should take her body down to her home, in Agaden Reach, and bury her there."

Heads tipped close together and whispering again broke out among them all.

"We will see to it, Mother Confessor," Niska said. "You are more thoughtful than she would have been for you."

Kahlan nodded. "I have known her for a long time, and while she intended to do something evil, the woman was more complex than this one act driven by the thought of such power going to her head. She has paid the price for that act."

"We hope your husband is safe," a woman in the back said, "but if he is not, we stand ready to help you in any way we can."

"There is one thing we could do," Shale said, looking around at the rest of the witch women. "When Shota made the Mother Confessor start to miscarry, Lord Rahl gave her the raw milk of mother's breath while I made up the preparation."

Worried whispers broke out among the women. They obviously thought that was troubling. They cast concerned looks at Kahlan. She fretted as to the reason.

Yara lifted a hand. "We could all join our gifts and cast a birthing spell to help ease your delivery, and also that the two babies might be born healthy."

Shale smiled. "That is what I was thinking."

Kahlan felt her worry ease a little. "I would be grateful for such a spell."

The women all gathered in a tight circle around Kahlan, their hands over each other's shoulders. They closed their eyes as they whispered a chant in unison. Kahlan didn't understand the words, but she understood the heartfelt intentions.

As soon as they had finished, they stepped back and, following Shale's lead, went to their knees and bowed forward.

Kahlan recognized the honor. She waited a moment in the silence and then said, "Rise, my children."

It was the Mother Confessor's formal recognition of those under her protection.

As they were coming up, Kahlan heard a sound and turned to see the red leather of the Mord-Sith emerging from the mist. In the gloomy swamp, such a flash of color was hard to miss.

She didn't see Richard.

43

Kahlan's eyes opened wide with dread as she saw all six Mord-Sith materialize out of the mist, but she didn't see Richard.

Panic started to rise up within her at seeing that he wasn't with them.

But then, off behind the Mord-Sith, she finally saw him emerge out of the swirling haze, like a good spirit come among them.

It felt as if her heart leaped up into her throat with relief at seeing him. She had been sick with worry that he was dead, but dealing with Shota was the problem at hand, so she'd had to set that worry aside to look after herself and the twins.

Kahlan cried out in excitement as she ran the dozen strides to meet him. She threw her arms around his neck and kissed the side of his face at least a half-dozen times. He squeezed her tight in return, momentarily lifting her from her feet. Finally, she separated from him and stood back to wipe tears of joy from beneath her eyes.

"What took you so long?" she asked him.

Richard shrugged. "Well, a building fell on me . . . ."

She blinked in astonishment that he had survived such a thing and was actually alive. "Shota told us that she had spelled your legs so that you couldn't run to safety. She wanted the whole palace to come down on you. How did you get out?"

He didn't seem at all concerned about what had happened.

"The good spirits watched over me."

"Actually," Vika said as she gestured among the Mord-Sith, "we dug him out. I don't recall seeing any of the good spirits there, helping, but we did have a lot of help from the people of Bindamoon. Lord Rahl didn't make it easy, though. He managed to stand under the center of the palace as the entire thing collapsed, so it was a lot of trouble getting him out, I don't mind telling you."

"We knew you would be angry if we just left him there," Berdine said, offhandedly. "So we thought it best if we got him out and brought him along with us."

Richard rolled his eyes. "The people in Bindamoon turned out to be a huge help in saving my life. They were more than thankful to be rid of Iron Jack, the palace, and the 'queen.' But it was Rikka, Nyda, Cassia, Vale, Berdine, and Vika who organized and directed them in the rescue effort. I am indebted to them."

"As am I," Kahlan said as she put a hand on the forearms of two of the Mord-Sith. "I was so worried. Thank you for not giving up on him. I don't know what I would do had you . . ." Her voice choked up and she couldn't say the rest.

"Kahlan killed the five evil witches," Shale said into the awkward silence. "One of them was Shota." She grinned, then. "With her bare hands."

The Mord-Sith all looked a bit astonished, but proud.

Richard nodded with a serious look. "I would have expected no less. I'm just surprised it took her so long." He winked at Kahlan.

She gripped Shale's arm, then, and pulled

her closer, as if presenting her to Richard. "I couldn't have done it without Shale. She gave me a snake to use."

"A snake?" Richard frowned. "You hate snakes."

Kahlan showed him a sly smile. "Not white ones."

"Ah, I see." He flashed a smile at Shale as he gripped her shoulder. "Glad you were able to help."

Kahlan turned and held her arm out toward the group of witch women all watching him with a mixture of awe and terror, fearing that, like so many others, he would think they were evil just because they were witches. Worse, they knew that he had the power to strike them down on the spot should he so wish.

"These ladies here were not willing participants in Shota's scheme. They were all forced to answer Shota's call to coven, the same as Shale. The ones who wanted to be part of it are now all dead."

"I know," Richard said. "I heard the last of it as we were coming in. I stayed out of sight and watched to make sure there wasn't going to be any more trouble. I wanted to be able to come in and surprise anyone who might still attack you. It turns out that, thankfully, it wasn't necessary."

"No," Kahlan said with a smile as she looked over at the women. "These women are all on our side. Shota was using them."

He bowed his head to the nervous women. "Thank you all for helping the mother of my children, my beloved wife, and the Mother Confessor. You have my most heartfelt gratitude."

There were giggles and nods as the witch women all finally stepped closer.

Richard turned to Niska, taking in the writing tattooed all over her flesh. He spoke words Kahlan didn't understand, but by Niska's wide eyes, it was clear she knew what he was saying. She bowed deeply.

"Thank you, Lord Rahl. Although I am their keeper, I have not heard these words spoken aloud since I was but a girl. It is a reminder to me of the importance of the messages I carry to preserve the ancient language of Creation."

"Keep yourself and the words safe," Richard told Niska. "Both are important for future generations."

With a slight smile, Niska bowed her head. "By your command, Lord Rahl."

He turned and gestured to the woman without any lips. "May I know your name?"

She bowed, too fearful to look up at him, or maybe too ashamed of her appearance. "I am Yara, Lord Rahl."

With two fingers, he beckoned her close.

Yara reluctantly stepped up to him, and then, upon his urging, up closer to him. Richard gently gripped her shoulders and turned her around. He leaned in and spoke softly in her ear.

"You know about Additive Magic, Yara, yes?"

She nodded. "Of course, Lord Rahl."

"Good. Now, I'd like you to close your eye for me."

She did, and Richard gently put his hand over her mouth from behind. As he held his hand there, he bowed his head until his forehead touched the back of her head. Kahlan didn't know what he could be doing, but as she watched, Yara brought her hands together in front of herself to twine her fingers together as if in anxiety, or maybe pain. She could see the witch woman's breathing grow short and sharp. They stood that way for quite a time, until Richard finally took his hand away from her mouth.

Kahlan was astonished to see that Yara now had normal-looking lips where there had been only lumpy scars before. Her disfigured nose, too, was restored to normal.

Her hand rushed up to touch them. She turned and knelt beside the water to look at her reflection. As she stood, she started crying.

"I'm sorry," Richard said as she turned to him, "but I don't know if it would be possible to create a new eye for you with Additive Magic. If it is, I'm afraid that I don't know how to do such a thing. But I could at least do this little bit to help fix some of the harm that was done to you by ignorant people."

Weeping, she fell to her knees before him and grabbed the bottom of his trouser leg, kissing it repeatedly.

"None of that, Yara," he said, reaching down to touch the back of her shoulder. "It's not necessary. It was my honor as the Lord Rahl to help you. More than that, it is my duty to try to set wrongs right where I was able."

She finally stood and returned to the others. Some of them touched her lips in wonder as they all expressed their astonishment.

Richard motioned then for the young

woman with the birthmarks under her eyes to come to him. Holding her hands together, she approached him with her head bowed.

Richard lifted her chin with a finger to look into her eyes. "Those aren't birthmarks, are they?"

"You know?"

He nodded. "Yes. Someone marked you."

She nodded. "I am called Thebe. When I was young, I was cursed by a sorceress with these marks. She said it was to let anyone who looks upon me know that I am to be shunned as a filthy witch."

Richard shook his head in disgust, then turned her around and spoke softly in her ear. "You know of Subtractive Magic, yes?"

She nodded. "Underworld magic."

Richard smiled as he put a hand over her eyes. "Well, yes, but it is also part of my power. And, as far as sorceresses' curses go, this one is relatively simple."

After a moment, when he took his hand away, the frightening bloodlike marks under her eyes were gone.

"Thebe!" Niska exclaimed. "The curse marks under your eyes are gone!"

Thebe started to go to the ground before Richard, but he caught her arm first. "Not necessary, Thebe. It was a simple thing and I was glad to remove the marks for you."

She bowed. "Thank you, Lord Rahl, for removing this curse from my face. It has long made people shun me. Some even spit on me. It has caused me great loneliness. People fear and hate me without knowing me. They wouldn't allow me to help them with my gift."

Richard smiled. "I think they will shun you no more. In fact, I suspect you will find that a lot of young men are bewitched by your beauty."

She lowered her head with a shy smile.

Richard gestured at the woman with the two peg legs. She immediately held up both hands to ward him off.

"Thank you, Lord Rahl, but I do not wish to have my legs back. My knees used to hurt me so bad that I could hardly walk. With these, I can walk. They do me just fine if it pleases you."

Richard showed her a smile. "Then I would not think of changing them."

Kahlan wasn't sure if Shale looked amazed, or concerned. She leaned close to whisper to him.

"How did you do those things?" the sorceress asked. "I didn't know that magic had such powers. How does it work?"

Richard stared off into the swamp a moment before he answered. "I have no idea. Sometimes when I need it badly enough, my gift works. This was one of those times. I sincerely felt the need of it, the need of helping them, and it worked. That is the way with war wizards, I believe. Or at least with my power. It is brought to life by need."

He turned his attention to the group watching him. "I'm sorry that Shota pulled you all into this. Thank you for your concern for the Mother Confessor, and your help, but we must leave at once. We have a long way to travel and I want to get us where we are going before our children are born."

"Lord Rahl . . . ?" Shale said, hesitantly.

Richard seemed to know what she was about to say. He dismissed her concern with a quick gesture.

"Of course you're coming with us, Shale. We need you with us. The children of D'Hara need you when it is time to be born, and after that, too. Besides, this is going to be a long and dangerous journey. We need to keep the Law of Nines intact. We can't do all that without you."

She sighed in relief and smiled as she gave him a single nod.

When Richard said that they needed to get going, Kahlan held the hand of each witch woman in turn, wishing them well on their own journeys home.

"Don't forget," the witch woman with the wavy white hair said. "If either you or Lord Rahl is ever in need of our help for any reason, we will always do what is within our ability."

Niska retrieved Kahlan's knife from near Nea's remains. Her pack was not far away. She brought both back and handed Kahlan her knife, handle-first. "We will do as you have asked and bury Shota down in Agaden Reach."

Richard rested the palm of his left hand on the hilt of his sword as he looked at all the women watching him. "Do you all know about the Glee?" There were worried looks all around. They obviously all knew what the Glee were. "The Golden Goddess, their leader, continually tries to get into the minds of people in our world in order to find out where the Mother Confessor and I are so that she can send the

Glee to kill us and prevent these babies from being born."

"What can we do to help?" Niska asked.

"You can all guard your minds. If you sense a power probing your thoughts, use your gift to shut it out."

All of them nodded and spoke up to say that they would be careful.

44

Richard put an arm around Kahlan's and Shale's shoulders and moved them away from the witch women over to the group of Mord-Sith standing a short distance apart under a dead tree draped with sheets of moss. He wanted to have a confidential conversation. He didn't necessarily distrust the witch women, but he didn't want to let anyone know his plans for where they were going, or the route he intended to take.

"Besides nearly killing us all," he told them once they were all back together with the six Mord-Sith, "Shota greatly delayed us in getting to the Keep. The diversion exposed us to attacks by the Glee. With Kahlan so far along, she is even more vulnerable. We need to avoid any more of those risky battles. Not only that, but Shota has caused us to go a long way off course in the wrong direction in order to come up here to Agaden Reach. It put us a long way from Aydindril."

"How far do you think we are from the Keep?" Shale asked.

Richard stared off to the northeast, as if he could almost see the Keep from where he stood. "We are farther from the Keep, now, than we were when we were at the People's Palace."

Shale clearly looked disheartened. Richard couldn't say he blamed her. They had already had a long and difficult journey, not even counting the time in Bindamoon and now up near Agaden Reach. They were all exhausted from that journey, and it turned out that for all practical purposes, the journey was only now beginning. They now had farther to go than when they started.

"We are going to need to hurry, then, if we are to get to the Keep before the babies come." Shale passed a look of caution among them all. "We certainly don't want to be traveling when the Mother Confessor gives birth. The Glee are danger enough, but if they ever caught us when the Mother Confessor was in labor, well, I think we all know how bad that would be."

Richard nodded. "I think we all agree on that. Fortunately, we brought plenty of horses with us from Bindamoon. They couldn't make it up here, of course, so we had to leave them down the mountains a ways. They are eating grass and hopefully resting up for the long and difficult ride ahead."

"Are you sure they will still be there?" Kahlan asked.

Richard had no trouble reading the concern in her voice or on her face. He reassured her with a nod. "We made sure they will stay where they are until we get back to them. We left them in a good-size box canyon. There's a stream through it, so they have water, and there is plenty of grass for them to eat. We made a quick fence of sorts with some deadfall to close off the narrow entrance to the canyon. They aren't going anywhere." He smiled at Kahlan. "I brought along a mare that is especially gentle riding for you."

She didn't look to care about that. She was obviously worried about bigger issues than an easy ride. "How far?" She ran her hand over her swollen belly. "We need to be on our way to Aydindril. How long will it take us to reach the horses so we can set off in earnest?"

Richard was probably more impatient than she was, but he was trying not to show his concern over the distance they still had to travel before the babies came so as not to discourage her. He didn't want Kahlan to worry they wouldn't make it in time, but it was a legitimate fear.

He could see that she looked spent from the battle with Shota and the other witches she had fought and killed. He knew she wouldn't give up easily, but he also knew she would be concerned about the twins. Carrying them, added to the difficulty of traveling, would have to wear her out all that much quicker.

He didn't really have an alternate plan if they didn't want to try to make it to Aydindril in time. There was no substitute that could begin to provide the same level of safety. That meant that they had to get there, and they couldn't afford to waste any time.

"You just went through quite the ordeal," he said. "Are you feeling strong enough for a difficult walk down these mountains?"

"I'm fine," she said without hesitation, almost sounding annoyed that he would think of her as fragile. "But I will be a lot finer when we get to Aydindril. Stop worrying about me—I can rest all I want once we get there. Now, though, is not the time for resting. Now is the time for riding. Get us to the horses, would you please?"

"All right," Richard said with a sigh at her determination. "If we push hard, I think we can reach where we left them by dark. It's a good place to camp. I saw wild boars on our way up here. I know where they will be bedding down late in the day. If we're lucky, I can get one with an arrow and we can have a good meal tonight and meat for our journey. We're going to need our strength, and our supplies of travel food are running low."

"Which way?" she asked, eyeing the path back through the gloomy and dangerous swamp, not seeming concerned about the details that worried him.

"I found a way that will keep us from having to go back up the peaks and over the snowpack that you used to get into this place. I saw your tracks," he explained when she looked over at him with a quick frown.

"That would be good. Then what?" she asked.

Richard flicked his hand toward the east. "Once we get back out of this swamp, we need to head east down out of these mountains as quickly as we can to get back to the horses. After that, we ride east."

Kahlan gave him a puzzled look. "Why not northeast? Aydindril is northeast of here. Northeast would be the straightest route."

"This spine of mountains runs northeast all the way up through the Midlands. You're right that it's the straight route, but it would take forever to pick our way through these mountains. Not only that, but we couldn't take horses if we went that way.

"Once we are down and out of these mountains we will head east, cross north of Tamarang to reach the Callisidrin, then we can follow the river up to its headwaters. That will be the flattest traveling, where the horses can make better time. After that, we jump east again between the worst of the mountain ranges over to the Kern River basin. Following that north will take us right to Aydindril and the Keep."

"Sounds simple enough," Shale said.

Kahlan looked over and arched an eyebrow at the sorceress. "Not so simple. Most towns and villages are along rivers. We don't want people to spot us. I really don't want to encounter any more Glee. If one of them hooks my belly with a claw, it's all over."

"Kahlan is right," Richard said. "That means we're going to have to stay close enough to the rivers to make riding easier and faster along relatively flat river valleys but stay far enough away from any of the towns or villages where people could see us ride past. We simply can't afford to let any people spot us before we get to the Keep. That won't be easy, but it's not so impossible."

"We're wasting time," Kahlan said. "By your lady's command, take me away from this dreadful place and get me to your keep, wizard. Our children are asking to be born."

Richard answered with a smile that made her smile in return, and that, more than anything, lit his world. He wanted to hug her and kiss her, but they needed to be on their way, and besides, he didn't want an audience when he finally had the chance.

They quickly wished the witch women safe

journeys home after they buried Shota; then they traced their route back out of the swamp. Once into the vast forests of the rugged mountain country, they ascended steep climbs through clefts in the mountains to get through a confined, narrow pass that Richard had found before. It was a difficult climb but, in the end, it turned out to be a lot easier than the frigid way into the Reach by going across the snowpack and then over the windswept, open ledges. The thickly forested cleft in the mountains had steep rises to each side and jumbled rock up the middle, so it sheltered them from the worst of the winds but was hard work that tired their muscles and at least made them warm with the effort.

Once through the pass, they were finally able to start down out of the mountains. The trees were thick, but that meant that the forest floor, so sheltered from the sun, was relatively barren, making travel quick and relatively easy.

Ahead of them lay a long and dangerous journey.

Richard intended to outrun any trouble.

45

As the nine of them rode through a woodland of massive oak trees with low spreading limbs, now bare of leaves, Kahlan worried about the people in Aydindril who had seen them arrive. They had taken out-of-the-way routes and bypassed main thoroughfares. Doing so enabled them to avoid being seen by most people, but they still had unavoidably been spotted by some. There was no telling how many more had looked down a rise, or out a window, or up a street and seen them race through the city. Still, it was only one of her worries, and not nearly the biggest one.

They all knew that being spotted created the danger of the Golden Goddess being able to look through the eyes of those people in her search for Richard and Kahlan, and then she would be able to find them. As soon as she did, there was no doubt in any of their minds that she would send hordes of her kind to finish them before they could reach the safety of the Wizard's Keep. But they were close and would soon be under the protection of the defensive magic of the Keep.

All the way from Agaden Reach, they had traveled as fast as possible and the whole time managed not to be spotted by anyone. It had been a swift and exhausting journey up through the Midlands. She only wished that the original journey from the People's Palace to the Keep had been as swift. Without the interference of the witch's oath, it would have been.

Aydindril, however, was another thing altogether. It was no longer possible to avoid detection.

There were also people out on the road, both on foot and on horseback, as well as in wagons as they went about their business. They were all surprised to see their group ride past. Many of those people waved. Some cheered. Word of the sightings of the Lord Rahl and the Mother Confessor, pregnant no less, would quickly spread throughout the city. By morning it was likely that everyone in Aydindril would know that the Lord Rahl and the pregnant Mother Confessor had finally returned. There would be rejoicing.

But with the Glee sure to attack at any moment, any rejoicing would soon turn to terror. While they would be safe up in the Keep, the people of Aydindril would have no such safety. Had it been possible to take a way in to the Keep without being seen, they would have done it, but there was no such way in. It had been inevitable that they were going to be seen, and even if it had been by only one person, that was enough to bring the Glee.

Kahlan's spirits lifted a little as she at last saw the magnificent Confessors' Palace. Set on an expanse of vibrant green grounds, the white stone of the palace atop a hill seemed to glow in the light of the setting sun. She slowed her horse to momentarily take in the sight. It had been so long since she had seen it that she had come to fear she never would again.

This was the ancestral home of the Confessors. It was where she had been born and where she had grown up. She ached to go straight there. More than anything, she wished the twins could be born there, where she had been born. Some of the same staff she knew growing up likely still lived and worked there. She knew they would be overjoyed to have the children of the Mother Confessor be born there, and to have little feet once more running through the halls. Kahlan wanted to bring life back to that home of the Confessors.

The palace, in addition to being the ancestral home of the Confessors, was also a seat of power for the Midlands. The larger lands of the Midlands had palaces down in the city for their ambassadors and members of the Central Council, which had ruled the collective lands of the Midlands. As the Mother Confessor, the last of a long line, Kahlan had reigned not only over the other Confessors when they were still alive, but, when need be, over the Central Council itself.

It was an authority that the Mother Confessor exerted only when the council could not reach agreement, or when they reached an agreement that she couldn't accept as the best course for the Midlands. Some of the larger lands occasionally manipulated the council to the disadvantage of other, smaller lands. When that happened, the Mother Confessor would intervene, but otherwise she let the council manage the Midlands.

Even so, her authority was such that kings and queens sought the Mother Confessor's advice and counsel. They were well aware that they ultimately answered to her, as did every ruler of every land of the Midlands. The council was the intermediary step to her final authority, and handled most of the mundane, day-to-day affairs. Kahlan used her role to sometimes speak for those in the Midlands who had no voice on the council.

That didn't earn her any friends, but Confessors, and the Mother Confessor in particular, didn't have friends anyway, because everyone greatly feared a Confessor's power. Richard had been the first real friend she'd ever had, the first one not to shy away from her because of that power, the first to stand with her and protect her willingly for the person she was, not because of her ability or status.

The irony was that wizards had always protected Confessors, and Richard was a wizard, although he hadn't known it at the time.

Up on the towering mountain beyond the palace they got their first glimpse of the dark, imposing walls of the Wizard's Keep. While the Central Council ruled the Midlands, and the Mother Confessor had authority over that council, it was the dark, brooding Keep embedded high up in the rocky face of the mountain that was the dark threat backing the word of the Mother Confessor. The Wizard's Keep had provided the wizards who always accompanied Confessors, including the Mother Confessor herself. The Keep, in a sense, was the muscle behind the Mother Confessor's authority. While it hadn't always been that way, during Kahlan's lifetime the wizards at the Keep chose not to use their power in order to rule, preferring instead to let the Central Council rule the lands.

As they rode higher up on the road to the Keep, it offered spectacular views of the city of Aydindril spread out far below. Smoke came from many a chimney, as most places had fires going not just for preparation of food but to ward off the cold. Lamplight glowed in most of the homes and buildings, making the city seem to sparkle in the gathering dusk. People, carts, and wagons filled the streets of the city. The view of the city from the road up to the Keep had always been one of Kahlan's favorite sights.

As they rode silently up the mountain along a series of switchbacks, the road finally emerged from a thick stand of spruce and pine trees before the bridge spanning a chasm that had always seemed to her like the mountain had split open, leaving a yawning abyss.

Beyond the bridge, the Wizard's Keep above them was embedded in the rock of the massive, imposing mountain. The complex of the Keep was vast, and it seemed to be perched menacingly on the side of the mountain, as if ready to pounce on any threat. The Keep was enormous, and its walls of dark granite looked almost like cliff faces rising up before them, as if it were a part of the dark rock of the mountain itself. Above those imposing walls, the Keep was an intricate maze of ramparts, bastions, towers, connecting walkways, spires, and high bridges between sections of the structure.

Wispy clouds drifted past some of the higher spires and towers, making the place seem as though it lived in the clouds.

Out ahead, off across the stone bridge, Kahlan

could see the gaping entrance of the arched stone passageway where the road tunneled under the base of the outer Keep wall. The portcullis was up.

Kahlan brought her horse to a stop to take it all in. The site of the Keep seemed to bring her mood to a low point of despair. They had spoken little the last few days, mostly because Kahlan had not been in a mood to talk and everyone seemed to realize it. When they saw her stop, everyone else slowed to a stop as well.

Kahlan turned in her saddle and looked back at Shale. "How long until I give birth?"

The sorceress was ready with an answer. "From my experience, the babies will come any day now. It is difficult to say precisely when, but I don't think it will be longer than three or four days, at most."

"You've been awfully quiet for the last few days," Richard said. "What's wrong?"

Kahlan felt tears well up. Fears she had been keeping to herself wouldn't let her have a moment of peace. Even when she slept, those fears haunted her. And now those fears were about to be realized.

Richard, right beside her, pulled in the reins

and rested his wrists on the horn of his saddle. When he glanced back at the others, they waited back where they were.

"Kahlan, what's wrong? I know you and I know that something is bothering you. This should be a joyous time. Our children are about to be born. We have reached the Keep, where they will be safe."

She nodded, too ashamed of her fears to speak. Richard's words only seemed to bring it to the surface, making the tears start to flow all the harder.

Richard leaned over in his saddle to get closer so he could speak privately, assuming it was something she didn't want the others to hear. "Kahlan, what's wrong? You can tell me."

Kahlan couldn't bear to tell him. How could she? These were his children, too, the children of D'Hara, the children the world needed.

Or were they?

"Kahlan, please tell me what's bothering you," he pressed in a whisper.

She couldn't hold it back from him any longer.

"You know what's wrong. Shota said that one of our children will be a monster. She saw into the flow of time. While she got her prophecies wrong in the sense of how they would come about, you know as well as I that in the end they always proved true. She was positive about this one because it was so clear-cut. I want these children so badly, but I'm terrified that one of them is going to be the monster she predicted."

Richard relaxed a bit. "Is that all?"

She wiped a tear from her cheek. "Is that all? It's everything. It's everything we have wanted, it's everything our world needs, and yet one of them is destined to be a monster who will destroy lives."

He smiled a little. "I don't believe in destiny any more than I believed in blindly following prophecy, and neither do you."

"This is not destiny. This is a vision from a witch woman who had seen it in the flow of time. Now that their birth approaches, I can't bear the thought of one of them being that monster that we bring into the world."

Richard took a deep breath and let it out as he considered a bit. "Do you think me a monster?" he finally asked her.

"You?" She frowned at him. "No. What does that have to do with it?"

Richard shrugged. "Darken Rahl was a monster."

"So what?"

"His father, Panis Rahl, was a monster, as was his father, and his father before that. The House of Rahl was a whole line of tyrants. Every Rahl who became a Lord Rahl was a monster and each bred a monster for a son."

"What does that have to do with it?" she said.

"I am the son of a monster. By that logic, I should be a monster as well."

"But you were raised by a good man and so you didn't turn out to be like Darken Rahl."

Richard winked at her. "Exactly."

Unsure, Kahlan squinted at him. "What's your point?"

Richard smiled. "Had Shota looked into her flow of time when I was conceived, what do you suppose she would have seen? Yet another monster in the making. Prophecy, after all, is in many ways merely the essence of potential. Though it would have been possible, I'm not the monster she would have seen. Monsters aren't necessarily bred and born to be monsters. Evil people are mostly created by how they grow up—either by the terrible way they were raised, or by the terrible things they experienced that shaped them into who they turn out to be.

"Our children will grow up to be good people because we will raise them to be good people."

Kahlan stared at him a moment. "Are you so sure of that?"

His smile widened. "Kahlan, if it wasn't true, then I would be a monster the way all of the men in the Rahl line of rule were monsters. But I'm not like them because I was raised differently, by a good man."

She gave him a look from under her brow. "Your brother was a monster."

Richard drew a deep breath. "True enough. But I don't think it was because of birth or that he was predestined to be a monster. I think he was weak and didn't use his head. He made a lot of bad choices. His friends and the people he associated with encouraged those bad choices. In a way, they urged him on to be the evil person he became. But I don't think he was born a monster the way Shota meant."

Kahlan finally smiled over at him as she wiped away the last of her tears. "You always make me feel better when I think things are hopeless. Please don't ever stop making me feel better."

Richard bowed his head to her. "By your command, my lady, it shall be so. Now, can we get you into the Keep so that you can bring our two children into the world?"

Kahlan leaned over and touched his arm. "You are going to be a good father."

At that, they started out again. The rest followed behind.

46

Kahlan rode close beside Richard as they crossed the stone bridge. She felt as if a weight of dread had been lifted from her. She had been secretly terrified that Shota's prediction that one of their children would be a monster would turn out to be true, but she hadn't wanted to burden Richard with her fears. The world had seemed a dark and threatening place. She had felt doomed, without a way out.

Richard had just made the sun come out again. Her spirits had been cheered to the point that dread suddenly turned to expectant joy at the thought of the fast-approaching birth. In the past, Shota's prophecies had always turned out to be true, but in ways that never brought about the kind of doom she had predicted.

With this one, like the others, they could work to make sure that things turned out well.

He offered her a smile, reassuring her, but she could see in his gray eyes that he was worried about things other than one of their children being a monster. She knew that, like her, he was worried about the lives of all the people down in the city once the Golden Goddess found out where they were. They both knew that she would use the lives of those people to try to force them to give themselves up.

On the one hand, she felt dreadful that their coming to Aydindril could result in the death of so many people in the city she loved. But on the other hand, if they didn't retreat to the safety of the Keep, then they and their children would end up being hunted and eventually slaughtered. If that happened, then in the long run, everyone in the world would be naked before the onslaught of the Glee and everyone in their world would be hunted to extinction.

That was always the dilemma with hostages, but the end result of giving in was why Kahlan never submitted to hostage negotiations. As cruel as it seemed on the surface, sacrificing hostages was for the greater good.

She hated that such a phrase was what Shota had used, but in this case, it was the cold reality. Giving in to such evil only resulted in more death in the end.

At least at the People's Palace there had been a lot of soldiers of the First File to help protect people. Even so a great many of those people had died. Here, there was no large force like that. There was only Richard, and he couldn't be everywhere at once.

The only solution she could see was that the threat from the Glee had to be ended by force, but she had absolutely no idea how they could accomplish such a thing. The Golden Goddess, after all, was off in another world. Even if they wanted to try to kill her, they had no way to get at her.

Kahlan smiled when Richard looked her way again, feeling better at least about how he had said they would raise their children. What he said made sense.

As they rode over the bridge, she looked down over the edge of the bridge's stone wall at the side. The rock walls below the bridge dropped away seemingly forever. In one place on the far wall of the chasm, a thin stream of water, as usually happened for several days after rain, emerged from a crack in the rock. The water tumbling down turned to mist before it ever reached the bottom far below. There were often clouds floating by below the bridge, but there were none this day.

"It's good to be home," she said to Richard.

He nodded. "It's been a long time, and a long journey."

It seemed too simple a statement for all the effort of finally arriving after deciding to leave the People's Palace and all they had gone through, from Michec to Shota to all the battles with the Glee.

Once across the bridge, they quickened their pace up the road. When they were almost to the opening in the outer Keep wall, and before they went in, Kahlan turned to have a look at the city she had so missed.

When she did, her breath suddenly caught.

Everyone else heard her gasp. They all wheeled their horses around to see what she was seeing.

To their astonishment, there on the bridge where they had been only moments before stood a lone Glee.

"Dear spirits," Kahlan said under her breath.

Everyone else drew their horses close together, both to protect Kahlan and as they prepared for a fight. All their heads swiveled as they frantically scanned the countryside for others, looked for the rest of the Glee about to ambush them before they could get into the safety of the Keep. The Mord-Sith all had their Agiel in their fists. Rikka and Cassia threw a leg over their horses' necks and leaped to the ground, drawing their knives in addition to the Agiel they had in their other hand.

Unlike Shale and the Mord-Sith, who looked ready for the expected battle, Richard merely stared at the single dark figure on the bridge. Kahlan was surprised that he didn't look alarmed. She could see that his posture was rclaxed in his saddle as he watched the Glee. Much to Kahlan's surprise, he merely studied the creature, which was just standing there looking back at them.

"Something looks a little different than I remember about the Glee I've seen before," Kahlan finally said when no one else spoke, "or maybe I just never before saw them standing still like that for so long."

Shale frowned back over her shoulder. "What do you mean? Different how?"

"I'm not sure, but I don't really remember them having that slight greenish iridescence across the tops of their heads."

"That's because the others you've seen before don't have that sheen of color." Richard sounded calm and not the least bit worried.

The way he said it made Kahlan think he had seen a Glee like this before.

She frowned over at him. "What are you talking about?"

Just then the Glee did the strangest thing.

It opened its arms out a little to the sides, and turned its claws palm-out, toward them. When it did it spread its arms a little. She saw webbing she had never noticed before between the individual claws of the Glee.

And then it bowed its head.

Kahlan, Shale, and the Mord-Sith stared in astonishment.

Richard let out a sigh. "Bags," he said to himself, but loud enough that Kahlan heard it.

"What in the world could this mean?" she asked him.

Richard finally looked away from the creature

and regarded her with an expression that bordered on regret.

"It means I want you all to get into the Keep."

Kahlan's frown tightened. "You know this creature, don't you? I can't imagine how, but you know it."

Staring off at the Glee again, Richard nodded as the Glee stared back at him.

"Get inside," he said. "All of you."

Kahlan grabbed his shirtsleeve in her fist. "Richard, what are you going to do? The twins are due any moment. I need you here. Our children need a father. I don't know what you're thinking, but I can see in your eyes that you are getting one of your crazy ideas."

He finally looked back to her with an iron determination in his raptor gaze. "I need to end this."

She shook her head, as if trying to clear what didn't make sense. "End it? What in the world are you talking about?"

"I'm not sure." He stared off again at the dark creature. "I want you all to get inside. I will be back with you as soon as I can. It may only be a few minutes . . . but I have a funny feeling it may be longer."

"Longer? What are you talking about? How much longer?" Kahlan quickly glanced around at the others all staring at him before she leaned closer. "What are you going to do?"

Shale was looking apoplectic. The Mord-Sith all looked back and forth between Richard and the creature, unsure if they should go attack it, or stand their ground. A firm look from Richard told them to stay where they were.

Kahlan again grabbed his shirt. "Richard, answer me. What are you going to do?"

He had that look she knew so well. The ferocity of it softened when he turned to her, but it didn't leave entirely.

"I don't know yet, but I suspect that this is a sign that the city is about to be attacked. I have to stop it."

He kissed the ends of his first two fingers, pressed them to her lips, and then pressed them to the twins.

"Richard—"

He gathered up his horse's reins. "I have to see what I can do, or this ordeal will never end, and countless people will die. I am the Lord Rahl, the leader of the D'Haran Empire. It is up to me to protect our people. I intend to do just that. Now get inside. All of you. Shale, I am counting on you to take care of Kahlan when the babies come."

"You mean you will be gone that long?" she asked.

"I don't know, but if I am, I want you to take care of Kahlan when she gives birth."

"Of course, Lord Rahl."

His gaze slid from Shale to the Mord-Sith. "Do as I say. I want you all to get Kahlan into the Keep where she will be safe. Don't delay for anything. Do it right now. The people in there will help you protect her."

"Only if you take Vika with you," Kahlan said.

"It's not his decision to make," Vika told her. "That decision has already been made. You had better do as he asks and get inside the Keep where you will be safe. I promise you, I won't leave Lord Rahl's side."

47

Richard dismounted and handed the reins to Berdine. Nyda took the reins to Vika's horse as she slipped to the ground. He gave the rest of them a commanding gesture to get into the Keep. They all recognized the seriousness of the command. Reluctantly, they all followed his orders and rode off toward the arched opening in the Keep wall. He watched Kahlan, with Mord-Sith surrounding her, ride in under the arch and then inside until he knew she was no longer in danger.

Just before she disappeared inside, she turned back to give him a last, brief look. Finally, she disappeared through the opening in the wall, to be greeted by people he could see waiting inside. He wasn't able to see who they were, but he hoped there were Sisters of Light among them who would be able to protect her. He hoped Chase was still at the Keep. He would certainly protect her.

"Lord Rahl, what are you planning?" Vika asked. "The Mother Confessor said that you have a crazy idea."

Richard nodded as he continued to share a look with the lone Glee. "She isn't wrong."

"So, what is your crazy idea this time?" she asked with a long-suffering sigh.

He flashed her a smile. "I think that Glee wants to talk to us. Let's go find out what it has to say."

"The Glee don't talk. They only come to kill."

"My crazy idea is that I don't think that this one intends us any harm."

She nodded as she started after him. "That is indeed a crazy idea. If you are wrong, and it's a trap?"

"Then we will deal with it."

Together, Richard and Vika walked back down the road toward the bridge, scanning the area for trouble as they went. He looked back over his shoulder, up at those ramparts and crenellations in the walls he could see from such a low perspective, but he didn't see anyone. Kahlan was now safe inside the fortress.

The Glee on the bridge had not moved from where it stood, waiting. Richard continually swept his gaze in every direction, looking for a mass attack, but not actually expecting one. Vika also kept up a sweep of the area, especially the woods, but unlike him, she did expect an attack.

Each time he looked back at the Glee, it hadn't moved. It watched him coming with big, glossy black eyes. Occasionally its third eyelid would blink across the surface to keep it wet.

The creature, with its soft, moist, mottled black skin, hairless head, big glossy eyes, two small holes for a nose, and wicked claws, looked completely alien standing there on the bridge built by men. Glee weren't typically anxious. But given how uneasy this one appeared, he thought it must be here for a reason it felt was important enough to overcome its apprehension.

As Richard slowed to a halt in front of the dark creature, he held his hand back and out to the side a little to let Vika know that he wanted her to stay back out of his way and give him room in case he needed to draw his sword. He really didn't think that was going to be necessary, but as he had learned so often before, it was better to be prepared to act and not need to, than to not be prepared and find out all too suddenly that you should have been ready.

The Glee tipped its head to the side and blinked with its third eyelids, as if studying Richard's face up close for the first time. It was a disconcerting appraisal by such a dangerous creature. At least its lips weren't drawn back to expose its needle-sharp teeth.

"I am called Sang."

Richard blinked in surprise. While it hadn't said the words out loud, and its mouth hadn't moved, Richard could clearly hear the words in his head. It was an unnerving sensation to have a voice talk to him from inside his own head.

Vika gasped. "I heard him talk in my head!"

"We can both hear him," Richard told her under his breath. He looked back at the Glee.

"How is it that I can hear you speak in my head"—he tapped a finger to his temple to show what he meant—"but you make no words that I can hear with my ears?"

Sang cocked his head the other way. *"It is*

how we communicate. The goddess comes into the minds of your kind in much the same way so that she may look through their eyes to see where you are. She has talked to some of you in the way that I talk to you now, in your mind. In that same way, I can speak into your mind in a way that you understand."

"Can all of your kind do this?"

"*Yes. This is how we communicate with each other. I have tried to speak to others in different worlds in this way, but they could not hear me in their minds. Only you and your kind can hear us speak in this way, as some have heard the goddess.*"

"Why did you try to speak to those others, in other worlds?" Richard asked.

"*For the same reason I speak now to you. But they could not hear me and unlike you, they could be of no help.*"

Richard didn't like riddles but decided to let it slide for the moment.

"I have seen you before, Sang," he said aloud.

"*Yes. I have watched you fight a number of times now.*"

"Why have you watched me fight but not participated in those battles with the rest of your kind?"

"I am also Glee, but I am not like those who attacked you. I watched because I wanted to learn about you."

Richard found that rather worrisome, but at the same time, it was what he had been beginning to believe.

"What have you learned?"

"I have watched and seen you finally discover how to fight the Glee. It is not easy, and no other has ever been able to learn what you have learned. The Glee are very, very dangerous. But you have grasped the way of fighting them effectively. You understand what I am meaning?"

Richard nodded. "Yes. I have learned that their claws, while deadly when used for ripping and tearing at people, are not really made for fighting. I think they are meant for something else. Even so, those claws are obviously very deadly. I have learned how those who fight us use them, and how to defeat them by using their weaknesses."

Sang cocked his head. *"And what are their weaknesses?"*

"Most of their arm strength is in close range, not when they extend their arms out to slash. Their shoulders and upper arms are not as strong when extended. I have learned the limitations of their movements, and where in those movements they are slowest and more awkward, and thus most vulnerable. The farther they reach, the weaker their ability to use their arms and the more cumbersome their strikes."

Sang nodded. *"Your kind thinks we are deadly, and that is obviously true in most cases, but in reality, you, Lord Rahl, are more deadly by far."*

Richard was somewhat troubled that Sang knew his name and title, but on the other hand, it told him that this individual shared information with others of his kind, which from what he had observed was rather unusual among Glee. This was obviously a thinking, reasoning creature, even if very different from him.

"Is there a point to all of this?" he asked. "A reason you have been watching me?"

Sang tapped his claws together several times, as if to demonstrate something. They made a clacking sound.

"My kind uses our claws to feed. We eat water plants called flutter weed and float weed. We harvest it with our claws. The webs between our claws help us to maneuver in water.

"We also use our claws to eat muscle snails that

stick themselves down to rocks and can hold tight. They are at least as big as your hand and have a broad, powerful foot to hold themselves against rocks. They provide us nourishment.

"We must get our sharp claws in under their broad, shallow shells and then pry and pull them off the rocks. We use our teeth—" He drew his lips back to expose his tightly packed, needle-sharp white teeth. *"—to rake the muscle snail's meat from inside the recess of its shell.*

"We also eat other kinds of water plants, delicious varieties of thick, ruffled plants that grow low and tight on rock. We use our teeth to scrape them from the surface of rocks. It is the only way we are able to collect and eat them. We also eat a variety of other snails and use our claws to extract the meat. Mostly, though, the flutter and float weed and the muscle snail are our staple foods which grow in abundance and what our kind has lived on for as long as any of us knows."

"But something happened, and as a result of that event some of you developed a taste for the flesh of creatures from other worlds?"

Sang let his claws drop back to his sides as he let out a kind of hiss that Richard took for a sigh. He looked somehow remorseful.

"*Yes. Some time back, before any of us now living were alive, we were visited by a race from another world. We thought of them as gods. These gods left us a gift. With this gift, we were able to visit other worlds much like they did. In these worlds the Glee visited, they eventually found other things we could eat.*

"*At first, it was a wondrous device to explore worlds with different kinds of edible plants. In some of these places the Glee found the kind of water weeds and snails that were similar to our favorites and they brought them back for our young.*"

Richard and Vika shared a look.

"You mean to say you care for your young?" he asked.

"*Of course. We love our young. A male and female Glee will together care for and protect her eggs until they hatch. From the time they hatch, the mother and father bring them food until they grow enough to be able to learn to gather food for themselves.*" Sang cocked his head again. "*Did the goddess tell your kind something different?*"

Richard let out a troubled sigh. "As a matter of fact, we were led to believe that the Glee simply reproduce, somehow, but that you don't experience love and bonding the way we do.

From what we were told, it sounded like your kind didn't pair together, and producing young was not a meaningful act."

Sang looked distressed. *"That is not true. When we find a mate, we bond for life."*

Richard hooked his thumbs behind his belt as he stole another quick glance at Vika. "This is not what the goddess led us to believe. She gave us a picture of a cold-blooded race that cared only about collecting other worlds and hunting creatures in those worlds for sport as well as to eat. She made it seem that they were born for this purpose and it was all they cared about. We were told that even if the goddess grew old and died, it was not important because they are all the same and of a like mind and basically interchangeable. She said her death would not matter because there would always be another to take her place."

Sang let out the same kind of hissing sigh as he had before. *"The one who calls herself the Golden Goddess lies as easily as she breathes. She lies in order to strike fear into the hearts of those she intends her followers to hunt. They have developed a taste for the flesh of other creatures, including, most of all, your kind."*

"A taste for people?"

Sang nodded. *"You are the only thinking creatures we know of that are in some ways similar to us. We have so far discovered no others. The other worlds we have discovered have at most lower creatures such as insects and other small creatures without the ability to understand our voice, much like float weed and muscle snails cannot hear our voices.*

"The goddess and her followers find great satisfaction in hunting down, killing, and eating your kind more than any that has been found before in the worlds she collects. She will tell anyone from your world anything that makes it easier for the Glee to succeed in hunting and killing, hoping your kind never learns any of our weaknesses, as you have. Creatures that are terrified don't fight back effectively. That makes them easier to kill.

"The goddess and her followers have come to highly desire the flesh of other creatures more advanced than the muscle snails of our world, and especially after the game of hunting your kind. The hunting has become the purpose of many, and they do not even devour all they catch. The fighters the goddess sends out to other worlds are all males,

like me. They bring some of their kills back to feed their females, the young, and the goddess.

"Those of us like me find the idea of eating thinking, reasoning creatures like you to be not only wrong, but abhorrent. Those with the goddess don't care about our objections, and as you have seen, they have embraced violence and they now eat your kind exclusively. They are even willing to use violence against their own kind in order to hold power so that they may continue doing as they wish."

Richard was disturbed to learn how much of what they had been told wasn't true. It changed everything.

"I have noticed that unlike all the rest of the Glee, you have a greenish iridescence to your flesh, especially over the top of your head."

Sang nodded. *"It is because of the flutter and float weed as well as some other plants of our world that we eat. Those plants we prefer to eat have this same shimmering green color. Those who have turned to eating the flesh of creatures in other worlds, especially your kind, no longer eat the food from our world and so they quickly lose this coloring."*

That certainly explained the color Richard

noticed on Sang that he hadn't seen on the other Glee. "I'm glad that there are some of you who don't want to eat us. I would much rather cooperate with you and those like you."

"It is the same with the others who side with me. You are the first creatures that I found who will fight back, which, of course, excites those who follow the goddess. And among your kind, you are the most effective at fighting and killing the Glee to stop them. I have been looking for one like you for a very, very long time, hoping all the time that I would find one."

"For what purpose?"

"To help us kill the goddess, of course."

"Of course," Richard said.

48

"*The Golden Goddess is smart, cunning, and knows how to win followers. She prizes the power she has. She craves the loyalty of her followers and is pleased that they would do anything for her. They would die for her. As you know so well, many have already died for her. As we speak, many more are preparing to come here and slaughter all the people living in this place.*

"*Those like me, who believe in consuming what our beautiful, wonderful world has to offer in abundance, have tried many things to make the others see that what they are doing is wrong. But they see us as simply weak and too timid for the dangerous hunts of your kind.*

"*More than for the food, they enjoy their power over your kind, much as the goddess herself enjoys her power over her followers. After trying everything to reason with the goddess and her followers, we now realize that there is no way to turn them back from their new ways.*

"If they are not stopped, she will see to it that the Glee come to roam this world and hunt your kind until there are none of you left. They think of eliminating your species as a goal and as an accomplishment. Finding new worlds for her followers to hunt, especially this one, gives the goddess power over them."

Richard stared into the large, glossy black eyes. "So why, exactly, are you are telling me all of this?"

"Because for your kind to survive, they must be stopped. For my kind to survive, they must be stopped.

"To stop them, the Golden Goddess must be killed. There is no other way."

Richard leaned back a little as he tried to judge the truthfulness of Sang's words. It was possible, after all, that there was a power struggle in Sang's world and he was just as bloodthirsty as the goddess, and simply wanted to win Richard's sympathy in order to help eliminate his opposition for power.

Richard supposed that it was even possible that Sang was trying to win Richard's trust in order to eliminate him for the goddess.

On the other hand, what Sang was saying did seem to ring true, and if it was true, this could be the key to ending the threat that Richard hadn't previously thought was possible. More than that, not ending the threat could very well result in the end of everyone.

"We were told that this goddess is merely one of your kind that takes the position of goddess, as others before her, and that if she is killed, another will simply take her place, and then another, and so on, so that killing her is not a solution to stop this madness."

Sang didn't hesitate to answer. *"It is true that if she is killed, her followers may not stop simply because she is killed. Hunting and killing has given them a taste for power, so another leader will likely emerge to take her place. If killing her would stop this war with other worlds and what she is doing to her own kind, we would have tried to kill her ourselves if we could.*

"But she is very powerful, with many who believe in her and do what she tells them. She teaches them that through eating the flesh of intelligent beings,

like your kind, they will gain the strength and wisdom of those they eat, making them superior beings. Unlike eating our traditional food of float weed and muscle snails, they find a thrill in the danger involved. It gives some of them the chance to rise to be champions of the kills. Champions gain the favor of the goddess. That means that if she is killed, another would very likely want to take her place.

"Those with me could never succeed in stopping them because they have learned to fight, and they are vicious at it. Those who believe like me that what they do is wrong are not fighters and we don't have their fighting skills.

"But on the other hand, if she is killed and if her followers are dealt a severe enough blow with many in their ranks killed on their home ground, they may then for the first time fear for their lives, fear for their world, fear for their offspring, and they may go back to the way we have traditionally lived for as long as any of us knows."

Richard studied Sang's emotionless face for a moment. "It's also possible that even if she and a number of her followers are killed, they could still hold to their belief in collecting and hunting other worlds, gather followers and revert to this savage life."

Sang nodded. *"Yes, this is true, and this is why, besides killing the goddess and enough of her followers as only you would be able to do, there is another important aspect to what must be done."*

Richard had thought there had to be more to it. "And what would that additional thing be that would need to be done?"

"The device that allows them to go to other worlds must be destroyed once and for all. If they are denied any possibility of ever hunting other worlds, they could not win over followers, and without followers—believers—they could not continue."

Richard felt goose bumps ripple up his arms to the nape of his neck. He didn't like the idea of being an assassin. He remembered telling Zedd once that if he took the sword, he would not be an assassin. Zedd had told him that he could be whatever he wanted to be. Not only the world, but he himself had changed since he'd taken the sword. He now understood that there were times when it was necessary to stop a deadly threat and that killing was often the only way to do that. The difference between him and those he had to stop, like the goddess and the Glee, was that they killed because they

wanted to; he killed because it was the only way
to survive and prevent killing from continuing.

"I presume you are here, then, to ask me
to somehow return to your world and kill the
goddess for you along with enough of her
followers to discourage them."

Sang bowed his head. *"Yes. You have it exactly
right."*

"Let's just say for the sake of argument that
I agreed. So then, if I went to your world and
could accomplish such a thing for you, you
would then send us back here and you would
then destroy the device so it could never be
used again?"

"No," Sang said with a sorrowful shake of his
head. *"You must also destroy the device with that
weapon you carry."*

"How could I possibly destroy a device that I
don't even understand?"

*"We cannot destroy the device because there is
nothing in my home world that would be powerful
enough to harm it."* With a claw, Sang gestured
to Richard's left hip. *"I have seen you use that
weapon. I have seen it do things that I find hard
to believe. I have seen it do things that nothing
else could do. We do not have anything like it. I*

believe it is the only weapon that could destroy the device."

Richard was feeling a rising sense of dread. "If I were to agree to come to your world and I succeeded in defeating the Golden Goddess and her followers, and then destroyed this device that allows them to go to other worlds, how could I come home, to my world?"

Sang reluctantly shook his head again. *"There would be no way. With the device destroyed, you would not be able to return to your world."*

49

Richard swallowed, trying to moisten his suddenly dry mouth, not entirely sure he had heard Sang correctly.

"You're saying that I could never return to my world? Never? There would be no way for me to return?"

Sang nodded sorrowfully. *"Yes. I am sorry. Once you destroy the device, you would not be able to return here. I am sorry, but it is the only way."*

Richard shook his head, not wanting to believe that he would have to stay there, in Sang's world.

"I don't know if I could leave my world for yours to fight for those on your side who can't—or won't—do it themselves, and then, even if I succeed, never be able to return home to my mate, my offspring, my people, and my world. That is too much to ask."

"I am sorry, but there is no other way," Sang said. *"But it would not simply be that you fight for those like me, it would be for the survival of those in your world as well."*

Richard blinked in disbelief. "I don't see how I could live in your world."

"I can tell you that of all the worlds the goddess has collected, none can begin to match the beauty of my own home world, so you would at least have that. Your world, here, is a harsh, dry place. My world is lush and warm and beautiful beyond anything you have ever seen before."

Richard had to remind himself to hold back his rising anger. This wasn't personal. Sang was trying to find a way to end the bloodshed, even if the solution he had come up with was unacceptable.

"I don't care how beautiful it is, it's not my home. Everyone I love is here, in this world."

Sang cocked his head to the side. *"But this is such a dry place. I don't know how you are even able to survive here. We have much trouble coming here because of how dry it is. We must put the jelly of the scrum plant on ourselves to help keep our skin moist while we are here, or it would dry out and crack. Then we would bleed, and we would die."*

That explained the gelatinous masses that Richard had seen slide off of them when the Glee first arrived, as well as the wet appearance of their skin.

"Sang, I'm not sure I could ever agree to such a thing—to leave everything I have here and everyone I love, never to return. As you may know, my own offspring are about to come into the world."

"I do know about the imminent arrival of your offspring. Please believe me when I say that I sympathize with your reluctance," Sang said, sounding sincere. *"If the situation were reversed, I don't know that I could stand to live in your world, never to return to mine."* He gestured at Vika. *"But you would have this female with you, at least."*

"That is not enough, nor is it a solution." Richard gestured up to the Keep. "My mate is there."

"I am sorry, but while I do admit to wanting my kind to return to their ways and no longer be able to raid other worlds, the more important

thing I am telling you is that this is the only way if you wish your kind here in this world to survive.

"As we speak, the Golden Goddess is right now preparing to send the largest number of Glee yet to come here to kill all the people of that place down the mountain. She wants none left alive to punish you for going into that place of magic to hide, rather than surrender. When that is finished, they will then be sent to other places in your world to hunt the people there until there are no more of your kind. This will not be attacks such as you have seen and fought against before. This will be mass attacks in many different places at the same time.

"The goddess knows of and fears your magic, and she also knows that when you retreat into this place of magic, here above us, she will not be able to reach out and take you, your mate, or your unborn children. But she also knows that with you hiding in there and not able to fight, or at least not able to fight in all the places of your world at once, there will be virtually no effective opposition to her and her forces. There will be the sport of some opposition of course, but the Glee enjoy some resistance. People in places all over your world will not be able to withstand the attacks. The resistance

439

they put up will not be enough for your kind to survive.

"The goddess knows that your magic protects the magic of this world. If your offspring live, their magic will do the same.

"Yet, as you hide and protect them in this place, she will see that vulnerability and exploit it. With you stuck in there protecting your mate and offspring, it gives her and her followers an opening to come here to this world in mass to hunt and devour your kind until there are none left other than you and those few with you in this fortress of magic.

"Although you may in that way be able to preserve magic in your world, and the few people inside there with you, there will be no people left out in the rest of the world. They will all be dead. Your world will be a dead place."

Richard looked over at Vika. When she realized the full extent of what was in store for their world, some of the color had left her face. What was coming was no less than the cataclysmic end of everyone and everything.

Sang was right; even if they stayed and fought, they couldn't fight in every city, town, and village all over the world at the same time.

He might be wildly successful against the Glee he faced, but he was only one man in one place and could not face nearly all of them.

"I am afraid that I am not offering you the ability to return to this place and the people you love," Sang said. *"Once you destroy the device, it will not be possible for you to return to your home. But what I am offering you is the possibility of destroying the threat that otherwise will hunt down and slaughter everyone in your world. You have seen what they have already done, how many they have slaughtered, and what they are capable of. They know no mercy and will grant none.*

"They will not stop unless you come with me and stop them, and then destroy the device to prevent them from ever again coming to this world. You can only do those things in my world.

"What I am offering you is the possibility of saving the lives of those you love and everyone else in your world. I will not deceive you; that is all I am able to offer.

"I understand the sacrifice you will be making, but you must decide now because they will be coming soon and if you don't come with me and stop them there, it will be too late."

50

Richard stood unmoving, terrified at the thought of never being able to see Kahlan again. She was his world. He would never see their children, never be able to teach them and watch them grow. Never see them have the life he and Kahlan had fought so hard for them to have.

He would never see Kahlan's special smile and her beautiful green eyes again.

Richard had never been so frozen in fear and uncertainty before.

Through that fear, though, he realized that if he didn't do this, it would be the end of his world and the end of Kahlan and their children's world. If he didn't take this chance, how could he ever look Kahlan in the eye again once she knew he might have been able to stop the slaughter of everyone in their world, and he hadn't tried?

Richard looked over at Vika. "What do you think?"

She arched an eyebrow. "You are the Lord Rahl. You care about everyone in this world or you would not have sacrificed everything you did to win freedom for everyone. You fought those long wars for those who depend on you, and because you care that they have a life.

"I know you are going, and I know that nothing I could say would stop you. So why are you even asking me?

"But I am going with you and that is final. I will fight beside you in the struggle you face there, in that world, no less than I have in this world."

Richard swallowed as he nodded. She was right, of course. She would also be sacrificing everything she knew and the possibility of what the future might bring for her.

He had only entertained the idea of not going as he desperately tried to think of another solution, but deep down inside, just as Vika said, he knew that he had no choice. This was the only way of ending the threat. He had to go, no matter what it cost him, personally.

The lives of everyone in the D'Haran Empire were his responsibility. Not only that, but he cared that the people of his world could live their lives as they wished and in peace. The Grace told the story of each of their lives and it needed to live on. It was not simply a matter of being the Lord Rahl and it being his responsibility. He sincerely wanted people to be able to live their lives as they wanted, to achieve their hopes and dreams. If he didn't do this, they would know only terror and death.

He was still filled with questions, though. Some, he knew, had no answer, but at least some did.

"How did you get here from your world? You had to have used this device you spoke of, but isn't it guarded by the goddess or her followers? That device is their way to raid other worlds."

"The device is in a high place that is very dry," Sang said. *"No one guards it because no one uses it except the goddess and her followers. Only they wish to go to other worlds, so there is no reason to endure such a dry place except when they use*

the device. They know that it cannot be destroyed, so there is no reason that they would need to guard it.

"Other than her followers, I am the only one who has used it. I went to other worlds they raided to try to find help but I could find none until I saw you fight. I needed to use the device to come here to observe you and see if I thought you could possibly be the one to help stop this. I finally came to know that you are the one."

"So then you simply went up to where it is and used the device to come here?"

"Yes."

As Richard considered it, he thought that it made sense. "But the device is not here, in this world, or any of the worlds the goddess collects for hunting grounds. So how do you return to your world without the device to send you back?"

"It is hard to explain."

"Do your best."

"You have seen my kind when they fear being killed and they simply vanish?" Sang asked.

"Yes. They sort of turn all scribbly and then they disappear. We all assume they are returning to their own world."

Sang nodded. *"They were. When the device sends us somewhere, it creates a link to our minds. So, when I desire, because I am connected to it through my mind, the device knows my thought that I want to return, and it pulls me back. It does the same with all the Glee you have seen vanish."*

Richard grasped the general idea but couldn't imagine how it could work. It sounded like magic of some kind, a very powerful, advanced, and incomprehensible magic.

As if he could see that Richard was having trouble understanding it, Sang idly clacked his claws as he tried to think of a better way to explain it. *"The way to think of it is that we become attached to the device by a lifeline that it creates when it sends us to another world. Imagine if you went in dangerous water, and you suddenly wanted to go back to shore. When you called out, others pulled you back to shore by that lifeline. In much that way, when we want to go home, the device pulls us back by that lifeline."*

Richard nodded as he considered, still not entirely satisfied. "What you expect of me will not be so easy. If I agreed to come to your world with you, would those who believe as you do fight with me to defeat the goddess and her kind?"

Sang stared at him a long moment. *"I cannot say for sure. They are not fighters."*

"This is about their world and their way of life," Richard pointed out with a rising sense of angry frustration.

Sang nodded. *"You are a great leader in your world. Leaders become leaders because they are able to convince others to follow them. The goddess is like this. Although those with me are not fighters, I believe that they might be willing to follow you. At the very least, they can help you in many ways, such as getting you to the goddess and her followers."*

"I need a lot more than having them point me in the right direction." Richard drummed his fingers on the handle of his sword as he considered. "I think I can understand what you say about how you are able to go back. But how could Vika and I go there, too? We don't have that link, that lifeline as you called it, for the device to use to pull us there."

"That is the easy part. When a number of injured Glee returned, they confirmed a theory many of us have. One time when they attacked

447

your people, one of the women with you used magic to create snakes. Many of those snakes bit the Glee, and while we do not fear the snakes in our world, these snakes from your world were killing those Glee with venom. The snakes, once they bit into a Glee, would not let go. The Glee being bitten panicked, called on their lifeline, and the device pulled them back. All they needed to do was to merely think to return, and the device that had sent them was able to know that wish, and it snatched them back to our world."

"What about this theory you had?"

"The important part is that when they returned, the snakes were still holding on tight to them. That confirmed our theory that if I hold on to something from this world, it will return with me. I myself tested this by holding a rock when I returned, and it came to my world with me. This was also confirmed when some of the Glee returned with parts of your people for the Golden Goddess and their offspring to eat. Those body parts were also used to convince others to join with her."

Richard remembered quite vividly how the Glee down in the bowels of the People's Palace had dismembered many of the bodies.

"You are saying, then, that we would hold on

to you and we would go there with you to your world when you return? You think it is really that simple?"

Sang gave him a single nod. *"Yes."*

Richard considered for a moment. He couldn't imagine a device with such power, but then, on the other hand, he had sent those who didn't want to live with magic, including his half sister, to another world without magic. He also had used a device that created a star shift and sent their entire world to another place in the sky. He had seen devices, such as the boxes of Orden and the omen machine, that had unimaginable power, power over the world of life and the world of the dead, so he supposed that even if he hadn't seen the device the Glee had, he knew that such powerful devices existed. He didn't really know where most of those devices came from, or who could have made them. For all he knew, it might as well be these same gods.

He looked over at Vika. She simply shrugged.

"If I were to agree to this crazy idea, what would we have to do? Simply hold on to you and we would be pulled back with you?"

"More than that," Sang said as he stared at

Richard for a long moment with a haunted look in his big black eyes. *"It is more than simply being pulled back by a lifeline. There is more to it."*

"What do you mean?"

"We must go into darkness."

51

R ichard's brow tightened. "Into darkness?"
Sang nodded again. *"I am afraid that it
is the only way."*

"I don't understand. What do you mean we
have to go into darkness?"

Sang stared off again with a haunted look.
He seemed to be looking again into that place
that obviously frightened him.

"That is the only way I can say it for you," he
finally told them as he looked first at Vika and
then at Richard. *"There is no way I can explain
such a thing in a way that would make you truly
understand. The only way I can say it is that we
must go into darkness. It is what happens when
we use the device. Once you have done it, you will
understand. You will know what those words*

mean. If you have not done it, then there is no way for me to make you understand."

"Into darkness," Richard said as he stared at Sang.

Sang nodded. *"Into darkness. That is really the only way I can begin to describe it, yet the words are so hollow. Into darkness is something such as you have never experienced before. It seems to consume you. It is falling into darkness, and it is . . . terrifying. You think that it will never end, that it never could end. Each time I go into darkness, I fear that this is the time it will not end, and I will forever be in that place of darkness."*

Richard wondered if it was anything like the underworld.

"So," Richard finally asked, "is there a risk that we would be lost there, in that darkness? Especially since we aren't attached to the device by this lifeline?"

The Glee bowed. *"To find what you seek, you must sometimes go into the darkness, even though there is always the risk that you will become lost."*

Richard thought that was a pretty vague philosophical answer. It didn't really tell him anything. He shared a look with Vika. He had of course been to the world of the dead. For that matter, he had actually *been* dead and then managed to return. In a way, he had been pulled back by his connection to those still living. That was a place of eternal darkness. A lifeline of sorts had pulled him back.

He couldn't imagine any place or experience that could be darker than that, but he got the impression from what Sang said that this place might be darker even than the world of the dead. Although he didn't think that Sang had ever been to the underworld to judge the difference.

Vika had been to the cusp of that world. She had looked into the dark world of the dead. He could see by the haunted look in her eyes that she was remembering that experience.

"The longer you think about it," Sang said, *"the greater the risk grows that the others will go to the device in order to come here before they can be stopped. If we delay too long, we risk arriving as they come up to the device, and then you would have to battle them when you are disoriented from having just come out of darkness and into my world. That would not be good. All three of us could be killed before we are able even to run."*

Richard knew Sang was right. To have the element of surprise, they needed to get there and meet with those who were on his side first to come up with a plan. The longer he considered, the greater the risk grew that the goddess and her horde would arrive in Aydindril first.

Plus, he had no idea how confused he would be upon arriving in that world. He knew that when he came back to the world of life after being in the underworld, it was difficult to again get his bearings. Light and colors and sounds were all overwhelming at first.

But this sounded somehow worse. He found himself immobilized with fear. Not with fear of going into darkness, although if he knew exactly what that meant maybe he would fear it more, but with fear of leaving everyone he loved forever.

It was fear of never again being with Kahlan.

He just didn't know if he could do such a thing.

It would be a living suicide.

"If you say no," Sang said, *"I would not blame you. I don't know that I could come here to your world and never be able to go home. But if you are willing to do this to have a chance to save the*

people of your world, then the time is now upon us when we must act."

Richard steeled himself. He hooked his bow over one shoulder and his pack over the other. Vika hoisted her pack up over one shoulder.

Finally, Richard reached out with his left hand and put it firmly on Sang's right shoulder. His skin was cool, soft, and moist, more like the skin of a salamander than that of a person. He looked over at Vika. When their eyes met, each of them placed a hand on the other's shoulder; then she put her right hand on Sang's left shoulder.

Sang reached up and laid a claw over each of their shoulders. Once he had, they were all locked together into a circle of three—an important component of the Law of Nines, Richard reminded himself. He hoped that added bit of magic would help him and Vika survive going into darkness.

"Do it," Richard said. "Call your lifeline."

52

Almost as soon as he said it, he thought of Kahlan and wished he could call his words back. But at the same time he knew he had to be strong if Kahlan and everyone else in his world were to have a chance to live free of the Glee. Besides, even as he had the thought, it was already too late.

Everything all around him—the stone bridge, the forest, the Wizard's Keep above them and the city of Aydindril below—all started to look scribbly.

Only Vika and Sang seemed solid. The air itself had streaks of empty darkness slashing through it, as if the fabric of the world of life were shredded apart. The whole world around them was rapidly dissolving into scribbles as holes tore open into voids in the very reality of existence.

Those voids suddenly expanded explosively.

All light, all sound, and everything else that made up the world around him seemed to be sucked out of existence, ripped away, leaving a universe of nothingness. Not even Sang and Vika were there with him.

He was totally alone as he was sucked into that darkness.

It felt in a way like tripping in the darkest night and tumbling off a cliff.

Richard felt himself falling without end.

He kept expecting to hit the bottom, or to hit something. He knew he couldn't fall this long without soon slamming into something. His muscles tensed and his nerves burned with the agonizing expectation of that sudden, bone-shattering impact.

It was terrifying. An eternity of fear was compressed into every second that he felt himself helplessly falling into darkness.

That fear of hitting the bottom—or of falling forever—became everything.

Richard worked at talking himself out of the panic that was clawing at his emotions. He tried to see his hand but couldn't. He tried to touch it to his face, but he felt nothing, either from his hand or his face. He felt nothing at all.

He put all his effort into focusing on reasoning out what was happening. As he did, he realized that he wasn't really falling. Once he concentrated and tried to make sense of what he was feeling, or rather not feeling, he became aware that there was no down, no up, no hot, no cold, no light, and actually no sensation of any kind. It was complete and total suspension of all sensation. There was nothing other than his own, free-floating thoughts.

He couldn't feel anything that made him feel alive. He couldn't feel his heartbeat or his breathing or anything that made him feel that he existed at all anymore. In fact, it felt as if he didn't exist, as if he were merely thinking that he had once existed. It was even becoming hard to remember his world.

Rather than let himself be pulled under by the overwhelming emotion of feeling that he no longer existed, and since he had absolutely no control over what was happening, he let himself relax as he tried not to think.

He lost track of how long it had been, and

as he did, it began to feel like something he was all too familiar with: the eternity of the underworld. That place, too, was darker than dark, and it, too, went on forever.

But this was a different kind of darkness. Not only was it a physical darkness, it was also a kind of inner darkness. The totality of it was different from the underworld. This was not a sense of being in the world of the dead, but a void of existence itself. The only thing that seemed to exist was his thoughts.

In the underworld there had at least been constellations of souls and he had been able to will his soul to travel through them. Here, there was nothing to travel through and he was not able to will himself to go anywhere. There was no "there" within this darkness.

Suddenly, it ended.

Existence imploded in on him from all sides.

He felt his own weight, and with that, solid ground under his feet.

He opened his eyes and as scribbles all around him were just vanishing, he saw a strange world of desolation beneath a heavily clouded sky. All the clouds were different shades of dark red, darker and thicker the lower they were.

Ruddy rock rose up in towering, otherworldly formations, seemingly shaped by the hot, moist wind that swirled around them. The muddy-reddish clouds that rolled by low overhead looked almost like smoke.

Everything in this world was some shade of sullen red. Richard felt like he was looking out through a piece of red glass that tinted everything.

It made him wonder if his eyes or even his brain had somehow been damaged by the journey from his world and maybe they weren't working properly, and as a result he could now see things only in shades of red.

He breathed in deeply. The air was damp and warm. So damp that in comparison to his own world it was heavy, humid, and uncomfortable. It felt almost thick. He could see why Sang said that his world was a dry world. This was an oppressively clammy, sticky, and moist world. He already longed for dryness.

They were standing in an area of sand that reminded him very much of the area of white sand in the Garden of Life in the People's Palace. Although, the sand here looked white only in that it was less red than everything else.

With all the smooth, towering rock formations, it felt almost like an eerie cathedral of stone sculpted by wind and weather. That muggy wind moaned as it moved through the strange, smoothly curved surfaces of the rock.

Vika was still holding his shoulder on one side and Sang on the other. Their arms were all still locked together. It had seemed he was totally alone once he went into darkness, but that wasn't true. The other two had always been there with him, he just hadn't been aware of them.

He finally released Vika's shoulder, and she his as they straightened. He could tell by the look on her face that she had experienced the same thing he had coming to this brooding, reddish, windswept world. He let his hand drop away from Sang.

He leaned toward Vika and whispered, "What colors do you see?"

She looked around. "Everything looks red. At least my outfit fits right in."

Richard nodded. "That it does."

As he looked around, he could see from the clouds between the reddish rock formations that they were someplace high. Over the edge, down below them, the ground was obscured by the rolling, roiling clouds drifting swiftly by the high place where they were.

"Come," Sang said to them. *"We must get away from this dry place before the others come."*

He turned and made his way between some of the surrounding rock formations. They were striated in layers of different colors of dark brownish reds and looked like the wind had eroded the soft rock, making smooth, round depressions and curving edges. It was disorienting to look at.

Richard could see by the clouds down lower that they were high up in some kind of desolate, mountainous terrain. There was absolutely no vegetation. He remembered Sang saying that it was a dry place. The wind carried a lot of moisture and made a ghostly moaning sound through the strangely shaped rock formations. Apparently, the air, as damp as it was, was not damp enough for the Glee.

Trying to focus his eyes in this reddish world was giving him a headache. The sand he and Vika were on was the least red thing he could see.

"This is my home world," Sang said as he waved

an arm, urging them on, *"the home world of the Glee. We have arrived safely. Now we need to get down out of this place."*

53

"Where is the device?" Richard asked, grabbing Sang by his arm before he could leave. "Is that it?"

Sang stopped and looked across the sand to what Richard was pointing at: something that definitely did not belong in this strange, windblown landscape of organic shapes.

There, across the way on the edge of the sand, stood a square piece of stone, each side about the length of his arm from his shoulder to his fingertips. It wasn't tall. It wouldn't quite come up to his rib cage. The top was slanted, so that if you stood before the stone at the edge of the sand on the other side, you would have been able to have a good look at that slanted top, but Richard couldn't see it from where he was.

The stone looked smooth, but not smooth in the same way the sculpted rock all around them was smooth. This thing was absolutely square and straight on all sides. And while it was smooth, it was not polished like so much of the stone in palaces.

With everything some shade of red it was hard to tell what color it might actually be, but Richard thought it would be dull gray in his own world. There were markings all over the stone. He was too far away to know what kinds of markings they were, but he could see that they covered the entire stone.

Richard wondered if he should draw his sword and destroy the device before the goddess could send more Glee to his world.

As if reading his thoughts, Sang was gesturing urgently. *"Hurry. We must get away from this place for now and get to those who side with me, against the goddess. I told them about you and said that I was going to see if I could get you to come back with me. They will be waiting."*

Richard and Vika followed Sang as he rushed off between the labyrinth of smooth, flowing shapes of the towering rocks surrounding the white sand. Once they were through the meandering gaps in the rock walls, the descent rapidly became steep. There was a path of sorts between the standing forest of rocks, at times with crude steps cut into the soft rock.

Below them, Richard could see a thick blanket of clouds covering the ground far into the distance.

As they moved down from the place with the device that sat at the edge of the area of sand, they gradually descended into that dark reddish cloud. As the visibility grew less and less, it was similar to moving down into clouds below high places in the mountains in Richard's world, and having those clouds turn to a dense fog once you were inside them. It was the same here, except the fog was a dirty reddish color.

The farther down they went, the wetter the air became with mist. At some point, the mist turned to drizzle. Even before the drizzle, the heat and humidity had Richard's shirt soaking wet.

Vika unbuckled some leather straps so that she could open her outfit at the neck. This was definitely not a place to be wearing leather, although the red fit right in. In fact, the red leather stood out brightly in the murky red world.

Sang looked relieved when they finally got into the heavier drizzle. He used his wrists to rub the water collecting on his arms around on his body, seeming to luxuriate in the wetness that he had missed for so long. He looked back at them and drew his lips back to show his teeth.

Vika glanced at Richard, wondering what it could mean.

"I think he is showing us a smile," he whispered to her.

She gave him a look of silent incredulity.

If it really was a smile, it was about as grotesque a smile as he had ever seen.

After about a couple hours of moving quickly down slopes of loose scree that slid out from underfoot, over ledges and down through canyons of towering rock walls, and then over yet more rock, but this time harder and more jagged, they emerged from the bottom of the cloud cover into a strange, wet-looking world. The ground for as far as Richard could see was relatively flat. The only mountainous area was behind them, as was the one they had just climbed down from out of the clouds. Haze and drizzle made the visibility toward the horizon poor, but he didn't see any hills or mountains off that way.

There was scattered, low vegetation among open swampy areas, and there were a lot of rather tall plants that resembled lush ferns. Mostly roundish rocks, most small, covered much of the ground where there wasn't the water or areas of the low vegetation. Among those small rocks were a few smooth, round rocks no bigger than about the right size to sit on. The rocks covered most of the dry areas above the water. In fact, they littered the ground endlessly. Some of the expanses of water in the distance looked larger, but most of the water nearby was in patchy areas much like the swamps he had seen before, but without the trees.

In the distance were peculiar trees with long, crooked, bare trunks. High up each tree had a single, dense clump of leaves. Widely spaced here and there, the trees seemed to march across the landscape beneath the cloudy red sky. They were the strangest-looking trees Richard had ever seen. None, though, were very close.

Flocks of birds moved through the air like current in a raging river. As some swept down closer, he could see that they weren't actually birds. They were large bats flying in colonies.

As they reached the bottom of the climb, Sang walked right into the first body of water he could get to until it was up to his neck. Richard could see several snakes writhing just below the surface of the water. Sang stretched out and swam for a bit, as if to refresh himself.

"Sang! There are snakes in the water!" Vika called out in alarm.

Sang kept swimming for a moment before turning back to them. *"Don't worry. The snakes are friendly."*

"Friendly? What if they bite you?" she asked.

"They eat small insects. They don't bite us and they do not have venom, like the snakes in your world. The only animals that sometimes cause harm to us are the boars. They are big and mean, and sometimes even kill Glee."

"Boars?" Richard asked. "You mean you have wild boars?"

"They live in the muddy places." Sang gestured off beyond the immediate swampy water. *"But sometimes they attack us. They are dangerous. They are big with tough hides our claws can't cut through and have sharp tusks, bigger than our*

claws. We must always watch for wild boars when we are not in the water. They like the mud, but they don't go near the water."

He then busied himself at the edge of the water, dredging up water plants with round nodules dotting their entire length. They were a sickly green color, with a slight iridescence to them. When he had an armful, he flopped them over on the rocks.

"Float weed," he told them.

As soon as he was free of his load of float weed, he started using his claws to pry at a large, flat snail stuck tight to a rock at the waterline.

"This is a muscle snail," he announced as he worked at prying it away from the rock. *"I want you to be able to try our delicious food."*

Richard thought the place smelled rather rank, like most any swamp he had been in; not as bad as some, worse than others. Vika looked around at the strange and forbidding reddish desolation, then looked over at him and spoke in a low voice that Sang wouldn't hear.

"He's right. This place is an absolute paradise."

Richard half huffed a laugh in answer.

"Sang," he said, "we're not hungry right

now. More importantly, we don't have time for this. We need to stop the goddess before she sends her hordes to my world to kill people. You said that there were those of your kind who wanted to see me if I returned with you."

Sang blinked up at him, then walked up onto the rocks. The water sluiced off him as he emerged from the swampy water, some of the string algae draped over a shoulder.

"Yes, you are right. My apologies. I was just so happy to be home that I wasn't thinking. I was eager to show you some of the wonderful things about my world, so that you would not be so afraid that you must remain here."

"Where are the others?" Richard asked, getting right down to business as he scanned the other swampy areas. They were dark, and it would be hard to see any Glee if they were in the water. "We need to talk to those who believe as you."

Sang stretched up on his webbed toes and peered into the distance. He pointed with a claw.

"There are some of them over there, on those rocks, harvesting muscle snails. I will go talk to them and ask them to gather the others right away."

"Good," Richard said, as he took Vika's arm and guided her up onto some of the rocks that were a bit flatter and easier to stand on without their ankles twisting.

In the distance, he could just make out the dark shapes of other Glee near the edge of some of the swampy areas. They were hauling up float weed. In other places he saw a few Glee swimming through larger bodies of water. They were so graceful in the water that they hardly disturbed the surface.

Richard was beginning to feel frustrated and annoyed. He had come to stop the Golden Goddess from sending the Glee to slaughter the people in his world. He and Vika had given up their futures—their lives—in order to accomplish that vital mission.

He hadn't known that he was going to end up playing mother hen trying to gather up groups of distracted Glee.

54

S ang met with Glee that were close by. They kept staring over at Richard and Vika. He then went off to talk to others. A crowd of Glee began to come over, gathering around Richard and Vika. The way they blinked as they leaned toward him and stared, they were making him feel like some kind of curious specimen.

By the time Sang returned with yet more of the Glee, a crowd of large black heads had spread out before him. They watched him, looking like maybe they expected he might fly, or breathe out flames or something. As they all crowded in around him, they made a kind of low hiss as they looked around at each other, as if mumbling, but he didn't hear any words in his head. Richard thought they must be talking to each other and they chose not to let the words come into his mind.

Richard and Vika shared a look, not knowing what to expect.

Sang finally stepped through the gathering of tall, black creatures. He held his claws in tight to his stomach so as not to accidentally catch on them, and they did the same as they allowed him to pass. Sang turned to the Glee assembled before them and held out a claw toward Richard and Vika as he waited for all those gathered to fall silent and pay attention.

Richard watched all the Glee, still wary. He was trusting Sang's word that they wanted his help, and that this wasn't some trick to get him away from his own people so they could eliminate him. He didn't really think that was the case, but he studied all the Glee before him, one at a time, looking at each face for any hint of trouble.

"These are the ones I spoke of," Sang finally announced. *"This is Lord Rahl with the weapon he carries on his hip, and the female is Vika, one of his warriors. Unlike us, their females fight alongside the males, and I can tell you, from having watched them fight, that this female is deadly.*

"They both have given up their lives and those they care for, given up any hope of ever returning to their world, in order to come here to finally stop the Golden Goddess and her followers. Lord Rahl has even given up caring for his new offspring not yet come into the world in order to come here to protect his world and ours."

This news seemed to create a lot of conversation that he and Vika couldn't hear, but he could imagine it well enough as Glee faced one another, nodding among themselves and occasionally glancing up at him and Vika.

Their animated gestures finally subsided until no one seemed to be saying anything, unless they were talking to Sang and only he could hear them in his mind. Richard didn't especially like the way the Glee could choose for others to hear them or not. He worried that if they were saying anything threatening, he wouldn't have any idea that he was suddenly on the verge of being attacked. If that were the case, there was nothing he could do about it before it happened.

"If we are to stop the goddess," Richard said aloud to get their attention, "we are going to need your help."

That seemed to send a fright through the group. A number of them started slowly moving back. A few at the edges of the crowd slipped into the water and glided away.

"They are afraid," Sang explained. *"These are not fighters, like the others. They are against what the others do, but they are not fighters. They don't like cruelty."*

Richard looked out at the sea of inky faces watching him. At least they weren't showing their teeth. As he scanned the group, he paid particular attention to one individual near the front. He was standing just behind a few others.

Richard pointed to that one. "You. Come here."

All the Glee looked confused. The Glee Richard had pointed to glanced around self-consciously but didn't move.

Richard stepped down off the rock he was standing on and gently urged several Glee in the front out of his way. Before anyone knew what was happening, he snatched the Glee he had been watching by the wrist, above the claw, before he could slip away.

The Glee twisted and turned first one way and then another as he tried to back away from

Richard's grip. Richard turned the wrist over and increased the pressure on it. He was glad to find that it had the same effect on the Glee as it did on people: it forced the Glee to his knees.

"What are you doing?" Sang's voice in his head sounded frantic and frightened.

55

Richard twisted the Glee's wrist harder. Doing so worked just as well as it did on a man, causing the Glee to squeal in pain as he cringed before him on his knees. Richard continued to apply pressure to keep him immobilized.

"This one here is a spy sent by the Golden Goddess," he announced to the shocked crowd.

At his words, the mass of Glee all moved back away from the one Richard had by the wrist as they hissed in fear, confusion, or Richard didn't really know what.

"She sent this one to watch the Glee she considers traitors to her kind. She considers all of you a threat. This one was watching and then intended to report back to her on what he heard you saying. Once he did, it would only be a matter of time before she moved against you."

Sang looked confused as he glanced around at the others watching them. *"What are you doing? What makes you think this?"*

Richard showed Sang a small smile. "He doesn't have the green sheen to his skin that all the rest of those gathered here have. This one does not eat flutter weed, float weed, and muscle snails. He eats the flesh of those from other worlds."

Along with everyone else, Sang stared at the Glee Richard had on his knees. *"Is this true?"*

"No!" the Glee screamed in Richard's mind and, he was sure, in the minds of all the Glee gathered around, watching.

"You are lying," Richard said as he gave Vlka a meaningful look.

Without hesitation she spun her Agiel up into her fist. She went to one knee to get down closer to the Glee, and without a moment's hesitation she gritted her teeth and rammed her Agiel into his midsection.

The Glee shrieked out loud, twisting, trying to get away, but Richard held him tight with pressure on his wrist as Vika kept the pressure on her Agiel. She finally pulled back away.

She leaned in, then, putting her face close to the Glee. "Tell everyone what you are doing here."

"I don't know what you are talking about," the Glee cried out in their heads. *"I am no spy! I am not with the goddess!"*

"We don't do this kind of thing to one another," Sang said as he held his arms out, trying to urge Vika and Richard to stop. *"This is not the way we behave to each other."*

Vika looked back over her shoulder, giving Sang the kind of look that only a Mord-Sith in a rage could give. He went silent as he backed up a step.

"We gave up our lives to come here," she said. "Lord Rahl gave up his wife and children who are about to be born to come here. He can never return home. All for you, all for the Glee. All to help you stop your own kind from killing and destroying your way of life. We are doing this as much for you as for the lives in our world. And I have to tell you, after sacrificing my life and my world, I am definitely not in the mood to be lied to."

"I would tell her what she wants to know,"

Richard told the Glee he was keeping on his knees.

The Glee defiantly shook his head.

Vika reacted by ramming her Agiel into his midsection again. The Glee twisted and shrieked. The first time had been a warning to talk. She held it there longer the second time and pressed it in harder. When she finally pulled it away, the Glee sagged, one arm raised up only because Richard had a firm grip on his wrist. Tears of agony ran from his big black eyes.

Vika held the Agiel up before the panting Glee's face. "The next time, unless you start answering our questions truthfully, I am going to shove this in your eye, blinding it, and when you don't answer, I will blind your other eye. If you still don't—"

The Glee held up his other claw. *"No! Please! I will tell you what you want to know."*

Richard lifted up on the arm, still putting pressure on the wrist, until the Glee was standing on trembling legs. "I want you to tell everyone the truth of what you are doing here."

The Glee looked around. He glanced timidly at Vika before beginning.

"The Golden Goddess sent me, just as this one

said. *She is gathering a large force to begin a mass attack.*" With a claw he gestured out at the crowd. "*She considers all of you traitors because you do not support her. You are traitors! She has promised those with her that she is going to let them hunt you for the sport of it and then eat you all. She will no longer tolerate any of you who talk to her followers, trying to get them to change their ways. She believes it would be better if you and your offspring were all dead.*"

Loud hissing that Richard took for a kind of collective gasp of shock spread through all the Glee watching. They clacked their teeth and claws, apparently in a display of anger.

"Why are you here, now?" Richard asked.

"*A spy up near the mountain saw that Sang was bringing two of the creatures from the other world down to here. The goddess sent me to find out your plans so that she might stop you. She is very angry. She wants your blood.*"

"I would be glad to tell her my plans," Richard said to the Glee. "In fact, I want you to go back and tell her my plans."

The Glee nodded eagerly. "*Yes, I will tell her what you say.*"

"Do you know who I am?"

The Glee shrugged a little. *"The one they call Lord Rahl?"*

"Yes, that and more," Richard said for all to hear. "I am also the one called *fuer grissa ost drauka.*"

"Fuer grissa ost drauka? I don't know what that means."

"It means 'the bringer of death.' I want you to tell your Golden Goddess that besides being *fuer grissa ost drauka*, I was born a war wizard. War is my calling. I live for fighting wars."

The Glee nodded furiously. *"Yes, I will tell her."*

"I want you to also tell the Golden Goddess that she has sent her kind to my world to kill us. Because of her, I have gone into darkness.

"Now I am here, and I mean to make war."

"Yes," the Glee said, still nodding. *"I will tell her your words."*

"I want you to also tell her that I demand she surrender her world to me."

The Glee winced a little as he shrank back as much as he could with Richard still holding pressure on his wrist. *"Surrender her world? What should I tell her are your conditions?"*

"No conditions. Her surrender must be unconditional. There will be no negotiations.

483

If she does not surrender her world unconditionally, I will come and kill her and all of her followers."

The Glee seemed to wince a little as he nodded again. *"I will tell her.* Fuer grissa ost drauka. *The bringer of death. She must surrender our world unconditionally. I will tell her."*

"One more thing."

"Yes?"

"Tell her that I am going to enjoy hunting and killing her."

Richard suddenly released the Glee's wrist. As he did, and before the Glee could leave, he drew his sword. The rage of the sword's magic instantly surged through him. The unique sound of steel rang out across the swampy water. Before anyone could say anything or had a chance to move, the blade flashed through the air and lopped off the Glee's claw.

The Glee stumbled back in shock, clutching the arm without a claw to his chest with the other as he shook.

"You tell the Golden Goddess that her kind has shown my kind no mercy, and I will show her none. Now go before I take your head in addition to your claw."

56

Richard watched the Glee stagger away and then gradually break into an awkward, stumbling run. As he watched the Glee leaving, he felt the magic of the sword pounding through him, matched by his own anger at how many people the followers of the Golden Goddess had killed in his world. He raged at what they had done to Kahlan's life, to his, and the lives of countless others left without a loved one. He finally slid the sword back into its scabbard to extinguish its fury.

He was glad, though, to learn that the sword's magic had joined with his and had worked in this world. His bond had also worked to power Vika's Agiel. It had confirmed that his own gift would function in this alien place. If he knew how to call upon it at will, that would be even better, but he had rarely been able to do that. He was relieved, however, that even though there were only the two of them, at least his magic would be there for him if he was in desperate need. He hoped that would be enough to see them through what lay ahead.

He turned back and looked out over the stunned crowd of Glee watching him.

"That Glee, had he not been discovered, would have betrayed you all. You could all have lost your lives before you even realized that the goddess was planning to send her followers to kill you. Now that you know they don't have the same greenish iridescence as all of you have, you need to be on the lookout for others. There is no telling if the goddess might have sent more than that one among you."

The Glee all looked around at those nearby.

"We will do as you say and watch for them," Sang said.

"I need to know the lay of the land and where the goddess and her followers are," Richard told them.

"It is some distance that way," Sang said as he pointed in the direction the lone Glee had

run off into the thick brownish-red haze that continually drifted past. *"She and her followers are off that way. It is an isolated area. There is only one way into the place where they are. There is not a lot to eat in that location, like there is here, but it is well protected. She does not care about what there is to eat there because her followers prefer to eat creatures from other worlds rather than the food our world has always provided for us.*

"But now that you have sent her spy back without a claw, she will be angry, and she will be expecting you to come for her. Her followers will be on alert and massed to protect her. I don't see how it would be possible to attack her now that you have told her that you will be coming for her."

Richard briefly glanced into the distance where Sang had pointed. "There is only one way in?"

Sang nodded. *"Yes. She chose that place because there is but the one way in, so it is easy to defend, should any others think to take her power."*

"Or think to end her ideas of taking other worlds," Richard said.

Sang nodded along with a few others. *"She will be preparing for you and prepared to protect the place."*

TERRY GOODKIND

Richard rested a fist on his hip again, thinking, as he looked off in the direction Sang had indicated. It was a gloomy, reddish landscape of swamps and low vegetation. In the distance there were more of the strange tall trees with the leaves in tight clumps at the tops of their long, crooked trunks. Colonies of the large bats flew among the trees.

In the far distance he could also see some higher ground, along with some imposing cliffs. He presumed that higher ground must be what protected access to where she and her followers were gathered. He looked back at Sang.

"What do you mean, there is only one way in? Why? Why can't we go around to come in another way, on another side?"

Sang and all the other Glee seemed to shrink back a little. *"It is impossible to go around and come in from another way."*

"You already said that. Why is it impossible?"

"Because," Sang said with a kind of whine that Richard could hear in his head along with the words, *"that way is far too barren and dry. Nothing grows there, and there is no water. None of us could survive there. We would die."*

"What do you mean, you would die? You

488

came to my world, and you said that was dry. You didn't die there."

Sang shook his head with conviction. *"This is a different kind of dry place. Do you remember the sand we were standing on when we came back from darkness?"*

"Yes. What of it?"

"All around the place where the Golden Goddess and her followers live is that kind of ground. Sand, as you call it. Nothing but sand and many towers of rock. In between those high rock walls there are hills of sand. Expanses of wind-driven sand make up all the ground there. When the wind comes up stronger, it creates a storm of sand and wind on the ground. Nothing can survive there."

Richard nodded. "Good. Then that's the way we will go."

There were gasps from the Glee and they turned to one another, seeming to murmur their fears. Richard ignored their obvious concern and instead squatted down and pushed some of the smaller rocks aside to clear an area of muddy ground.

"Here, draw a map for me. Show me where everything is located in relation to us."

Sang leaned in and looked at the bare ground. *"I don't know what you mean."*

Richard pointed out at the areas of swampy water, then drew a quick map of the ponds in the sandy dirt. "Like this. A picture on the ground of where places are. See this?" He pointed again out at the nearby landscape. "I have drawn a map, a picture on the ground, of where the water is"—he gestured—"out that way. See each of the areas of water I drew?"

Sang and the others looked back at the water, then leaned in to peer down at the map Richard had drawn on the ground.

"I see what you mean, now," Sang said.

Richard smoothed out the ground, covering the map he had just sketched. "Now, you draw a map of where we are, where the goddess is, and the kind of land around her place—what is the area of dry sand. Try your best to show their relative sizes."

Sang squatted down and lifted one single claw out and away from the other two, like pointing with a finger. Richard hadn't known they had that much dexterity with their claws. Sang then used the single claw to sketch out a lay of the land. All the while he was drawing, he pulled his lips back over his sharp teeth, the way some people stick out a tongue when drawing.

"This," Sang finally said, tapping the ground with the single claw, *"is the area of sand and tall rock. Here are mountains that are too high to climb. Here, on this side, is the way that the goddess and her followers go in and out of her place to then go to the mountain with the device they use to travel to other worlds. All of this, around here, is the impassable area of sand. We would die if we tried to go that way to get to the place where they are gathered."*

Richard studied the map and then tapped a finger on the area that Sang said was impassable. "Good. We will go in this way. They won't be expecting us."

All the Glee gathered around looked at each other, again hissing their fright. Sang held up his claws to ward off the very notion of Richard's idea.

"You can go that way to kill the goddess if it is your choice, but we cannot guide you into her place if you wish to go that way around. Besides, even if we could go that way with you, we are not fighters. This is why I asked you to come to our world to kill the goddess. I have seen you fight. We,

*here, cannot fight the way you do, or the way those
with the goddess have learned to fight and kill. We
are peaceful."*

Richard raked his fingers back through his
hair as he let out a sigh of angry frustration.
"Look, I intend to do my best, as I said I would.
I have proven my willingness to help end this
threat to both of our worlds by coming here, to
your world, with you. But this is not my fight
alone. It is your fight as well."

"But we cannot—"

"This is about your future more than mine."
Richard gestured off in the direction of the
goddess and her followers. "You heard what
that spy said. The goddess intends to slaughter
and eat all of you for disrespecting her. What if I
die in the attempt to kill her? Then what? What
will you do then? Just let them kill you all?

"Brutal leaders like the Golden Goddess
cannot long tolerate those who don't believe,
follow, and do as they are told. She views all
of you as a disease that could spread to her
followers if she does not cut you out before she
loses any of her followers and then her power.
She cannot allow you to live. She will send
her followers for you and they will kill every

one of you, along with your females and your offspring. You don't need to believe me. You all heard what that spy said.

"I have fought wars before, and this one is really not all that different. Such brutal leaders always seek to eliminate any who don't believe in their cause.

"You all are a bigger threat to her than I am. If I am killed, she continues to rule. But if you are not eliminated, you all pose a continual threat that could make her followers turn on her. Leaders need the support of those they lead. All of you threaten to cause her to lose her support. For that reason, she must kill all of you.

"It is not up to me to do it for you. You all must be a part of your own futures if you want to protect not only your own lives, but the lives of your offspring. If you do not help me, your offspring will have no future."

One of the Glee in front gestured to be heard. *"You told that spy that you are a war wizard, the bringer of death. You said that war fighting is what you were born to do. We are not war fighters. We were not born to do this. This is something you alone must do. We cannot fight."*

Richard fought back his urge to yell some sense into them.

"I realize that," he told them, trying to maintain his patient, reasoning tone, "but you all need to listen to me. You are a gentle race. You are peaceful. You love your young. You do not wish to harm others.

"I understand all of that because I was once very much like you. I did not want to fight. I learned hard lessons that if I stand aside, then those I love lose everything. They lose their lives. I have seen many good friends die.

"I learned that to save those I love, and even others who believe in peace as I do, as you do, I had to fight even though I did not wish to fight. I am telling you this from my harsh experience. If you wish to survive, you must fight for your own lives. I can help a great deal, but I can't do everything for you. This is about your lives, and the lives of your kind. If you don't take your world back from the goddess, she will take everything from you.

"She already has plans to come and kill you all, so, in a way, you all are already dead. Your only choice now is to decide to live."

57

S ang looked around at the silent Glee watching them. They seemed to be shaken by
Richard's words as they looked at one another,
but Richard didn't hear their voices. At least
they weren't running away. He wondered if
they were talking among themselves or voicing
their objections to Sang alone, or maybe even
arguing among themselves and they didn't want
him to hear.

It was even possible that they were all about
to decide that they couldn't, or wouldn't, fight
and in the end they would all walk away, leaving
it to him. He couldn't do this alone with only
Vika to help him. He feared that they were so
shaken by all they had heard that they would
end up saying no. He knew that once the Glee

had made that switch to hunting and killing, they lost all reluctance, but these Glee had not made that transition to being killers.

He knew that he might be able to kill the goddess, but that would not by itself stop the beliefs that she and her followers held. If these Glee would not fight for their own lives, then in the end, the most realistic thing he could do would be to save the people in his own world by destroying the device that allowed them to go to different worlds to hunt people. That might be enough to save his world, but it would not save this one, and he and Vika were going to have to live out their lives in this world.

Finally Sang turned back to Richard, as if having heard what the others had all had to say. *"Lord Rahl, we understand and appreciate the very meaningful sacrifice you have made to save your kind, and your world, as well as to help save our world and preserve our way of life. We have helped you in coming here so that you might stop the goddess and save your world. We also understand the threat the goddess poses to our lives.*

"But even if we agreed to do this, you must understand that we would die out there in those barren, dry, empty lands. It is too far for us to

travel away from here, away from the water where
we gather our food and live. We could not survive
out there. We would die."

"And what you need to understand is that I
know about fighting wars. I'm telling you, if the
goddess believes there is only one way in, then
that is the only place she will guard and the only
place they will stand ready to fight. If we could
instead go in behind where they least expect us,
and surprise them—"

"I am telling you, we could not do it," Sang
said, lifting his arms in frustration. *"We would*
die out there."

"Not necessarily," Richard said.

Sang shook his head in apparent exasperation.
"We cannot go that way and hope to live to fight
them."

Richard smiled. "That's what the goddess
believes. That is why it would give us the
element of surprise on our side, and surprise is
one of the best weapons you could have in a
fight. Surprise will help all of you prevail even
though you are not experienced at fighting. It
would be even better if we could come in at
night. When does it get dark here?"

Sang hissed his frustration that Richard just

didn't seem to get the point. He gestured to the sky. *"There is always at least some light in the sky. When the sun goes down, there are moons that provide light."*

"Moons?" Richard asked. "How many moons are there?"

"Two. It does get darker when the sun goes down, but with the light of the twin moons it never gets to be such a dark night like it sometimes does in your world."

"Is that when they sleep? When the sun goes down and it's darker?"

"Yes. When the sun goes down and day grows still, we all sleep then. When night comes, we sleep partly in the water to stay wet, and also to be safe. The wild boars like the mud, but they are afraid of water, so they won't come right up to the banks to attack us."

"How much longer until then?" he asked. "Until they sleep?"

Sang looked to the sky, shielding his eyes with one claw. With such thick, continually heaving and rolling clouds, it was hard to tell where the sun was, but apparently the Glee had learned how to judge it. Sang thought a moment, trying to think of a way to explain it. Finally he did.

"You know how long it took us to come here from the device on the mountain? It will be the quiet time when the Glee sleep in probably three of those journeys. That long. We have never crossed the drylands, but it would be at least two days and nights. We could not survive that long there."

Richard pinched his bottom lip as he considered. It was a problem that it wasn't darker at night. Still, if the goddess and her followers were asleep, that helped. He consulted the map Sang had drawn on the ground, and again looked at the sky.

"Then we must go now, around the way they would not expect us, in order to arrive at their place when it is dark," he announced to the crowd watching him.

Sang shook his head along with many of those in the crowd watching. *"You are not listening to my words. We would die, so we can be of no help to you in fighting them if we go that way. If you wish to go that way, then you and Vika will have to go alone."*

"If there was a way that you could cross the drylands, without getting too dry or suffering, would you all agree to come with me, show me the way, and fight with me against them?

If there was a way, would you help me for your survival and your world?"

Sang looked around. A number of the Glee finally nodded. Richard knew that they were probably all nodding because they felt it was impossible, so they could easily commit to something they thought they would never have to do.

Sang shrugged. *"If there was a way, then yes. But there is no way for us to do this, so we cannot go with you."*

Now Richard knew for sure that he had just gotten them to commit to something they all thought was impossible. It was easy to agree when you never thought it was possible and so you wouldn't have to do it. He was about to use that commitment to his advantage.

He looked over at the pile of float weed Sang had pulled up before and thrown on the rocks. He turned back to Sang.

"I would like you to show me the water plants you use to get the jelly that protects you when you travel to my world."

"The scrum?" Sang asked.

"Yes," Richard said. "Collect a big pile of the scrum plants for me."

58

Richard watched as a few dozen or so of the Glee waded through the swampy water, bending down and pulling up water weeds here and there. As they collected it, they threw their loads on the bank beside the pile of float weed.

While they were doing that, he directed others to collect more of the float weed and an even bigger pile of flutter weed. They had no idea why he wanted them to do it, and he knew that they possibly thought he was crazy, but as he and Vika watched, they all went along with his odd request and collected the water plants. As they worked, the piles grew quite large. Every time they asked if they had gathered enough, he had them continue adding more to the piles.

As the Glee brought ever more of the water weed up onto the bank, Richard finally squatted down and pulled some of the scrum plants from the pile. The plant was tough and fibrous, and almost transparent. The broad, flat blades were almost as wide as his fingers would be if he spread them all the way out. Each piece was longer than he was tall, and a relatively uniform width.

The most remarkable thing about it, though, was how slimy the long blades were. If he pulled one through his fingers, he could collect globs of the sticky, gelatinous coating. The broad leaves themselves remained quite slimy despite some of the coating being removed.

The other plant, the float weed, had groups of nodules that apparently caused the ends of the plant to float, probably so that they could reach up to get more sun. Below the nodules, the broad blades of the plant were almost as wide as the scrum, but it was only slightly slimy, as was any plant growing in water, and the leaf texture was thick and strong. It was hard to tear.

The flutter weed was similar to the float weed, but without the nodules and even more flexible.

Both sides of the broad blades were wavy, but they were pliable enough that they could easily be flattened out.

Richard looked up at the puzzled Glee watching him. "I need the help of one of you so I can demonstrate what we are going to do."

Looking around at the others and not seeing any more volunteers, one of the Glee finally stepped forward. *"I am Iben, Lord Rahl. I will help you. What would you like me to do?"*

Richard stood, bringing up a bundle of scrum plants in one hand. "I would like you to simply stand there so I can demonstrate to everyone that it is possible to protect yourselves so that you can survive a good long time in any dry land."

Iben shared a look with Sang before finally coming up to stand in front of Richard. Richard immediately began layering the slimy scrum plants over and around Iben's body. Next he wrapped his arms and legs with lengths of the wet, slippery plant. He draped some over Iben's large, black head and around his chin and then around his neck. He directed the others watching to pay attention as he explained how to lay down the strands to weave the long plants together in order to give them more strength together and hold them in place.

All the Glee watching were fascinated. Richard thought that since they so enjoyed being wet, this must be something that felt luxurious to them. A few of the Glee stepped up to help by smoothing down the scrum in a few places or filling in missing spots. As they did, Iben made a low, guttural, cooing sound.

"Now," Richard told his eager audience, "over the top of the scrum, we are going to do the same thing with the float and flutter weed. On the flutter weed, pull off the round nodules, like this. We don't want that part of the plant. We only want the long, broad parts."

When he did, several of the Glee scooped up the discarded nodules and tossed them in their mouths. He could hear them softly pop as the Glee chewed them.

As they watched, Richard began covering Iben in the same way he had done with the scrum plants, but this time covering it over with the thicker types of water weeds. He wove the layers together so that they had strength in all directions.

"How does this feel, Iben?" he asked.

"Actually, quite wonderfully wet."

"Good. Now, walk around to make sure it stays put."

Another Glee called out for them to wait. Soon, it brought long, thin, flexible vines out of the water. They were about as thick as string, but stronger.

"Use this," the Glee said. *"Put it around and around to help hold the scrum, flutter weed, and float weed in place."*

Together Richard and the one who had brought the vine used it to quickly weave a net of sorts to help hold the water weeds down on Iben. Richard remembered quite well how the gelatinous material always slid off the Glee when they arrived in his world. Now the flutter and float weed, layered over scrum, kept the slime against Iben's skin so it couldn't slide off.

Richard gestured. "Move around. Run and bend." Iben hopped about, following the instructions. "See how well it stays in place?"

Iben demonstrated his new suit of water weed to the others, walking among them so they could inspect it. It worked better than Richard had dared hope.

"Now, I want all of you to do the same thing

with each other. Put the scrum on first, as I showed you, and then the other weeds over the top both to hold it in place and to keep it from drying out. This way, even if the top layers of flutter weed dry out, it won't matter because underneath it will still be wet and comfortable."

The Glee were all eager to try both being the one wrapped and the one doing the wrapping. It almost seemed a game to them, something new and unheard of. They cooed excitedly.

With an eye to the sky, keeping track of the day and how much time they had before dark, Richard saw that the afternoon was wearing on. He urged them to hurry. If Sang's map was at all accurate, it was a long journey across the drylands, and Richard wanted to arrive at the enemy camp while they were still asleep.

It never ceased to surprise him just how much dexterity the Glee actually had with their big claws. They could pinch the first two on one hand together to hold things, much like fingers. Of course, without thumbs, it was still somewhat difficult, but they managed and were obviously good at it. In fact, maybe because they were used to handling the water weeds, they were faster at it than Richard had been. Along the way, they perfected the weaving technique, making the suits of water weed fit snugly yet still allow them freedom to move.

As they worked at wrapping each other, more of the Glee collected the water plants needed. Before long they had an entire trade in full swing. The Glee found the wrapping exciting and interesting. None voiced any complaints. He knew that when they came to his world, if they became too dry, they could always activate their lifeline and return to their own wet world. Out in the drylands, they would not have that ability.

He was sure that somewhere along the line, they had to have figured out what he had in mind, and why he was doing this, but if they had, none of them balked or refused to join in.

As they worked, he realized it was building a sense of camaraderie, like soldiers working on their armor to get each other ready for combat.

He hoped they would maintain that sense of spirit when they headed out into the drylands, and even more so, when they met the enemy.

As they were wrapped, the Glee drew their lips back to show him a kind of frightening smile. He returned a similar smile, hoping it satisfied them despite his not being able to quite match the display of teeth.

Sang came up to him, completely wrapped from head to toe. *"I am amazed by this, Lord Rahl. I thought crossing the drylands would be impossible for us, but I really think this will work. Not only now, but in the future, after we are rid of the goddess, this will give us a way to expand our world and discover new places and more food."*

Richard put a hand on Sang's slimy shoulder. "I'm glad to hear it. But the day is wearing on. We must hurry. We need to get to the goddess's followers while they are still there and before they leave to come here. We still have a long way to go."

Sang nodded. *"As you say, we must get started, then. You are right that it is a long way around through the drylands in order to get to the place the goddess holds. Unfortunately, none of us has ever traveled there, so we are not exactly sure of what that place is like or what we might encounter there.*

"We will not be able to get there in one day. We will have to stop along the way tonight for some sleep for at least a little while, because it will be a

longer day tomorrow and then tomorrow night we will arrive there."

Richard looked around at all the Glee, wrapped in water weed, watching him. "You all look wonderful. Let's get moving."

59

Sang had been right. As the sun set and night descended on them, the two small but bright moons certainly did provide enough light to see by, especially out in the windswept drylands. Everything, though, was a different shade of gloomy, dark red that seemed to weigh down Richard's spirits. He wanted to rub his eyes to clear away the bleak shades of reddish color to everything. He had never really appreciated color so much as he did after being in this place. He longed to see the simple colors of his world again.

Thick, heavy clouds frequently scudded past to sometimes obscure the moons, but when that happened they were backlit by the moons and in that way provided enough light to see where they were going. When the moons came out from behind the clouds, it was about as bright as a night with a full moon in his world. It was easily bright enough for their journey, especially in such an open, sandy landscape.

Although the ominous clouds scudding past looked thick and heavy, they didn't bring rain to this desolate place, and didn't look like they ever had, making Richard wonder if they could actually be more dust than rain clouds. If they did carry rain, he guessed that for some reason they didn't release the rain they carried until they reached the swampy parts of this strange world.

Richard had thought at first that the sand would be hard to walk across, but he found instead that in many places it had been packed hard by the howling winds that left ripples in their wake across the face of the dunes. In other places, especially on the lee side of the dunes, the sand was deep and loose, making progress difficult and time-consuming. They hadn't been traveling long and Richard's legs already ached from the effort of walking through the places of deep sand.

Enormous, soaring rock peaks thrust up

through the sand to impossible heights in random spots all around them, like islands in the sea of sand. The massive stone monarchs watched them pass at their feet. In places when they passed close to the stone towers it hid the two moons, casting them into gloomy shadows.

The rock of those strange peaks was so rough and rugged, composed of faceted, stacked, sheer cliff faces, that Richard couldn't imagine they could be climbed. He was happy to instead make their way past in the shadows of those rocky peaks.

It looked to Richard that those craggy, monumental prominences of rock stood so tall that they often pierced up into the dark, ruddy clouds continually sweeping past, and that had over the ages caused them to crumble under the forces of wind and weather. All the decaying rock created both the sloping skirts of crumbled rock, and the sandy surface between each of those monstrous stone outcroppings. As the decomposing rock gradually and continually added pieces of debris to the low places between them, the wind tumbled it around and around, breaking it down, until it all turned to sand. Once it was small and light enough, the wind lifted it and carried it across the face of the landscape, shaping it into dunes.

Some of the dunes couldn't be avoided without a long detour and had to be climbed. The windward sides were sloped gradually enough to be an easy climb, but the lee sides were often quite steep and the sand soft. They had to run down the steepest sections to keep from falling face-first. A few of the dunes were quite high. At the top it gave them a good view of the bleak landscape out ahead of them. From those views, Richard thought it looked endless.

That landscape greatly concerned the Glee, but in their wet wrappings of water weeds, they at least weren't complaining about being dry. The weeds were tough and were proving surprisingly durable. Richard thought that they were surely mostly worried about fighting the followers of the Golden Goddess. These were not warriors, but they seemed to grasp the necessity of what they were doing and were so far willing.

Some of the followers of the goddess had already visited Richard's world and fought the people there. Those that hadn't yet had that experience were probably eager for it. The Glee with Richard were not at all eager to fight.

None of them carried weapons, but of course they didn't need to. They had wicked weapons at the end of each arm. He had discovered just how skillfully those claws could handle the most delicate of tasks. He hoped that when the time came, they would also be able to fight with them. Their lives would depend on it.

As if reading his thoughts, Vika leaned close. "Do you think they will fight, or run?"

Richard leaned over slightly to speak to her in a low voice. "To tell you the truth, I've been wondering that very thing myself. I think, though, that their usefulness may actually be in the shock value they will provide.

"It's a sure bet that the other Glee with the goddess will never have seen anything like these Glee all wrapped in water weeds come walking out of the drylands. I'm hoping that surprise will make them stop and stare. That hesitancy will give you and me the opportunity to get to the goddess."

"You're thinking, then, that if you can take

her out quickly, that may take the fight out of her followers?"

Richard nodded. "I'm hoping so. If nothing else, it should cause a lot of confusion. Confused people—and Glee—are easier to take down."

"What if another one of them is eager, once they see her killed, to become the leader?"

Richard tucked his head down and turned to the side as he leaned a shoulder into a hot gust of wind-driven, reddish sand. He had to wait for it to die down a little before he could answer.

"Then we will simply have to take out any of them who think they would like to become the leader. I have my doubts that the Glee with us will have the nerve to do that. It's going to be up to you and me. If a different Glee steps up to be in charge only to swiftly meet our blades, I'm hoping that will take the fight out of any of the others who would think to be a leader, and the ones who would be followers willing to fight. If they don't have a leader, then their whole defense may very well collapse like an army without officers."

Vika lifted an eyebrow. "Well, that's not the

craziest idea you've ever had, but it's certainly one of the more optimistic ones."

Richard didn't want to tell her his doubts and fears. "I'm glad you are with me, Vika."

She smiled. "I wouldn't have it any other way."

The thought of living in this strange world for the rest of his life had hopeless depression continually clawing at him to take over his emotions. He tried his best to tell himself to worry about one thing at a time. For now, they had a big enough problem to overcome with a fighting force of Glee that had never fought before and seemed more kind and cooperative than vicious. He worried about what they would do when they saw their kind dying.

"When this is done, I need to get back to the device and destroy it," he told her. "If there are Glee that escape during our attempts to get to the goddess, they could eventually get the same notion as the goddess had to travel to other worlds. We can't allow the Glee to ever again get to our world."

"You will get no argument from me."

Richard glanced over at her. "When that time comes, before I destroy the device, I am going to first have Sang activate it so we can send you back."

Vika stopped in her tracks and glared at him. "You are going to do no such thing."

"Vika, there is no reason for both of us—"

"Yes, there is every reason. I am Mord-Sith. I have sworn to protect you with my life."

"I don't want you to sacrifice a future you could have in our world."

Vika stepped closer as she flipped her single braid forward over her shoulder and gripped it in a fist, as if deciding on using that instead of pointing her Agiel at him.

"You gave me a choice in the beginning of how I wished to live my life. This is how I wish to live my life—at your side, protecting you. I never wanted anything else. If I returned without you, my life would have no meaning. This, here, is the choice I made for my life."

Richard would want her to return and then devote herself to protecting Kahlan and the twins but decided that this wasn't the time and place to task her with that duty. She would say that there were other Mord-Sith to do that. He didn't want to argue with her. She still existed partly in that place of madness.

The Glee behind them had slowed to a stop, waiting.

"But you would have a life, Vika," he said, simply.

"It is my choice, not yours, and besides, maybe I like this world much better than a world full of people. I often find people intolerable.

"You once told me to choose what I wanted to do with my life. I am here by that choice. Do you now intend to revoke your word and deny me the right to choose for myself what I will do with my life?"

Richard slowly let out a deep breath as he scanned the horizon. "No, Vika. I will not deny you the right to choose what you want to do. If it is really your wish to stay here with me, then I will be happy not to be so alone."

"Good."

Sang came a little closer and pointed to an outcropping of rock. *That place there will protect us from the wind so we can get a little sleep. There is still a long way to go.*

In was deep in the night. Richard knew they were all tired. He nodded. Sang started back to the others, motioning for them to gather in the protection of the rock for a bit of sleep.

Vika gestured to a spot in the shelter of an overhang of rock where the Glee were headed. "Now that that subject is closed, let's get some sleep. We have a war waiting on us tomorrow."

60

The next day, after hours of walking, rocky areas began to break through the sandy ground. Here and there off to the sides, enormous rock towers also appeared to erupt up through the sand and thrust toward the sky. Their size made Richard feel very small. The debris that had gradually fallen as the rock decayed had accumulated over eons around their bases, creating massive slopes of scree that gradually became almost vertical near their tops. The way it rose up ever more steeply, it gave the rock monoliths a flared appearance at the bottoms, but it was really their rock faces gradually shedding material.

Between two of the towers off to their right, one of the moons between the massive rock mountains lit the billowing clouds that seemed to boil up from the distant landscape, the reddish color making them look almost like smoke from distant, raging fires. With those silent monoliths, that sand, the rolling clouds, and the moons, it was a frighteningly beautiful, if ominous, sight. The isolated islands of massive rock towers reminded Richard of the plateau that held the People's Palace rising up from the Azrith Plain, except these in this world rose up considerably higher.

It had been a long journey from that palace, a journey unlike any other that had taken him to a different world. It was turning out to be a journey that could never see him reach home again. It was depressing to think that this world of sand, desolate rock, and in places stagnant swamps, would be where he had to live out the rest of his life.

Richard had to put those thoughts from his mind. Being distracted by turbulent emotions was a good way to die in battle. He had to stay alive at least long enough to be sure his home world would be safe from the Glee ever coming there again. He had to make sure that Kahlan and their children would be safe.

As they went farther into the drylands, he understood the fear the Glee had of this desolate place. While the areas where they lived were swampy, there was abundant life there, providing food and safety. For good reason they were most at home there. This was an empty place where it would be all too easy to die a very lonely death. If they died out here, it was unlikely that anyone would ever come along to bury their bones. Eventually those bones would be ground to dust by the wind-driven sand.

The one good aspect of what they were doing was that he could see why the Golden Goddess and her followers would never expect that anyone would come around this way into the place where they lived. They wouldn't be expecting Richard, Vika, and the Glee with them.

"How are you doing?" Richard asked Sang.

Sang held his arms out, wrapped in water weeds with just the claws sticking out the ends. Water weeds were also draped over and around his head, so that his eyes could barely see out of his suit.

"I thought that you were foolish to think we could cross this land, but this way you thought

to wrap us with the water weed is working. It is amazing for us to explore this strange dry land we have never seen before. My skin is warm and wet. I no longer fear that I am about to die."

Richard thought that maybe Sang should reserve judgment until they met the enemy.

Areas of rocky ground breaking through the sand became ever more frequent, with large stretches of the rock joining with others until before long they were walking over jagged, uneven rock rather than sand. The rock was pitted and sharp. The terrain was even more harsh, and that worried the Glee with him. As they continued onward the rock seemed to tilt upward so that they had to continually climb the ever-rising, massive shelf of rock.

Having never been through the drylands, the Glee didn't really know much about the terrain and could offer no advice other than general guidance about the direction they needed to go to reach the area held by the goddess and her followers. Richard worried about what other surprises they might encounter in the vast trackless drylands.

As they went farther, many of the enormous peaks began to line up, with numbers of them joining in chains of towering rock making it appear that they were one long mass of rock wall rather than individual peaks. In some places the rock did completely cease to be individual towers, becoming long, sheer rock walls hemming them in. By their size and orientation across the landscape, those rocky outcroppings seemed to bend the wind, deflecting it off to their right, rather than channeling it through the drylands the way they had up until then. Those winds, while still hot, became heavy with moisture and felt stuffy. Richard could see the thick overcast being funneled past the walls of rock to head off away from them.

The uneven ground, littered with sharp, pitted, crumbled rock, was difficult to walk on. They all had to be careful lest they twist an ankle. He was worried that the Glee might fall and tear their suits of weeds, as well as their soft flesh.

As they came to the crest of the rising ground, they all slowed to a halt.

"There," Sang called out, pointing off into the distance. *"That place down there is where the Golden Goddess and her followers live. They like this place because it is near the mountain with the*

device, it is wet, and there is a lot of room for their great numbers to assemble."

Richard nodded as he studied the landscape out ahead. It looked to be a low, swampy area, with abundant vegetation. It was indeed a vast area that would hold great numbers of Glee. In the far distance, he saw more of the tall, crooked tree trunks with the single, high clumps of foliage.

"When we get down there," Richard told the Glee in a low voice as he scanned the area in the distance, "I want you all to stay behind me."

"Why?" Several Glee asked in his mind at the same time.

"Because if things get rough, anything in front of me is going to die."

That seemed to bring the seriousness of what they were doing into sharp relief for them. Richard urged them back a ways, out of sight of any of the Glee down below that might happen to look up. If they did look up, they would easily be able to see them silhouetted against the sky. Once back a ways, they all watched as he quickly strung his bow.

"What are you doing now?" Iben asked.

Instead of answering, Richard gave him a

meaningful look and then nocked an arrow. Without a word, he drew back the string, let out a deep breath, settled his aim. He drew the target to him as he had long ago learned to do and then let the arrow fly. Even as the arrow left his bow, in his mind, it had already hit its target. Several seconds later reality caught up with what he was seeing in his mind.

The arrow went right through the head of a Glee sitting on a rock outcropping down closer to the swampy area. He had been looking away from Richard and his group, keeping watch from higher ground toward the only way they believed others could enter their home ground.

Watching the Glee crumple in the distance seemed to sober those with him even more. None spoke, but they glanced around at their fellow Glee, having never seen anything like it.

"That one was standing watch," Richard whispered to them. "Had he turned, he would have seen us. We don't want any of them to sound an alarm. We need to catch them by surprise."

"We will let you know if we spot any others standing guard," Iben said. A few others nodded their agreement.

61

"Where do they sleep?" Richard asked back over his shoulder after he had moved forward in a crouch and taken a peek.

"We like to sleep in beds of water weeds where it grows thick on the banks of the water," Sang told him, *"often with our legs in the water."*

"So then most of them will be sleeping right beside the areas of water?" Richard asked.

"Yes," Sang said. *"That is where Glee like to spend the night. It is comforting."*

Richard found the concept disturbing but didn't say so. "But these Glee don't eat the water weeds or the muscle snails like you eat," Richard told them. "These Glee eat those like me. So do you think they would still sleep on water weeds the same as they used to do?"

Sang thought about it a moment. *"Now that you mention it, I'm not sure. But I believe they would still want to sleep the same way as Glee have always slept. They still want to keep their skin wet, and stay where the boars won't come."*

Richard nodded, thinking. He turned back and peered into the distance, trying to spot any of them sleeping at the edge of the water. Richard finally looked back at the others as they waited.

"The Glee who have been eating people from my world don't eat the float weed anymore, so they lose the green sheen to their skin that all of you have."

"Like that spy you found," Iben noted.

"That's right. All of you have that green coloring. The ones down there won't have it."

Iben nodded. *"Now that you showed us that with the one you caught watching us for the goddess, we can easily know any who are followers of the goddess."*

"That's exactly right," Richard said, "so remember that if things get confusing in a battle. I don't want any of you to accidentally slash those with us if some of you lose the water weeds wrapped around you." After another quick look, he turned back to the Glee with him. "Is there a way to tell the goddess apart from the rest of the Glee down there?"

Almost all the Glee were nodding even as he was finishing the question. Iben stretched up, looking over the rise to be sure of the lay of the land, and then gestured off toward the swampy areas.

"I don't see her," he said.

"But how would you recognize her?"

"The one who calls herself the Golden Goddess hatched in a nest of eggs that had unknowingly been built almost on top of a rare plant," one of the other Glee with them said. *"It was the first thing she ate when she emerged from her shell. She then broke open the other eggs and ate her sibling offspring so that she could grow fast and strong."*

"None of you eat the other eggs in the nest with you, do you?" Richard asked.

They all looked horrified at the very notion. Just about all of them were shaking their heads, not wanting to be associated with eating their siblings.

"That is not something our kind does when they hatch," Sang told him. *"The parents would prevent it. I don't know why her parents did not, but maybe she did it while they were asleep."*

"What does all of that have to do with recognizing the goddess?" Richard asked.

Iben spoke up first. *"That rare plant growing by her nest, the one she ate when she first hatched, is somewhat poisonous. As a result, it scarred her skin and gave it a golden color unlike any of the other Glee. Also, she is big for a Glee, at least a head taller than any of us. Her whole life she has always used her size to torment and intimidate others."*

Richard realized then that all the Glee were very similar in stature. They were all lean, and their skin all looked the same. From the description it certainly seemed like he would have no difficulty at all recognizing the goddess.

Although, he couldn't imagine how she would look golden in this world. Everything was tinted some shade of red. Only Vika's red leather outfit looked normal to him. But the rest of her was tinted red. Her blond hair was a rather lovely rose color.

He guessed that maybe the golden color was simply relative to everything else. But finally, with an easy way to recognize the goddess, Richard felt like they at least had one advantage on their side.

"Do you think she will be down there with the others?" Vika asked.

"Oh yes," Sang said, nodding confidently. *"She likes the others to see her among them so they can admire her. Her golden skin color is the envy of all for its exotic appearance. She likes others groveling and seeking her approval, so she is always among them."*

"Besides, she never likes the others to be out of her sight," Iben said. *"She doesn't easily trust that they will stay loyal."*

Not wanting to waste what darkness there was, preferring to have that on their side along with the element of surprise, Richard finally gestured for them to move out. With Vika beside him, he started out in a crouch, heading down the long slope into the place of the goddess and her followers. He worried about their numbers. When they had attacked back in Richard's world, there were sometimes large numbers of them, so they were likely to encounter even more of the enemy Glee here.

All the Glee wrapped in water weed followed Richard down the rocky slope. None of them seemed to grasp the concept of sneaking up on an enemy. He urgently signaled for them to crouch down the way he and Vika were doing. They did their best considering the wrap of water weeds but found it awkward.

The Glee they were after were quite familiar with being vicious. Most of the Glee with Richard and Vika apparently had not yet met any of their fellow Glee with such a capacity for brutality. The spy had said that they were coming to kill Sang and all those who weren't followers of the goddess. This was going to be a savage encounter.

To say that he greatly feared for those with him was an understatement, but this was their world, and this was about their lives and future. Richard couldn't simply fight this war alone and then hand them their freedom from the Golden Goddess, or others who would eventually spring up from her legions of followers to take her place. Sang and his group had to take part in stopping the threat to their world and way of life.

He hoped that when it came right down to a battle, they would show the same capacity for ferocity as those they were about to face.

62

Richard moved in a low crouch from one thick growth of vegetation to another, relieved that, since they were coming in from an unexpected direction, they had managed to get down close without being spotted. He knew that the closer they could get before they struck, the greater the surprise, the more confusion it would create, and the more effective the attack would be.

Vika was close behind him as he silently slipped through the moon shadows, going from cover to cover. He had told the Glee to stay back a little because he wanted room to draw his sword and fight. If he had the chance, he would rather use his bow to take the goddess down from a distance than engage in close combat

with her. He already had an arrow nocked and
ready.

He had learned to fight Glee, but he had no
idea what her capabilities might be. She was
taller than the others, so she very well might
be stronger as well. But Richard was also tall, a
little taller than the rest of the Glee.

The biggest problem would be their numbers.
It would be hard to take out one individual,
the goddess, if masses of her followers were
charging in all around him. It would be much
better if he could simply drop her with an arrow
and then they could deal with her followers.

It tended to take the fight out of followers
when they saw their leader be the first to fall. If
he could, he wanted to dispirit them by killing
the goddess first, before he had to fight the rest of
them, or before the Glee with him had to engage
in battle. He wanted the important part over
first. He knew, though, that in battle things rarely
went as planned. In such unfamiliar territory, that
made the situation even more difficult.

So far, they hadn't seen any sleeping Glee,
but they were still some distance from the areas
of water. The ground back where they were was
muddy, but Sang and Iben had said that the

Glee favored sleeping in the wet water weeds on the banks and often partly in the water.

All of a sudden, there was a loud squeal, and it wasn't from a Glee.

Richard turned just in time to see something low crash through the thick brush close to him. He heard grunts and high-pitched squeals. When he spun to the sound, he saw several Glee upended, their legs knocked from under them as they were flipped through the air.

He just caught sight of a bunch of piglets scattering through the underbrush in every direction. Almost immediately he saw the sow charging through the brush to protect her young. The sow was bigger than any wild boars he had ever seen. The tusks were enormous, and no doubt lethal. The sow charged at the Glee with Richard. Fortunately, they were all able to dive out of the way just in time.

The piglets' piercing squeals seemed to be all the louder in the stillness of the night. The sow let out angry snorts as she wheeled and charged the Glee before racing through the dense brush toward the squeals from her young.

The boar was not the problem, though. The squeals and screeches of all the piglets were the problem because the sound pierced the quiet night air.

Richard heard the warning cries of the Glee rising from their sleep, furious at discovering other Glee sneaking up on them in a surprise attack. He saw frightening numbers of the dark shapes rising up everywhere out of the swampy areas and then the shadowy shapes of all the Glee were suddenly racing toward them.

Searching frantically, he finally caught fleeting glimpses of the Golden Goddess as she raced through the dark masses of Glee. Iben had been right. There was no mistaking her. Her long legs carried her faster than any Glee Richard had seen before.

Richard tracked her as he let the first arrow fly. Although the aim was true, it hit another Glee that got in the way of the shot at the last second. She charged ahead without pause, pushing some of them out of her way as she wove through the throng of her followers, clearly infuriated. The same thing happened with the second and then the third arrow as others passed in front of the arrow before it could get to her.

Richard realized that his plan to take her down at a distance with an arrow was not going to work. There were simply too many Glee in the way to have any hope of getting a clear shot and she was closing the distance fast.

As he momentarily lost sight of her, Richard threw his bow to the ground and drew his sword in a rush. The unique sound of the blade that had been touched by the world of the dead rang out across the swamp. That clear, pure sound could easily be heard above the mass of angry howls as it announced the arrival of a lethal rage of its own.

Some of the advancing Glee in the front stopped in their tracks at the sound as those behind kept coming, packing them together even tighter. Maybe some of them had heard that sound before, or heard descriptions of it from returning Glee, or maybe the danger it represented was simply obvious.

Off to Richard's right, Iben raced out ahead, calling out, bent on urging the Golden Goddess to stop and listen, hoping to stop the battle before it could begin.

The goddess suddenly burst through the throng of dark Glee and with one powerful swipe, tore out Iben's throat.

Shrieking her anger, she turned and raced

toward Richard even as he was charging toward her.

As they came together, she swung at him with a claw. He dodged to the side and it just missed his face. Without pause, he brought his blade around and severed the claw before she could withdraw it. The sword flashed in the moonlight and just as quick the other claw was off.

She stopped dead in her tracks as her big black eyes blinked in stunned surprise.

While her followers had gone to Richard's world to fight, she never had. Because of that, she was all angry bluster and intimidation without the fighting skills or experience to back her threats. She had never come face-to-face with anyone like Richard who was not intimidated by her.

Before she could react, Richard was already using all his strength to power the blade around in an arc. It severed her head in one clean strike.

The goddess's head, as it flew up and back, made one slow turn through the air as strings of blood were pulled around after it. Glee stood frozen as they watched what they could never have imagined.

The clawless, headless Golden Goddess dropped straight down as if she didn't have a bone in her body.

The crowd pushed back to be out of the way as her head completed several revolutions in midair before it thudded down heavily on the rocks in their midst and took a few odd bounces before rolling to a stop. Her stunned followers backed out of its way as if it might bite them, or yell at them.

All the howling rage and fury came to an abrupt halt.

A number of the Glee with Richard cried out then and fell to their knees around Iben's body. Their distress at his tragic death was sad to see.

Richard immediately turned to the threat from the goddess's followers, expecting a furious onslaught of claws and teeth. Instead of charging in to fight them, he stopped as he saw them slow to a stop. They all briefly gazed down at the body of the goddess before moving on to come forward and stare at the dead Iben.

Glee wrapped in water weeds protectively surrounded their dead friend, many on their knees beside him, weeping. They all crowded around, reaching out to touch their friend, clearly devastated that he had been so violently slain by one of their own kind.

After Sang, grieving, had gently touched Iben's body, he stood in a rush to face the enemy. Tears of rage ran from his large black eyes, his third eyelids trying to blink them away, but more continued to flow.

He gestured angrily with a claw down at Iben's body.

"Look at what you have done! This is what you all wanted? Look at what you all have done to one of your own kind! Look! Glee should never harm Glee! Never! Your Golden Goddess did this! You all did this! You are all responsible!"

If Glee could look shamefaced, those Glee watching him standing over the body of his friend certainly did. Many hung their heads. Others looked away in disgrace.

"This is what you wish for our world?" Sang cried out as he swept an arm out in anger. *"This is what you wanted? This is your way, now? To kill other Glee?"*

Other grieving Glee behind Sang stood after touching the body to gesture down with a claw, demanding that the enemy look at what they had all been a part of.

"Is this how you want to live now?" one of the others asked as he got up from kneeling by Iben. *"This is what fills your hearts? This is what you wanted? Your own kind to be murdered? This is what you all would do to other Glee? To us? None of you are as good as this one was. He rushed forward because he wanted to tell you all to please stop your ways and return to the way we have always lived. But you instead killed him! What kind of beasts have you become?"*

The guilty Glee stood around, watching but not interfering, some holding their claws behind their backs, while others hung their heads, all of them clearly not knowing what to do.

The fight had been taken out of them.

Finally, in the unbearable predawn silence, one of the enemy slowly approached and pointed with a claw. *"You are covered with water weeds. Is that so that you were able to cross the drylands to come in and surprise the goddess?"*

Many of the Glee who had come with Richard nodded.

Then, the masses of Glee that had been hanging their heads began to step forward and do the strangest thing.

63

At first, a few of the enemy Glee slowly, timidly, began approaching the Glee still kneeling around their fallen friend. When the first reached Iben's body, the Glee who had been kneeling stood and moved back so that the others could see what their beliefs had wrought. Many of Sang's Glee bared their teeth as they hissed. Richard thought that their meaning was clear enough.

The first Glee to slowly shuffle up to Iben went to a knee beside the body. Richard and Vika shared a look, wondering what it could mean, and what was going to come next, but with that look they wordlessly decided to let it play out and see what happened. Richard still had his bloody sword in his hand, so if things suddenly turned violent, he intended to show them what violence really was.

The twin storms of rage were still roaring through him. His blade had come out in anger and tasted blood. It wanted more. This time, if a battle broke out, they were already in their home world and would not be able to vanish to escape certain death.

The Glee that approached first and went to a knee gently pulled off a strip of the float weed from Iben's body. As Richard and Vika watched along with all the silent Glee, he ate the piece of water weed.

To Richard, it looked almost like some kind of sacred ceremony or statement that this one Glee, at least, wished to give up the path he had been on and return to their traditional ways.

As that Glee stood and moved aside, another came forward and took his place. He, too, pulled off a short piece of water weed and ate it while the Glee with Richard stood back beyond Iben's body, out of the way, and watched.

Soon, all of the Glee were lining up to come and kneel before the dead body of one of their kind. Each in turn took a piece of float weed and ate it in a kind of reverent expression of their sorrow. Richard took it as a wish to return to their ways.

Before long, the flutter and float weed, and the scrum under it, had all been eaten, except for the layers around Iben's neck that were covered with blood. There were still a vast number of followers of the goddess who hadn't had a chance to eat some of the water weeds that had protected Iben, so instead, they began mingling in among the Glee who had been with Richard, looking like they wanted to take pieces of the water weeds off of them as a suitable substitute. The Glee covered in water weeds all held their arms out so that their former enemies could all partake of the water weed in a symbolic gesture.

If any of them were speaking, they were not doing so in a way that allowed Richard and Vika to hear anything they were saying. He supposed they didn't want outsiders to hear their apologies and pleas for forgiveness.

It took quite a while for all the Glee to come up and take a piece of the water weed. As they gathered around, waiting their turn, some of the Glee wrapped in the weeds began pulling off strips and handing them to the ones waiting their turn in order to speed up the process.

Richard didn't see a single Glee leave, or express defiance. They all looked genuinely remorseful at the death of one of their own kind.

He finally sheathed his sword. He was thankful that it had done enough.

He also didn't see a single Glee pay any attention to the body of the Golden Goddess lying in a heap by itself. None of the Glee mourned her death. There were so many of the Glee, it took over an hour before all of them were able to collect and consume a symbolic piece of the water plants that had long been part of their staple diet and way of life.

"I have never seen anything like this," Vika whispered as she watched the silent ritual. "I'm sorry that Iben had to die, but I am thankful to be able to see others make the kind of decision I once made."

Richard put an appreciative hand on Vika's shoulder. Having been prepared for a bloody fight to the death, and now seeing that fate turning aside, he feared to test his voice.

The piglets had all run off and the sow had gone after them, so the scene was hushed as each of the Glee ate some of the water plants after they paid their respects to the dead Iben and finally greeted their long-separated brethren.

Richard, too, was sad at the death of Iben. He had been open, friendly, and eager to help, and along with Sang had completely turned Richard's view of the Glee upside down. They were not all what he expected. They were far more than that.

Iben had wanted to talk his fellow Glee out of violence against their own kind. He had wanted to try to get them to stop and think about what they had been about to do. He thought he could persuade them.

In the end, he had.

64

Late in the afternoon, the Glee took turns using their claws to dig a grave. When it was finally deep enough, they gently placed Iben's body in it and covered him over.

After they had put Iben to rest, they then slashed the body of the Golden Goddess until it was covered with ribbons of deep cuts. Richard and Vika couldn't imagine what they were doing. Once satisfied, they threw the body and the head into one of the swampy lakes. The body floated for a short time among standing reeds before small creatures Richard couldn't see began tearing at the flesh. After a few hours most of it had been eaten, leaving only bones. It was apparently a disrespectful burial to show their displeasure with what she had brought to their kind.

The strange celebration and socializing went on into the evening. As it grew dark, the Glee began finding places to sleep. Some curled up in thick beds they made from fronds. Others laid their heads down on the banks of ponds and let their legs float out into the water. Whatever had eaten the body of the goddess apparently didn't bother with living Glee. They slept peacefully with half their bodies in the water.

Richard and Vika found a place nearby beside a beautiful bush that was more like a small tree. They gathered fronds to make sleeping mats. Neither one of them liked the idea of both of them sleeping at the same time, so they took turns taking naps while the other stood watch. Richard wondered how long they were going to have to do that in their strange new world.

By late morning of the next day the odd reunion was still going strong, with the Glee mingling together and talking with one another. Richard and Vika weren't aware of much of what was being said, because while they occasionally heard some of the talk, most of the Glee chose not to have their voices, or possibly their confessions, heard by these strangers from another world. Richard wasn't overly concerned, though, because everything appeared to be friendly enough, but he did wish he possessed that talent to deny others the ability to hear his words. It could come in handy at times.

As he casually watched, he remained vigilant and ready to draw his sword at the slightest sign of trouble. He didn't think it looked like there would be trouble, but he felt it best to be ready just in case. He saw Vika idly spinning her Agiel on the end of the gold chain around her wrist as she, too, watched.

He and Vika stood out of the way, not wanting to intrude. From time to time many of the Glee slipped into the water, where they seemed most at home. Groups congregated in the water as they floated together. Others would periodically bring bundles of water weeds to the banks, where yet others could take some to munch on. Others, apparently tired from the reunion and celebration, rested their chins on a pillow of their folded arms while the bottom half of their bodies floated in the water. Yet others sat cross-legged on the banks to talk. Richard supposed they had a lot to talk about.

Richard had been to a number of fancy banquets and gatherings of officials. This seemed very much the same, other than the trappings of power and social standing, and of course the claws and needle-sharp teeth. Other than those trappings, he recognized the body language and the interplay of different personalities. The whole thing was, in a word, weird.

Richard was getting hungry himself. He wondered what he and Vika were going to be able to eat in this strange world. He certainly didn't have any cravings for the smelly water weeds. He supposed he might be able to catch some fish, or he could hunt wild boar. There might even be fruits and berries that they could eat. Fortunately they still had some travel rations in his pack, but not a lot. As they watched the Glee, he and Vika idly chewed on strips of dried meat.

It occurred to him that as time went on maybe the Glee could provide the meat of some muscle snails for him and Vika to roast over a fire or smoke. He glanced around and realized that he didn't see much that they could use for firewood.

All the Glee Richard had brought through the drylands were easy enough to spot, because their skin had the green iridescence. They seemed somewhat somber that Iben had died, but also recognized that his death had resulted in the end of the reign of the Golden Goddess. Iben had been the catalyst that had brought all the Glee together again. Richard didn't know if, or how long, that would last. He hoped it did, but he worried that it wouldn't.

He was also all too aware that at some point after those former raiders of other worlds ate enough water plants, it would give their skin the same green iridescence. He worried that once that happened, he wouldn't be able to tell the formerly hostile Glee from the peaceful ones. If they ever turned hostile again and decided they wanted to eat Richard and Vika, he would have no way of telling them apart. That would put surprise on their side.

Richard supposed that, while he didn't want to die, he didn't really have much to live for anymore, except the one thing that he was growing impatient to finish.

As he and Vika watched, some of the former followers of the goddess came up to them and made a point of telling them that besides ending the tyranny of the Golden Goddess and her oppressive rule over their lives, what Richard had done had lifted them from a terrible future in which they abandoned their traditional ways and instead went to other worlds to hunt for food where many of their kind had been killed.

Some told him of beloved offspring that had been eager for the adventure of going off to other worlds and had only ended up dying there. Richard wondered if he had killed some of those Glee, or offspring. They had been vicious killers and had died as such. He hoped their minds didn't turn to revenge.

Those engaging him in conversation ex-plained that they had done what they had done because the Golden Goddess made them do it. Richard didn't necessarily believe a word of it, but he let them have their excuses in order for things to remain friendly. If that was what they wanted to claim in order to soothe their consciences, he didn't really care as long as it meant an end to the fighting.

At this point, stuck in their world with Vika, never to be able to return home to Kahlan, he didn't really care how they justified to themselves what they had done. He only cared that it stop. Now that it had, he was relieved that he didn't have to face yet another protracted war in which he and Vika would be vastly outnumbered.

But this new peace still had to prove to him that it could last. It was possible, or even likely, that there were Glee among them who harbored very different sentiments and they simply hadn't come forward to express them. He realized that he might never again be able to sleep with both eyes closed.

He had always been skeptical that when the time came, those Glee who came across the drylands with him would actually fight. Now, he didn't need to fear that bloody conflict, or all of them being slaughtered. If, that was, a new leader didn't rise from the ranks of the former followers of the goddess.

Richard's patience finally came to an end. He pulled Sang aside to talk to him privately.

"Before any of these former followers of the goddess start to think that maybe they might like to have the power she had and be in charge of a vast army that could raid other worlds, we need to destroy the device so that can never happen again."

Sang nodded, looking apologetic that he had forgotten all about it, and handed the long piece of the float weed he was munching on to one of the others passing by.

"Everything is back to the way it was, thanks to you and Vika. I don't think we could ever adequately express our gratitude. With peace restored, we have nothing to fear, now. We can take care of the device any time. There is no longer any worry or any rush."

"There is to me," Richard said in a firm voice. "I want it taken care of now. I don't want to have to worry that I might have my throat torn out in my sleep by followers of the goddess who decided to resume their ways and will then go to my world and kill the people there."

"I don't think you need to worry about—"

Richard held up a warning finger. "I came here to do what was necessary to protect my world. I sacrificed my life with my kind, my wife, and my offspring to do this—both for my people and for your kind. I have nothing left for me, now, other than a lonely future here in this world where Vika and I don't really belong.

"I made that sacrifice to be able to destroy that device that made all of the terror and bloodshed possible. That job is not yet done. I want it finished."

Sang could see the determination in Richard's face and hear it in his voice. He nodded.

"Of course, Lord Rahl. I understand. Of course you are right. We will go there now. I will show you the way."

Richard would simply have left the days-long celebration and gone there on his own, and he actually would have preferred to do that, but with the clouds obscuring much of the landscape, he wasn't sure exactly how to find the place up in the mountains. They had come into the territory of the Golden Goddess via a long, roundabout way through the confusing maze of rocky spires in the drylands in order to surprise the goddess and her followers. With the clouds, the wind-driven sand, the maze of rock towers, and not being able to see exactly where the sun was in the sky, he wasn't confident that he had been able to keep track of direction or distances.

He had a general idea where he could find the mountain where the device was located, but with visibility so poor, and the low clouds always obscuring mountain peaks, he feared that if he looked for the site on his own it could end up taking him days to find the small trail. He knew that Sang could show him the way and then he could destroy the device much sooner.

He worried about the possibility that in the meantime, if it wasn't quickly destroyed, it might be used again without him being aware that some of the Glee had snuck away to travel to his world. He didn't want to risk it existing any longer. Better to destroy the device once and for all. That was the only way to make sure Kahlan and everyone else would be safe.

Sang spoke with some of his followers, apparently letting them know that they were leaving to go to the mountain where the device was located. But as they started out, Richard saw that a large number the Glee were following behind—both Sang's followers and many of the followers of the goddess. He didn't know why, but as long as Sang got him there so he could use his sword to destroy that strange square block of stone, that was all that mattered.

His sword had cut through steel before. Not all that long ago his blade had cut through massive stone pillars and blocks to get at Moravaska Michec down in the complication.

Neither steel nor stone ever proved to be any obstacle to the Sword of Truth, so he had no doubt that it would cut through the stone device.

Although, in the back of his mind, he realized that it was possibly neither steel nor stone. It was, after all, a device that allowed travel to other worlds, so it was possible that it only looked like stone and would in reality prove much more difficult to destroy than he had at first thought.

When he looked back over his shoulder at the line of Glee following him, it reminded him of a funeral procession.

In a way, that's exactly what it was.

65

A warm rain accompanied them along the climb up the mountain. It made the air wet and heavy, and difficult to breathe. At times it came down in sheets, harder than any rain he had ever known before, almost like standing under a waterfall. It was so heavy that they could barely even see.

When the rain increased to an intensity that Richard and Vika found unendurable, they had to crouch behind some of the forest of rock towers that had overhangs enough to shelter them somewhat. Sang warned him to stay out of any low places because this kind of rain often created flash floods that could sweep him away before he realized what was happening. It could easily be disastrous to be rolled down the mountain in such floodwaters. From time to time they came to those kinds of sudden, rushing, muddy rivers and had to find a way around them.

The Glee didn't at all mind the rain, at times standing in it with their arms held out and their faces turned up to the sky, but Richard and Vika found it miserable. Traveling into the heaviest of the curtains of rain was arduous. It was also hard not only to see where they were heading, but also where they were stepping. He worried that either Vika or he might fall and break a leg. Richard had grown up outdoors, and so he was familiar with walking in challenging terrain, but Vika hadn't, so it was harder for her to walk among the jumbles of rock during the downpours.

There were no healers that he knew of among the Glee, and he didn't think that they had any. They seemed to be too simple a species to have healers. If he or Vika was injured, there could be no help. They had only each other, and while he knew about healing, both with magic and with herbs, he could certainly heal Vika, but she couldn't heal him. He also didn't know if this world had any healing herbs they could use.

The landscape they had to travel through was completely devoid of any kind of life; there was just rock and, in the rain, mud, much of it rushing down at them. There were no plants, not even a blade of grass. Just continual rain. Since starting up into the mountains, he hadn't seen a single bird, or even one of the bats that he had seen in large groups down in the swampland. He remembered that Sang had said that where the device was located was a dry place, but getting there beneath the leaden overcast certainly wasn't dry. He was looking forward to getting up into the mountains above the clouds that were dumping so much rain on them.

A lot of the rock was sharp and crumbly, making walking difficult. This world was a strange mixture of lush swamplands, sandy drylands, and desolate, lifeless mountains. The skies seemed to be an odd mix, too, of dark clouds that carried no water and heavy, wet overcast. From what he had seen so far, it seemed that nothing lived anywhere other than the swampy lands down lower, where all this water running down the mountainsides eventually collected in the swamps.

Richard came across holes in the upslopes of grainy rock. They appeared almost big enough that he might be able to crawl inside. He wondered if they might be able to be enlarged and in the future provide some kind of cavelike shelter for him and Vika. He stuck his head inside one of the holes, trying to see how deep it was. All he could see was blackness.

Suddenly, Sang put both claws around his arm and urged him back out. Richard pulled his head out of the hole and turned to look back at Sang. Sang shook his head in warning. It seemed clear to Richard that Sang didn't want to talk about whatever lived in those caves. Richard could tell from the looks of the others that whatever was in the holes scared the other Glee speechless.

Right then, the device was Richard's priority, so he didn't want to waste the time to be concerned about the holes and what might be in them. He would have to ask later.

After he nodded his thanks for the warning to Sang, he turned back to the trail and kept going. But now he was concerned about what lived in those holes that he and Vika might one day have to deal with. Unlike the Glee, the two of them weren't equipped with claws for protection.

Lightning flashed nearby, and the ground shook with a sudden thunderclap. While the rain didn't bother the Glee, the lightning clearly made them nervous. It made Richard nervous as well. The Glee looked around, as if they thought they would have time to run if they saw lightning. Some of them sought shelter behind rocks whenever there was a particularly bright flash and crack of thunder. Richard knew that hiding like that was pointless, because by the time you saw a close bolt strike, it was already too late to run from it. Richard disregarded what some of them did and kept climbing.

"Being up high like this is dangerous when there is lightning," Sang said, almost apologetically.

Richard looked back over his shoulder as he pulled himself up over a projecting shelf of rock. "I understand. I know the way from here, so you don't need to go the rest of the way up to the device. You can all go back, now, and when I'm finished destroying it, I will come back and join you."

As he and Vika waited, Sang consulted with a number of others. Richard couldn't hear that debate in his mind, so he didn't know what was being said, but he was hoping they would turn back. He didn't particularly want an audience. Flashes of lightning lit clouds from the inside in a frightening display of the power of the storm that was rolling in on them. The heads of some of the Glee sank into their shoulders as they cast worried looks to the sky.

Finally, Sang returned. *"We will go with you. I want to see the device destroyed, and so do many of the others. It has ruined many Glee lives. We want it ended once and for all. The ones who used to follow the goddess wish to go as well."*

Richard worried about those Glee, but didn't want to get into any kind of disagreement that could prevent him from destroying the device. So, he simply nodded and then turned back to the trail up through the rocks.

They had to scramble up steep areas of scree, almost running in order to make progress against the ground sliding away underfoot. The rock was loose and difficult enough to climb in the dry, but when it was wet it was even harder to get up because the water coming down helped it to slide out from underfoot. After an exhausting climb up through the loose, wet rock, they finally made it up into rock that was still slippery in the wet, but at least solid and much easier to climb. Richard's legs ached, but he didn't want to stop to rest. He could rest once the task was completed.

As they climbed higher into the low clouds, the fog became so thick that it was difficult to see very far. Richard could see Vika's dark shadow behind him, along with a couple of the Glee, with what looked like ghosts following them, but the rest were lost in the poor visibility.

Thunder rumbled almost continually through the desolate landscape. Lightning flickered somewhere off in the distance, illuminating the cloud they were in. Because they couldn't see where it was coming from, the light and sound instead seemed to be everywhere. It was unsettling.

Richard didn't like the idea of being on a mountain in a storm with such violent lightning, but his need to destroy the device made him ignore the danger and drove him onward. After he destroyed it, they would be forever trapped in this awful, wet world.

After hours of climbing, they finally began to emerge above the cloud cover and into the strange, dry forest of small rock towers. The sun was still obscured by an even higher layer of clouds, but at least it wasn't raining, and it was brighter. The lightning moved some distance away along with the huge, dark, billowing clouds, but Richard could still see the near-constant flickers of lightning inside those clouds down below them, lighting them with an eerie reddish, firelike glow.

He didn't know that he would ever be able to get used to this strange world, but he knew that he didn't really have a choice. It made him wonder if life would be worth living here after he destroyed the device.

As Richard and Vika wove their way through the maze of rock spires that had been carved, shaped, and softened by the weather, they finally reached the cathedral of those stone shapes surrounding and overlooking the device. It sat across the way at the edge of an expanse of white sand.

He could tell that Vika, not usually given to emotion, was feeling as despondent as he was at the prospect of destroying their way back to their own world. But it had to be done.

Richard drew his sword.

66

The sound of the blade being drawn from its scabbard rang out, echoing back from the complex shapes of the stone walls all around them. It was the forlorn sound of finality, of all his hopes and dreams ending. That distinctive ringing sound caused the massive crowd of Glee following them, who had seen the sword kill the goddess, pause with concern before backing away. Many moved back among the safety of the standing stones.

In his mind's eye, Richard could see Kahlan's smile. He had to force the image from his thoughts lest it be too unbearable or even prevent him from doing what he knew he had to do to protect her and all the people in her world. He hoped that one day his home world would again have a Lord Rahl, one who cared about his people: his son. One day it would also have a new Confessor to help protect them: his daughter.

For now, though, Richard was the only protection for that world, and to protect it, he had to destroy the device that allowed the Glee to go there. None of his people would ever know what he had done to save their world, and one day the Glee would only be a terrible memory. New generations would likely not even know anything about them or the horrors they had brought to the world.

He looked up overhead when he noticed that it was getting brighter. He saw that the clouds had parted enough to give them a rare glimpse of the sky. The sun itself wasn't in view, but the sky was a bright reddish orange. Because it was still late in the day, he thought it likely that it was near sunset. He couldn't yet see the stars, but if he could, he knew that he wouldn't be able to recognize them from a strange world he didn't want to be in.

So far, since he had arrived, the sky was rarely visible. The continual, heavy, rolling, boiling clouds seemed to make this world all that much gloomier. He didn't know if it was simply a seasonal weather pattern, or a habitual one.

Kahlan was out there, somewhere, among stars he couldn't yet see. He wondered if in her world, when she looked up, she might one day look toward the forsaken place in the sky where he would be forever stranded.

His joy at having a glimpse of the reddish sky instead of the continual overcast vista was short-lived when his gaze reluctantly settled on the device waiting for him across the sand.

"Are you sure you want to do this?" Vika whispered from close behind him. "Once you do, there is no going back."

He looked over his shoulder into her blue eyes. She questioned his choices and decisions quite often, sometimes in the form of a cutting remark, but he knew that it was her way of testing his confidence in a course of action, a way to get him to reaffirm his decisions within his own mind. When it came down to it, he knew that she had complete confidence in him.

This time, it was a critical, consequential question.

"What choice do I have?"

Vika's face said it all as she nodded slightly.

"None, I guess."

Richard could feel the power of the sword storming through every fiber of his being. That power pulled and tugged at him, wanting his anger to join with that power. But this time, he knew that venting his anger on the device that would forever separate him from Kahlan seemed out of place. This was an instance more of solemn duty than rage.

Besides, Richard couldn't seem to bring forth any anger of his own to join with that of the sword, or at least none he dared unleash.

Finally he decided that it was best to simply get it over with and not dwell on it, so that he could at last rest easy in the knowledge that it was done and that Kahlan and their children would not have to live in fear of Glee coming to slaughter them. So many had already died a horrific and senseless death. He couldn't realistically do anything for them, but he could at least see to it that the ones still alive would be spared the terror the Glee could bring.

As he crossed the expanse, with the tip of the sword dragging through the sand behind him, he was reminded again of the round area of white sand in the Garden of Life at the People's

Palace. That was a place of great significance. So much had started there, and ended there, and now it was all ending in a similar circular area of white sand in a world far away.

As Richard got closer, something about the symbols on the stone device made him pause for a moment, staring. He moved closer then to have a better look, to see if his initial thought could actually be possible.

When he realized that he was right, he sheathed his sword.

Vika looked suddenly concerned. "What's wrong?"

Richard hardly heard her as he dropped to his knees in front of the stone and reached out to run his fingertips lightly over the symbols on the smooth surface.

"Lord Rahl, what is it?"

He could hardly believe what he was seeing.

"These symbols are in the language of Creation. It's not precisely the same as the symbols I've seen before, but they're awfully close. I can tell right off that most of them are substantially the same. There are some differences, but they're close enough that I think I might be able to translate them."

Vika rushed up and fell to her knees beside him. "Really? What does it say?"

"It's not that simple."

"Well, if you can recognize it as the language of Creation, and you understand that language, then it only makes sense that it must be something you can read, right?"

"Yes, I think I can. Some of it, anyway. From the parts I am able to read, what it says is incredibly complicated."

"What do you mean by complicated?"

"Well, in many ways, it reminds me of a complex constructed spell."

"A constructed spell?" She leaned closer to him with an astonished look. "You mean magic?"

Richard nodded as he tried to decipher one of the symbols having to do with intersecting lines of power.

"Yes. Like magic."

Vika let out a sigh as she sat back on her heels. "I'm afraid that I can't help you there. But are you sure? How could magic possibly be involved with this device?"

"Magic is involved with all the devices I've seen before."

"You would know a lot more about that than

I would," she said. "I try to avoid anything having to do with magic. You seem to always be involved with it in one way or another."

He nodded, not really hearing her as he leaned in and frowned. "It's saying something about a ring."

Vika stared at him. "A ring? What kind of ring?"

Richard ran his fingers over the symbols, trying to understand what he was reading out of order and out of context. Doing so always made translations much more difficult. The language of Creation was not easy to read as it was, but a lot of it had to be read in context to be understood.

He searched for the beginning to try to read it from where the description started. The problem was, he wasn't entirely sure, yet, exactly where that starting point was.

He read several of the symbols looking for the beginning when he recognized something. He looked to the sand at the sides of the stone.

"It's talking about a ring beginning and ending here."

"What could that mean?"

"I'm not sure." He pointed beside the stone.

"Dig in the sand, right there, and see if there is a ring of some kind."

As Vika did as he asked, Richard went to the other side and started digging with his hands.

"I found something," Vika called over to him.

As he dug, his fingers touched something hard and smooth. "Me too."

He started clearing away the sand, exposing what was buried there. He brushed sand away to expose more of it. Vika was doing the same. In a few moments they each had uncovered gleaming metal. It was the color of gold and perfectly round, about as thick as his forearm. It was not cold to the touch like some metals. It felt more like real gold.

As he and Vika both followed it along, un-covered more and more, they began to see that it went out in both directions from the stone, and by the way it curved as it moved away from that square stone, it soon became obvious that it was a gold ring that, from what they had so far uncovered, looked like it encompassed most of the round area of sand.

"What should we do?" Vika asked.

Richard was using his hands to sweep away sand from the top of the ring. "It's not buried very deep. Let's uncover it all and confirm if it really does go all the way around in a ring."

They worked with urgency to solve the mystery. They both felt driven by the discovery, wanting to excavate it to see if it told them anything important. Richard couldn't imagine, though, what use it could be to them. After all, the whole thing would soon be destroyed.

The hundreds of Glee watching them from around the whole area and back in among the stone formations didn't say anything or try to interfere, but it was clear that they were as astonished as Richard and Vika. They had lived with and used this device all their lives, and yet they had never known that the ring was right there, connected to it, just under the surface of the sand.

In a short time Richard and Vika had uncovered the entire ring. Both of them stood and stepped back to look at it.

Richard thought that it was either made of or covered with gold. The golden ring went in a full circle, interrupted only by the stone sitting at one side of the sand. The ring was polished and so perfectly smooth that Richard could see his distorted reflection in it. It was simply a smooth, polished golden surface. It had no writing or symbols on it.

Richard looked over at the stone. It had a massive amount of writing on it.

He rushed across the white sand to see if he could tell if the writing on the stone might reveal something about the purpose of the golden ring.

67

"Anything?" Vika sounded impatient. "You've been looking at it long enough that you must be able to read at least some of it. You should be able to tell something from the symbols, right? So, what does what you've translated so far say?"

Richard sat back on his heels and looked over at her. "The Glee are wrong in calling it a device."

"Really? Why? What is it called?"

"It's called a gateway."

Vika stared at him a long moment. "A gateway?"

"That's what it says."

Vika gestured at the stone. "You mean . . . like a gateway to other worlds?"

Richard nodded. "It would seem so."

She frowned as she considered. "I guess that makes sense. But it seems like an awful lot of writing just to say that it's called the gateway. Does it really take all of that to say it's called the gateway?"

Richard let out a deep sigh as he looked back at the stone. He gently ran his fingers over the symbols as he considered them.

"No, that's only a small amount of what this says. There's a lot more to it. The symbols are similar to those in our world, and many are the same, but not all are and there are key differences from any I've seen before. Some of the more complex symbols are meant to convey concepts by using underlying elements, but not all of those use the same elements as the ones I'm familiar with. Even though it's in many ways different, it's still hauntingly similar to what was once a common form of writing in our world."

"You mean it's the same as the writing all over that witch woman, Niska, back in our world? The one in the swamp by Agaden Reach where we caught up with the Mother Confessor."

"The very same. And it's close to the same as in a lot of other places in our world. It predates everything else. All other writing, which involves words rather than pictorial elements and concepts, came after the language of Creation."

Vika gave him a blank look. "So . . . what, exactly, are you trying to say?"

Richard shook his head with a sigh as he looked back at the stone. "I don't know. I'm just saying that this has to be very old. But more than that, don't you think that it's more than strange for the language of Creation to be on this stone in another world besides ours?"

"It has been here for a very long time," Sang said from back beyond the sand, trying to sound helpful. He had stepped a little closer, away from the others watching. Richard had forgotten that the Glee packed in among the stone spires were listening. *"Maybe that is what you mean? That it has been here for a very long time?"*

Richard knew that Sang didn't grasp the significance of what he had discovered. There was no way he could. He wasn't in the mood to give lessons, though, so he kept it simple.

"Longer than that."

All of the Glee looked to be confused as they whispered among themselves. They clearly had a hard time grasping anything Richard was saying. The language of Creation, after all, had no meaning for them.

Vika slapped a hand onto the stone. "But it could be that this thing, this gateway, may have once come to our world and given us the language of Creation, don't you suppose? Much like it came to this world?"

Richard shook his head. "I have absolutely no idea, Vika. That seems like it could be true, but I don't think that's the case. I simply have no way of saying for sure. What I do know is that these symbols are instructions."

Vika withdrew her hand from the stone as she leaned close to him. "Instructions?" she whispered. "Instructions for what?"

Richard leaned in toward the stone again to put his fingers on the symbols. "I'm not ready to say, yet. I need to read some more so I can try to piece it all together."

Vika stood to leave him to it. She walked the perimeter just beyond the gold ring. Richard thought she looked like she might be making sure the Glee stayed back out of the way. The more he read, the more he thought that might be a very good idea.

On one of her rounds, as she went past him, she bent close. "Anything useful, yet?"

Richard looked up at her. "Tell Sang I'd like him to come over here. I want to ask him something. Be casual about it. I don't want the others to hear me."

When she strolled back with the tall, nearly black Glee, Richard stood.

"What is it?" Sang asked. *"Why are you not destroying the device? I thought that was why you were—"*

"How did you use this device to come to my world? You came a number of times. How did you do it? How did you make the device work for you?"

Sang was taken off-guard by the question. He thought about it briefly, and then looked over at the device.

"There is a place on the top, on the other side, that I used to make the device work so that I could go into darkness. That is how I reached your world."

"Show me," Richard said.

Sang nodded and then led them around the square block of stone to stand just outside of the ring, facing the slanted top. Richard came around with him and watched.

Sang spread his right claws to extend just the first one, much as a person would extend their first finger to point.

"When I wished to go to your world, I would put one claw into this place, here."

Sang used the claw to tap the sloped top of the stone. There was a slot right next to where he tapped. It looked like he would be able to fit the single claw all the way down into the slot. That was what Richard had thought from what he had read so far. But he knew that there had to be a lot more to it.

"How did you know where to go? When you went into darkness, it didn't just spit you out somewhere at random. How did it allow you to come to our world?"

"In the beginning, long before we all came alive, it is said that Glee would sometimes try putting their claw into that place. They were never seen again. No one knew what happened to them. So maybe, as you say, the device sent them someplace where they died. Or maybe it sent them

nowhere at all and they long ago simply vanished into darkness.

"The Golden Goddess, besides being bigger than other Glee, was also smarter. She was the first to learn that she could ask the device to send her to other worlds where she could survive. I believe that was the key. The device then picked places like that.

"She learned right at first that she could return by what we now call the lifeline. She would travel to other worlds and then come back and tell others what she had discovered. As she found worlds for them to raid, they came to call her the collector of worlds.

"After she found a world she liked, she would then insert one claw, and think of the place she wished to go back to, and the device would send her into darkness until she arrived at that world. They began to call her a goddess, much like they thought of the ones who had left the device as gods. Because she alone knew how it worked, she began to gain followers who called her goddess, and then the Golden Goddess. She liked having followers who worshipped her.

"After a time, she would stand here, where we stand now, and in that way send her followers to the places she had found where they would hunt for food. That eventually evolved into sport for them."

Richard knew that when the gods, or whoever it was, had brought the gateway to Sang's world and left it where it now stood, it had to be adjusted so that the Glee could use it. It had protocols, shown in the symbols, that had to have been set so the Glee could use a single claw to activate it. From what Richard had read, once it had been set for the new use, such as had been done when it had been left here in this world, nothing else would work.

Until the gateway was reset.

From what Sang had just told him, the Golden Goddess was the first to finally figure out how to make the gateway work successfully. Now, all the Glee knew.

The implications were racing around in Richard's mind as he tried to piece together all the things he had so far been able to read on the stone.

"Thank you, Sang. That explains a lot." Richard lifted his sword halfway from its scabbard to show it to Sang. "You better go stand back there with the others where it will be safe."

Piecing together what he had read so far, and what Sang said, Richard knew just how dangerous this gateway was in the hands of the Glee. It had to be destroyed.

Sang nodded, having seen the destructive power of the sword before, and rushed out of the circle of sand to stand back with the others among the rock formations.

Richard stood staring at the symbols on the stone gateway for a long moment. He let the sword slide back down into its scabbard.

Vika frowned at Richard and lowered her voice. "Lord Rahl, what's going on? Are you going to destroy this terrible thing or not?"

Richard rubbed his chin as he looked from her to the stone and back again. "I'm getting an idea."

Her brow tightened. "What kind of idea?"

"The crazy kind."

"Is it going to get us killed?"

"Probably."

68

"What kind of crazy idea is it this time?" she asked, sounding weary of such ideas and the likelihood that it would get them killed.

Richard waved off the question. "Do me a favor and keep making sure the Glee stay back. I need to be left alone for a while to study these symbols. They're complicated."

Vika waggled a hand at the stone. "What do you think all those are for? What is their purpose? You said before that they're instructions, but instructions for what?"

Richard looked into her blue eyes. "Instructions to reset the gateway."

"What do you mean, reset it?"

Richard wiped a hand across his face. He was

already weary of this damp world. He dreaded the thought of living out his life among the Glee in this hot, red, often wet world. He supposed he wouldn't have to live too long until one of them eventually got the idea to eat him.

"Well, when whoever brought this gateway here left it for the Glee to use, they had to reset it so that it would work for the Glee."

"Maybe they didn't really intend to leave it here," she suggested. "Maybe the Glee captured them and forced them to reset it so they could use it. After all, we know all too well how vicious they can be."

Richard pulled his lower lip through his teeth. "I suppose that's possible, too. There is no real way to tell for sure."

"So, what are you considering?"

He waggled a finger at the stone. "I'm thinking that if I can figure out enough of the symbols to activate it, I may be able to reset it."

Vika cocked her head as she suspiciously scrutinized him with her left eye alone. "Why would you want to reset it? For what purpose?"

"Well, think about it. If I'm able to reset it so that it works differently, then they could never again use it to go to our world—or any world for that matter. They wouldn't have the means to reset it to work for them, so that would render the gateway inert."

Vika's mouth twisted as she tried to follow his train of thought. "Why bother with all that? Wouldn't it be a lot simpler to just break it apart with your sword? If you did that, they certainly wouldn't be able to ever use it again, right? I mean, you wouldn't need to understand the symbols to do that. If you simply break the stone apart with your sword, that would be the end of it. Forever."

Richard glanced over at the stone before looking back at her. "We don't know what this thing really is."

Vika was giving him a wary look, like she was trying to figure out what he could really be thinking. "You said it's called a gateway. Obviously, it's a gateway to other worlds. That's what it is."

"Yes, but what I mean is we don't know what powers it, what makes it work. How does it send people"—he gestured with a hand in the direction of the throng of Glee watching them—"or Glee, or whatever, to another world? What if it uses some kind of magic, or what if inside it has mechanical components powered by magic like the omen machine used to have?

"I've found things in our world that are incredibly powerful and in many cases I have no idea exactly how they work or who could have made them or, for that matter, even where they came from. But I learned that they were profoundly dangerous, and had I tried to simply destroy them with my sword so that no one could ever use them, it could have caused unimaginable consequences. Some of those devices could have destroyed the world of life. In some things involving unknown magic that has the potential to be profoundly dangerous, such as this, here, you have to think it through before you do anything that can't be undone."

Vika glanced over at the stone in a new light. "So, you're saying that it could be so dangerous to try to destroy it that you think it might kill us all?"

Richard shrugged. "I don't know. From what I know about magic that's a possibility. If I hit it with my sword it could kill me, or, for all I know, it might even unleash enough power to destroy everyone for miles around, or even render this entire world a dead rock."

He leaned closer to her. "Or, for all I know, it might even act as a weapon and send that destructive power to the last place the Glee used it to visit—to our world."

Vika flipped her braid forward over her shoulder and held it in her right fist as she considered.

"You mean, you think it could possibly be dangerous to try to destroy it, even dangerous to our own world, so instead you are thinking it might be safer for us, and our world, if you try to reset it so that the Glee can't possibly use it, and that would accomplish the same thing. It would render it useless and prevent them from ever harming our world again."

Richard gave her a firm nod. "That's right. For all I know, it could kill me if I try to destroy it, and then it would still be here and still work and remain a threat to our world."

"Well," she said with a deep sigh, "that's not crazy, so it's obviously not what you are actually thinking of doing. What is the crazy thing you are really considering doing?"

Richard showed her a small smile and gestured off to the other side of the ring. "Would you please go keep an eye on them. Once I start,

I think I may need to keep going and I don't want to have any nosy Glee interrupting me."

Vika studied his face for a moment. "What are you not telling me?"

"I'm not telling you what you don't yet need to know."

Vika folded her arms as she looked at him from under her brow. "I'm here alone in this world with you. Forever. I'm going to grow old and die in the world along with you—if we live that long. We are in this together. Tell me."

Richard pursued his lips. "We are starting to sound like an old married couple."

She kept the look leveled on him. "Tell me."

He sighed. "All right. Well, first of all, if I simply reset the gateway, it's always possible that someone else could come along, figure it out, and reset it back again. If that happened, then they could use it for who knows what purpose. There's more to it, though."

"Like what?"

Richard gestured toward the gateway without looking over at it. "These symbols are starting to look to me like they could actually be a constructed spell."

69

With her arms still folded, she shrugged. "That's the big deal you couldn't tell me? That it might be a constructed spell?"

"If you mess with them and accidentally do the wrong thing, some constructed spells can kill everyone within dozens of miles."

Her arms came unfolded. "Oh."

"They can also be incredibly dangerous in other ways as well. Unexpected ways. If it really is a constructed spell, or even if it isn't but it functions something like one, it's not any kind of constructed spell I'm familiar with, and yet it has many of the routines and protocols I recognize. On top of that, not all the symbols are close to the same as those in the version of the language of Creation that I'm familiar with.

That makes it hard to know precisely what each of those protocols means, how they function, and if there is a specific order to using them.

"Some constructed spells have fail-safes built into them that can kill you if you do the wrong thing at the wrong time. I will need to study it some more, first, before I can say for certain exactly what we are dealing with, here."

Vika looked at the stone and then back to him. "But if it really is the language of Creation, you should be able to understand it, shouldn't you?"

"I believe that the language of Creation may have different dialects. The markings here might simply be one of those different dialects, and that's why I'm having trouble understanding it. That makes it a little more difficult to translate all these symbols. It won't prevent me from translating what they say, but I first need to be sure of what some of the more familiar ones mean. Once I'm sure of the meaning of the symbols in those, that will help me translate others. That's going to take me some time. I don't know how much time, but I need to be left to it."

She shrugged. "All right, so study it."

He gave her a meaningful look. "I would

appreciate it if you went over there and watched the Glee to keep them from getting too curious so I can concentrate in this."

"Oh. All right. Well, why didn't you just say so? But if you really think it is a constructed spell, wouldn't that mean this thing is powered by magic?"

Richard shook his head, feeling frustration that he had a hard time explaining all the technicalities. "I don't know. Maybe. I understand constructed spells, and I know how they function. I've even made a number of them myself. This looks in many ways like it could very well be a constructed spell, but in other ways it's different, so I'm not yet entirely sure.

"It may simply share some aspects with a constructed spell. It may be a coincidence that it looks like one to me in part because I'm not able to read all the symbols. I might also be reading too much into it. I just don't know yet. But these symbols are the key to learning how this thing functions, and if it actually is a constructed spell, so that's why I need to study it. Got it now?"

"What difference could that make?" She frowned at him. "If you simply reset it so they can't use it, that's all you really need to do, right?"

"Sure, unless someone comes along who can recognize the symbols or figure them out and then reset it for themselves so they could use the gateway. I'm trying to figure out if there is a way to lock in the reset, or better yet, use a fail-safe. So, unless you know how to work a constructed spell or you understand the language of Creation, would you please go over there and watch those Glee? And be prepared in case something happens."

Vika glanced to the Glee and then back at him. "Something like what?"

"Are you going to ask questions all the time for the rest of our lives in this awful world?"

Vika only smiled.

Richard looked over at the Glee out of the corner of one eye. "I don't know for sure what might happen, but if this thing really is a constructed spell powered by magic and something happens, they may become alarmed."

"What should I be prepared for?"

Richard let out a weary sigh. "Vika, Sang is going to soon grow impatient that I am not destroying this thing. I don't know what the other Glee will do if this stone starts making noises or something. After all, they seem to regard this thing as some sort of sacred object given to them by gods."

Vika finally relented. "All right. That makes sense. But if I have to start using my Agiel on them, things could get messy."

"Well, I don't want you to do that. Just keep your eye on them. Strike up a conversation or something. Divert their attention. Ask them about their offspring. Parents love to talk about that."

As soon as he said that, he wished he hadn't.

"I'm not all that experienced at small talk, but I'll give it a try."

"Is life with you in this world always going to be this difficult?"

Vika smiled again. "You wouldn't want life here to be boring, would you?"

Richard shook his head before turning back to the stone as Vika walked over to Sang.

70

Richard glanced over to check and saw Vika talking to the Glee. Things seemed peaceful enough. They looked interested in whatever she was telling them. He turned his attention back to what he was doing, bending close to continue studying the series of symbols and emblems on the stone, trying to figure out what the parts he didn't recognize meant.

He rubbed a temple with a finger as he worked to understand the connecting links. They were in fact different in a number of ways from the language of Creation he had learned, but he hadn't told Vika everything he already knew about them. He wasn't sure she could understand it—or would care to. Mord-Sith were famous for their dislike of anything to do with magic. Richard wasn't yet positive that this gateway stone really did possess magic, but the symbols certainly did have a lot of the characteristic elements of magic as expressed through constructed spells. He almost had a hard time believing it could be something other than magic.

In large part, they did comply with the precepts of a constructed spell. And yet, in some ways, they didn't.

He had created constructed spells before, and in his studies, he had learned a great deal about their complexities and how they functioned through principles of magic, both Additive and Subtractive. He knew a number of their key provisions. But that hardly meant he knew everything about them.

While this was in many ways the same element he knew, and understood, there were differences he couldn't yet fathom. He traced components of things he knew, struggling to identify exactly how this was different so he could fill in the blanks.

In his studies of books of magic and in working with constructed spells he had access to, he had also learned a lot about his own gift.

For reasons that eluded him, he had an easier time using his gift with constructed spells, perhaps because they were so technical, and the steps made sense. When he followed the steps in constructed spells in the proper way, the spell came to life. In other situations when he needed his gift, it didn't always respond, so he naturally gravitated toward the type of magic with structure he could analyze.

He also suspected that those technical aspects that required him to concentrate distracted him enough to call upon his gift without really thinking about it when his magic was needed in procedures along the way. When he was relieved of the conscious pressure to call forth his gift, it simply naturally worked as required to assist him. Importantly, one of the things he had learned in his studies was that it took his gift not only to work with constructed spells, but to understand them.

It had always been difficult for him to call up his gift consciously, except in a certain kind of crisis, but here, with these emblems, he could sense them with his gift. It seemed like here, in this world, with this complicated spell he was able to touch his gift in order to understand elements in ways that were difficult or impossible to do back in his home world.

He realized that it felt to him like he was having much the same kind of ease with using his gift as he had experienced before, only in the underworld.

Because constructed spells were so rare, he hadn't been able to study a lot of them. Having seen only a relative few, that left a lot of questions in his mind with the gateway.

He came to realize that, rather than trying to decipher every element of every symbol along the way to understand all of the language of Creation the way it was written on the stone, if he simply assumed it was a constructed spell and treated it as such, that very well might be the best way for him to come to grasp the entirety of what all the writing meant.

As he became more familiar with the symbols he hadn't seen before, he began to learn by their context that it wasn't really all that different from the language of Creation he already knew. This simply said things in a slightly different way. It might use the symbol for a bat to express flight, rather than the bird symbol he was familiar with. But it suddenly clicked in his mind that the larger concept was really the same. They were both referring to the concept of the air, or the sky. That realization helped him start to make faster progress in deciphering the overarching meaning of what he was reading.

When he glanced up, he noticed that the Glee across the sand were starting to look restless. Vika was walking back and forth, talking to them, distracting them. He certainly couldn't afford to have the Glee suddenly decide that they didn't want Richard messing around with their device, as they called the gateway.

But what was worse, he now realized that he was going to need to ignite a verification web if he was to learn more of how the gateway functioned, and he didn't know how the Glee might react to that. He finally decided that there was no other way around it. He was simply going to have to do it.

Richard finally located the sequence of symbols that would initiate the verification web. He touched those symbols with a finger in the proper order, letting his gift flow into each of them to begin to unlock the constructed spell. It should work if the symbols were what he believed they were.

He held his breath and briefly tapped the last one to let a bit of Subtractive Magic feed the emblem.

Suddenly, all the symbols on the entire stone lit up as if they were made of glass and there was a light inside the stone. Every one of the symbols glowed a pale bluish color that stood out all the more because of everything else being some shade of red. More alarming, the thing started giving off a low humming sound.

Richard didn't know if he had merely activated the stone in some way, or it was doing what he intended. He quickly went back to the symbols and tapped the next series in the proper sequence to add Subtractive Magic to them in order to find out if this really was a constructed spell. Subtractive Magic would break the necessary seals if it actually was a constructed spell. If it was, then something should happen to give him some kind of indication.

At first, nothing happened.

He held his breath as he waited.

All of a sudden, one of the emblems on the top of the stone, on the side opposite the sloped top, lit with red light. He touched it with a finger, letting it have a bit of Additive

Magic. As soon as he did, it abruptly threw a series of lines through the air similar to the way a fisherman would toss out a net. But instead of sinking to the ground, this net of lines hung in midair over the sand. The lines all glowed the same pale bluish color as the other symbols on the gateway stone. That was a sign, but not yet the right sign.

He heard the Glee across the sand, crowded in among the rocks, start to hiss. It sounded to him like a hiss of impatience.

He glanced up at the intricate pattern of the lines hanging in midair only to see Vika rushing back to him.

The alarm on her face was clear.

71

Richard motioned frantically to get Vika to go around the glowing lines rather than run straight toward him and through them. She had no idea how dangerous they were, but fortunately she instinctively avoided anything having to do with magic, so as soon as she spotted the glowing lines she dodged to the side and changed course to avoid going into the gold ring altogether. He breathed out a sigh of relief.

She skidded to a stop beside the stone. She put a hand on it for support as she panted.

"Lord Rahl—"

Richard pushed her hand off the stone. "Don't touch it. It's active. I don't know what it could do if you touch the wrong thing."

She drew her hand back as if she had touched fire. "Lord Rahl, the Glee are not at all happy about what they're seeing."

Before she could elaborate, Sang raced up behind her. *"Lord Rahl! You must not do this,"* he shouted in Richard's mind. *"You said that you intended to destroy the device. That is what you must do. The others, the others who were followers of the goddess, are growing angry. They consider this device a sacred gift from the gods."*

Richard frowned up at Sang. "Then why didn't they object when I came up here to destroy the thing?"

Sang looked back at the massive throng of Glee among the rocks on the other side of the white sand. They were all waving their arms, apparently arguing among themselves. He looked back at Richard and bent down as if to speak confidentially, although the Glee had already proven their ability to have others hear them selectively. Or maybe it was only an ability to make Richard and Vika selectively not hear them.

"They did not know that you intended to destroy the device."

"What?" Richard rose to his feet. "You mean you didn't tell them what I intended to do?"

Sang shook his head. *"No. I dared not. You must understand that we have only just been reunited with them after you struck down the Golden Goddess. I thought you would come up here and do the same thing with the device and it would be over before they realized what you were going to do, and in that way have it ended once and for all before they could object."*

"What did you expect them to do once had I destroyed it with my sword?"

Sang hesitated. *"I thought that since it would then be over and too late for them to do anything about it, we could more easily convince them that it was for the best. With the Golden Goddess dead and the device destroyed so we could no longer go to other worlds, I thought they would then realize they had no choice but to go back to our traditional ways and then they would come to be at peace with it. I thought they would even realize that the fighting and violent death of so many was finally ended and be pleased."*

Richard realized that even though they had the ceremonial eating of the water weed from Iben's body, they hadn't fully committed to giving up all their beliefs or using the device to go to other worlds. They had enjoyed the sport of hunting, and they had developed a taste for the flesh of people. There were probably Glee among those watching who craved power and were waiting to later use the device to win followers to themselves.

"This is more complicated than I realized," Richard told Sang. "I can't simply use my sword to break this stone apart. It's not just a piece of rock. If it were, I could shatter it. But it's a powerful device that uses magic to send you to other worlds. If I use my sword to try to destroy it, it could end up killing us all, or even killing everyone in this world. I need to disable it in another way."

"Do what you must, but hurry," Sang urged. *"If you do not destroy it quickly, you may never get another chance."*

"I will go as fast as I can, but it will take some time. I need you to go back and convince them that they need to stay away because these lines you see above the sand are dangerous."

Sang looked across the sand toward the Glee for a moment and then back to Richard. His third eyelids blinked across his large, glossy black eyes.

"What lines?"

72

Richard was shocked. "You mean to say you can't see the glowing lines above the sand?"

Sang briefly looked again and then back at Richard. He shook his head.

"I see only sand and beyond it, the Glee who are growing angry."

Richard hadn't expected that the Glee couldn't see the lines of light. He knew that everyone in his world had at least a spark of the gift within the Grace they were born with. That spark, even though it usually wasn't powerful enough in most people to use it to do magic, still allowed them to see and interact with magic.

The only explanation was that the Glee had no such spark of the gift. They were completely devoid of even that infinitesimal spark. That was why the goddess had been so fearful of the magic of Richard's world. She had never experienced it before and didn't understand it. It was a fearsome unknown to her.

Sang drew back his lips, exposing his needle-sharp white teeth, as if in apology.

Richard gestured. "Can you see the symbols on the stone light up?"

Sang leaned past Richard to look at the stone. *"Light? I see no light. Only the markings as they were always there."*

The sun had set, and it was rapidly getting darker. Sang should have had absolutely no difficulty seeing either the glowing lines of light above the sand or the glowing symbols on the stone gateway.

Richard looked over at Vika. "You see them both, right?"

She shrugged her confusion that Sang couldn't see them. "Of course. I don't know what the lines over the sand are, or what they mean, but I can see them."

Richard was at least relieved by that much of it. "It's the initial stages of a verification web. The lines mean that I was able to get the gateway to ignite its constructed spell. There's no explanation I can see other than whatever this gateway is, it uses a constructed spell. It's built right into it."

"What is a constructed spell?" Sang asked.

"Magic," Richard told him. "Dangerous magic."

"Dangerous to you, or to us?"

"Extremely dangerous to the Glee," Richard told him. "You already know that this device has the ability to send you into darkness. That should tell you something about how powerful it is. That power is dangerous."

"But we have used it since long before any of us were alive," Sang said. *"It never harmed us."*

"It was never activated before, but now it is. Because it uses a very powerful form of magic, I need to use that power built into the device to destroy it. It's the only way."

Sang gestured back across the sand. *"But the others are angry at not knowing what you are doing with their device, and they may soon decide they must stop you."*

"You need to go talk to them. Tell them how you have seen the power of magic in my world. This device uses that same magic. If you want to, tell them that the device is malfunctioning, and it is about to kill anyone up here. You need to get all of the Glee away from here or they might be killed. Get them all to go back down the mountain to safety."

"I don't think they will want to leave you alone with the device. It is too important to them."

Richard growled his frustration. He gestured up at the darkening sky. "It's getting dark. You need to go now while it is still light enough to see your way down the mountain or you will all be stuck up here in this dry place all night." Richard leaned toward him. "All night. Without water."

Sang touched a claw to his lip. That concerned him, but he was still hesitating. Because he couldn't see the glowing bluish lines, Richard didn't know if he understood and feared the magic of the gateway, but like a boulder falling off a cliff from above, you didn't need to see it to be killed. He knew, though, that fear of being stuck in this dry place overnight was probably more alarming to him than anything else. He looked across the sand to the others. Some of them were clacking their claws in a threatening manner.

"Sang," Richard said, drawing his attention back to him, "something is about to happen that will likely kill all of you up here. You need to convince them they must leave, right now. You need to tell them that darkness will soon trap them here in this dry place and they must leave now, while they can still see the path down. Tell them they can come back tomorrow if you have to."

Sang nodded. *I will try. I will tell them what you say about being trapped up here in this dry place where it will soon be dark. That may convince them to go back down from here right away.*

"I'm serious," Richard said. "Dangerous magic is about to begin and if anyone is up here when it does, they will die.

"If they refuse to leave, then you and your friends must leave as quickly as you can or you will be killed, too. You must believe me, Sang. You must leave now. I don't want you or your friends to be harmed. But if they stay up here, you all will die."

Sang again touched the tip of his claw to his black lower lip as he studied Richard's face. Finally, he nodded. *You have done what we needed to stop the Golden Goddess. You have helped us. I will tell those with me that we must run. I will tell the others, too, that it will soon be too dark to see, and they will be trapped here so they must leave until tomorrow. They will be warned. If they don't leave . . ."*

Richard put a hand on Sang's shoulder. "You have been a friend, Sang. I wish you a good life."

Sang's dark skin bunched above his big black eyes in a kind of grotesque frown. *"Are you saying that you will be here when the magic starts, and you will die?"*

Richard continued to gaze into those black eyes. "I'm afraid so. This is what I need to do to protect my world. Thank you for your part in this, and for coming to help me protect my people as well as yours. Now go. Hurry. Get to safety."

"You have been a friend to me and to my friends."

Sang laid a claw on Richard's shoulder, as if to thank him, and then he quickly turned and rushed away. He paused once to look back, and then he ran to the others off among the forest of tall rocks to warn them that they must leave at once.

73

Vika leaned close to Richard once she saw Sang join the others. "This is it, then? We are really going to die?"

Richard glanced over at her. "If my crazy idea doesn't work, most likely."

She frowned in a way that only Mord-Sith could frown. "And if your crazy idea does work, then the gateway will be destroyed, and we will have to face who knows how many thousands of angry Glee that will want to rip us apart for destroying their precious device?"

"Maybe they will cool off once they get back to their ponds."

Richard didn't want to tell her what his crazy idea actually was.

"So, if your crazy idea doesn't work, we will

likely die in the attempt, and if it does work and doesn't kill us, the Glee likely will."

"I tried to get you to stay back there in our world," he told her. "You are the one who insisted on coming with me."

Vika made a sour face as she folded her arms. "I guess coming with you was my crazy idea."

He showed her a small smile that was more forced than real.

She looked across the sand at the Glee. They were all engaged in an animated discussion. There was even some pushing and shoving. Sang threw both arms up in the air as he jumped around, frantically trying to make his point. They didn't look to be convinced. He gestured at the sky and then toward the way down the mountain, urging them that they had to leave before it was too dark.

The former followers of the goddess who had followed them up the mountain didn't look like they had any intention of leaving before it was too dark, apparently more upset about Richard messing with their precious device than anything else. The way they were pointing across the sand, they looked like they were more set on stopping Richard.

The Glee Richard had brought across the drylands finally heeded Sang's urgent warnings and started for the path down the mountain. Richard looked up and he could already see the first stars. They soon wouldn't have much light to help them make it down the mountain. The moons would help, but only until they were in the dense fog of the heavy cloud layer lower down the mountain.

"I don't know what you have planned," Vika said, "but you had better hurry up before they decide to come over here and kill us to keep you from harming their sacred device."

"I know, but I need time."

"Time for what? How much time?"

"I already activated the verification web." He gestured toward the sand. "That's the bluish lines in the air above the sand. It doesn't tell me enough about what I need to know to reset the gateway. In order to understand the gateway and the process to reset it, I need to do an aspect analysis of the verification web from an interior perspective."

"Oh, of course." Vika rolled her eyes. "I don't know why I didn't suggest that in the first place."

"Vika, this is serious. This is our only chance.

I'm going to have to use both Additive Magic and Subtractive Magic. It's the only way to activate an interior perspective."

That sobered her. "What do you need me to do?"

"Once I ignite that kind of power, anyone up here is going to die."

"I hope you don't really expect me to leave with Sang."

"No." He gestured to the bluish lines above the sand. "I want you inside that web with me. It's the only way to protect you."

"Inside magic?" She looked at him like she thought he had lost his mind. "You want me inside some kind of powerful magic with you? That's your crazy idea?"

"You need to trust me. You have already let me take you to the world of the dead. Compared to that, this should be a breeze."

"Sure, a breeze." She glanced briefly at the glowing lines above the sand. "I don't know a lot about magic, but what I do know is that mixing Subtractive Magic and Additive Magic is beyond dangerous. If you need reminding, that's what brought Shota's palace in Bindamoon down on top of you."

"I know, but this time there is not a witch unleashing the same thing at me."

"Will we be safe in your web thing?"

Richard nodded to reassure her. "Yes. I've done it before, and I know how to do it. But there is a problem."

"Of course there is." She let out a deep sigh. "What's the problem?"

"While I know what I'm doing with the constructed-spell portion, I don't know for sure how the gateway is going to react to a mix of that kind of power."

She gestured across to the sand. "Well, whatever you're going to do, you had better hurry. I don't think Sang is convincing those angry Glee of anything."

Richard saw that she was right. The last thing he needed was to get into a battle with Glee in the middle of complex protocols. He grabbed hold of Vika's upper arm and urgently pulled her with him toward the center of the maze of glowing, bluish lines, working his way carefully but quickly through the maze without touching it to get to the center. Fortunately, there weren't yet a lot of the bluish lines; that was why he needed to do the more extensive interior perspective from inside the verification web.

Once there in the center of the sand, Vika looked all around at the glowing lines, like they might bite. She wasn't necessarily wrong. But they were far from as dangerous as they were going to get.

"I don't have magic," she reminded him.

"You have the bond to me," he told her in a distracted voice. "I have magic. That gives you all the magic you will need. You will be protected by that bond."

She looked around at the lines. "If you say so."

"I do."

"Well, do I need to do anything?"

"No. Just try not to move around too much or touch the glowing lines. Stay close to me. Once everything starts, don't move away or try to run."

She gestured. "Sang is still here, trying to convince them to leave."

Richard turned. "Sang!" he called out. "You have three heartbeats before anything living up here is killed. Go now! If they won't go with you, leave them!"

74

At Richard's urgent warning, Sang and the rest of his followers still up on the mountain raced away and disappeared through the contorted rock spires toward the path that would take them down the mountain. A few of the other Glee looked about and then changed their minds when they saw the others running for their lives. A number of them decided to go with them. Many more watched them go but didn't follow.

Richard had given them a chance to get to safety. They refused to take it.

He saw the masses of Glee that were left behind, apparently wary because of Sang's warnings about dangerous magic, cautiously begin to move out from between and behind the smooth, flowing shapes of the rock. Cautious or not, he recognized Glee with murderous intent.

"Lord Rahl—hurry!" Vika yelled.

"Don't stare at the lightning," he told her.

"What lightning?"

Instead of taking precious time to answer her, Richard simply reached out and touched two separate primary intersections of converging, glowing, bluish lines and then closed his eyes. To cast the proper interior perspective of a verification web, he needed to use his gift. He could feel the power of the gateway's constructed spell as it pulled his gift up from the depths of his soul.

He knew by the way it functioned that the gateway had to be powered by a constructed spell. It was clear that it was simply a type of constructed spell he had never encountered before. That being the case, he hoped that everything at least worked in the same way with the same procedures he knew.

As he felt the power from those bluish lines radiating up his arms, he didn't try to resist. They were seeking within him what they needed. He knew that without Subtractive Magic the verification web would be sterile. He quickly opened his mind to what they were trying to pull from him and released his restraints.

His gift responded with such a rush of power it took his breath.

Time and movement outside the golden circle seemed to stop.

Inside that circle, almost instantly, both Additive and Subtractive Magic ignited from his outstretched arms with a deafening thunderclap. From his right hand, Additive Magic flashed in a twisting arc that would blind a person were they to stare right at it for more than a brief glance. Beyond the gold ring, Glee tried to shield their eyes with an arm. They might not be able to see magic, but this kind of power was something that even they could see. With his eyes closed, Richard could still see the bright, searing lines of the lightning right through his eyelids.

Almost at the same time, from his left hand, Subtractive Magic thundered into existence, shaking the ground. Unlike its opposite, it wasn't at all bright. His eyes were closed, but he had seen it enough times that he could sense the cold void in the world of life that was blacker than death itself.

Now that his gift had responded and the

full verification web had been ignited, Richard held both arms out as he squinted just enough to see the blindingly bright threads of crackling Additive lightning and shrieking threads of totally black Subtractive threads flickering and twisting all around him and Vika. Those threads of power arced upward from his hands and then cascaded down to the golden ring. The way they each turned and tumbled, they reminded him of wild beasts on a chain.

In his peripheral vision Richard could see the dark shapes of the Glee that had started racing toward the gold circle suddenly stop where they were as they saw power they couldn't comprehend exploding into existence before them. They didn't run, maybe because they were waiting for an opening to attack to save their precious device, or maybe because they couldn't understand what it was they were seeing, or maybe because they were simply paralyzed by fear.

The whole perimeter of the golden circle that he and Vika had uncovered in the sand drew a network of thin Subtractive threads of inky black lightning as well as blindingly bright threads of Additive Magic, all of them flickering as they jumped and raced around the entire perimeter of the gold ring as if it were alive and trying to find a way to escape. But the golden circle prevented any escape. At least for the moment.

Richard closed his eyes again and swiftly raised both arms. Using all the power of his gift he abruptly brought the main trunks of those crackling, flickering discharges of Additive and Subtractive Magic up with his hands feeding them everything he had. Both of those arcing streams of thunderous power slammed together, rocking the mountain.

Instantly, all around the perimeter of the gold circle about waist high, a burst of dark energy powered by Subtractive Magic exploded outward in an ever-expanding ring. As it shot off in all directions, it instantly cut cleanly through the Glee where they stood and the rock towers behind them as well as those all around the mountaintop.

Richard saw what had just happened as if watching from outside his own body. With the threat stopped, he immediately used his gift to pull the Subtractive Magic he had allowed to escape back within the boundary of the gold ring.

The Glee had all been sliced cleanly in two and were dead before they tumbled to the ground. Some of the tops of the rock towers, suddenly separated by a void cut cleanly through them by Subtractive Magic, dropped straight down with a thud and stayed there, as if joining into one again. Others that were out of balance slowly began to tip over until they crashed down. Any of the Glee that had been behind the rock had also been cut in two and killed. No Glee that had come up on the mountain, other than those with Sang who had fled, escaped alive.

Everything had happened in a blinding flash of pure elemental power. What only a second before had been a dangerous threat, was no more. With the threat eliminated, Richard turned his attention back to the procedures for the ignition of the interior perspective of the verification web.

He allowed both kinds of lightning to twist and dance together. Countless threads of the combined power crackled all around them, forming a dome shape over Richard and Vika. The ends of all those thrashing threads grounded on the golden ring, like lightning drawn irresistibly to a tree. It didn't seem to do any harm to the ring.

That part was unlike any verification-web procedure Richard had ever seen before, or heard of, but he realized that just because he hadn't seen it before didn't mean it was wrong, and was no reason to stop.

Within that dome of crackling power, all around Richard and Vika, the constructed spell rapidly built a network of yet more lines, confirming that everything about the spell was unfolding properly and as he had expected. As Richard concentrated on giving those lines the power they needed from his gift, they traced their way through the air, building a three-dimensional series of glowing lines.

Unlike the previous lines, these glowed orange, which was a rather discordant contrast in the red world. The bluish lines from before turned green when the orange lines intersected with them, changing them and adding to their structure. Lines of light raced through the air to support and reinforce geometric shapes. Triangles merged and formed complex angles and shapes of pure white light that lit the remaining towers of rock all around them in their soft glow.

The lines swiftly grew in purpose, creating an

intricate web around Richard and Vika. Richard understood those lines and the elements of magic they represented. As they multiplied, the glowing lines continued to build, crisscrossing around the two of them at a dizzying rate. As they did, Vika pressed her back to his as yet more lines shot like arrows through space close in around them.

The lines, Richard knew, were routines of the spell-form, protocols that created the web to confirm what elements made up that spell-form. They were, in essence, a three-dimensional diagram of the constructed spell.

The lines continued to trace their routes with purpose and precision as the dome of crackling lightning overhead protected them. The symbols on the stone flashed in sequence. In the fabric of the web around them made of orange, white, and green lines, in the angles and junctions, Richard could read purpose and procedure, revealing how the spell and the strange power used by the gateway functioned.

Even though it was unlike any constructed spell he had seen before, in the complexity of glowing lines all around them, there was profound beauty of purpose.

Richard now understood how it all fit together and the underlying mechanism for how the gateway worked.

And, he now understood exactly what he had to do to alter the gateway.

75

Richard looked back over his shoulder at Vika. "Are you all right?"

"Peachy," she said above the crackling noise of the lightning flickering all around them.

Richard smiled. "Good."

She cast a worried look around the dancing and glimmering dome of power, then gazed back at him. "As far as your crazy ideas go, this one might be the craziest."

"Well, I have to tell you, I haven't yet gotten to the crazy part."

She carefully avoided touching any of the glowing lines as she used her hands on him to twist herself around until she was facing his back. She circled one arm around his waist to make sure she stayed close enough in case he moved. He was glad, at least, that she was taking the danger of the glowing lines seriously.

"What?" she yelled out. "This isn't the crazy part?"

"No. I just wanted to make sure you are all right because I'm about the do the crazy part. I'm going to need your help to do some of it with me."

She shook her head. "Sure, why not. I have nothing better to do."

He gestured around at the complex network of luminous blue, green, orange, and white lines of the verification web. "I'm going to have to extinguish some of these glowing orange lines in order to open up a corridor of sorts that you and I can move through to get to the gateway device."

"Should I go with you?"

"Yes. Once I clear away enough of the lines, then when I start to move toward the stone, I want you to move with me, like you are my shadow. Can you do that?"

"Of course. But that doesn't sound like it's the crazy part."

"It's not. When I'm ready and we start to move, keep your arms in close. Be careful not to let any part of you touch the lines, because they will cut a slab of flesh right off you."

"I understand."

"I'm going to extinguish some of the lines, but I can't get rid of them all quite yet or the web will collapse, and I still need it, so it will be a narrow space and we will have to be careful."

"I understand. But there is something that I think you should know, first."

"What's that?" he asked.

She pointed down. "We're not touching the ground. We're floating about a foot above it."

"I know. It's part of the process. When I extinguish some of the lines, we will settle down to the ground and be able to walk to the stone."

Once he was sure that she wasn't going to panic and do something that might get her killed—he realized as soon as he had the thought that Mord-Sith didn't panic and they didn't necessarily fear getting killed, as long as it was in service to protect him—he began reaching out and touching his first finger and thumb together at key intersections in the web. Since the lines were in part a creation of his own gift, he knew that as long as he was careful, they wouldn't harm him the way they would harm Vika.

As he touched the first intersection of lines above and a little to the right, two of the lines crossing in front of him vanished. He continued to pinch off primary junctions of lines, in a way cauterizing the flow of power so that it wouldn't bleed away, and the web would remain viable.

As he pinched off intersections at the proper nodes, it extinguished lines in midair between him and the stone at the edge of the ring. With each that vanished, he could reach farther in to touch other prime points where complex networks of glowing orange lines came together. As he worked, he and Vika gradually sank toward the ground.

Once their feet touched the ground, he spoke to Vika back over his shoulder. "I'm going to move closer to the stone. Stay close."

"Don't worry. Just think of me as your shadow."

Richard worked as he moved deeper until he had an adequate corridor opened to the stone. It wasn't roomy, but it provided enough space for them to get through. Once there, he started clearing the glowing lines from all around the

stone to give himself the access he would need
to all the symbols.

"All right, I'm ready for the next part. Don't
be alarmed."

"Nothing you do alarms me anymore."

He smiled as he pulled his silver-handled knife
from the sheath at his belt. It had an ornate
letter "R" on it for the House of Rahl. It was
a reminder of home, Kahlan, and all he had left
behind, as well as his responsibility to his own
world.

As Vika watched over his shoulder, Richard
gritted his teeth and drew the razor-sharp blade
across his forearm, cutting deep enough to
bleed sufficiently to provide the blood he would
need. He ignored the stinging pain of the cut
and wiped the knife in the blood, turning it
over, collecting all of it he could on the blade.

He held the knife level so that the blood
wouldn't all run down and drip off. Leaning
over, he touched a series of three emblems
in the language of Creation with just enough
Additive Magic to initiate a reset of the gateway.
Each one he touched confirmed that touch of
magic with a slight vibration and a tone.

Once done with that, he held the knife over

the stone to let the blood drip from the tip of the blade into the slot on the top where Sang had shown him they put their claw.

"What are you doing?" Vika sounded apprehensive.

"I thought you said that nothing I do alarms you anymore."

"I'm not alarmed. I'm Mord-Sith. I'm curious."

Richard held the knife steady to make sure all the blood continued to drip into the slot. "I'm altering the protocols with my blood so that the gateway will only recognize a Rahl from now on."

"That's actually not crazy."

"Just wait," he whispered.

"What?"

"Nothing."

Richard swiftly stroked the edge of the blade up his arm again to collect more blood. Once he had, he quickly held it over the slot, letting more of his blood drip from the tip into the slot. He didn't know how much would be needed to accomplish what he wanted to do, but he decided it would be best to be sure it was plenty rather than risk having too little.

As he dripped the blood in the second time, the ground began to rumble like distant thunder. A soft glow appeared in the air over the sand within the gold ring.

Richard looked back at Vika. "Now comes the crazy part."

Her mouth dropped open. "You mean none of this was the crazy part?"

"No, not really."

"What are you going to do?"

"I don't have time to explain. The reset is active. I need to complete the series."

"What can I do to help?"

"I need to hold an arm around this stone. I will reach back with my other arm. I want you inside the gold ring as close as you can get to the center of that glowing light and still be able to stretch out an arm and hold my hand."

Seeing his grim expression, she nodded. "All right. Anything else?"

"Just don't let go of my hand no matter what happens."

"I won't," she said earnestly before she started carefully working her way back through the corridor in glowing orange lines. She turned and stretched her arm out, waiting for his hand.

Richard put his right arm around the stone, with his wrist hooked up over the top on the other side so that he could hold the knife, still dripping his blood, over the slot in the slanted top of the stone.

With his left hand, he reached down and touched the reset sequence with his palm. He used enough of a flow of Subtractive Magic to close the verification web. As soon as he felt the final emblem vibrate under his palm, confirming that it accepted the instruction, all the glowing lines instantly turned to smoke. Those lines of smoke swirled a little in the air before they quickly began to vanish. In a moment they were gone.

But in their place the softly glowing air within the golden ring began to vibrate with an ever-increasing roar that hurt his ears.

Richard looked back at Vika. She was wincing against the pain of the thundering roar.

"You will need to bend over a little more to be able to reach me!" He had to yell to make sure she could hear him over the strange vibrating, rumbling noise.

She nodded as she did as he asked, bending at the waist and stretching her arm out toward him while keeping her feet in the center of the sand. She held the position, waiting for him to grab her hand.

With his left hand, Richard quickly pressed his palm to the final reset authentication emblem. It pulsed a bright red to confirm that it recognized him. As soon as it did, he immediately stretched his left arm back to Vika. She grimaced against the pain of the sound as she grabbed and then gripped his hand like her life depended on it.

It did.

He again read the critical emblem in the language of Creation that was facing him. Because it was so important, the same emblem was on all four sides of the stone so that it couldn't be missed. Each emblem was the same. It translated roughly to "Keep your target in mind."

He didn't need to know what that meant to tell him. He understood it from using a bow and arrow. When he shot, he called the target. That was what the gateway meant him to know. As strange as it seemed, it felt to him as if the gateway, now that it had his blood, was reading what was in his mind and using what he already knew in order to guide him.

It was like they were now of one mind and one purpose.

Richard looked back at Vika. "Once more into darkness!" he cried out over the roar.

Hugging his right arm around the stone, target firmly in mind, he reached over the top with his right hand and slammed the silver knife down into the slot in the stone.

76

The air within the gold ring that had been glowing with a roar abruptly began to flare with points of light packed together so tightly that it almost looked like the air itself was burning white hot. All of those sparkling points of light gave off a crackling sound that replaced the roar but was just as loud.

Richard hugged the stone with all his might as he gripped Vika's hand as hard as he could. He dared not lose his grip on her hand. He thought he might be hurting her, but she was squeezing back just as hard.

He closed his eyes, trying to empty his mind of all the thousand worries questioning everything he had just done. No one had taught him these procedures. He had learned them from the gateway itself through its verification web. In essence, the gateway had shown him what it needed at each step.

His grandfather Zedd had taught him that many dangerous things of magic had fail-safes that prevented anyone who wasn't supposed to from using them. He worried that maybe the things the gateway had revealed it needed to function and reset might be one of those fail-safe traps to not only prevent him from successfully using something that he was not meant to use but kill him in the process.

Many fail-safes were, after all, lethal.

He mentally ran through everything he had done, trying to make sure he hadn't overlooked anything. He knew he had done a thorough analysis and as a result he had disarmed all the fail-safe sequences he had found from the interior perspective of the verification web. He tried to think if it was possible there had been any that he could have missed. But if there were, it was too late now.

He knew he needed to focus, so he finally put those concerns from his mind.

He called the target.

He tried as hard as he could not to let any

other thoughts but that target enter his mind. Around the fringes of his awareness, though, a continual stream of little things nagged and nibbled, calling to him, trying to pull him away to think about each of them. He redoubled his effort to put them from his mind.

As he did when he shot his bow, he saw the target in his mind, centered on it, and pulled it toward him.

He didn't feel anything trying to force him from the stone, or Vika from his grip, but he dared not loosen his hold on either. He had to remind himself what mattered and put both of those thoughts from his mind as he concentrated on calling the target.

He stole a quick peek. It was hard to see anything through the sparkling points of light, but he could detect the windswept stone all around them rapidly getting increasingly wavy. He thought it might be that his eyes were watering, so he blinked and returned to concentrating on calling the target.

He had done everything to the best of his ability. He knew he could no longer dare to spare the mental effort to worry about any of it. Now, he simply focused on calling the target.

That was all that mattered. It was everything that mattered.

Suddenly there was a thunderous rumbling sound, low, intense, powerful. Even with his eyes closed, he could see the flash of light that had caused it.

The next thing he was aware of, before he could begin to understand what had just happened, was darkness beyond dark.

Abruptly, there was no longer any sound at all. The profound silence rang in his ears until it hurt, and then even that sensation was gone.

Richard felt nothing. It was a complete lack of any sights or sounds or sensations. He couldn't tell up from down.

He couldn't feel if he still had hold of Vika's hand or if he was still holding the stone. He desperately hoped that he was. If he wasn't, then it had all been for nothing and he would go forever into darkness until even his thoughts gradually disintegrated into nothing and became part of the void.

He had absolutely no sense of time. He didn't know if it had been minutes, hours, or even days since the silent darkness had abruptly collapsed in on him. Even that sensation of falling and the awful expectation of hitting the bottom left him. Having done this before made it easier to do again. He told himself that this was no different than it had been last time.

But somehow, in some indescribable way, this was different.

Very different. Profoundly different.

Despite having done this before, it was a sensation of no sensation that left him feeling hollow and lost.

Since he had done this before, it was relatively easy to talk himself out of any panic. He knew that eventually it had to end—in one way or the other—so he tried his best to disregard the sensation, or rather, the lack of sensation, and focus only on calling the target. That was his only job, now.

To keep his mind from wandering into disturbing places even as he concentrated on calling the target, he thought of Kahlan in the background behind the target.

He pictured her face in his mind.

He smiled when she smiled.

77

Suddenly, light and sound and sensation slammed in all around him. It was such a powerful awareness that it made him gasp. It was so totally different from the void of all sensation that the abrupt weight and light and sound hurt.

He could feel himself still holding Vika's hand and he still had his other arm around the gateway stone.

Richard opened his eyes, afraid he would see the same terrible place in the Glee's world.

Instead he saw his target brought to life all around him.

Despite having expected it, he blinked in surprise.

Vika turned all the way around, her eyes wide with wonder.

"You did it! You did it! Lord Rahl, you did it! You got us home!"

The gateway stone was right there beside him the way it had been, except that now wisps of vapor rose off of it. The gold ring sat in the white sand, like it had been before. But this sand was white. Really white.

All around him, in all its glory, was the Garden of Life.

He could see the stand of trees off to one side, with the path meandering back through them. It made him feel so good to see trees again that he thought his chest might burst. When he looked up, he saw the glassed skylight overhead that let in the sunlight . . . sunlight of his world. The sky was a clear, bright blue, not red. All around him there was color—greens of every shade and browns and whites. Color had never looked so luscious, so vibrant before.

He and Vika stared around at the place. It didn't seem possible that it could be real.

This was the target he had called, and it was all around them, and it was real.

They were in the People's Palace. They were home again in their own world.

Vika finally gripped him by his shoulders as

she looked into his eyes. She had to swallow to be able to use her voice.

"Lord Rahl, I will never ever again, for as long as I live, doubt any of your crazy ideas."

Richard smiled as he used a thumb to wipe tears from under her eyes. "Don't be so quick to make that pledge. You have not yet heard what other crazy ideas I have."

By the look in her eyes, she didn't care. He turned more serious.

"I expect all those I love to occasionally doubt my crazy ideas, because questions from ones I care about and trust make me have to be sure, for their sake, before I act. So don't ever stop questioning my crazy ideas."

She smiled. "All right. But now what? I'm afraid that we're back where we started. The Mother Confessor and the rest of them are a long way off at the Wizard's Keep."

He looked over at the gateway stone sitting beside him. The vapor was finally beginning to abate. It was still making a soft humming sound, as it had back in the Glee's world when he had activated it.

Vika gestured at the slanted top. "Don't forget your knife."

TERRY GOODKIND

Richard could see that several of the emblems were still glowing red and a couple were blue.

"I'm not done yet. While the reset process is still active, I have to put in a fail-safe."

"A fail-safe?"

"Yes, a procedure that prevents just anyone with the gift from being able to reset it or use it. Believe it or not, if you activate the gateway in the way I've done, you can actually create a duplicate."

Vika frowned. "What for?"

Richard shrugged. "I don't know. Maybe so that you can play that you are gods by gifting a gateway to other worlds. Maybe this one is a duplicate and that is how the Glee came to have it. Maybe the ones who gave it to them wanted to play at being gods."

"But you know for sure that there was no duplication this time, right? Are you sure this device is the one from the Glee's world, and that they don't have one anymore, maybe a duplicate of this one?"

"I'm positive. The procedure for creating a duplicate is completely different. This is the original from the Glee's world and there is no duplicate left behind. The Glee are going to be trapped in their world. They can never again travel to other worlds. I think Sang and his friends will be happy about that."

"And only you can ever do that with this one?"

Richard nodded. "Only a Rahl, yes, with fail-safes to prevent just anyone from figuring it out and using it. The knife I used is only used by special people. The gateway will recognize only it, the same way it was set to recognize the claw of a Glee, before. That's one safeguard. My blood created another protocol so that the gateway will only recognize Rahl blood."

"That should be specific enough, shouldn't it?"

Richard shook his head. "With something this dangerous, you can't be too careful. It needs something more, another fail-safe that no one would likely know to use. Something that only the right person would know."

"Like what?"

Richard flashed her a smile before squatting down before the stone. Most of the symbols in the language of Creation glowed a soft blue. One of them in the series of final emblems still glowed red, indicating that the reset was still open. He knew that once he touched it, the protocols would lock in and set.

Before he put his hand on the pulsing red symbol, he reached down to another series of emblems designed to accept additional properties. He recognized that this was a way he could set a fail-safe protocol.

He tapped that lower emblem once each time he counted out loud.

"One, two, three, four, five, six, seven, eight." Each tap elicited a soft chime along with a pulse of brighter light. He tapped the emblem one last time. "Nine."

He spread his fingers to touch two green emblems at the same time. The gateway stone made a soft dull sound as it recognized and accepted the new fail-safe.

Finally, he pressed his palm against the glowing red, pulsing symbol. He felt it make a soft vibration to confirm that the fail-safe was set and all the new protocols he had initiated were locked in.

Vika leaned close, looking at the symbols as the light within them gradually faded away and finally went out. The gateway stone once more looked like the inert stone it had seemed to be the first time they had seen it. It now appeared to be nothing more than a smooth but not polished stone, with symbols inscribed on it.

Vika looked puzzled. She gestured at the gateway stone.

"What were you counting?"

"This thing is obviously dangerous. As dangerous as the most dangerous magic. I'm not sure how to destroy it, or what harm it could cause if I tried, so instead I decided to make sure that it will be incredibly difficult for anyone to ever use.

"To make the gateway work, I locked in protocols that one now has to use a special knife like the one I'm carrying, and Rahl blood. But it's always possible that those requirements could be met, even against the will of a Rahl, by using a knife like this to kill him. This kind of knife, with Rahl blood on it, would meet the initial procedures. But it's too dangerous to leave it at that.

"So I set into the gateway a protocol that, in addition to this kind of knife and Rahl blood, the Law of Nines is also required for the gateway to work. Without the Law of Nines, no gateway. It will remain an inert piece of stone."

TERRY GOODKIND

Vika rose up. "You are a devious man, Lord Rahl."

Richard let out a deep breath now that it was finalized. "You've said that before."

"It bears repeating."

He looked to the path out of the Garden of Life. "We need to get to the Wizard's Keep. Kahlan was about to give birth back when we left her there."

78

"It was a long and difficult journey getting to the Keep the last time," she reminded him. "We had better get some fast horses."

"I have a better way," Richard told her.

"Another crazy idea? Please tell me you don't intend to use the gateway to get us there."

Richard shook his head at the very notion. "Dear spirits no. I'm not sure that would even be possible. But I know a better way, and it's not crazy at all. Let's go."

As they went through the double doors and out of the Garden of Life, there was a very surprised knot of men of the First File standing right there. They all stepped back, stunned at seeing the Lord Rahl and Vika.

It looked as if they had heard sounds and

were all gathered by the doors. At seeing him, all of them snapped to attention after stepping back and clapped fists to their hearts.

One of the Lord Rahl's personal guard stepped forward. The man was even bigger than the men of the First File. He was armored with fitted leather and had metal bands around his massive arms, just above his elbows. Those bands had razor-sharp projections on them that were used in close-quarters combat. They could tear an opponent apart with ease in short order.

The big man blinked in astonishment. "Lord Rahl, we weren't . . . expecting you."

"I suppose not," Richard said. "To tell you the truth, I wasn't expecting me to be here ever again."

When the man only frowned in confusion, Vika showed him a smile. "We went into darkness to get here."

He clearly didn't have a clue as to what she could mean.

"We've been keeping extra guards on this place since you told us to before you left," the captain of the guard said. "Not a soul has gone in there, but we heard noises and thought that maybe it was more of the Glee." He leaned over to look around Richard and through the open doors into the Garden of Life. The man looked painfully puzzled. "How did you get in there?"

"I just returned from the world of the Glee," he told them. The eyes of all the men widened. "They were killing people in our world, and they killed a lot of people here, at the palace. I had to make sure they can never come here to harm anyone again."

The captain looked grim. "There was an attack not long after you and the Mother Confessor disappeared, some time back, but none since then, thank the Creator."

"That wasn't the Creator's doing," Vika told them. "It was Lord Rahl's."

Richard ignored her and addressed the captain. "I'm sorry to hear about that, but at least there is no longer any need to ever again have to worry about attacks from those monsters. They will never be able to come here to our world again."

The captain frowned his concern. "Lord Rahl, how can you be so sure of that? Those demons could just show up out of thin air—we never knew when or where. How can you be sure they will not come again?"

Richard gestured back through the open double doors. "Because I stole the device they used to travel to our world and brought it back with me."

Jaws dropped. "Weren't they angry you did that?" the commander asked.

"Well, yes, actually they were, but the ones who objected are now dead."

They all looked at Vika, like maybe she could explain the incomprehensible to them. "I know, it sounds crazy," she told them, "but Lord Rahl sometimes does crazy things. If he didn't, we would be the ones who were dead by now."

The captain cleared his throat. "We are certainly happy to hear that you are safely back in our world with us, Lord Rahl. But what of the Mother Confessor? You were going to the Keep for her safety."

"Yes, well, and therein lies the problem. I wanted to bring the device I stole from the Glee here, where I know it will be safe under the protection of the First File. Now that I've done that, I need to get to the Keep as soon as possible."

"What can we do to help?"

"Get me to the sliph."

At that command, he sensed Vika tense up, and he saw her glance down at the Sword of Truth.

He showed her a small smile. "Since the sword had been touched by the world of the dead, and this time there isn't any risk to Kahlan's pregnancy, I can take my sword with me in the sliph."

Her expression eased. "That's a relief."

Richard nodded his agreement and then turned to the Captain. "The fastest way to the sliph, if you please."

The man clapped a fist to his heart. "Come with us."

Richard could see in Vika's face that she had lost weight. They had eaten hardly anything in the days they were in the world of the Glee. He was feeling weak himself. He knew that the sliph would take at least a day to get them to the Keep.

Before they started out, he took one of the other soldiers by the arm. "It's going to be a long journey. Please bring me and Vika something to eat. Nothing fancy or anything that would take time to prepare. Some kind of meat. Whatever is already cooked. Bring it to the sliph and be quick about it."

79

Breathe . . .

Richard had traveled with the sliph a number of times, and as was usually the case it was both breathtaking, in more ways than one, and utterly terrifying.

The only difference this time was that he didn't need to be told twice to breathe when they arrived and the sliph pushed him to the surface. While the sliph could be an experience of profound wonder, his sense of urgency meant that he didn't care about any of that. He simply wanted out.

He threw one arm over the side of the sliph's well to hold himself up as he forced her fluid from his lungs, returning it to her, and then pulled in a deep breath. The shock of air made his body want to reject it. Despite the burning discomfort, he quickly pulled another deep breath as he grabbed a fistful of red leather as a limp Vika bobbed to the surface nearby.

He pulled her up from the churning silver liquid to the edge where he was holding on with one arm over the side of the stone well. Slipping his other arm around her, under her arms, he helped keep her head up above the sliph's quicksilver surface. She was limp and unresponsive. The silver fluid sluiced off her hair and red leather.

"Breathe!" he yelled in her ear.

He knew from experience that the sliph would be telling her the same thing, but in her mind, much the same way the Glee had talked to them. She didn't respond.

He put his mouth closer to her ear. "Vika! Breathe! I need you! Do it for me!"

She abruptly opened her eyes wide and exhaled the silver fluid as if she had just been surprised awake. She gasped a deep lungful of air and immediately winced in pain. The first few breaths after breathing the sliph were painful, not just physically but also mentally, because all your mind wanted was to stay in the velvety silver dreamworld.

She coughed, spitting up a little blood. In her mind, he knew, she didn't want to breathe air again and at first had to force herself to do it. The quicksilver-like fluid of the sliph was an otherworldly, spectacular experience unlike any other. It was a release from the bounds of the world of life, a sensation of free-floating, flying, and drifting all at once. It was in a way like being with a good spirit in a different kind of existence, where the concerns of the world no longer mattered. Once in the sliph, breathing her silver fluid, you never wanted it to end.

Except this time Richard had been eager for it to end.

Richard threw a leg up and over the side of the stone well. He pulled Vika up, helping her to get her arms up and over the wall. She was still limp.

"Breathe, Vika."

"I'm breathing," she complained.

The silver fluid in the well swelled up in the center, pulling upward until it formed into a beautiful, shiny, reflective face.

"Were you pleased, Master?"

"Yes," Richard said. "Very pleased."

"I know how painful death was for you, but I

am glad that your sword now knows death as well so you can take it with you when we travel again."

"It is always a pleasure to be with you."

"Then come. I can take you many places. Where would you like to go? You will be pleased."

"I would like that very much. But I have some business right now. Maybe later."

"When?"

"I'm not sure yet. But really, it was wonderful. I was pleased."

The silver face smiled. *"I am glad, Master."* A bit of a silver frown formed. *"You are sure you were pleased?"*

"Yes," Richard said, nodding, as he hauled Vika's upper body over the edge. As she finally got a leg over, he helped her down to the ground. "Very pleased. You may go back now and be with your soul. I will call on you again just as soon as I wish to travel."

"Thank you, Master, for traveling with me. I enjoyed it. When you wish to travel again, I will be waiting for your call."

With that, the silver face melted down into her churning silver waters. The reflective fluid began sinking down inside the well. Richard looked over the edge to see the choppy surface receding at an ever-increasing speed until in a blink it was gone down into the darkness.

When he looked back, Vika had her fists on her hips. "That was just plain weird."

"I know, traveling in the sliph is a strange experience."

"No, I mean that conversation was weird. Why were you talking to that thing like that?"

Richard waved off the question. "It's a long story. Come on. Let's go."

They raced out of the sliph's room and along the railing around the pit with the dark rock sitting in the center of dark water. Their sudden appearance caused small creatures on the rock to leap into the surrounding water.

The lower reaches of the Keep were dark and gloomy. Occasionally there was a long shaft that reached to the outside to let in light and fresh air.

Richard took them the shortest way he knew to get to the massive lower chamber that was kind of like a central hub. From there, one could go to any number of different places and levels in the Keep. The chamber was so long that he couldn't recognize a person's face from one end to the other. It wasn't nearly so wide, but it was immensely tall. Up near the top there were long openings that let the Keep breathe, changing the air down deep in the place and letting it flow through the halls. It also let birds and bats come and go. Both came for the bugs.

It was a long climb from the lower Keep. They went up both narrow, dark stone stairs and more elaborate staircases. Together they raced down passageways and through elaborately decorated rooms.

Higher up in the Keep, when they finally rushed around a corner, Richard heard voices. He looked down a broad hall to see two women standing at a window, looking out and talking.

Richard trotted down the hall with Vika at his side. He slowed to a breathless stop near the women. Both stared with wide eyes as he and Vika caught their breath.

"Sister Phaedra, right?" he finally asked.

She curtsied. "Lord Rahl, it has been a very long time. I am surprised you remember me."

Both women stared at the red leather. "This is Vika," he told them as he held a hand toward her in introduction.

The Sister likewise lifted a hand out to the side. "This is Jana, one of the women from

TERRY GOODKIND

down in the city who come up here to help out at the Keep."

Richard offered her a quick tip of his head in greeting.

She blushed, and then performed a shaky curtsy, too intimidated by the Lord Rahl to speak. It was something that he'd gotten somewhat used to. He didn't have the time to talk her out of her mute fright.

"Where's Kahlan?" he asked the Sister. "She is—was—pregnant. Did she have the babies yet? Is she all right? Where is she?"

The woman blinked at the burst of questions. She turned to the window and pointed out.

"She went down there. She said she wanted to have her children where she was born."

"She went down to the Confessors' Palace?"

Richard was astonished that she would take that risk before knowing that she would be safe from the Glee.

"That's right," Sister Phaedra said. "She has been down there for quite some time now."

80

As he and Vika raced into the majesty of the Confessors' Palace, two of the women who lived and worked there were already rushing toward them, skirts held in a hand as they ran.

"Lord Rahl! Lord Rahl!" one of them called out, waving an arm overhead to make sure they saw her.

They both ran up to meet Richard and Vika as they came into the bright, airy, grand central entryway. "Lord Rahl—"

"Yes?"

"I'm Ginny. This is Nina."

"A runner just arrived to tell us that you were on your way," Nina put in as if it were exciting gossip, or maybe she was just excited to see him.

Richard had been in a hurry to get there, so

he was surprised to hear it. "A runner? A runner beat us here?"

"Rachel," Ginny said with a grin. "She knows the shortcuts."

Richard frowned. "Rachel? You mean Chase's daughter? That Rachel?"

Ginny nodded. "Yes, she is such a big help to everyone. She has long legs, that girl. She was so excited to tell us that she had spotted you and a Mord-Sith that she had to race all the way down here as fast as she could to tell the Mother Confessor." She pointed toward the ceiling. "She is up there with her now."

"Where is Kahlan? Has she had the babies yet? Has—"

Ginny held her arm out, directing him. "Come. Everyone will be so excited that you have returned. To be honest, we all, well, we all thought you were dead. Everyone except the Mother Confessor. She said . . ."

Richard wanted to strangle the words out of her. "She said what?" He looked over at the other woman instead. "What did she say?"

"Well," Nina stammered, "she said that you weren't dead, that you would . . ."

"Would what?"

Nina blushed furiously. "She said that you would get some crazy idea and be able to come back to us. I guess she was right. Oh! I don't mean she was right that you would have a crazy idea—I'm sure your ideas aren't crazy—but that you would return."

When Richard swished his hand to urge them to get them moving and show the way, Ginny immediately turned and led him and Vika up a grand stairway of white marble to a spacious balcony that ran most of the way around three sides of the palatial entryway. Around one side of that balcony they went up a second stairway to the third floor, and then turned down the central hall.

As they hurried down a wide, elaborate hallway with comfortable-looking chairs in groupings, Shale came racing around a corner out ahead. "Lord Rahl!" She rushed up and seized him by his shoulders. "Dear spirits! We thought for sure that you were lost to us!"

Vika cocked an eyebrow. "He got a crazy idea how to come back."

Shale stared at her a moment, but had no answer. She turned back to Richard. He was surprised to see her in such a fine dress.

"The Mother Confessor will be relieved to see you. She was so worried, but she would never admit it. Whenever one of us would look at her, concerned for her and what she must be fearing, she would just smile and tell us not to worry. That you would be back."

Richard threw up his arms. "Where is she! Bags, would one of you take me to her?"

Ginny and Nina blushed at the language.

"Come on," Shale said, rolling a hand to urge him to follow. She started him down the hallway toward another grand stairway.

Richard was beside himself. "Has she had the babies yet? Are they all right? Is Kahlan all right?"

"Just come on and you can see for yourself."

Shale led Richard and Vika up the stairs two at a time. Ginny and Nina hastened along behind. The palace was white and quiet and beautiful, but it was all a blur to Richard. He hardly saw any of it. He just wanted to get to Kahlan.

And then as they came to another hallway, he saw a group of people all milling around down the hall. He recognized the Mord-Sith, but they were all in white leather, which was a shock after having seen them in their red leather for so long.

Berdine spotted him coming and broke into a dead run. When she got to him, she leaped up into his arms, nearly knocking him down. She threw her legs around his waist.

"Lord Rahl! Lord Rahl! You're back!"

Richard grabbed her by the waist and set her down. He flashed a quick smile as he turned her around and pushed her ahead as he rushed onward to the group outside a doorway.

He saw Chase there, with his wife Emma. He paused long enough to squeeze the big man's arm in a silent greeting.

"Richard!" Rachel cried out as she suddenly hugged him. He ran a hand down the back of her head of long hair. He was surprised to see that she was now nearly as tall as him.

Richard looked around at the small group. "I need to see Kahlan."

Shale smiled as she opened a white door with ornate carving on it. She held the door open for him and motioned him in.

Richard stared at her.

Shale grinned. "Go on, then."

81

Richard walked into a beautiful room decorated with cream-colored curtains with a textured pattern and white frame and panel walls. The reflector lamps mounted on the walls were all silver, but none were lit. The carpets were leaf patterns in various shades of off-white. It wasn't a large room, considering the size of the palace, but it looked special. The bed had four posts draped over the top with a white, filmy material that hung down on each side near the headboard. Through the open window Richard could hear birds chirping outside. In the distance the looming Keep looked down over them, a dark protector of the Confessors.

From that bed, Kahlan's green eyes were

locked on him from the moment he walked through the doorway.

His heart hammered as he stared at her.

She was so beautiful he felt tears well up in his eyes.

In each arm, she held a bundle. He could just see the tops of the babies' heads.

"Are you all right?" he asked in a hushed tone, feeling stupid because he couldn't think of anything better to say.

"Now that I see you, everything is good," she said in a soft voice. "Everyone was so worried. But I knew that you would find a way to come back to me."

"I'm sorry it took me so long. I wanted to be here when the babies came. But I—"

She was still smiling. "You are back with me now. That's all that matters to me."

"You don't have to worry about the Glee coming after us ever again. No one in our world ever has to fear them again."

"The Golden Goddess is not the new golden age, then?" she asked.

Richard shook his head. "No. A golden ring helped me get back to you and make our children safe. That golden ring is with us, now, here in our world. I think that is what it really meant when I promised you the beginning of a new golden age. That's where that promise really comes from. I wanted you to know. It's nothing else, nothing bad."

She nodded against the pillow she was propped up on. "One day you can tell me about your crazy adventure, but right now, come and meet our children."

At long last, Richard carefully stepped to the edge of the bed, close to her. He didn't think he had ever felt more nervous and expectant all at once.

Kahlan smiled with bliss, with tranquility, and in weariness. It somehow calmed him. Her green eyes calmed him.

"Lord Rahl, I would like you to meet your children." She lifted the one in her left arm, on the other side of her from Richard, out a little. "This is your daughter, Cara Amnell."

He stared in wonder a moment at his sleeping daughter.

Kahlan looked down as she lifted the other one, asleep in the crook of her right arm, out a little. "And this is your son, Zeddicus Rahl."

Richard stared at his son a moment, then

bent and gently kissed the top of his head, then leaned farther and kissed the forehead of his daughter.

At last, he finally kissed Kahlan, making everything he had been through melt into nothing.

He straightened as he smiled down at her. "Their names are perfect. They are perfect. You are perfect."

Both babies reached a tiny hand out, then. They looked almost like they were searching for each other's hands. Using her fingers on the bundles she held, Kahlan gently smoothed their hands back inside the blankets.

She smiled her special smile at Richard as her eyes closed.

Shale came up behind him and took his arm to urge him back.

"She needs to rest, now," the sorceress whispered. "You can talk to her again after she gets some much-needed sleep."

Richard didn't want to leave, but he wanted all three to rest.

82

Once they were outside the room, Shale gently closed the door. "She wanted so much for you to see the babies that she has been trying to stay awake until you came back to her. She knew you would be back. And she wanted to see that you were safe. She can rest easy, now."

The Mord-Sith were all beaming at him. Vika put a hand on his back for a moment, a touch of congratulations that meant more than words. In that simple human act, Richard saw far more. He saw a journey back from madness.

"She looked so tired," he said. He gave Shale a meaningful look. "Is everything all right? Did it go well? The birth, I mean."

Out of the corner of his eye he saw the

Mord-Sith all share a look. Shale glanced over at Rachel as an excuse to divert her gaze for a moment. She finally looked back up at Richard.

"Yes. The babies finally arrived. They are all well."

"Why is she here, at the Confessors' Palace?" Richard asked suspiciously. "We went through a lot of trouble to get to the Keep so she could give birth where she would be safe. What is she doing here?"

Rachel touched his arm to answer. "She said that she was born here, and she wanted her children to be born in the Confessors' Palace as well."

"But the danger of the Glee—why would you all let her come down here to give birth?"

"Have you ever tried to tell the Mother Confessor no?" Shale asked. "It is not so easy, let me tell you."

Richard realized that he knew the truth of that.

"We tried to tell her to stay in the Keep where she would be safe," Berdine said, "but she said it wasn't a problem because you would see to it that she and your children would be safe."

"But—"

"He did," Vika said. "He saw to it that they were safe. He didn't let her down. He didn't let any of us down."

Richard looked back at the sorceress. "You helped her, then, when the babies came?"

"I did," she said as she was overcome with a peaceful smile. "As I promised you. I wouldn't let you, or her, down."

Richard could sense an odd tension in the mood of all those in the hallway.

"Was the birth difficult?"

Cassia, standing next to Shale, turned her back on Richard and whispered to Shale. Richard could just barely hear her say, "Tell him."

Richard looked back at Shale. Her smile faltered.

"What is it? Was there a problem with the birth? I should have been here. I'm sorry. I came as fast as I could. What is it? What happened?"

Shale folded her fingers together, holding her hands together in front. "Well, to be honest, it was a difficult birth. Partly because of all the mother's breath we gave her. But there was . . . more to it. Kahlan was in labor for days. She finally gave birth not long ago."

"But . . . she looks all right. She looks just fine. The twins look beautiful and are sleeping peacefully."

"No, no, she is fine. That's not it. The babies are fine as well."

Richard gestured as he grew impatient. "Well then, what is it that all of you know about and none of you are saying?"

Shale cleared her throat. "The thing is, Lord Rahl, she had a very difficult birth. The babies . . ."

"You already said that. The babies what?"

Shale glanced away from the intensity in his eyes. "The babies had a difficult time being born."

Richard had been with Zedd when he had helped with a few difficult births. He knew how tense that kind of situation could be. "Why? What was the problem?"

"Well, actually," Shale said, "I've never seen anything like it before, so it's rather hard to explain."

Richard was at his wits' end. He threw his hands up in the air. "What was the problem? What happened?"

Shale cleared her throat again. "The thing is

we were having a difficult time helping her in delivering the babies."

Richard looked from face to face. "Were they breech?"

"No, that wasn't it, exactly," Shale said.

Richard planted his fists on his hips. "What was it, then? Why was it difficult? Tell me."

Shale finally looked back up into his eyes.

"When the twins were being born, they were holding hands as the Mother Confessor was trying to give birth."

Richard stared at her a long moment. "Holding hands."

Shale nodded. "We had a very hard time getting them to let go of each other so they could finish being born. After we finally pried their hands apart, Cara was born first. Zeddicus came immediately after. For a time we didn't know if we would be able to get their hands apart so they could both be born. It was a tense situation."

Richard frowned. It didn't make any sense.

"They are newborn infants. How difficult can it be to pry their little fingers away from each other?"

Shale looked up at him from under her

brow. "You do realize they are both gifted, right? They were holding on to each other not just with their hands, but with the power of their gifts."